The Ferryman

By

Wendy Saunders

This book is the intellectual property of the author and as such cannot be reproduced in whole or in part in any medium without the express written permission of the author.

ISBN:10 1519667760
ISBN-13: 978-1519667762

For my mother, Isobel
Who taught me how to love unconditionally.

CONTENTS

1.

Olivia sat restlessly in the old armchair, her legs curled under her. Even staring into the flames in the small fireplace in her room watching the strands of red and gold didn't soothe her, she still couldn't sleep. She glanced over to the bed to where Theo sprawled naked and tangled up in the sheets, one arm stretched across her side of the bed reaching out to her even in his sleep.

She sighed and turned back to the fire. It had been a month since that night in the woods and there was still no sign of her mother or the demon Nathaniel. It had been almost too quiet and that was what worried her. After the last murder life had pretty much returned to normal in Mercy. The case had been conveniently pushed to the back of the shelf and marked unsolved. Thomas Walcott had been laid to rest in Mercy cemetery. He'd had no surviving family and few friends, being a very private man, which should have ensured him a pauper's grave but at the last minute the funeral had been paid for by an anonymous patron. Olivia had a pretty good idea who'd paid for Walcott's funeral. She shook her head resolutely as if trying to rid herself of the thought. She was still mad at her father and she didn't want to think of him doing something so kind for the man he'd once called brother, despite what

Thomas Walcott had become in the end. Even the Mayor had stepped in at the last minute and pulled some strings to get him buried next to James Talbot, the man he had loved so desperately. She only hoped he was at peace now and maybe somehow they would find each other in whatever afterlife they believed in.

Unfortunately thinking about Thomas Walcott drew her thoughts back to her father. She'd been dodging him for weeks; in fact she'd been dodging everyone. Her agent Mags had been calling her almost non-stop after she returned to Boston. She'd only seen Louisa when medically necessary as her shoulder was healing well apart from a little lingering stiffness. After the initial round of statements and the police investigation into Thomas Walcott's death she'd even managed to avoid Mac and Jake. She'd pretty much holed up in the house licking her wounds and brooding. Theo was the only one whose presence she seemed able to tolerate. He was the calm at the eye of the storm while chaos raged around her. He soothed her in a way she'd never experienced before and wasn't ready to examine in intimate detail just yet.

Suddenly she heard a deep chiming somewhere in the house. She listened as the chimes struck three o'clock, before it occurred to her how weird that was. She didn't have a grandfather clock in the house but that was exactly what it had sounded like. She dropped her legs to the floor, and stood slowly. The small carriage clock sitting on the mantle above the fireplace also read three a.m. Frowning to herself she headed out the door. Beau, sensing her move, stretched and yawned before trotting out of the room behind her.

She moved down the stairs slowly but was barely half way down when she shuddered uncontrollably. It was freezing and a shiver danced up her spine making the tiny little hairs on the back of her neck rise. She kept moving but the further down the stairs she went the colder it was. Her fingers and toes were starting to feel numb and her breath was expelled from her mouth as a vaporous mist.

She moved warily down the hallway, her bare feet
flinching as they touched the floor. She felt a rush of icy
air coming from the kitchen, brushing against her face and
wafting her hair back. She could still hear the monotonous
ticking of the grandfather clock she didn't own. It seemed
to be everywhere. Beau cowered behind her which was
unusual for him. She approached the kitchen
apprehensively and as she reached the doorway she could
see that the back door stood wide open and wet footprints
trailed across the floor into the house.

Theo tossed restlessly in his sleep, a frown creasing
his brow. He was standing on the shore of the icy lake
looking out across the dark waters which were shrouded in
a mist so thin it looked like lace. The sky was black as
pitch, lit only by the pale full moon.

He saw a figure standing on the shore gazing out
over the restless water and opened his mouth to speak but
found he could make no sound. The figure turned, her
hood falling back to reveal a face so heartbreaking similar
to his beloved his heart clenched. His fists tightened in
anger as he beheld the woman who had caused Olivia so
much pain.

Isabel West's gaze swept past without seeing him.
Her coldly beautiful face fixed upon the two figures in
front of her. The demon Nathaniel returned her stare, his
eyes burning in equal measures of pure hate and reluctant
obedience. His face resembled a mis-matched assemblage
of the men Isabel had murdered in order to build him a
mortal body but Theo knew it was him. He would always
recognize the demon regardless of whose face he was
wearing.

Isabel's gaze dropped to the dirty and bloodied
figure held tightly by Nathaniel. 'Where is she?' Isabel
asked coldly.

The captive man raised his head, fixing her with

dark eyes, his lip bloodied and torn.

'I know what it is you seek Witch,' he spat contemptuously; 'you will not find it this way.'

'Where is she?' she repeated calmly.

He clamped his lips together and stared at her, his eyes burning with hatred.

'Very well' she whispered as she leaned in close, her lips almost brushing his intimately, 'we'll do this the hard way.'

He laughed, a cold humorless sound.

'There is nothing you can do to force an answer from me Isabel West.'

Her eyes locked on his as she casually appraised him.

'I'm not the only one who knows who you are and what it is you seek,' he warned. 'You are being watched.'

'It makes no difference,' her mouth curved in amusement, 'let them watch.'

'Release me.'

'Oh I don't think so; you have some information I want.'

'And I told you I will not give you what you want, despite your pet demon.'

Nathaniel growled at the insult and twisted the man's arms tighter, until he hissed in pain.

'Not quite as untouchable as you thought are you?' she smiled, before looking back to Nathaniel.

'Bring him,' she commanded.

'Stupid woman,' the captive laughed derisively, 'you cannot take me from the lake.'

He watched as her hand disappeared into the fold of her jacket and she drew out a large thick black metal ring. Deep blue letters were etched into its face and it glowed as the moonlight caught its shiny surface.

'Where did you get that filthy thing?' he hissed.

'Let's just say I have friends in not so high places' she smiled as she swung it nonchalantly from her fingertips.

'I can't give you what you want.'

'We'll just see about that.'

She headed towards him slowly and as she took the ring in her hands it separated to form two halves.

'No!' he inched back trying desperately to get away from her but Nathaniel simply laughed and held him tighter. 'NO!'

He struggled and fought desperately but it was no good. Nathaniel held him firm and as Isabel placed the metal ring around his neck it fused back into one to form a thick metallic collar. Nathaniel let him go and he dropped helplessly to the ground. He tried to raise his head but it was as if the collar was simply too heavy for him to move, pinning him to the freezing snow covered ground.

'You can't do this,' he gasped as if every breath was a struggle.

'I already have,' she replied sharply. 'That's the difference between us. I take what I want, whereas you...for all your power you are still nothing more than a servant.'

'If you take me from the lake the doorway will remain open,' he panted. 'You have no idea of the chaos you will unleash.'

'Tell me what I want to know,' she spread her hands innocently, 'and you may go free.'

'I can't,' he growled clawing desperately at the ground, trying to return to the waters of the lake.

Nathaniel laughed mercilessly and grasped his ankle, dragging him away from the water.

'Please,' his eyes met hers, his voice an exhausted whisper. 'You don't know what you've done.'

'Bring him.'

Nathaniel grabbed the nearly unconscious man and effortlessly hauled him over his shoulder before disappearing into the darkness.

Isabel turned and took one last look at the lake as

thin misty insubstantial figures began to rise from the depths. Hovering above the churning water they began to drift ominously towards the shore.

Theo woke with a start, his body drenched with a cold clammy sweat. In his panic the last vestige of the dream was almost forgotten. Reaching out for Olivia his eyes widened as he realized she was no longer there. Hauling himself out of bed he pulled on his sweatpants and t-shirt and headed down the stairs, his disturbing dream all but forgotten as he went in search of her.

Olivia stepped into the kitchen and her heart lurched in her chest. She could barely breathe, her breath catching in her throat as every muscle in her body froze.

A girl stood motionless with her back to her. She wore a thin white muslin shift; wet, torn and streaked with mud. Her black hair hung in thick wet tangles down her back and her skin was chalky white. Olivia blinked and the girl was suddenly facing her, the pupils of her eyes white and lifeless and the shadows under her eyes like dark purple bruises. She looked no more than eighteen years old. Suddenly she stepped towards Olivia, a strange twitchy movement like she was watching an old film reel.

Olivia couldn't move, it was like her muscles had been petrified. She could feel her hair standing on end and she just couldn't make her voice work. The girl was now standing barely a foot in front of her, just staring. She slowly opened her mouth as if to speak but instead dirty water spilled from her lips in a huge gush.

'What the hell?'

Theo's voice split the atmosphere and the girl simply turned to water and dropped to the floor like someone had just emptied a bucket. Water sloshed across the kitchen floor butting up against the cupboards like mini waves.

Olivia knelt down and scooped up some of the water, examining it thoughtfully and letting it pour from her palm back to the floor.

'It's lake water,' she looked up at Theo

'Was that what I think it was?'

Olivia nodded in confirmation. 'She was a spirit.'

'Has this ever happened before?' Theo asked a little wild eyed and she couldn't really blame him. Her own heart was still hammering in her chest.

She shook her head, 'I've never see anything like this before.'

'Shouldn't the protective wards have kept her out?'

'I guess not,' Olivia murmured thoughtfully, 'I wonder what she wanted?'

'What she wanted?' he repeated incredulously.

'I don't know,' Olivia frowned, 'don't get me wrong she scared the shit out of me but I don't think she was trying to hurt me. It felt like she was trying to tell me something.'

Theo looked at the floor, an inch deep in dirty water.

'I'll go and find the mop,' he turned and headed out into the laundry room where she kept her cleaning supplies.

Olivia turned back to the kitchen and shivered. Realizing the back door was still open she stepped forwards intending to close it, when Beau suddenly rushed past her barking madly as he disappeared into the darkness.

'BEAU!' she yelled after him. 'Damn it!'

She rushed to the door and yanked on the green rubber boots tucked neatly behind it. Grabbing her coat off the coat hook she pulled it on over her pajamas and ran out after him.

Halfway down towards the dock she realized she should have brought a torch. She reached down inside herself for the light and heat of her magic. She flicked her hand irritably and one of her dragonflies appeared, burning brightly and composed entirely of flames. It hovered over her shoulder, lighting her way. Hearing Beau bark down by the lake she took off, trudging as quickly as she could through the snowdrift and shivering against the cold wind.

She could see a small form on the jetty. Trying to move quickly but carefully she headed towards him. Her feet slipped beneath her on the wet wood and she slowed even more, knowing the last thing she needed was to fall into the icy waters of the lake.

'Beau,' she scooped him up into her arms as he continued to bark madly at something.

She looked up and through the pale moonlight she could see the lake was shrouded by a thick fog. For a second she thought she saw a light out on the water, a small orange glow. She unconsciously took a step forward as she peered out, and as the fog parted momentarily she saw a small wooden skiff drifting on the water. It was empty; at one end mounted on a pole was an old fashioned lamp which burned in the darkness. This must have been the light she'd seen. Another roll of fog swept in and the small boat once again disappeared from view.

Frowning to herself she turned to leave but her gaze was caught by something floating in the water lapping up against the jetty. Putting Beau down carefully and telling him firmly to stay, she knelt down on the damp wood and leaned over the edge. Her dragonfly hovered above her, highlighting the shape in the water. At first she thought it was just a piece of driftwood, maybe a stray branch, but as it drifted into the light she could make out some sort of carving on it.

Unable to resist she stretched for it, frustrated when it bobbed just out of her reach. Now she was determined to have it and she leaned out further. It lapped against her hand in the icy water, not once but twice, but as her fingers finally wrapped around it, a chalky white hand shot out of the water and grabbed her wrist.

Letting out a bloodcurdling scream she felt herself pitch forwards towards the water.

Suddenly familiar arms wrapped around her and

yanked her backwards. Both she and Theo tumbled back against the jetty. Her heart pounded wildly in her throat as she fought to suck in a deep breath, aware that her fingers were still wrapped tightly around the piece of wood she had found floating in the water.

'Livy, what the hell were you doing?' Theo shouted angrily.

'Sorry,' she breathed heavily, 'grab Beau before he falls in would you.'

Theo stood and scooped the puppy up, tucking him under one arm safely while he reached down and hauled Olivia to her feet.

'We'd better get back to the house before you end up with a fever, its freezing out here.'

She realized it was better not to argue with him after all she'd probably just scared another ten years off his life. At this rate she'd probably turn the poor guy prematurely grey.

They struggled through the snow back to the house, shutting and locking the door behind them.

'Why are you holding a stick?' Theo asked in confusion.

'I don't think it is just a stick,' she replied as she pulled her coat off and hung it on the rack. Turning it over in the bright light of the kitchen she studied it. It was about three feet long and quite thick. There was a gnarled knot at the top although she couldn't quite tell if it was part of the wood or whether it had been chiseled that way. In fact she couldn't even tell what kind of wood it was. But it was the engravings that ran the length of it that fascinated her.

'Are those letters?' Theo looked closer, 'I don't recognize them.'

'I think they might be Greek,' Olivia mumbled thoughtfully.

Theo picked up the mop and turned to clean up the wet floor.

'Here I'll do that,' she dropped the stick down on the island and took the mop from him. 'Where's Beau?'

'He's thawing out in front of the fire.'

'I think he's got the right idea,' Olivia replied, before yelping and dropping the mop as Theo scooped her up and tossed her over his shoulder.

'You don't need to worry; I'll thaw you out.'

Olivia laughed as he carried her out of the kitchen, the mop forgotten on the floor as he flipped off the light switch on their way towards the bedroom. But as their laughter drifted down from the stairs, forgotten on the island in the darkness of the kitchen, the strange ancient lettering on the staff began to glow pure silver.

2.

Olivia looked up, her mouth full of toast, as Theo wandered into the kitchen with the paper in one hand and Beau winding happily in circles around his legs. Setting her toast down while Theo poured himself a coffee she began to absentmindedly butter a slice for him. As he joined her he saw her gaze was still locked thoughtfully on the stick she'd pulled from the lake the night before.

'Why have you still got that dirty stick?'

'It's not just a stick' she murmured as she dipped the knife into the jam, 'I'm not sure what it is yet.'

'You're lucky you didn't end up in the lake last night' Theo frowned.

'That wasn't exactly my fault; something grabbed me and tried to pull me in.'

'That's even worse' he sighed, 'and yet you say it so calmly. Look can you just avoid the lake for a while. I still can't swim, and although that wouldn't have stopped me from jumping in after you, we would have both drowned.'

'Are you kidding' Olivia smiled, 'the Lake in January? We'd both have died of hypothermia before we drowned.'

'Is that supposed to make me feel better?'

She shrugged, placing the toast on his plate. 'That is unless the crazy ghost in the lake didn't get us first.'

'This is the strangest breakfast conversation I think I've ever had.'

Olivia laughed quietly as he took a bite and almost purred.

'What's this?'

He turned the jar around and tried to read the scrawled handwriting on the homemade label.

'Liddy Mayberry,' Olivia took a bite of her own toast. 'The woman's turning into something of a cottage industry. She's decided to branch out from baking cakes and pastries and has been trying her hand at jams and jellies.'

'Where does the woman find the time?' he shook his head taking another bite.

'Never underestimate the ingenuity of a woman suffering from a severe case of empty nest.'

'Empty nest?' Theo's gaze locked on hers questioningly, 'I don't understand this reference.'

'All her children have grown up and left home,' Olivia replied taking a sip of her tea. 'I believe her husband Alistair Mayberry owns and runs the local newspaper and puts in long hours and with her children gone she's lonely and bored.'

'I see,' he answered as his hand disappeared under the table with part of his toast and she heard the distinct sound of a wagging tail thumping enthusiastically against the floor.

'Theo' she sighed, 'stop feeding him from the table. You're giving him bad habits, no wonder he follows you around like a shadow.'

'It won't hurt him,' he grinned.

'Stop smiling at me like that,' she shook her head, 'it's not good for him to have sugary foods. She stood up and leaned down to drop a kiss on his lips, 'he'll end up with a sweet tooth like yours.'

He watched her with a smile as she turned to fill Beau's bowl with some of his own food. Hearing his food bag being opened Beau scrambled to his feet and headed for Olivia.

'Good boy,' she bent down and stroked him lovingly as he clumsily stuck his face deep into the bowl, causing the food to spill up and over the sides like a small tsunami.

'So what are we going to do about the visitor we had last night?' Theo asked.

'I'm not sure yet,' Olivia shrugged turning to pour herself a fresh cup of tea. 'I don't have much experience with spirits. Apart from that time in college when a couple of my friends decided to get drunk and have a séance I've never given the idea of spirits much thought. Last night was definitely the first time I've seen one up close and personal.'

'I wonder who she was.'

'I have no idea,' Olivia sat back down with her fresh tea cradled in her hands.

'It's a pity there is no one we can ask.'

'Someone we can ask,' Olivia murmured thoughtfully as her eyes fell on the newspaper, 'I wonder?'

'What?'

Setting down her tea Olivia picked up the paper and opened it. Flipping through it to the page she wanted she scanned down the list of ads.

'There,' she replied pointing to a name.

'Fiona Caldwell, medium and spiritualist,' Theo read out loud. 'A medium?'

'Someone who speaks with spirits' she clarified.

'Speaks with spirits,' Theo replied skeptically, 'we had those where I come from, but they were either charlatans or in league with the devil.'

'Careful sweetheart,' she smiled, 'your Puritan is showing again.'

'Regardless,' he replied dryly, 'this person is

probably a fraud; it's a waste of time.'

'Well it's my time to waste,' she shrugged. 'It's either Fiona Caldwell or...' she squinted slightly as she read the ad underneath, 'the mysterious Madame Magini, purveyor of mystical and fantastic communications from the other world.'

'Fine,' he conceded after a moment, 'Ms Caldwell it is.'

Olivia rose from her chair and walked over to Theo, climbing into his lap with her legs astride his. She wrapped her arms around him and brushed her lips against his.

'You know,' she replied slowly, 'as we're going to be out anyway we could always swing by the coffee shop afterwards, I think they're still doing the caramel bruleé latte.'

'You're a devious woman,' he chuckled lightly as his hands slid around her pulling her in closer.

'I don't know what you mean,' she smiled against his lips.

His hand slid up under her hair and cupped the back of her neck. He took her lips softly as if he had all the time in the world and in that one moment everything faded away and he was every breath she took.

An hour later they pulled up to the address listed and climbed warily out of the car. Stepping onto the sidewalk Olivia looked up curiously at the two storey house in front of her. It was like a rainbow had exploded all over it, the boards were painted a bright happy yellow with poppy red shutters. The front door was an eye catching cerulean blue, and hanging everywhere were brightly colored glass jars, wind chimes, sun dials and weather vanes. Opening the gate which was painted grass green she picked her way up the snow covered path, closely followed by a bemused Theo. Small bundles were placed at random intervals throughout the front yard, each covered with a fine dusting of snow, showing splashes of color here and there. They reached the porch and she realized the small heaps were actually garden gnomes, dozens of them clustered together in corners.

She raised her hand to knock but before she could the door swung open and Olivia's mouth fell open at the short well-built woman regarding them both suspiciously. She wore cat's eye glasses attached to a gold chain and sported a wild grey beehive which would not have looked out of place on a 1950's school mistress. She had two curls either side of her face by her ears, but rather than falling in sweet little ringlets they stuck straight out from her head like mad grey corkscrews. She wore a bright blue hand knitted jumper with a reindeer on the chest and a tweed skirt which fell to just below her knees. Her green argyle socks were pulled up to mid calves and on her feet she wore bright red Birkenstocks.

'Uh...Ms Caldwell,' Olivia stepped closer offering her hand, 'I'm...'

'The West girl,' she nodded, 'I know. I used to play bridge with your aunt Evelyn every Thursday.'

She took her hand and shook it brusquely before turning to look at Theo. She pushed her black rimmed glasses up her nose and squinted as she scrutinized him thoroughly.

'This is...' Olivia began.

'Not from our time line are you?' she interrupted pursing her lips thoughtfully and then releasing them with a smacking sound. 'Fascinating.'

She stepped back from the door and waved them inside.

'Come in come in, don't loiter,' she closed the door behind them, 'jolly cold out.'

'Um, okay,' Olivia stepped into the foyer. The house looked even bigger inside; the walls were decorated with huge flowers and a dark wooden banister wound alongside a curved staircase.

'What the hell is that?' Theo whispered with wide eyes.

Olivia followed his gaze to the cat sitting upright on the curved end of the banister.

'It's a Sphinx cat,' she replied.

'That's a cat?' His brows rose in alarm, 'what's wrong with it?'

'It's supposed to look like that.'

Theo stared at the strange wrinkled hairless cat.

'Oh don't worry,' Fiona interrupted brusquely, 'that's just Penelope.'

Another cat identical to the first appeared and wound itself around Fiona's legs.

'And this is Pandora,' she chuckled as she bent down and scooped her up, nuzzling her wrinkled face.

Another cat shot out of a nearby doorway and taking one look at the new guests, bolted down the hallway and disappeared.

'That's Priscilla,' Fiona told them as she set off down the hallway, 'she's a little shy of strangers.'

'I think we might've been better off with the mysterious Madam Magini,' he muttered under his breath.

Fiona huffed.

'Madam Magini my foot,' she snorted. 'Her name's Delores Lebinski and she's about as mysterious as a can of baked beans,' she stopped abruptly and looked Theo up and down. 'She'd have eaten you alive boy. If she ever offers to read your tea leaves, my advice is decline, politely.'

'I'll bear that in mind,' Theo murmured as she ushered them through a doorway.

His eyes fell on another two of the strange hairless felines sitting regally on the arm and the back of a deeply cushioned couch of bright sunshine yellow. A mewling came from across the room and he spotted another three cats sprawled idly along the deep window ledge.

'This is Primavera and Primrose,' she nodded towards the two on the couch, 'don't mind them they're quite friendly.'

'Is she aware of the other twenty five letters in the alphabet?' Theo whispered to Olivia.

'Over there is Pomona and Poppy,' the small woman continued, 'then we have Prudence and... Colin.'

'Apparently she is,' Olivia replied dryly.

'Sit, sit, sit,' she bustled them towards the couch as she dropped Pandora to the ground. We don't stand on ceremony here, take a seat. I've just put a pot of tea on, I'll be back in a jiffy.'

The strange little woman hurried from the room muttering to herself. Olivia watched Theo in amusement for a moment as he and Primrose eyed each other with mutual distrust, before turning her attention to the room itself. The walls were painted bright blue, several large art canvases covered one wall, each a riot of bright primary colours. The effect was hectic and slightly nauseating. Everywhere she turned she could see loud jewel colours and nothing seemed to match. The final effect was almost psychedelic.

Fiona shuffled back into the room carrying a large tray and set it down on the coffee table with a loud clatter.

'Coffee for you Theodore, black and sweet,' she handed him a steaming mug.

'How did you know?' He took the mug, staring into it with frown, and then at their hostess with suspicion.

'You'll find I know a great many things young man.'

She sat down and began to pour out a cup of tea from a chipped red teapot. 'Tea for you Olivia dear,' she handed her a cup and saucer.

'Thank you Ms. Caldwell.'

'Fiona,' she took her own cup, 'and don't slouch girl, knew a girl like that once. Perpetua Lancastry, went to school with her. Spine like a question mark, always slouching. Ran off with a second trombone from the Bromley brass band, ended up with a dose of the clap before he left her high and dry in a B&B in Scotland. Dreadful business that.'

'You're English?' Theo asked curiously.

'That's right,' she nodded.

'How did you end up in Mercy?'

'How do most people end up in Mercy.' Fiona pulled out a small slightly tarnished silver cigarette case from the deep pocket of her skirt, 'you'll find people with a preternatural gift naturally gravitate towards this town. It's a place of power and it's old, very old. I'm not talking about the town itself; back in England we have buildings older than this town. No, I'm talking about the land itself. It runs just beneath the surface, magic, far older than anything you can possibly imagine. It calls to those with abilities, draws them close. You must've felt it yourself,' she looked directly at Olivia as she pulled a cigarette from the case and closed it with a snap. 'Mind you, with that demon calling you back to Mercy, I expect his voice drowned out everything else.'

'You know about Nathaniel?' Olivia's eyes widened.

'Of course I do,' she pulled a box of matches from her pocket and flicked it open. 'Of course I do, pay attention girl, your Aunt Evelyn and I didn't sit around discussing the weather during our bridge nights.'

'Do you mind?' she indicated the cigarette before shrugging and lighting it anyway. 'Of course you don't mind, I know about your proclivity for fire.'

'You seem to know an awful lot,' Theo frowned.

'The advertisement may say medium and spiritualist,' Fiona took a long drag and breathed out a cloud of smoke, 'that pays the bills. Most of my clients just want the comfort of knowing their loved ones are still watching over them. But make no mistake my talents run far deeper than that.'

She rummaged around in her pocket once again and this time came up with a tartan covered hip flask.

'Hot toddy anyone?' she offered, pouring the deep amber coloured liquid into her teacup.

'Sure,' Olivia held out her own cup, charmed by the eccentric middle aged woman.

'That's a good girl,' Fiona chuckled in approval, 'so let's cut to the chase as you Americans say. Why don't you tell me what it is you want from me?'

Olivia took a sip from her teacup and sucked in a sharp breath.

'Are you alright?' Theo frowned at Olivia, 'your eyes are watering.'

'I'm fine,' her voice came out as a husky rasp.

Fiona slipped the flask back inside her pocket and took another drag of her cigarette.

'You like it?' she beamed, 'I brew it myself, not unlike your moonshine I think.'

'I can tell,' Olivia coughed weakly.

'So?' Fiona indicated for Olivia to continue.

'Last night,' she began, setting the cup down on the table, 'I heard a grandfather clock chiming. I don't own a clock like that, so I got up to see what was going on. I went downstairs and the temperature had dropped to below freezing. When I reached the kitchen the back door was open and there were wet footprints leading into the room.'

'You saw a spirit?' Fiona leaned forward intently.

'Yes,' Olivia nodded, 'a girl. I'd probably put her at about eighteen, nineteen years old. About my height, long dark hair, she was wearing a white muslin shift, torn and dirty. She opened her mouth to speak but water poured out of it.'

'What was the water like?' The question appeared somewhat random.

'Why does that matter?' Theo asked.

'Because it does,' she answered irritably, 'stop

interrupting.'

'It was dirty, like lake water,' Olivia replied.

Fiona nodded and indicated for her to continue.

'Theo walked into the kitchen and she just...' Olivia held her hands up looking for the right word to describe what she'd seen, 'dissolved.'

'Disappeared?'

'Not exactly,' she shook her head, 'it was more like she became the water and just...'

'Dissolved,' they both said in unison.

Fiona nodded and sat back thoughtfully, sucking on her cigarette so hard it almost burned straight down to the butt.

'I'll need to take a trip out to your house and see what we're dealing with,' she replied after a moment. 'Did you feel threatened by her?'

'She scared the absolute crap out of me.'

'I'm not talking about the initial jolt of seeing her; I mean did she try to hurt you in any way?'

'No,' Olivia shook her head, 'it felt more like she was trying to say something to me.'

'Interesting,' Fiona stubbed out her cigarette in a cow shaped ashtray, 'well there's no time like the present.'

'For what?' Theo asked as Fiona stood abruptly.

'To visit the scene of the crime as it were,' she replied. 'I can get a better reading if I'm standing where the manifestation took place.'

'You want to come to my house?' Olivia stood.

'Isn't that what I just said?' She strode out into her hallway and kicked off her Birkenstocks, replacing them with bright orange snow boots. 'Come on, come on, my time is not limitless you know.'

She ushered them out briskly as she zipped up a thick red jacket and yanked on a purple striped woolen hat, grabbing her keys on the way out as she followed them onto the porch.

'You head back I'll follow you,' she told them as

she headed towards an old green mini cooper.

'I guess we'd better do as she says,' Olivia grinned and shrugged as she glanced at Theo.

'You're enjoying this aren't you?' his eyes narrowed suspiciously.

'Of course I am; that woman is exactly my brand of crazy.'

'Well you're right about the crazy part,' he murmured turning to follow Olivia to the car.

They drove back in silence for the most part, followed by the strange little green car which seemed as quirky as its owner and as Olivia parked up in front of the house, it swung in behind her. She watched as Fiona unfolded herself from the pint sized car and stared out towards the woods. She pursed her lips thoughtfully as her eyes narrowed. After a moment her gaze wandered from the woods, tracking slowly across the panoramic view from the land in front of Olivia's house, past the road they'd just come down and then across to the lake with its small lonely wooden jetty.

'Is everything alright Fiona?' Olivia asked as she approached the distracted woman.

'Yes, yes,' she answered absently although her eyes seemed firmly fixed on the waters of the lake.

'What is it?'

Fiona turned to Olivia and stuck her hands in her pocket jingling her keys restlessly.

'Nothing,' she replied, 'shall we have a look in the kitchen then?'

'Sure.'

Olivia turned back towards the house and followed Theo up the steps to the porch. She could hear a scrambling of claws on wood followed by an enthusiastic bark and as Theo opened the front door Beau shot out past them heading straight for Fiona.

'Well hello young man,' she laughed delightedly and hunkered down to his level while he jumped up at her and tried to lick her face. 'You're a handsome chap aren't you.'

'His name is Beau,' Olivia told her.

'It certainly suits him,' she laughed standing and heading up the steps with the puppy following her happily.

Fiona stepped across the threshold and stood in the hallway. She removed her purple hat and several hairpins dropped harmlessly to the floor. Her crazy iron grey beehive, streaked with the odd stripe of pure white, stood out in all directions making her look like a banshee.

'Shall I take your coat for you?' Theo asked politely.

'No,' she shook her head, 'no need I won't be staying, I don't like to leave the cats for too long.'

'Well the kitchen's through this way,' Olivia indicated.

'I remember well enough,' Fiona replied jovially and sauntered off in the direction of the kitchen. 'Is this the only place she has manifested?'

'Yes,' Olivia nodded behind her.

Olivia watched in fascination as Fiona stepped into the room and inhaled deeply.

'I see there are protection wards around the house, they weren't here before.'

'No, they're mine; I put them around the house when the murders were going on.'

'I see.'

'How much do you know?' Olivia asked curiously, 'how much did my aunt actually tell you?'

'I know about the demon, I also know that he has escaped. I felt it the moment he set foot on Mercy soil.'

'Well, I set the wards around the house to keep out any supernatural creatures. What I don't understand is how the girl's spirit was able to cross the line.'

'She didn't,' Fiona turned back to face Olivia.

'What do you mean?' she frowned.

'She didn't cross the line, she has been here all

along,' Fiona told her seriously. 'When you raised the protective circle around the house all you did was trap her on the inside.'

'Oh.'

'Although,' she mused, 'I don't know that your wards would have made much of a difference anyway. You said you adapted it to keep out supernatural creatures?'

'Yes.'

'Spirits aren't technically supernatural creatures; even though they're deceased they were still once human.'

'Great,' Olivia muttered sourly.

Fiona turned back to continue her thorough perusal of the room. She crouched low to the ground, her knees cracking loudly as she did. She placed her hand on the floor and closed her eyes.

'She's always been here,' she murmured, 'this was her home once.'

'Do you know who she is?'

Fiona opened her eyes and stood.

'She's yours,' she replied, 'she's a West, I can feel that much. I can't seem to get her name though, which is strange. Usually that's the first thing I pick up on.'

'She won't tell you?' Olivia frowned.

Fiona shook her head. 'It's more like she can't tell me; something or someone is stopping her.'

'Someone?' her eyes widened.

'I can sense more than one presence in this house.'

'Well that makes me feel better,' she muttered sarcastically.

'Do you recall anyone in your family ever mentioning a girl in your family who drowned in the lake?'

Olivia cast her mind back for a moment and then shook her head in frustration.

'No, I don't remember anything like that. Is that what happened to her then? She drowned in the lake?'

'Yes,' Fiona nodded slowly, 'it may have been an

accident, or maybe not. I can sense her spirit is restless, for whatever reason she never passed over to the other side but remained here, tied to this house. Up until now she has been dormant,' she tapped her chin thoughtfully, 'what happened to change that? What pushed her out of her pattern?'

'The demon rising?' Theo suggested.

'Maybe,' she mused, 'you said you felt like she was trying to tell you something?'

Olivia nodded.

'Yes, but she couldn't seem to get the words out. Water just kept pouring from her mouth.'

'She's trapped in a cycle, reliving her last few moments of life. You have to understand spirits aren't linear as you and I are. Time has no meaning for them, nor does reality. They often get confused and don't make sense. If this poor unfortunate girl has been trapped in a death cycle she wouldn't have been aware of any living person in this house, which would probably account for why no one has mentioned her. She hasn't shown herself to anyone else, so the question is why did she show herself to you?'

Olivia blew out an exasperated breath and cast her eyes to the ceiling.

'Why is it always me?' she sighed.

'That my dear,' she replied sympathetically, 'is a question I can't answer for you. But I'm sure you'll figure it out. You said she is trying to tell you something, so listen. Sooner or later she'll show up again.'

'Thanks,' she replied dryly, 'that'll help me sleep better at night.'

'Here,' she dived into her deep skirt pocket and handed Olivia a slightly rumpled scrap of paper. 'Don't call the number on the newspaper ad, that's the line for clients and I don't always answer. This is my personal number; call me anytime day or night if you need to. In the meantime I suggest you try and figure out who she is.'

'How do I do that?'

'I didn't get much from her, but I will go out on a limb here and place her sometime at the end of the nineteenth century beginning of the twentieth. We know she was part of your family and that she was around eighteen when she died. We also know she drowned. It's a start, so look at your family history, the history of the town, at anyone who drowned in the lake. Sooner or later we'll find out who she is, maybe that'll be enough to put her spirit to rest. Sometimes spirits just want to be acknowledged.'

'But you don't think so,' Olivia's eyes narrowed suspiciously, 'do you?'

'No I don't,' Fiona shook her head, 'I think it took something pretty significant to break a spirit out of a death cycle. She is trying to reach out to you for a reason, we just need to figure out what that reason is.'

'I'll see what I can find out.'

'Good,' she nodded in approval, resuming her usual brisk business-like tone. 'I must be going now, Theodore, if you wouldn't mind walking me out.'

'Certainly,' he turned to lead her back out of the room as she said goodbye to Olivia.

Fiona followed him to the door, pulling the purple hat out of her pocket and yanking it down over her ears.

'A word if you don't mind Theodore,' she marched past him and out onto the snow covered porch.

Theo stepped out behind her curiously and pulled the door to.

'Is there something I can help you with Ms Caldwell?'

'Fiona,' she corrected in a clipped tone, 'I have a question.'

'Okay?'

'When are you going to tell Olivia about your wife?'

Theo's eyes widened in shock and then darkened.

His back stiffened and his jaw clenched.

'I don't know what you're talking about.'

'Yes you do boy, don't play the innocent with me,' her eyes narrowed. 'You need to tell Olivia about Mary.'

His arms crossed in front of his chest as he regarded her dangerously.

'Olivia doesn't need to know.'

'Yes she does,' Fiona puffed out her chest drawing herself up to full height and still she only reached Theo's chest. 'You need to tell her about your wife...about what happened to her.'

His eyes flashed angrily and his mouth tightened into a thin line.

'Olivia will never find out about that.'

'Stop looking at me like that,' Fiona muttered irritably, 'I have no intention of telling her but you should. If you don't you'll lose her.'

'If I tell her I'll lose her,' Theo replied quietly.

'That's her choice to make,' she told him pointedly, 'not yours.'

'What do you intend to do?'

'Nothing, for now,' she regarded him with dark serious eyes, 'but I will give you a warning. The dead never stay dead; your visitation last night should have taught you that. The past has a way of refusing to stay buried. The truth will out boy,' her voice dropped low as she turned towards the steps, 'you would do well to remember that.'

3.

It had been two days since Fiona's visit. Two frustrating days, Olivia thought as she slammed another journal shut, and still she hadn't found any clue as to who her mystery ghost was. To make matters worse, for the past few days Theo had been surly and withdrawn which was unlike him. He'd disappeared into the dining room which they had cleared to make into a studio for him. Whatever was on his mind he seemed to be working through it by painting so she'd left him to it. But she missed talking to him, having him to bounce ideas off.

Leaning back in her chair she took a deep breath; she was getting nowhere. She'd been through all the family records she could find, as well as her grandmother and her great aunt's journals, but there were quite literally hundreds of years of the West's history tucked up in her library and they were in no kind of order. It would take her years at this rate to make sense of her family history.

There was one avenue she could explore although she had been deliberately putting it off. If the girl had drowned in the lake, whether it was a suspicious or accidental death, there should have been an investigation, especially as the victim belonged to one of the founding families of Mercy. At the very least there should have been a police report somewhere. It was time to stop avoiding everyone. She was going to have to go and see Jake to ask for his help.

Closing the journal she pushed back from the desk and stood, stretching out the kinks in her back. Wondering what Theo was up to she wandered into the dining room and stopped in the doorway to watch him for a moment. He was asleep in the deep tatty chair they had hauled in from the parlor and placed in front of the huge bay window. His head had fallen back against the threadbare cushion and his chest rose and fell in slow measured breaths. An open sketchbook lay in his lap and a pencil dangled from his loose fingertips.

Frowning she watched him in silence, she knew he wasn't sleeping at night. She'd felt him toss and turn restlessly next to her and a few times he'd even given in and disappeared into the dining room to paint into the small hours of the morning. But whatever it was that plagued his thoughts he refused to open up to her. She'd tried to be understanding and give him some space, hoping that he would talk to her, but so far he showed absolutely no inclination to speak of it.

She stepped into the room and walked quietly across to him. An easel stood in the centre of the room with a canvas resting on it. She guessed from the wet paint blotted on the floor that he'd spent the morning painting. Although burning curiosity gnawed at her she resisted the urge to lift the sheet covering his latest creation. She knew if he'd covered it he didn't want anyone seeing it. Resolutely turning her back on it and avoiding the paint splatters on the floor, she crossed over to stand beside him. Beau slept curled up at his feet as if he were guarding him and as she reached them the dog opened a sleepy eye. Lifting his head to look at her he thumped his tail on the floor a couple of times in greeting then laid his head back down on Theo's feet and promptly went back to sleep.

She gazed down at his face, aware of the frown

which marred his brow. Whatever he was dreaming about it wasn't peaceful. Reaching out with gentle fingers she smoothed back the dark lock of hair which had fallen forward onto his face. Her gaze was drawn down to the open sketchpad in his lap where he had drawn a very detailed gnarled ancient looking tree on a hilltop. From its lower branches hung several nooses.

Frowning Olivia reached out, her fingers closing around the book so she could get a closer look. As she tried to lift it Theo's hand shot out and grasped her wrist firmly. He silently looked up at her with unreadable dark eyes; wordlessly he took the pad from her and closed it.

'That was Gallows Hill wasn't it?' she whispered.

He stood abruptly, causing Beau to scramble out of his way and turning away he placed the sketchpad on top of the pads he had stacked on the table, dropping his pencil back in the pot with the others. Although she could argue he was just tidying his things away, it felt like he'd slammed a door in her face.

'I wish you'd tell me what's bothering you,' she spoke so quietly he almost missed it.

He released a slow breath and turned back to her. 'There is nothing bothering me.'

'No lies Theo, isn't that what we agreed.'

'We also agreed we didn't have to share everything.'

'Fine,' she answered in a clipped tone forcing back the sudden sting of hurt. She wasn't used to him shutting her out and after the lies and betrayal of her parents, his slight cut deep.

'Suit yourself, I'm going out.'

She turned and walked out of the room without waiting for his response. She stalked out into the hallway and yanked on her coat, thrusting her feet into her boots. Picking up her keys and purse she was about to open the door when she heard his voice behind her, low and troubled.

'Don't leave like this Livy.'

She closed her eyes and leaned against the door, feeling a heavy weight settle on her chest.

'I'll be fine,' she replied quietly, 'I'm sorry I disturbed you.'

She moved to grasp the handle of the door but suddenly found herself trapped by Theo's body against her back and his arms either side of her, his palms pressed flat against the wood of the door.

'I'm sorry,' he whispered.

'What's going on Theo?' she turned her head so she was looking into his eyes. 'You've been ignoring me for days.'

'It's...' he shook his head unable to find the words, 'it's not you it's me.'

Not wanting to hear him give her the old brush off speech she abruptly turned away from him. She opened her mouth to speak and then thought better of it, not trusting the words that might tumble out. Her chest was tight with need and an uncomfortable ball of emotion burned at the back of her throat. Suddenly she found herself blinking back tears. Determined not to let him see her cry she shoved him back and yanked the door open.

'I'll be back later,' she muttered as she stepped out on the porch, unable to look back as she headed towards her car.

Theo sucked in a breath as she slammed the door in his face, pressing his forehead against the door much as she had, his fist clenched in anger. Dammit, he'd hurt her, he knew he had. Turning around he slumped back against the door and rubbed his hands over his face in frustration.

What the hell was he doing?

He let his head fall back against the wood with a dull thud and dragged in a deep breath. He knew he'd been pushing her away and he hadn't meant to. He just didn't know what to do. The crazy physic woman was right he did need to tell her about Mary but he just couldn't bring himself to do it. It was his deepest darkest sin, the one thing he was most ashamed of. If Olivia ever found out the truth about what he'd done he didn't see how she could possibly forgive him, especially as he'd never been able to forgive himself.

The truth was he didn't want her to know. Their relationship was still so new, not that she would even admit they were in a relationship. Whenever he tried to bring the subject up she simply shut down or changed the subject. She seemed content to just coast along enjoying each other without any of the work and commitment that came with loving another person, not that she would admit that either. He tried not to let it bother him, tried to give her time but he had to admit it stung that she couldn't say the three little words he was desperate to hear from her.

He pushed away from the door and moved back into his studio. Stopping in front of the easel he dragged the sheet off the canvas and stared into the one face in the world he wanted to forget.

Icy blue eyes stared coldly back at him framed by a pale face. Her blonde hair was tucked neatly under a plain linen cap; although only her shoulders were visible he knew she wore a dark severe dress.

Theo continued to stare at the portrait of his wife. He should never have painted it; he wasn't even sure why he had. Unable to sleep and plagued by guilt, nightmares had driven him from his and Olivia's bed. He'd wanted to turn to Olivia so badly, to breathe her in, to feel her soft warm skin against his, to lose himself in her. But he couldn't while his mind was trapped in the past. He wouldn't let it touch her, wouldn't let what he had done taint her in any way.

He'd started to paint; unaware of what he was creating until Mary's face emerged to stare at him accusingly. Unable to stand looking at her a moment longer he picked up the first tube of paint he could reach, regardless of the color, and squeezed it into his palm.

Swiping his hand across the picture in a jagged motion he watched as part of her face disappeared behind a violent slash of red. How apt he thought to himself dryly. Picking up another tube again he squeezed out the contents into his hand and this time swiped a blue streak across the canvas. Lost now in a maelstrom of conflicted emotions he grabbed tubes of color at random and continued to rake his hands across the canvas in the most primitive way until nothing was left but a mad riot of colours.

He stepped back breathing heavily, his hands caked in the thick sticky paint. He still didn't feel any better, maybe he should just take the stupid canvas out back and burn it. He reached for the canvas intending to throw it out the back door but he suddenly paused, his fingers outstretched towards the offending canvas. A cold chill danced down his spine causing him to shiver. Just for a moment he thought he heard a breath exhaled against his ear. He turned to look but as his gaze caught on the mirror mounted on the wall, his heart clenched and his head snapped around. Everything was just as it should be and he let out a breath of relief. Rolling his shoulders, he tried to shift the knot of unease planted between his shoulder blades. Just for a moment, in the mirror, he could have sworn he had seen the reflection of a tall blonde woman standing in the doorway.

Olivia pulled into a parking space outside the police station and killed the engine. Taking a deep breath she leaned over to retrieve her purse, before stepping out of the car locking it carefully behind her. Smoothing down her coat she headed towards the main building trying not to let her thoughts slip back to Theo. She shouldn't have had a pop at the guy just because she wanted him to spill his secrets. She'd been unfair; he hadn't pushed her when she didn't want to talk. She should have at least given him the same courtesy. Sighing in resignation, she pulled the station door open and stepped in. A wall of heat hit her and she almost took a step back. Jeez, someone liked the heat up high. Pulling off her hat and jamming it into one of her pockets she unzipped her coat and loosened her scarf as she headed for the main desk.

Ada Bradley gazed up from her computer screen as Olivia's shadow fell over her screen.

'Miss West,' she nodded after a moment, 'what brings you by today?'

'Ms Bradley.'

Olivia deliberately plastered a cheery smile on her face. After the damage the previous Chief of Police had done by half convincing everyone she was a deranged murderer it was going to take a while to rebuild her reputation. Of course her reputation had not been stellar to start with, on account of everyone believing her father was a murderer. It turned out that was not true but unfortunately no one knew her mother was still alive and that the charges against her father were false.

'I was wondering if Jake is in today.'

'Might be,' she picked up the phone and held up a finger indicating for Olivia to wait. 'Carl,' she spoke briskly, 'is Jake back there with you or is he out on a call?'

She listened to the muffled reply for a moment, her gazed locked on Olivia's.

'Tell him Olivia West is here to see him,' another muffled response caused her to roll her eyes to the ceiling, 'that's what I said.'

She hung up abruptly and turned back to Olivia.

'He'll be out in a moment.'

'Thank you,' she tugged the collar of her sweater, starting to feel a little clammy in the heat, 'warm isn't it.'

Ms. Bradley's mouth curved at the corner.

'Heating's busted we're waiting on an engineer,' she indicated the seated area. 'You can wait over there, enjoy the sauna.'

'Thanks,' Olivia smiled taking a seat.

Removing her coat and laying it over her lap while

she waited, her mind was inadvertently drawn back to Theo. Maybe she should give him some space; perhaps he was having second thoughts about them. After all they were kind of thrown together in the middle of a massive supernatural crisis. They'd barely known each other a few weeks before they ended up pretty much living together. Everything had been so intense and dangerous it wasn't surprising they'd ended up in bed together. Okay, so he'd said he loved her but really, how could she believe that? Despite the visions he'd had of her they really didn't know each other that well. Now that the danger and urgency had faded she wondered how much of his feelings towards her had been colored by the situation they had found themselves in. A slow unwelcome thought began to creep in; what if he wanted to leave but just didn't know how to tell her? What if he was only staying because she was the only thing in his life that was familiar?

'Olive!' a warm welcome voice pulled her from her morose thoughts.

'Hey Jake,' her face broke into a genuine smile as she stood. Before she could utter another word she found herself crushed in a bear hug.

'Missed you,' he muttered, 'are you okay?'

'I'm fine,' she wheezed, 'Jake...need oxygen.'

He released her with a laugh.

'I'm sorry I haven't seen you for a while,' she frowned, 'I just needed some time to process everything.'

'And have you?'

'I'm getting there,' she shrugged.

'Is this a social call?'

'Not exactly,' she smiled ruefully, 'I wanted to ask a favor.'

'Come on,' he tugged her with him, 'I'll get you a really bad cup of coffee and you can tell me about this favor.'

She followed Jake back through the double doors, past the front desk and the ever assessing gaze of Ada

Bradley and into a large open plan office, bustling with activity. Edging her way around clusters of desks, she dropped into a seat at Jake's desk while he disappeared towards the coffee machine.

'Sorry it's black,' he handed her a Styrofoam cup, 'we're out of milk again.'

'No its fine,' she took a sip and grimaced. 'I take it back it's not fine, it's like tar. How can you drink this poison?'

'You get used to it after a while,' he shrugged. 'I guess I've just got a cast iron stomach.

'You'd need to,' she slid the offending cup towards the corner of his desk.

'So what's up?'

'I'm looking for any police files, incident reports or any kind of documentation about a girl who drowned in the lake.'

Jake pulled out a notepad and picked up a pen.

'Name?'

'I don't know yet.'

'Date?'

'About a hundred to a hundred and twenty years ago.'

Jake dropped his pen and turned to stare at her.

'I'm sorry what?'

'A hundred to a hundred and tw…'

'Yeah yeah that's what I thought you said.' He held up his hand, shoving the pad out of the way and turned to face her more fully. 'Why don't you tell me what's going on.'

'Are you sure you really want to know?'

'Start talking Olive,' he leaned back in his chair and crossed his arms.

'I have a ghost in my house.'

'Huh?'

'Jake, this conversation is going to take all day if I have to keep repeating myself.'

'You have a ghost?'

'She just showed up out of the blue, a few nights back. Scared the freaking crap out of me, so Theo and I went to see a medium, Fiona Caldwell.'

'Caldwell,' his brow furrowed in thought, 'that crazy British woman over on Fairfield Avenue? The one with all the garden gnomes?'

'That's the one,' she nodded. 'Anyway I'm trying to figure out who she is, so maybe then I can figure out what she wants.'

'So tell me what you know.'

'Young girl about eighteen years old, drowned in the lake, don't know if it was accidental or not. She was related to me somehow, she's part of the West family and would have lived and died sometime around the turn of the nineteenth century.'

'Well I'd like to help you Olive, but back then record keeping was practically non-existent. Most of the cops weren't even trained. Hell, I don't even know if we have records that go back that far.'

He watched as the desk clerk passed by on the way to the coffee machine and waved her over.

'Ms Bradley, I don't suppose you know how far back our records go do you?'

'Why?' she asked suspiciously, eying Olivia.

'Just trying to solve a little family mystery is all,' she smiled easily. 'I'm looking for records that go back to the turn of the nineteenth century.'

Ada pursed her lips thoughtfully.

'Not sure how far back the records go; the archives used to be kept down in the basement but about ten years back we had that busted pipe, basement got flooded. We lost a lot of paperwork, whatever they managed to salvage was moved up to the third floor. Can't say what's actually there and it's in a hell of a mess.'

'Thanks Ms Bradley,' Jake nodded.

She grunted and walked away.

'Stop giving me the puppy eyes,' Jake turned back to Olivia, 'you heard her, it's a mess.'

'Jake,' she smiled.

'Urgh, fine,' he sighed. 'I'll take a look but I'm not promising anything.'

'Thank you Jake I really appreciate it.'

'Don't thank me yet,' he frowned, 'I'll only be able to take a look in my free time and even then it's probably going to take a while.'

'Still thanks anyway,' she stood up and pulled her coat back on. 'You should come by the house sometime this week, I know Theo would like to see you.'

She kissed his cheek lightly and turned away, pausing when he caught her wrist lightly.

'What's wrong Olive?'

'You mean apart from my psychotic parents and a scary ass ghost loose in my house?'

'Stop avoiding the question.'

She sighed.

'I don't know, Theo is different,' she shrugged helplessly. 'He won't talk to me about it, I just figure he might need a guy to talk to.'

'I'll stop by,' he tugged her pony tail affectionately.

'Thanks Jake.'

'Stop thanking me, he's my friend too.'

'Okay,' she nodded, 'I'm gonna head out now. I have some other ideas on how I can track down our mystery girl.'

'Call me if you find anything out.'

After promising to contact him with any further information Olivia left the station and headed straight for the museum. It was time to catch up with Renata Gershon, the sweet old curator of the museum. The woman was a goldmine of information, she'd made it her life's work to not only make sure Mercy had a museum to rival the Peabody in Salem but she'd also amassed a comprehensive paper history of Mercy and its residents. There wasn't much the woman didn't know.

Olivia opened the door expecting to find quiet and stepped into a frantic whirl of chaos. She watched in fascination at the mad bustle of workmen and staff. Plastic sheeting hung like giant shower curtains across the cordoned off exhibits.

'I'm sorry we're temporarily closed for renovations,' a young woman around Olivia's age scurried forward.

She was a pretty little thing with glasses and wild curly hair she'd tried to tame back into a ponytail at the nape of her neck, although several errant curls had sprung free and now framed her face. She wore sensible heels and a practical skirt. Her sweater was buttoned up over her blouse and she carried a clipboard.

'I'm afraid we won't be open to the public again for at least two weeks,' she spoke again softly.

'It's alright Veronica,' a familiar voice interrupted.

Olivia turned and smiled at the old woman walking towards her, leaning heavily on her cane.

'Hello Olivia dear.'

'Renata,' Olivia wrapped her arms carefully around the small woman, noting how fragile she felt. 'It's good to see you.'

'Veronica this is Olivia West,' she introduced them.

'The historian?' Veronica smiled widely offering her hand. 'I've read your work, and I'd love to discuss your theories on the role of women in the New England colonies some time.'

'Sure,' Olivia replied shaking her hand lightly.

'Olivia,' Renata spoke softly, 'this is Veronica Mason. She's the new assistant curator.'

'You're not retiring are you?'

'Heavens no, this place is my life I plan on dying at my desk.' Renata chuckled as she shuffled over to a nearby chair and eased herself into it carefully as if afraid of jarring her bones. 'I'm old Olivia, I'm not going to be here forever. I started looking for my replacement five years ago; it took me a long time to find Veronica here and to convince her to move to Mercy.'

'Boston, judging by the accent,' Olivia turned to Veronica.

She nodded. 'Renata is exaggerating though; I didn't take much convincing. When she offered me the job I nearly bit her hand off.'

'Well congratulations,' Olivia replied.

'Thanks,' she smiled warmly.

'So what brings you to my door?' Renata placed both gnarled hands on the handle of her cane, tapping her fingers curiously.

'A family mystery.'

'Ah,' Renata's eyes glittered with interest, 'I do love a mystery particularly when it involves the Wests.'

'I'm trying to track down a member of my family; she would have lived and died sometime around the turn of the nineteenth century. She died drowning in the lake and she would have been about eighteen years old at the time,' Olivia explained. 'I tried online at the office of vital records but they only go back as far as 1921. Anything before that I'd have to go to the state records office. But seeing as you keep such comprehensive local records I thought I'd try you first.'

'So you should,' she rapped her cane against the floor in approval, 'you've come to the right place. What you need is the archive room on the second floor.'

She offered her arm and Olivia took hold of her gently and helped her to her feet.

'Veronica be a dear and go and keep an eye on those workmen, I don't trust them near the founders' exhibit.'

'Of course,' she nodded.

'So what's with all the renovations?' Olivia asked as she helped Renata towards the elevator.

'We're outgrowing ourselves,' she smiled proudly. 'The town council have finally figured out how important this place is. Not only for tourism but it's becoming a hub of research and information.'

'Renata,' Olivia smiled as they headed up to the second floor, 'I'm so pleased for you. What you've done here is just amazing.'

'Well,' she chuckled, 'I'm glad to have had a part in preserving so much of Mercy's history. This place has been my home for such a long time and when my time comes I'll be glad to have left my mark on it.'

'You're not sick are you?' she frowned.

'No sweetheart,' she patted Olivia's hand reassuringly but her skin felt as dry and thin as paper. 'I'm just old and beginning to feel it now.'

'Is there anything I can do?'

Renata shook her head as they stepped from the elevator and wandered down the corridor, the quiet punctuated every now and then by a loud crash or the high pitched whine of a buzz saw.

'So what exactly are you doing here?'

'Well the Mayor has given us funding to expand the research rooms so they can be opened to the public. The plan is to open out a couple of the storage rooms and update the fire suppression system. Eventually we're hoping to be able to expand into the building next door. The lease expires next year and the current tenants are not planning on renewing. We've put in a bid and submitted plans for the expansion and we've got the town council backing us so I'm hopeful.'

'Wow,' Olivia stopped as Renata reached out to open the door in front of them.

'Right,' Renata flipped on the light and stepped into the room.

It was a fairly large size room; the walls lined with functional metal shelving each containing dozens of box files. There was a photocopier tucked into the corner and in the centre of the room sat a large conference table and chairs with several computers set up.

'So we have copies of most of the births, marriages and death certificates for Mercy. You'll find them all indexed on the computer, we also have copies of the local churches' baptism records although,' she smiled, 'I doubt you'll find any of your family in the church records.'

'Probably not,' she laughed lightly, 'thanks Renata, I really appreciate this.'

'No need for thanks. This is what the records are here for. Now once you've looked through the indexes, if there are any records or certificates you would like to view or have copies of just write down the reference numbers. I will send Veronica up in a little while to help you.'

'There's no need,' Olivia insisted, 'I'll be fine on my own.

'Some of the records are very fragile and need to be handled by a member of staff,' she answered matter of factly, 'besides you should get to know Veronica. She's about your age and has only just moved here. She barely knows anyone, I'm certain she could use a friend, I'm sure you can appreciate what that feels like.'

'Ok, send her up,' Olivia smiled and dropped an affectionate kiss on Renata's pale cheek.

The old lady nodded in approval and shuffled from the room.

Olivia laid her coat over the back of a nearby chair, sitting down and firing up the nearest computer. By the time Veronica stuck her head around the door an hour later she had a list of three names.

'Hey Olivia, Renata said you needed some help?'

She looked up from the computer screen and nodded.

'Yeah, I have three names that fit the time line roughly. I'll need to look at their death certificates to see if any of them are the actual girl I'm looking for.'

'No problem, did you write down the reference numbers?'

She handed Veronica a piece of paper, watching as she disappeared to the back of the room and started scanning the file boxes. She pulled one from the shelf and moved back to the table placing it down carefully. She removed the beautiful large leather bound volumes and Olivia watched curiously as Veronica selected one and began to leaf through the death certificates.

'Ah here we go,' Veronica pushed her dainty gold framed glasses back up her nose and began to read, 'Eleanor Josephine West born 3rd March 1863 and died 20th October 1887 age 24 at Mercy infirmary. The cause of death is listed as complications due to childbirth.'

Curious, Veronica flicked to the next record. 'Look here, there was also a stillborn female listed.'

Olivia turned back to the computer and searched again.

'Twins,' she nodded, 'I thought so. It seems Eleanor died giving birth to twins, one didn't survive and the other was named Katherine Margaret West.'

'She's the next name on your list,' Veronica confirmed.

'Yes, it seems she died young as well.'

'May I ask a question?'

'Sure,' Olivia shrugged.

'I can see Eleanor's father was listed as James Walker and Katherine's father is listed as Jonathan Douglas.'

'You want to know why all the West women take their mother's name not their fathers.'

She nodded curiously.

'It's a family peculiarity, for some reason as far back as we can trace my family history, only girls are ever born into the West family.'

'Really?'

'It's almost a single unbroken female line, each

generation usually only has one child. Every so often we get twins, but always identical and always girls.'

'That's weird,' Veronica breathed, 'no boys ever?'

'Nope.'

'Well, Eleanor is obviously not the one you're looking for, she was slightly too old and she didn't drown. So let's take a look at Katherine, did you want copies of these records?'

'Yes please, I'm probably going to be spending the next twenty years trying to sort out my family history. I don't think anyone's ever done a comprehensive family tree of the West's. But they kept everything, my house is full of journals and family papers, it's going to take forever to sort through it. It's a wicked mess.'

'I'd love to help you sort through all that history,' Veronica replied dreamily.

'You really are perfect for this job aren't you?'

'Yes,' Veronica laughed, 'I love history; nothing makes me happier than sorting through layers and layers of it.'

'You won't be saying that when you've been through the layers of my family.'

'Seriously, I'd love to help out.'

'Well I might just have to take you up on that once you've finished the renovations here.'

Olivia waited patiently as Veronica took a copy of the certificates and reappeared at the table with another box and was soon sifting through another dusty volume of records.

'Here we go, Katherine Margaret West born 20th October 1887 died 30th November 1918 age 31, cause of death is listed as Influenza.'

'Okay so not her either.'

'The last name on the list was Charlotte?'

Olivia nodded, although Veronica's gaze was firmly fixed on the records in front of her.

'Charlotte was another twin; she and her sister

Elizabeth Laura were born in 1905. From the date of birth, I guess they were Katherine's daughters.'

'You'd be right, here it is. I think we have a winner. Charlotte Lilly West born 20th May 1905 to Katherine Margaret West and Henry James Dover. Died 18th July 1924 age 19, place of death, Mercy Massachusetts and the cause of death is listed as accidental drowning.'

'We found her,' Olivia's gaze dropped to the page as Veronica turned the book around so she could get a closer look. 'It has to be her.'

'Do you mind me asking...why are you looking for her in particular?'

'That's depends, do you want the crazy insane answer or do you want me to lie?' the corner of her mouth curved.

'The truth,' Veronica replied curiously.

'I have a ghost,' Olivia sighed and waited.

'I'm sorry what?'

'A ghost is haunting my house and I am trying to figure out who she is.'

'You're right that is insane,' Veronica frowned.

'You asked,' Olivia shrugged.

'But ghosts aren't real.'

'You come and spend a night in my house then we'll have this conversation again,' Olivia replied nonchalantly.

'Okaay...' Veronica turned skeptically back to the book and wisely chose to drop the subject, 'this is odd.'

'What?'

Veronica was reading through the death certificate in more detail.

'I have a Mr. Augustus Philip Swilley listed as informant on Charlotte's death certificate.'

'Why's that odd?'

'Because I recognize his name from one of the displays downstairs. Augustus Swilley was the Mayor of Mercy from 1920 to 1926 until he died unexpectedly from a massive heart attack.'

'Why would the Mayor of Mercy be registering Charlotte's death?'

'Exactly,' Veronica mused, 'we do seem to have stumbled onto a bit of a mystery.'

'Well it's a start,' Olivia murmured, 'at least I know her name now.'

'You know,' Veronica began thoughtfully, 'Renata was just telling me yesterday that she'd loaned a few of her interns to Mr. Mayberry at the Mercy Chronicle last summer. They were helping him and his staff scan the newspaper archives and upload them into a virtual library, which we have access to.'

She pulled a small pink flowered notepad from her pocket and leafed through it.

'I haven't learned all the passwords yet,' she replied sheepishly as she caught Olivia staring at her.

Settling down comfortably into a chair next to Olivia she logged in to the archive and began searching.

'It was 18th July 1924 wasn't it, Charlotte's death?'

'Yes,' Olivia replied absently as she sent a quick message to Jake with the name and date of death. When he had the time to look into the police records he'd at least have a time frame to work with.

'Here we go,' Veronica spoke after a few moments. 'It is with great sadness Mr. Henry J. Dover and Miss Elizabeth L. West announce the death of a beloved daughter and sister Charlotte L. West. Miss West's body was discovered on the shore of the lake near to her home having accidentally drowned on the evening of 18th July. The burial is to take place on the 20th at Mercy Cemetery.'

'Wow,' Olivia leaned back in her chair, 'Charlotte West...she was only 19 years old.'

'I'll print out the death announcement and get all the copies of the certificates for you,' Veronica told her softly.

Olivia looked down at her watch. It would be

getting dark by now and she wondered if Theo even remembered she wasn't there or if he was still brooding in his studio. She sighed heavily; she supposed she would have to face him sooner or later.

'I have to get going now,' she shut down the computer and stood, grabbing her coat as she went. 'Thanks Veronica, I appreciate all your help.'

'It's my pleasure,' she smiled handing the papers to Olivia, 'if you need anything else give me a call.'

'I will.'

By the time she stepped back out onto the sidewalk, the temperature had dropped again and the sky was already dark. Pulling her gloves and hat on she hunched down against the biting wind and headed for her car. Just one more stop and then she could head home.

There was little in the way of traffic and the drive back was short. Trudging up the frozen steps to the porch she opened the door, expecting to find the house quiet and dark with Theo back in his cave. Nothing prepared her for the roll of smoke which greeted her, nor the curse words coming from the kitchen, accompanied by enthusiastic barking.

'I don't think I've ever heard you swear before.'

Theo's head snapped up at the familiar voice in the doorway to the kitchen. He paused in the act of pulling something unrecognizable from the oven and stared at her with unfathomable eyes. But as the heat from the tray slowly penetrated the potholder he yelped in pain and dropped the tray with a resounding crash.

'Shit.'

She couldn't help the smile tugging at her lips; he looked so flustered and cute.

'I was cooking you some dinner,' he frowned.

'You cooked for me?' she replied softly.

'Yes,' he gazed down at the charred mess on the floor, 'I don't think it's very edible though, even Beau won't touch it.'

'Then it's just as well I brought dinner with me,' she held up a bag.

'Chinese?' Theo smiled hopefully.

'Yes,' she replied as she dumped the bag on the island and walked past him to open the back door, letting the last of the smoke clear from the room.

She turned back towards him and found herself caught up in his arms, his lips fused to hers. Unable to help herself she relaxed into the kiss as his fingers tangled in her hair and he took her down into a deep drugging kiss.

'I'm sorry,' he murmured against her mouth. 'I'm sorry about earlier, I'm sorry about the last few days.'

She nodded slowly as he released her. She didn't say anything; she wasn't ready to but she knew they would have to have a talk sooner or later. Theo needed to know he wasn't bound to her, that he could leave anytime he wanted to, whether she wanted that or not.

'Where did you disappear to today?' he asked.

Glad for the change of subject she felt her shoulders relax and she even smiled.

'Get the wineglasses, I'll get the plates and then I'll tell you what I found out.'

4.

Olivia fumbled for the phone on her night stand as the ring tone blared out unexpectedly.

'Lo,' she mumbled.

'Olivia?' a soft voice spoke, 'I'm sorry dear it's Renata, did I wake you?'

'No, it's okay,' she glanced at her watch realizing how late in the morning it was. Beau must be desperate by now. She swung her legs out from under the covers trying not to disturb Theo, who grunted and rolled over.

'How are the renovations going?' Olivia yawned as she padded from the room closely followed by Beau, who danced expectantly around her legs.

'That's what I wanted to speak to you about.'

'Oh?'

'We finally got around to sorting through the last storeroom which one of the research suites will extend into and we came across some of your belongings.'

'Mine?' Olivia frowned in confusion as she pulled an over sized sweater over her pajamas.

'Well, they are now,' Renata explained. 'These

items were loaned to the museum by the West family about thirty years ago as part of a display. After that particular exhibit was dismantled they were put into storage and I suppose they were forgotten about. But as you are the only West left they belong to you now.'

'Oh I see,' she trotted down the stairs, 'do you want me to come by and pick them up?'

'No, no dear, a couple of the items are quite large,' she replied. 'The work isn't due to start in that section until next week, so I'll have someone bring them by the house for you in a day or so.

'Well if you're sure,' Olivia frowned as Beau hit the last step and rushed into the kitchen barking happily.

'It's no trouble.'

Olivia wandered into the kitchen and froze at the familiar face that greeted her.

'I'm sorry Renata I need to go,' she murmured into the phone.

She barely registered her response as she hit the disconnect button. 'What the hell are you doing here?' she asked coldly.

Her father finished making a fuss of Beau before looking up at her.

'You look well Olivia,' he replied conversationally, as if they'd only just seen each other days before, instead of the nearly two months that had passed since that night at Boothe's Hollow.

'Haven't you heard of knocking?'

'Would you have let me in?'

'No.'

He raised a brow knowingly.

She stormed past him and opened the back door. Sensing imminent relief Beau rushed outside.

'You can go too,' Olivia glared at her father fiercely.

'Not until I've spoken to you,' Charles replied easily, 'this conversation is long overdue.'

49

'There is nothing you could say to me that I would possibly want to hear.'

'Aren't you at least going to offer me a coffee?'

'No,' she crossed her arms.

'Olivia, it's about your mother.'

'Like I said,' she replied coolly, 'there is nothing you could say to me that I want to hear.'

'Stop being childish, this isn't about what you want; this is bigger than either of us.'

'Then you go and deal with it,' she shook her head in disgust, 'I'm done with both of you. You can go after her, or you can go back to Morley Ridge or you can go to Hell for all I care. I didn't want anything to do with this and yet both of you dragged me into it and for what? You screwed up my childhood, lied to me, betrayed me, left me all alone for the last twenty years and then finally, as the icing on a really crappy cake, I got shot for my trouble. Thanks but no thanks, you can clean up your own mess.'

'It's not as simple as that, you're a part of this whether you like it or not.'

'Only because the two of you dragged me into the middle of this crap heap.'

'No, because you are a West. It's your blood that makes you a part of this and like it or not you have a responsibility.'

'Fuck you and your responsibility,' she muttered angrily.' 'You left me all alone, passed from family to family because no one wanted me, because no one wanted to adopt the child of a murderer.' Her voice cracked as she ruthlessly bit back the tears which threatened to fall.

'For twenty years you let me believe that you were a monster, that you killed mom and even when you found out that she was alive, you still didn't tell me the truth. You let me go on mourning a woman I thought loved me.'

'Olivia,' he sighed, 'despite everything the woman you knew, the mother you remember, did love you.'

'Yeah,' she replied bitterly, 'because nothing says

"I love you" like a bullet wound.'

'I can see you're not ready to discuss this,' he stood and smoothed the rumpled line of his jacket. 'I wish I could give you more time but we simply don't have that luxury. Unless you have forgotten there is a demon loose in Mercy that needs to be caught and shoved head first back into whatever Hell dimension he came from. We don't have time for you to feel sorry for yourself.'

'You're such an asshole.'

'It has been said,' he shrugged.

'I tried everything to stop him from being raised with no help from you,' she hissed furiously, 'so don't you dare blame me for this.'

'No,' he replied quietly, 'there's plenty of blame to go around and most of it falls squarely on your mother and I. She was obsessed with raising the demon and I didn't see it until it was too late. It was my job to stop her and I failed. I hope you can believe me when I say to you truthfully; I never ever wanted you to get hurt. I would've taken that bullet myself if I could have gotten to you but I couldn't and for that I am truly sorry.'

'How can I trust a word that comes out of your mouth?'

'I know it will take time for you to trust me again,' he answered and for the first time she could hear the remorse in his voice. 'Theo has my number, please use it. I know this is a hard situation for you but like I said earlier we simply don't have the luxury of time. You mother isn't going to wait. Raising the demon Nathaniel was simply a step in a much more elaborate plan, it was not her end game. I know you want to walk away from all of this and I wish I could let you. But things are only going to get worse and this time you do need to be prepared.'

Olivia stood quietly watching him.

Stepping towards the door, he paused and looked back at her.

'I know that you lost your childhood. I took that

from you and that is something I will never be able to make right. But there wasn't a single second I didn't think about you. I made sure that you were watched over and protected. You said you always felt alone but you weren't… because even though you couldn't see me I was always with you.'

Olivia watched as he disappeared out of the door. She could feel the tears and pain burning the back of her throat as she stood motionless in the cold doorway. Beau suddenly reappeared having relieved himself outside, but instead of jumping up at her for his breakfast, he scurried happily past her, wagging his tail. She followed him numbly with her gaze until it fell upon Theo standing in the kitchen doorway propped against the door frame, watching her intently.

'How long have you been standing there?' she asked, her voice sounded rough and foreign to her own ears.

'Long enough,' he replied softly.

Turning away from him she closed and locked the back door taking a minute to draw in a shaky breath. Seeing her father brought everything flooding to the surface and all she wanted to do was turn and burrow into Theo's arms. She wanted to have him hold her so tightly that it would knit back together the pieces of her that felt as if they were flying apart. But she couldn't, she wouldn't let herself. It wasn't fair to him, he needed to come to terms with his new life in the present day and choose what path he wanted his life to take from this point on. She didn't want him to feel guilty or obligated in any way to her.

No, she squared her shoulders and straightened her spine, this she would have to deal with on her own. After all she'd spent the last two decades taking care of herself, she couldn't start relying on someone else now. If the last few months had taught her anything it was that even the people she was closest to, could and would betray her.

When she turned back to him, her eyes were guarded and her voice casual.

'Would you like some breakfast?' she switched the coffee machine on and reached for a new filter.

'What I would like is for you to talk to me the way you used to,' he frowned.

'You pretty much heard most of that' she shrugged, 'what else is there to say?'

'You could tell me how you feel.'

'I think that's pretty obvious.'

He caught her arm gently as she moved past him and turned her to face him.

'Livy,' he replied quietly, 'I know I've had a lot of things on my mind recently but I feel like there is a distance between us now and maybe that's my fault, but nothing has changed.'

'Everything's changed,' she whispered pulling her arm free, 'you just don't want to admit it.'

'Olivia,' he began but suddenly froze as a loud chiming began somewhere in the house.

Olivia tensed as the phantom clock continued to chime. 'Can you hear that?'

'It's a bit hard to miss.'

'Not the clock,' she frowned, 'it sounds like running water.'

Turning she moved towards the hallway, warily following the sound of water. Beau whined, and trembling, hid behind Theo's legs.

'It's okay boy,' he bent down and stroked him soothingly, 'go to your bed, I have to stay with Olivia.'

Beau licked his hand and trotted off to the corner of the kitchen climbing onto his cushion and curling up to stare at Theo with watchful eyes. Satisfied Beau was okay he followed Olivia out into the hallway.

Water ran like tears between the spindles of the staircase and down the wooden paneling. She rounded the corner and stood facing the stairs; here water trickled down the steps like a tumbling stream over small rocks to pool at her feet. Shivering, she felt the temperature plummet and as she breathed out heavily to calm her racing heart her breath fanned out as a fine mist. Grasping the banister purposefully she raised her foot and placed it on the first tread.

'Olivia don't,' Theo warned as he grasped her wrist to prevent her from going any further.

'I have to' she shook her head; 'she's trying to tell me something. I'm not going to figure out what it is unless I face her.'

He sighed heavily. 'Then let me go first.'

Everything in her softened at his genuine concern and she reached out without thinking to stroke his face softly.

'She's mine,' she whispered, 'I have to do this for her.'

'All right' he conceded, 'but I'll be right behind you.'

She nodded and turning towards the stairs she began to climb slowly. The higher she went the colder it became. She ignored the numbness in her hands and feet and the fact that the hem of her pajamas were now soaked. Her heart was pounding so hard she could feel it in her ears. Her mouth ran dry and her hands trembled as she reached the top step and turned towards the landing.

There she stood in the corner, much as she had the last time, in a dirty cotton nightgown her long midnight hair tangled and hanging forwards, partially concealing her pale face. She seemed to be swaying, unaware of Olivia's presence.

The hairs on the back of her neck rose and everything inside Olivia was screaming at her to turn and run but she didn't. She braced herself and took a hesitant step forward.

'Charlotte?' Olivia spoke softly.

The dark haired girl stopped swaying and with an agonizing slowness turned towards Olivia, but still she didn't look up, just stood motionless, waiting.

'Aunt Charlotte?' she whispered.

Charlotte's head suddenly snapped up and her white eyes fixed on Olivia.

Olivia felt her stomach swoop, that sudden jolt as you step down and accidentally miss a step. She tried to fight her way through the layers of fear and draw on her logic. Charlotte recognized her name but only truly responded when Olivia had acknowledged the familial connection between them. So part of her had to be aware, if she could just reach it.

'Aunt Charlotte?' she took another small step forward, 'I know you recognize me. I'm yours, I come from the same blood as you.'

Feeling a little bolder she moved closer. 'I know you are trying to tell me something important and I'm here, I'm listening. Can you tell me what you want?'

Charlotte suddenly moved with the same jerky movement, disappearing and reappearing directly in front of her. With her heart pounding at the sudden shock, Olivia gasped and took a small involuntary step back.

Charlotte opened her mouth to speak. The noise that came from her throat was a kind of choking sound, a stuttering kind of rasp. Water once again oozed from her lips and she held out her hands imploringly towards Olivia.

It took everything in her to look past her fear, to look past Charlotte's white eyes, pale face and bruised skin to see the girl underneath. Once she got past her own fear she could see the scared girl trapped beneath, the one who was desperately trying to tell her something but couldn't force the words out.

In that one moment Olivia's heart broke for her and she would have done anything to help her. Without realizing it she reached out towards the girl and stepped forward. Everything else faded away and all she saw was

Charlotte, all she felt was her pain and desperation. If she could just reach her. Her heartbeat slowed, her breath was expelled as a slow even roll. It was as if they were trapped in a single moment of time. Her fingertips were mere inches from Charlotte's and all she had to do was stretch a little further and they would meet.

Suddenly she felt warm arms wrap around her and yank her back. At that moment everything roared back into clarity, too loud, too bright. She fell backwards as both she and Theo tumbled to the floor.

Charlotte's shriek of frustration echoed through the whole house like a banshee, shaking door frames and rattling windows. She collapsed to the floor in a violent wave of churning water and swept through the hallway slamming open the bathroom door. The surge of water reared up with a final echoing wail and plunged into the sink, cracking the basin and disappearing down the drain.

Olivia lay on top of Theo with his arms still wrapped around her protectively.

'Why did you do that?' she breathed heavily.

'You couldn't see yourself,' he answered as she rolled off him. 'You were turning blue.'

He climbed to his feet and help her up. 'I was afraid of what would happen if you touched her.'

Olivia took a deep breath as her heart rate settled.

'Thank you,' she shook her head to try and clear her thoughts. 'I don't know why I reached for her. It was like a compulsion; I couldn't seem to stop myself.'

Theo nodded and tucked an errant strand of hair behind her ear. They both turned towards the bathroom and stared at the huge crack in the porcelain.

'Where does the water come from?' Theo asked suddenly.

'The town's water supply all comes from the lake.'

'The lake where Charlotte drowned,' he replied.

'Yeah,' Olivia muttered quietly.

'What is it?'

'I just,' she shrugged helplessly, 'for a moment, I thought I got through to her and I saw...'

'What did you see?'

'She was just a girl Theo, she's trapped and she's afraid. She's desperately trying to break free.'

'You feel sorry for her.'

'Yes I do,' she replied slowly, 'does that make me crazy?'

'No,' he ran his hands down her arms comfortingly, 'it makes you human.'

'I feel helpless.'

'You said they recovered her body?' he asked after a moment.

'That's what the newspaper announcement said,' she nodded. 'As far as I know she's interred at Mercy Cemetery.'

'Why don't we go and find her.'

'What?'

'Why don't we go and find her grave,' he stroked her neck gently, 'we could take her some flowers and pay our respects. It might make you feel better.'

'Really?'

'Yes,' he nodded smiling slowly.

'I'd like that.'

'Then go get dressed,' he dropped a slow soft kiss on her lips, 'we'll skip breakfast, it's nearly lunch anyway. I'll feed Beau and make us a sandwich then we can go grave hunting.'

'That sounds so much cooler than it actually is.'

'Regardless,' he laughed lightly, 'go get dressed.'

Nodding in agreement she disappeared into the bedroom and Theo trotted down the stairs to check on Beau.

Despite the cold and the snow, it was a bright clear crisp day and as they were going to go trudging through a snow covered graveyard for the most part of the afternoon they decided to take Beau with them, a prospect which delighted the enthusiastic pup. After a brief stop at the coffee shop and the florist for provisions they headed out to the cemetery which was located on the outskirts of town.

They parked up outside the cemetery and climbed out. The place had a decidedly Victorian feel to it with its imposing black wrought iron gates. They passed underneath the archway which read Mercy Cemetery in ornate lettering and stepped into the cemetery itself.

'Wow,' Theo muttered.

It was huge, way bigger than Olivia had been expecting. It was going to take them forever to find the right grave, especially as everything was covered in layers of snow. But despite that, everything looked so peaceful and undisturbed. Obviously not a lot of people visited in the winter.

'Who's that?' Theo asked suddenly as his gaze fell on a hunched figure in the distance, shoveling snow from the path.

'He's probably the custodian,' Olivia's eyes narrowed. 'Let's go talk to him, with any luck he might be able to point us in the right direction.'

Beau wove back and forth, happily plowing through the snowdrifts towards the figure in the distance, pulling impatiently on his leash at the prospect of a new friend.

The figure looked up as Beau barked happily. He raised his hand in acknowledgment and started up the path towards them.

'Hi,' Olivia said breathlessly as Beau dragged her nearer.

'Afternoon,' he nodded. 'Don't get many visitors this time of year.'

He hunkered down to pet Beau who collapsed to the ground and rolled over in sheer delight.

'I'm Olivia West, this is Theodore Beckett.'

The old guy stood and offered his gloved hand to each of them. 'Jed,' he nodded in response, 'I take care of this place.'

'It's nice to meet you Jed,' Olivia smiled, 'I was hoping you could help us. We're looking for a specific grave, an ancestor of mine. She would have been buried sometime late summer 1924.'

'West eh?' he scratched his stubbled chin. 'I do have records of all the plots if you can't find it. But the truth is the West family being one of the oldest in Mercy have a huge plot all to themselves, over in the North East corner.'

He pointed them in the right direction.

'What's the name of the one you're looking for?'

'Charlotte West.'

'Oh that one,' he replied.

'Why do you say that?'

'No reason,' he shook his head, 'you go on now and head out that way, you shouldn't have any trouble finding her. If you need anything else I have my own little cabin just down there a ways. I'll be putting the kettle on after I've finished clearing the path, so feel free to stop by.'

'Okay,' she replied a little suspiciously, 'we might just take you up on that.'

With a nod of thanks they set off up the steep incline towards the section Jed had indicated.

'What was all that about I wonder?' she muttered once they were out of earshot.

'What?' Theo replied.

'I don't know,' she frowned, 'I just get the feeling he knows more than he's letting on.'

They climbed higher towards the North East corner and soon were passing by small mausoleums and ornate graves. Some of them had only small stone headstones whereas some had huge columns and angels standing over them.

'A little ostentatious,' Olivia murmured.

'These are all graves?' Theo asked absently as he took in his surroundings. 'Why are their markers so elaborate?'

'I forget you're not used to things like this,' she mused thoughtfully, 'there are various reasons. Sometimes it was just the fashion; back in the 1800's Mausoleums were all the rage.'

'Mausoleum?' he frowned.

'See those little square buildings scattered throughout the cemetery?'

'Yes.'

'Well each one would belong to a family; inside you will find the remains of up to five or six family members. The parents usually and due to infant mortality back then quite often some of their children. Those who grew into adulthood may have had plots of their own.'

'I see.'

'As for the graves, well sometimes it was a demonstration of the deceased's wealth and position or sometimes just because their loved ones wanted to honor them the best way they could.'

Theo nodded in understanding as they came to the first Mausoleum marked West 1819-1842.

'That won't be it, the timescales wrong,' Olivia dismissed it and moved on.

It was hard to see the gravestones clearly as they were mostly covered in a fine dusting of snow. They moved further along and Olivia leaned down and dusted the snow off the stone with her glove and froze.

'Evelyn Patricia West Born 31st January 1934 Died 29th July 2015,' Theo read aloud. 'Your Aunt Evie?'

She nodded as she dusted the stone next to it.

'Alice Louise West Born 31st January 1934 Died 29th August 1994. 'My Nana,' Olivia murmured.

She turned to face the stone next to them. Although she couldn't read the writing she was fairly certain she knew whose grave this was, just as she also knew it was empty. The headstone had been split right down the centre and sat forlornly, cleaved in two, covered with snow.

Kneeling down Olivia brushed the stone clean and stared at the inscription.

'Isabel Katherine West Born 4th September 1968 Died 29th August 1994. Beloved Wife and Mother,' she whispered.

The words beloved wife and mother sat like lead in her stomach and she wanted to lash out and break the stone herself, to erase the words of hypocrisy and smash it to pieces. She wondered idly if her father had broken the stone, feeling the same helpless rage at her mother's betrayal or if it had been her mother who had done it, trying to symbolically sever herself from the West family. It didn't matter either way, it changed nothing. It didn't heal her broken heart or lessen the sting of betrayal.

Beau crunched through the snow at her side and sniffed the stone before promptly lifting his leg. She couldn't help the ridiculous laugh that bubbled out of her mouth. She stood and stepped back from the grave and stroked Beau lovingly.

'Do you want a moment?' Theo asked gently.

'No,' she breathed.

She pulled two red roses from the bouquet Theo was holding and laid one each on her grandmother's and great aunt's graves. Kissing her fingers lightly and touching each of the headstones she turned back to Theo.

'There's nothing to say,' she told him quietly, 'wherever they are I'm sure they know how I feel.'

He nodded and took her hand, gently pulling her away from the graves. They moved further back and suddenly something caught her eye. A flash of bright red amongst the pure whiteness of the snow. Tugging Theo's hand to get him to change direction they headed towards the pinprick of vibrant color. As they got closer she could see random splashes of color and realized it was another grave.

Letting go of Theo's hand she knelt down next to the headstone. It was made of white marble and covered with some sort of vine. Tapping the plant carefully she watched as the snow shook loose revealing a deep green vine with hundreds of small bright red flowers in full bloom. Frowning to herself Olivia brushed huge handfuls of snow from the grave to reveal more of the flowers; it seemed to cover the entire grave, releasing a sweet aromatic scent. Dusting off the headstone she realized the writing itself was in gold and in a strange lettering.

'Charlotte Lilly West Born 20th May 1905 Died 18th July 1924 Agapiméne échase , vreíte to drómo sas píso se ména.'

'This is very odd,' Olivia frowned.

'Those flowers shouldn't be blooming this time of year,' Theo commented.

'You're right, but it's not just that. These are poppies, not only are they growing out of season but I've never seen them grow on vines before and yet the whole of her grave is covered in them. Also, look at her headstone and the inscription.'

'What about them?'

'They're completely out of character, I mean look at the other graves. No one else from the early twentieth century has a white marble headstone with gold lettering and the grave itself is 91 years old but it looks brand new, there's not so much as a chip or a scratch on it.'

'Someone is caring for the stone?'

'Possibly,' Olivia murmured as she pulled one of the delicate blood red flowers from the vine and twirled the stem absently between her fingers.

'What is that inscription?'

'Agapiméne échase, vreíte to drómo sas píso se ména,' Olivia read aloud.

'Is that Latin?'

'No,' she shook her head pulling her phone from

her pocket and taking a picture of it. 'It's not Latin, I'm not sure what it is.'

'Beau, No!' Theo scolded him and tugged his leash.

Olivia looked down to the edge of the grave where the puppy had begun to dig furiously. As Theo scooped Beau up and held him firmly, a flash of metal caught her eye. Scooping some more of the snow out of the way she dug her fingertips into the frozen soil and pulled out a chunk of mud with something sticking out of it. Peeling away the excess soil she found she had a tiny metal disc. It was badly tarnished and very dirty so she couldn't make out the markings on it but it looked like an old coin.

'What is it?' Theo leaned down to get a closer look.

'I'm not sure yet, we'll have to clean it up once we get back home, I mean get back to the house,' she corrected herself. She tucked it into her pocket and stood up, not noticing Theo's frown at her choice of words. She absently rolled the flower stem between her fingers, 'I think it's time we had a little chat with Jed.'

He handed her the bouquet of flowers they'd bought for Charlotte and watched silently as she tucked them into a small copper urn which sat at the footplate of the headstone. Her expression was troubled as she lay her hand lightly on the headstone in a moment of silent contemplation. She turned towards Theo, who was waiting patiently.

Satisfied the pup wasn't going to start digging again, Theo dropped Beau back down to the ground and they headed off down the hill to the small cabin where a small wisp of smoke rose from its chimney.

'Thought you'd be by,' Jed smiled as he opened the door and stepped back allowing them to enter.

'I'd like to ask you some questions if you don't mind,' Olivia replied as he shut the door behind them.

'Figured you would,' he nodded as he turned up the heat under the small tin kettle. 'Would you like a hot drink? I got tea or coffee?'

'Tea would be great thanks,' Olivia answered.

'Coffee,' Theo spoke up as Jed turned to look at him.

'Take a seat then you two, might as well be comfortable.' He picked up a small bowl and filled it with water before setting it on the floor for Beau.

Olivia unhooked Beau's leash and settled herself into a hard wooden chair next to the small wood burning stove as Theo took a seat next to her.

'So you found Miss Charlotte's grave then?'

'Yes I did,' she replied, 'and its strange that she has a white marble headstone with gold lettering and as for the inscription on it, well its seems like an odd thing for her father and her sister to have put.'

'Well I don't know as it was them.'

'Pardon?'

'That wasn't her original headstone,' he answered handing them a steaming mug each.

'It wasn't? Are you absolutely sure?'

Jed turned to a low table covered in a blanket and tucked into the corner of the cabin. But when he pulled up the corner of the blanket it wasn't a table at all but a small heavy looking safe. He opened it and pulled out a fairly large leather bound book. He limped over and placed the book on the table in front of them and began to leaf through the dry dusty pages.

'Are you supposed to have that in here?' Olivia asked in horror. 'That should be locked up safe in the town archives; what if there's a fire?'

'Don't you worry about these,' he chuckled, 'what the council don't know won't hurt them and besides the safe is fireproof.'

Olivia shook her head in disapproval.

'Here we go,' Jed read aloud, 'plot 347. Charlotte

West, grey stone marker reading beloved sister and daughter, rest in peace.'

'That's not the one she has now.'

'No,' Jed agreed, 'but there's no record of it being changed. I've been here myself since 1974 and my predecessor was here from 1952. I asked him once about that particular grave and he couldn't recall it being moved either. So sometime between '24 and '52 that marker was changed, but when and by who I couldn't say.'

'Do you know who planted the flowers?'

He shook his head.

'They've just always been there.'

'It's a bit odd that they bloom in winter though,' Olivia persisted. 'They're poppies; they're not supposed to flower in winter.'

'That I can't answer,' he shrugged, 'alls I can tell you is that they bloom all year round.'

'That's not possible.'

'But it doesn't stop it from being true,' he took a sip from his mug and studied Olivia's puzzled face. 'You look like her you know.'

'Who?'

'Your Grandmama, Alice.

'You knew her?' Olivia asked softly.

'Aye, knew her and your Granddaddy.'

'She never spoke of him.'

'No she wouldn't, hurt her too much when she lost him but Sam Jones, he was a good man. Jonesy and I went way back, came up through school together and were both assigned to the same unit when we shipped out to Nam.'

'That's where he died wasn't it?'

'It was,' Jed nodded. 'Boy he sure did love Alice. Her and little Izzy was all he ever talked about and that when he shipped back home he was going to teach his little girl how to ride her bike. He adored them.' Jed sighed deeply, 'he didn't deserve the way it went down.'

'What did happen?' Olivia asked curiously.

'Shot, by a kid if you can believe that.'

'A child?'

'Yeah, barely more than a babe, nine years old and already a killer, Jonesy took four bullets before I could get to him. Died, right there in my arms, in the rice paddies of North Vietnam. Less than a week later our unit was caught in the crossfire...Napalm,' he frowned, 'last thing I remember was an explosion and a bright light. Next thing I know I'm being shipped out. Jonesy came home in a box and I came home minus a leg.'

'You lost a leg?' Theo frowned staring down, obviously confused by the fact that the guy very clearly still had two legs.

Jed smiled and lifted his pant leg to reveal his prosthetic limb.

'It's a false leg?' Theo gasped, clearly fascinated, 'what is it made from?'

'Carbon fiber and covered with silicone,' he told them, 'it's a hell of a lot more comfortable then the first one I had, but then again they've made a lot of advances in artificial limbs since Iraq and Afghanistan,' he sighed. 'It seems we never learn from our mistakes.'

'I'm sorry.'

'Don't be,' he shrugged, I was a lot luckier than some guys I knew.'

He stood and pulled out a bottle of Devil's Cut.

'Anyone?' he offered the bottle before pouring a shot into his own coffee.

Swirling the mug, he inhaled deeply and sighed.

'To Jonesy,' he lifted his mug, 'and all the others.'

'To Jonesy and the others,' they all lifted their mugs as they toasted the dead.

5.

Olivia sat at the island in her kitchen idly twisting the flower in her fingers. It was still pristine. Even after being stuffed into her pocket for the last few hours the petals showed no sign of bruising or wilting. Theo sat opposite her, scrubbing away at the coin with a rag and a bottle of metal polish.

'There's something about this flower,' she murmured.

'You mean apart from the fact it seems to be unnatural and indestructible.'

'Apart from that,' she frowned, 'something about poppies in general that I'm missing, or forgetting, I'm not sure which. I know that they are used to symbolize the dead soldiers of the World Wars.'

'World Wars?'

'World War I and World War II.'

He stared at her blankly.

'Oh, I guess we haven't covered that yet,' she pursed her lips thoughtfully; 'those were pretty major points in history. We should really take some time to fill you in on them.'

'But not today?'

'No, not today,' she shook her head, 'it would take

too long and it's getting late.'

'Here,' Theo handed her the coin, 'that's the best I could do. It's not just tarnished it's corroded so it's pretty hard to make out the details but it's definitely some sort of coin, probably made of bronze or copper.'

'Let me see.'

He dropped it into the palm of her hand and she studied it intently before cupping it between her hands and whispering.

> *Little coin of brass or steel,*
> *Make it whole make it real,*
> *Turn back the seasons turn back time,*
> *Bring back what is mine,*
> *Its original form let me see,*
> *As I will it so mote it be…'*

She opened her hands slowly and the coin sat glimmering in her palm like a shiny new penny, with no hint of a patina or any kind of corrosion. Theo snatched it up and turned it over in his fingers.

'What did you do?'

'It's a simple housewives charm.'

'You could've just done that from the start,' he stared at her accusingly.

'I could have,' she shrugged, trying not to smile, 'but you seemed to be enjoying yourself.'

He shook his head not trusting himself to speak, returning to his perusal of the coin.

'Do you remember that film we watched the other night, the one with Achilles in it?' he murmured after a moment.

'Of course,' she replied, 'who could forget naked Brad Pitt?'

'That was Greek wasn't it?'

'Yes.'

'Well this sort of looks like him.'

'Wow a coin that looks like Brad Pitt, seriously?' she snatched it back from him and turned it over in her hands to look at it.

'Not Brad Pitt, Achilles.'

'You're right, look at the markings. It does look Greek doesn't it.' Her brow furrowed thoughtfully, 'I wonder.'

She turned to her laptop and brought up the search engine.

'I knew I was missing something about the poppies,' she looked up at Theo. 'Listen to this, its original name is the Greek Anemônê. It's sacred to the Goddess Aphrodite, it's said she created the red anemone flower from the blood of her lover Adonis after he was slain by a wild boar.'

'So the flower's Greek in origin,' Theo replied, 'and the coin.'

'It could be a Greek drachma, maybe even an obolus or danake. I guess it depends on how old the coin is.'

'What about the inscription on the headstone. If it's not Latin, maybe it's Greek.'

'That's a good point,' Olivia mumbled turning back to the laptop and bringing up an online translator. 'Why didn't I think of that?'

She pulled out her phone and scrolled through to the photo she had taken earlier of the grave and typed in the inscription slowly letter by letter.

'Well I'll be damned,' she murmured sitting back, 'you're right it is Greek. The reason I didn't recognize it is because it was the Greek language, but written using the English alphabet not the Greek one.'

'So what does it mean?' Theo asked curiously.

'It says, "Beloved lost, come back to me".'

'That sounds more like something a lover would say, not a father or sister.'

'I wonder if she did have a lover,' Olivia replied

thoughtfully, 'she was certainly old enough but there's really no way to find out. Anyone who would have known Charlotte will be long since dead and buried.'

'Did she have a journal?' Theo asked. 'The women in your family seem to be obsessed with writing journals.'

'If she did I haven't come across it yet.'

They both looked up suddenly, at a knock on the front door.

'I'll get it,' Olivia slid off her seat and disappeared down the hallway.

She opened the door to find Jake, holding a six pack and a deck of cards.

'Hey Olive,' he grinned. 'Is Theo around, we thought we'd teach him how to play poker.'

'We?'

She looked around him and climbing the steps was a cute dark haired guy wearing a dark khaki jacket and army fatigues. He reached the top step and shifted the six pack and bag of chips he was holding.

'Hello Olivia,' he smiled shyly, his dimples winking to life. 'It's been a long time.'

It took her a moment to place him. 'Tommy Linden?' she smiled at Jake's brother in law. 'Louisa didn't tell me you were coming home.'

'I wanted to surprise her,' he scratched his shaved hair. 'I've been back a couple of days now and she's working the night shift tonight so Jake thought he'd introduce me to Theo.'

'Well come in then,' she smiled stepping back, 'he's in the kitchen so go on through.'

Shutting the door she turned to follow them when her phone rang. Pulling it out of her pocket she hit connect.

'Hello?'

'Hi Olivia, its Veronica from the museum. I hope you don't mind but Renata gave me your number.'

'No, I don't mind at all, what can I do for you

Veronica?'

'Um, well again I hope you don't mind but I kinda got caught up the other day when we were researching your ancestor Charlotte. I did a little further digging into the records and I have some information for you. I was just wondering if you wanted to meet me for a drink at the pub tonight, I know its short notice.'

'Actually,' Olivia interrupted her nervous ramble as she listened to the raucous laughter coming from the kitchen, 'it's perfect timing. I can be there in about half an hour.'

'Great, I'll see you then.'

Olivia hung up and headed into the kitchen. Picking up her laptop she shoved the flower and coin into her pocket.

'So as it's guy night we need you to make yourself scarce, no girls allowed' Jake grinned.

'Yeah, yeah I get it,' she rolled her eyes.

'You don't have to go,' Theo frowned.

'It's okay,' she smiled, 'I have plans.'

'Since when?'

'Since Veronica from the museum phoned and asked me if I wanted to meet her at the pub for a drink. She's only just moved to Mercy and she doesn't know many people yet.'

'Oh,' Theo replied sliding his arms around her and pulling her close. 'Are you sure you'll be alright.'

'I'll be fine,' she smiled, 'it's okay. Go have fun with the guys.'

'Put her down and get over here,' Jake cracked open a beer. 'It's time you learned the most sacred male bonding ritual and poker be thy name.'

'Amen brother,' Tommy raised his own beer in salute.

'Should I be worried?'

'Probably,' she laughed as Theo leaned down and kissed her. 'Don't let them take all your money.' She leaned around him and glared at Jake, 'and don't get him drunk.'

'Can't make any promises Olive.'

She shook her head and let out a long sigh.

'I'll see you guys later and don't feed chips to my dog,' she called over her shoulder as Jake snatched his hand back guiltily.

By the time she reached The Salted Bone, it was dark and the pub was already starting to get busy. She eased her way through the crowd and spotted Veronica at the bar.

'I saved you a seat,' Veronica smiled as she approached. 'I'm afraid there weren't any booths left when I got here.'

'It's fine,' Olivia climbed up onto the stool and smiled at Jackson who threw her a wink in response. 'These are the best seats anyway; we can share a bowl of chips and stare at Jackson as he's so pretty.'

'Well I don't like to brag,' Jackson grinned as he placed a fresh bowl of chips in front of them. 'What can I get you Olivia darlin'.'

'A large coke and something delicious to eat, I'm starving.' She turned to Veronica, 'have you eaten yet?'

'Um, no I haven't,' she confirmed quietly.

'What have you got for us tonight Jackson?'

'Guinness stew and mashed potato with green beans.'

'Sounds amazing,' she turned back to Veronica, 'trust me, Jackson's cook Owen is a genius. I don't usually like Guinness, I don't know what the hell he does with it but I swear it turns out incredible every time he cooks with it.'

'Uh alright then.'

'What do you want to drink with that darlin''' Jackson asked.

'Coke please,' Veronica blushed.

'Don't worry about it,' Olivia whispered dipping her hand into the bowl and nibbling on a chip. 'It's not just you, the man is ridiculously good looking.'

'It's the baby blue eyes and black hair,' Veronica agreed.

'Just your type?'

'No,' she blushed again, 'I don't have a type. I'm not very good at talking to guys if it's not work related.'

'There's nothing wrong with that,' Olivia laughed.

Suddenly the door to the kitchen swung open and a heavily pregnant red haired waitress stepped out carrying a tray of food. The minute she clocked Olivia she threw her a vicious glare before heading to a nearby table.

'She doesn't seem to like you very much,' Veronica murmured.

'That's an understatement.' Olivia sighed as Veronica turned to look at her curiously, 'and a very long story.'

'I wouldn't worry about it too much,' a familiar voice spoke from behind them.

'Hey Shelley,' Olivia turned around and greeted her warmly, 'how's things?'

'Not too bad,' she nodded dropping her tray of empties down on the bar. 'Like I said, I wouldn't worry about the death glares Kaitlin's throwing you; she seems to have a problem with everyone these days.'

'She's looking very pregnant, are you sure she's only got the one in there. She just seems to have gotten big, really quickly. It's only been, what, three months since Adam died?'

'Yeah,' Shelley sighed, 'well it seems she was actually quite far gone when she finally did a pregnancy test. She'd missed a lot of the early warning signs.'

'So how far along is she?'

'About seven months,' she replied uneasily, 'it hasn't given her much time to get used to the idea.'

'Did you order food?'

'Yeah,' Olivia nodded.

'I'll go hurry it along for you.'

'Thanks,' she replied as Shelley disappeared.

'What was all that about?' Veronica asked curiously.

'Well I guess you might as well hear it from me, you're bound to hear it from the town gossips sooner or later,' she sighed. 'Did you hear about the murders a couple of months back?'

Veronica nodded.

'It was on the news, my mother nearly had a cardiac arrest when she found out I was planning to move to Mercy.'

'Well, Kaitlin was seeing the first victim, Adam Miller and she found out she was pregnant the same day she found out Adam was dead.'

'How is that your fault?' she asked in confusion.

'Because at the time there were some nasty rumors going around about me, mostly spread by the former Chief of Police. I'd not long moved back to Mercy myself and he'd got it into his head I was the murderer.'

'Why would he think that?'

'It's a bit complicated but the short version is, my dad was arrested and charged with murdering my mom back in the nineties. It was the reason I left Mercy in the first place. But because my dad was a convicted murderer the Chief was convinced I was too. The guy was severely emotionally unhinged, having lost someone he loved deeply in a very violent way.'

'Oh.'

'I can assure you I am not, nor have I ever been, nor do I have any intention of becoming, a murderer. If you're uncomfortable about me in any way you can ask the Mayor and the current Chief of Police and they will assure you I was cleared of all those accusations.'

'I'm not uncomfortable,' Veronica replied.

'Okay,' Olivia relaxed, taking a sip of the coke

Jackson had slid onto the bar in front of her as he collected Shelley's empties.

'So anyway,' Veronica began, 'Charlotte West.'

'That's right; you said you found some more information?'

'I did,' she nodded, 'I think I figured out the connection to Augustus Swilley.'

'The Mayor?' Olivia cast her mind back, 'the one who signed the death certificate as informant?'

'Yes, well it turns out Charlotte was engaged to his son Clayton Swilley.'

'Really?'

'I found the engagement announcement in the archives of the Mercy Chronicle.'

She took out a folded piece of paper and handed it to Olivia to read.

'Mayor Augustus Swilley would like to announce the engagement of his son Clayton Swilley to Miss Charlotte West of Lakeside Drive. The Wedding will take place on the 19th of July at All Saints Church.'

'At All Saints Church,' Olivia murmured, 'that's odd.'

'Why?'

'Because my family aren't exactly church goers,' she shrugged.

She really didn't think this was the time to tell her it was because she came from a long line of witches. But this also meant that if Charlotte was marrying her fiancé in a church then it was likely he also didn't know she was a witch. She looked back at the date again.

'Didn't her death certificate say she died on the 18th July?' Olivia frowned.

'Yes, poor thing,' Veronica nodded sympathetically, 'she died the night before her wedding.'

That was like a red flag to Olivia. She was beginning to wonder if Charlotte's death had been an accident after all. She glanced back at the newspaper copy trying to make out the details of the photograph.

'Was this a photo of them both?'

'Yes, that would have been their official engagement photograph but unfortunately the original paper was damaged before it was scanned and uploaded. There's no way to clean up the image, I'm sorry.'

She could just about make out some of Clayton's features but the rest of the picture was a blurred mess.

'I don't suppose you know what happened to him?'

'Clayton?'

Olivia nodded.

'I did look him up, just out of curiosity and he moved to Salem and married in 1926 to a Madeline Rosser. I couldn't find what happened to her but I have him marrying again in 1933 this time to a Colleen Barton. She gave birth to a daughter a year later in 1934 who she named Catherine. Clayton himself died in 1935 from a self inflicted gunshot wound. It was during the Depression after the Wall Street crash; they moved from an extremely well to do neighborhood to one of the less fashionable areas so I can only assume the crash hit his business hard. Maybe that's why he killed himself.'

'What a coward,' Olivia frowned, 'to take the easy way out and leave his wife and child to fend for themselves.'

'My thoughts exactly, Veronica nodded, 'but they seemed to do alright for themselves. Colleen remarried a few years later and lived to a ripe old age and her daughter Catherine is still alive. She's 81 years old now and lives in Salem.'

'You are just a goldmine of information,' Olivia shook her head in amazement. 'No wonder Renata tracked you down and begged you to come work for her. I just may have to start using you for my research projects.'

Veronica glowed with pleasure.

'I just like figuring stuff out.'

'You said Catherine lives in Salem?'

Veronica nodded.

'I wonder if we could visit her.'

'I have her current address, I could write to her and ask if she would mind speaking with us? That is if you don't mind me tagging along.'

'I don't mind,' Olivia smiled. 'I wonder what happened to the other wife?'

'The other wife?'

'You said Clayton married in '26 to a Madeline?'

'Rosser, yes I couldn't find her. That is going to take a little more digging, there has to be either a death certificate for her or divorce papers. I'll keep looking.'

'Here we go ladies,' Shelley swung through the doors from the kitchen and dropped two steaming plates of stew in front of them, 'enjoy.'

'Thanks Shelley,' Olivia handed Veronica a set of cutlery and they both settled down into a companionable silence as they ate.

'So I have an Ace, King, Queen, Jack and ten, that's a...what did you call it? A straight flush?' Theo leaned back in his chair and took a deep swig of his beer.

Tommy stared at the five diamonds laid out so innocently in front of him and shook his head in defeat as he threw his three Jacks down.

'That's a royal flush man, the most unbeatable hand.' His eyes narrowed as he looked at Theo, 'are you sure you haven't played before?'

'Beginners luck,' Theo grinned.

He didn't have the heart to tell Tommy that after the first hour of playing he'd started to see a pattern emerging. By the end of the second hour he'd figured out he could count the number of cards. By the time they hit hour three they'd managed to plough their way through a six pack each and he could predict which cards were being dealt, fairly accurately considering he was pretty impaired.

It wasn't about the money though, he'd enjoyed the challenge and he'd enjoyed Tommy's company. Jake had barely drunk half of his beer when he'd been called out on an emergency, which had left Tommy and Theo on their own. Tommy had patiently explained the rules of the game and Theo found that he genuinely liked the quietly spoken young marine.

'Man, Louisa's gonna kick my ass,' he chuckled as he pushed the pile of money towards Theo.

'How long have you two been married?'

'Must be...' he leaned back in his chair and gazed at the ceiling thoughtfully, 'six no wait seven years now.'

'No children yet?'

Tommy shook his head.

'There wasn't a good time,' he absently began to peel the label off his bottle. 'Lou was training to be a doctor and I was posted overseas. It wouldn't have been fair to the kid with us not being around. When we do decide to have a kid we're gonna be a family.'

'Tommy can I ask you a personal question?'

'Sure,' he tipped his beer back and took a sip.

'Did you always know with Louisa?'

'What, that she was the one?'

He nodded.

'Yeah, I did,' his mouth curved fondly in remembrance, 'right back in grade school, she was so pretty. Blonde pigtails and baby blues, I was a goner the second I laid eyes on her.'

'How did she feel about you?'

'I don't think she knew I existed,' he laughed. 'I was a short nerdy kid with dimples and glasses who used to get shoved into lockers fairly frequently.'

'The other children caused you injury?' he frowned.

'You're a weird guy Theo,' Tommy shook his head in amusement. 'They never caused me any real harm especially not after the ninth grade when I seemed to grow six inches overnight and lost the glasses. After that they pretty much left me alone.'

Theo fell quiet as he stared contemplatively into his almost empty bottle.

'I take it Olivia's 'the one'' Tommy said after a moment.

'Yes,' he sighed, 'yes she is.'

'So what's the problem?' he shrugged. 'I saw you two earlier, you looked pretty solid.'

'I love her,' Theo slurred slightly; 'I love her so much it's making me crazy. I'd walk through fire for her and I did, sort of.'

He turned his hand over and stared at the tattoo which began at his palm and wound around his hand and up his arm.

'That's some wicked ink you've got there Theo.'

'Yeah,' he muttered as the light caught the lines and it shimmered. Only he and Olivia knew that it was no ordinary tattoo, that it was in fact the melted metal of a supernatural blade deeply embedded in his skin. It had become a part of him that night at Boothe's Hollow and now, to many, it simply looked like a tattoo but he could call forth the blade anytime he wanted. The metal would flow down his arm to pool in his hand, reforming the weapon, separate yet still a part of him.

'What is it Theo?' Tommy asked him, 'doesn't she feel the same?'

'That's the problem, she won't say,' he frowned. 'She shows me all the time how she feels about me, the way she talks to me, the way she touches me but she won't tell me how she feels. It's like she's holding a part of herself back and sometimes it feels like she's just waiting.'

'For what?'

'For me to disappoint her,' he shook his head. 'For me to walk out, it's almost like she's expecting me to.'

'Theo, I'm not surprised she acts that way, after what happened with her parents. Her dad killed her mom, right in front of her from what I hear. After that kind of betrayal, I'd worry if the girl didn't have trust issues.'

Theo didn't bother to correct him about Olivia's parents, after all it still wasn't common knowledge that her mother was still alive.

'You my friend need another drink.' Tommy stood abruptly, swaying slightly on his feet.

'Probably shouldn't,' Theo murmured.

'Why?' he shrugged, 'it's not like you gotta drive anywhere.'

'Can't anyway.'

'What?'

'I don't know how to drive.'

'What?' Tommy repeated.

'Amnesia.'

'Oh right got ya,' he nodded.

Jake had decided that as Tommy wasn't aware of Olivia's powers or the fact that Theo not only had visions but that he'd been pulled forward in time to the present day from seventeenth century Salem, that the best way to explain any lack of knowledge was just to plead amnesia, especially as Theo had briefly been hospitalized and it was listed in his medical records.

'So as you can't drive,' he grinned, 'let's have another beer.'

'There aren't any left.'

'Oh,' he frowned, 'well where does Olivia keep her booze?'

'In there somewhere,' he gestured absently.

''Kay,' Tommy headed for the nearest cupboard in a somewhat less than straight line.

'You know,' Theo spoke up loud enough for Tommy to hear as his head was stuck in the cupboard, 'Olivia might be right to worry about me.'

'What do you mean?' his muffled voice replied.

'I mean what if I do disappoint her?'

'Ah ha! Now we're talking,' he came up grinning

and holding onto a bottle. 'Don Julio.'

'What's that?'

'Tequila my friend,' he scooped up two glasses and set them down on the table pouring them both a generous glass. 'So why do you think you'll let her down?'

He slumped back in his chair and knocked his drink back in one go as Theo, following his example, did the same.

Theo coughed slightly and held his glass out for a refill.

'Have you ever done something so bad,' he replied quietly, 'that you've never been able to forgive yourself and knowing that if anyone ever knew the truth they'd never be able to forgive you either.'

'Yeah I do actually,' Tommy swirled the liquid around in his glass before knocking it back. 'Can you keep a secret?'

'Yes,' Theo nodded.

'I'm not going back to Afghanistan; the doc's think I might have PTSD. Louisa doesn't know yet but she will soon enough as I won't be able to hide it from her.'

'What's PTSD?'

'It's post traumatic stress disorder,' he shook his head sighing bitterly. 'You know, all I ever wanted to do was serve my country but the things I saw...the things I did...'he sucked in a shaky breath and his hand trembled on his glass. 'I have so much blood on my hands Theo, sometimes I think they'll never wash clean.'

They sat quietly for a moment both lost in a drunken state of contemplation, realizing how much they actually had in common, until Theo's quiet voice suddenly broke the stillness.

'I had a brother once, he was older than me. I looked up to him. I wanted to be just like him.'

Tommy reached out and filled his glass.

'What happened?'

'Our younger sister died unexpectedly. He

changed, he was so angry. He was,' Theo shrugged helplessly, 'looking for answers, looking for someone to blame. He'd joined this…group,' Theo decided that was a safe enough word to use.

'What like a gang?' Tommy frowned.

'Sort of I guess,' he replied, 'they hurt so many innocent people. I could see my brother changing, disappearing. I was so desperate to save him before he became as lost to me as my sister was, I joined them too. I thought I could exercise some sort of restraint, maybe convince him to come home but somehow I ended up doing terrible things too. They just had this way about them, especially their leader Nathaniel. He had a way of making you do things without even realizing it. People died because of me Tommy, my hands are no cleaner than yours but at least you were serving your country, you were fighting for honor and freedom. I on the other hand was too stupid to know when I was being manipulated.'

'Does Olivia know?'

'She knows some of it,' he shook his head, 'but not the worst of it. There was someone I cared for, someone I was supposed to protect and she ended up dead because of me.'

'It seems to me you need to find a way to forgive yourself.'

'Will you ever forgive yourself?' Theo asked him seriously.

'Touché,' Tommy smiled bitterly as he refilled their glasses.

Taking a deep remorseful breath, he held his glass up. 'To our damned souls.'

'Our damned souls,' Theo repeated as they both downed the fiery liquid.

Olivia threw her head back and laughed as Veronica smiled behind her glass.

'I can't believe your mom did that,' Olivia shook

her head. 'No wonder you took the job with Renata and moved to Mercy despite the recent murders.'

'I think I'd rather take my chances with a murderer,' Veronica stared into her nearly empty glass of wine. 'That came out a little harsher than I meant, I do love my mom it's just that she's a bit...controlling.'

'It's probably just because she loves you and she wants what's best for you.'

'Do you know she actually forbade me to take the job at the museum?'

'Really?' Olivia asked in surprise.

'Yeah,' she took a sip of her Cabernet, she was on her third glass and beginning to get very chatty. 'She said it wasn't ladylike to work so many hours in a dusty old museum and that no one would ever want to marry me if I didn't make more of an effort.'

'No offense,' Olivia replied, 'but your mom sounds like a bit of a bitch.'

'She is,' she sighed and then suddenly giggled. 'You should have seen her face when I told her I didn't care what she wanted, that this was my choice and I was going whether she liked it or not.'

'You rebel,' Olivia laughed in delight.

'Yeah, my teen rebellion came about ten years late but I finally got there,' she looked up and smiled at Olivia. 'I didn't realize that I was slowly suffocating in that house with her and my father. My brothers were all allowed to pretty much go and do whatever they wanted but I was like mom's own personal little doll. Piano lessons which I hated, ballet lessons which I was absolutely no good at and she would buy all my clothes for me and even tell the hairdresser how to cut and style my hair.'

'Damn,' Olivia pursed her lips thoughtfully as she looked Veronica up and down, taking in her sensible shoes and ugly skirt, not to mention the sweater that buttoned up to her neck with what she guessed was an equally sensible blouse underneath. 'How old are you Veronica?'

'I'm twenty eight,' she glanced at Olivia, 'you?'

'Same,' she replied. 'I'm not trying to be rude here but you dress like you're forty; is this one of your mom's choices too?'

Veronica nodded.

'I've been so busy with the move and setting up my apartment and then the renovations at the Museum I haven't had time to get anything new. There again I wouldn't know where to start, do you know I've never owned a pair of jeans?'

She eyed Olivia's jeans enviously.

'You looks so casual but so feminine and sexy,' she sighed again. 'I'll never look like that.'

'Yes you will,' Olivia answered purposefully, 'when's your next day off?'

'Thursday.'

'Okay it's a date then.'

'Eh what is?'

'We are going to buy you some new clothes and get something done with your hair,' she patted Veronica's hand reassuringly. 'You'll be amazed at how much of a confidence boost it will give you.'

'You don't have to do that?' she blushed.

'It'll be fun,' Olivia smiled. She glanced around the pub, which had quietened down to one or two customers. Checking her watch her eyebrows rose in surprise. 'Wow, I didn't realize it was that late, Jackson will be closing up soon.'

'Um Olivia…' Veronica twisted the stem of her wine glass nervously.

'Yes?'

'I have to admit that I did have a bit of an ulterior motive when I asked you to meet me for a drink.'

'Really?'

'I…um well, there's something I wanted to talk to you about and I don't really know where to start. I just…well I suppose I don't have many people I can talk to and I think you're possibly the only one who won't think I'm completely crazy.'

'Well now you have my attention,' she replied curiously, 'why don't you just spit it out and we'll deal with whatever it is.'

'I...talked to my grandmother this morning.'

'Oh,' Olivia frowned in confusion, 'that's nice, is she well?'

'That's just it,' Veronica drained her glass, 'she's been dead three years now.'

'What?'

'It started about a week or so ago; at first I thought I was just getting forgetful. Things wouldn't be where I left them or they would just go missing and then reappear days later in the same place. The temperature in my apartment kept dropping even thought the heat was on full blast, the lights would flicker, I even had someone out to check all the fuses and I went around the place myself replacing all the light bulbs with new ones. I kept dreaming about my Grams and then I woke up this morning and there she was just sitting in the chair in the corner of my bedroom as if she'd just been waiting for me to wake up.'

'Bet that gave you a bit of a jolt,' she murmured.'

'You can say that again,' Veronica shook her head.

'So what happened next?'

'She just smiled and said, 'good morning buttercup.' It was what she always used to call me and then she just started chatting away like we'd only just seen each other last week.'

'I'm assuming nothing like this has ever happened to you before?'

'No, I shrugged it off the other day when you mentioned you had one in your house. I've never believed in ghosts before, but then again I've never had a two-hour conversation with one before.'

'Were you scared?'

'I was a bit at first but then when she started

talking it was just Grams and it felt so natural.'

'If you don't mind me asking what did you talk about?'

'Just normal stuff,' she shrugged, 'the family, the weather. She was asking me if I was enjoying my new job.'

'What was your relationship like when she was alive?'

'We were really close,' her eyes filled suddenly, 'she was always there for me. She accepted me just the way I am, something my mother has never been able to do. I was heartbroken when she died.'

Olivia took her hand and squeezed comfortingly.

'What should I do?' Veronica wiped a stray tear and looked at Olivia.

'Nothing,' she smiled softly, 'she's not trying to hurt you in anyway. You have been given something few people experience. Another chance to see someone you have loved and lost. Just enjoy whatever time you have together.'

'You don't think I'm crazy then,' she sniffed.

'No, I don't,' she told her quietly, 'but I will give you a friendly warning. Mercy is no ordinary town and strange things have a habit of happening around here, so you shouldn't question your sanity every time something does.'

The bell rang for last orders and Olivia looked up as the door opened and a familiar face wandered in.

Jake stepped aside as two customers left and noticed the pub was now empty except for Olivia and a petite mousy woman who were sitting at the bar.

'Jake,' Olivia frowned as he approached, 'what are you doing here? Where's Theo?'

'Relax,' he sauntered over casually, 'your boy's fine. I got called out on an emergency but he's back at your place with Tommy.'

'This is Veronica,' she introduced them. 'She's new in town and working at the Museum with Renata.'

'Hey,' he nodded in her direction.

'Hi,' she mumbled uncomfortably.

Olivia's brow rose in at her friend's sudden change of tone. Boy she wasn't kidding when she said she didn't know how to talk to guys.

'I...um I'm just going to use the restroom,' she slid off her seat but as she turned to move she caught her foot in the leg of the bar stool and went down in an ungraceful tangle of limbs.

Olivia bit back an amused smile as she watched Veronica disappear below the bar.

'You okay?'

'I'm fine,' Veronica suddenly reappeared on her feet, smoothing down her skirt, her cheeks flaming red. 'I'll be back in a minute.'

'How much has she had to drink?' Jake watched her disappear through the door to the restrooms.

'Only a couple of glasses of wine,' Olivia smiled at him. 'I think you make her nervous.'

'Some people are just naturally skittish around cops,' he shrugged.

'I think it's more that you're ridiculously good looking.'

He grinned at her.

'It's a curse.'

'I'm sure,' she rolled her eyes, 'so what was this emergency?'

'Car accident out on Oak Lane.'

'Oh,' she frowned, 'was anyone hurt?'

'No thankfully,' Jake picked up what was left of her coke and drained it.

'Hey!' she complained, 'that could have had alcohol in it for all you know.'

'No it wouldn't.'

'How do you know?'

'Because your car's out front and you're too sensible to drink and drive.'

Sighing and shaking her head she turned to face him more fully.

'So what happened with the accident? Are the roads getting icy again?'

He shook his head. 'Oak's not too bad actually, they've just been out and ploughed the road. Fact is I'm still not too sure what happened. It was Jerry Foggert, he lost control of his truck and swerved off the road into a ditch and hit a tree.'

'Is he okay?'

'Yeah the old guy's tough as nails, few bruises and scrapes is all, but we did haul him off to the medical centre just in case. I think he might have a bit of a concussion. When we tried to ask him what had made him swerve he wasn't making any sense.'

'Why? What did he say?' Olivia asked curiously.

'He said his brother had appeared in the passenger seat next to him.'

'Appeared?' she repeated slowly.

'Yeah,' Jake shook his head, 'Problem is Brian Foggert died, had a major stroke last spring. I tested Jerry but he came up clear for alcohol so must've hit his head harder than he thought.'

'Yeah must've,' Olivia murmured thoughtfully as Veronica rejoined them.

'I should probably be getting home,' Veronica frowned.

'What's wrong?'

'I left my boots at the Museum.'

'You walked down?'

She nodded.

'It's alright I'll give her a ride home,' Jake interrupted, 'then I'll drive out to your place Olive and pick up Tommy.'

Olivia nodded.

'Oh you don't need to do that,' Veronica stammered, flustered at the thought of being trapped in a car with the hot blonde haired blue eyed cop and having to make conversation with him.

'Sure I do,' he smiled easily, 'it's all part of the job. Now where do you live?'

'The apartment complex on Louis Street.'

'I know the one, that's just around the corner from my place,' he nodded.

Olivia stood and shrugged into her coat as did Veronica.

'Hey Jackson,' Olivia called out, 'Thanks.'

He lifted his head to look at her and smiled. Suddenly several of the glasses which Shelley had lined up on the bar to be stacked in the dishwasher, began to shake and tremble as if they were caught in an earthquake. Everyone froze, including Jackson, as the glasses shot along the length of the bar skidding to the end where Olivia and the others stood. They stopped abruptly as if they had encountered some kind of invisible shield and then one by one they exploded violently sending glass shards flying.

'What the hell?' Jake swore as the pub once again fell silent and still.

'I'm so sorry,' Jackson rushed over to them, 'is anyone hurt?'

'No,' Olivia dusted the glass from her coat, 'I'm okay, Veronica?'

'I'm okay,' she replied her eyes wide behind her golden framed glasses. 'Jeez you weren't kidding when you said weird stuff happened in Mercy.'

'What's going on Jackson?' Olivia asked suspiciously.

He blew out a deep breath. 'We seem to have a visitor.'

'By visitor you mean?'

'A ghost,' he sighed.

'Looks more like a poltergeist,' Olivia frowned, 'Jackson when did all this start?'

'About a week or so ago,' he frowned, 'I started noticing cold spots, flickering lights, strange smells.'

Veronica and Olivia threw each other a glance.

'Then the knocking began, but whenever you walked into the room there was nothing there. This is the first time things have been moved or it has acted violently.'

'This can't be a coincidence,' Olivia shook her head.

'What can't be?' Jackson frowned.

'A couple of weeks ago a ghost showed up at my house, a young girl. Turns out she's an ancestor of mine. Veronica here started having cold spots and flickering lights then this morning her dead grandmother showed up. Jake's just been out to an accident where the guy driving swore blind his deceased brother had appeared in the passenger seat next to him, which caused him to lose control of the car and crash. Now this?'

'What the hell is going on?' Jake frowned.

'I don't know yet,' Olivia shook her head, 'but I'm going to find out. I don't think Veronica or I are in any immediate danger as our visitors seem to be pretty benign, but I have to say Jackson what I just saw concerns me.'

'I'll be alright darlin' I'm made of sterner stuff.'

'I don't like the thought of you being here on your own tonight. You can come back with me and stay in one of the spare rooms if you want.'

Jackson smiled affectionately at Olivia. 'I appreciate the offer love, but this is my home. I'm not leaving.'

'Fine' she sighed heavily, 'but I'm going to be by in the morning with a friend of mine who can help.'

'Who?' Jake asked before realizing who she meant, 'not that crazy British woman?'

'What crazy British woman? Jackson asked in interest.

'Her name is Fiona,' she threw Jake a warning look, 'she is a little eccentric but she really does know what she's talking about. She'll at the very least be able to figure out who or what we're dealing with.'

'Alright, come on around the back in the morning to the private entrance,' he told her as he walked them to the front door.

'Are you sure you'll be okay?'

'Stop fretting Olivia I'll be just fine.'

Not really happy to leave him but resigned she allowed him to usher them out and lock the door behind them. After saying goodbye to Veronica she left Jake to see her safely home and headed back herself.

Jake pulled up outside Veronica's building and glanced across at the stiff woman sat next to him. She'd barely said two words to him since they'd left the pub.

'The paths are pretty icy, you need any help getting to the door?' he asked.

'I'm fine,' she fumbled with the door handle and stepped out of the car.

Jake rolled down the window as she slammed the door shut.

'Thank you for the ride,' she told him awkwardly as she leaned down to the open window.

'No problem, just be...' he watched her let out a yelp and then disappear, 'careful...'

Shaking his head he climbed out of the car and headed around to the sidewalk where she was laying sprawled out on the ice. Grasping her gently he hauled her to her feet as if she weighed nothing.

'Thank you,' she mumbled, her cheeks blazing red.

'Are you sure you don't want a hand,' he glanced down at her really ugly shoes. 'You're not exactly wearing the right shoes for this weather.'

'I said I'm fine,' she snapped, completely mortified.

'You're from Boston right?'

'Yes why?'

91

'Figured as much, the accent,' he smiled. 'I'd have thought you'd be used to winters like this.'

'I am,' she hissed. 'I'm just having a bad day.'

She turned abruptly, intent on heading into her building as quickly as possible but her heel caught on the ice and she felt a whoosh of air leave her lungs as she went down again.

'You're going to give yourself a concussion at this rate,' Jake shook his head.

She felt herself once again hauled to her feet, but this time she stumbled into him, causing him to falter back himself. He wrapped his arms around her tightly and tried to get his balance before they both went down.

'You should come with warning labels.'

Her heart was pounding in her chest as he pressed her firmly against him, her glasses sliding down her nose as she gazed up at him.

She had really blue eyes was all he could think as he held the tiny woman in his arms.

'I ah,' he frowned shaking his head to clear his thoughts; 'I think you should probably just let me help you or we're both going to end up at the emergency room tonight.'

Not trusting her voice Veronica simply nodded as he relaxed his grip on her. Taking her arm in his he managed to get them across the path and up to the front door to her building without further incident. Taking out her keys she unlocked the door.

'Thank you deputy.'

'Jake,' he replied.

'Jake,' she repeated softly, giving him a small hesitant smile she turned and smacked her head on the door.

Holding her head with one hand she turned back to Jake, who was watching her with a straight face although his eyes danced with amusement. Leaning forward wordlessly he turned the handle and opened the door for her.

Unable to force another thank you out of her mouth she locked the door behind her and headed up the stairs to her apartment with her dignity trailing mournfully along the floor behind her.

6.

Olivia glanced across at Theo who was slumped in the passenger seat. His head had fallen back against the headrest and his mouth hung slightly open. Due to the dark glasses he was wearing she couldn't tell if he'd fallen asleep again but from the light snore escaping his mouth every now and then, she guessed it was a definite possibility.

'Theo,' she nudged him, her mouth curving in amusement as she pulled up to the curb.

'What?' he murmured.

'We're here, wake up.'

He lifted his head gingerly, swallowing slowly.

'I think I'll just stay here, you go.'

'Oh no you don't,' she nudged him again as his head fell back against the seat; 'the fresh air will do you good.'

'Nothing will do me good,' he pulled off the glasses wincing at the bright light as he tried to focus through bleary eyes. 'I appear to have a headache in my left eyeball.'

'Sorry honey, I have no sympathy,' she laughed lightly. 'That was a big boys' drinking session, now you have a big boys' hangover. There's nothing you can do but pay the piper.'

He groaned again and she took pity on him.

'Here,' she handed him a 'to go' cup, 'I stopped at the coffee shop while you were out cold. It's fully leaded and full of sugar. That'll get you up and moving.'

He pulled the lid off and swallowed deeply.

'Ah,' he sighed happily, 'I love you.'

Choosing not to answer she climbed out of the car and moved around to his side.

'Come on,' she opened the door, 'get up and get moving, you'll feel better for it.'

'You're a cruel woman,' he unfolded himself from the car and took another gulp of coffee.

'What on earth possessed you two to go through the two six packs Jake brought, all my beers and then an entire bottle of Don Julio?'

'It seemed like a good idea at the time,' he mumbled.

She shook her head in amusement and started up the path, leaving Theo to drag himself along in her wake. As she raised her hand to knock, the door was suddenly wrenched open forcing her to take a step back in surprise.

'Morning Fiona,' Olivia smiled pleasantly.

Fiona glanced at her through narrowed eyes. She was still wearing her bright lurid colored flannel pajamas buttoned up haphazardly over a gaudy orange t-shirt. Her wild grey hair was sticking out all over the place and her mouth was set in a grim line.

'Been expecting you' she moved aside, 'get in here you two.'

Olivia stepped through the door, closely followed by Theo who only nodded silently in greeting.

'Something wrong?' Olivia asked as Fiona slammed the door shut.

'You tell me,' she frowned. 'Ever since that girl showed up at your house my phone has been ringing off the hook with reports of sightings.'

'What?'

'I've never heard of spirit activity on such a large scale. Even Kennicott, Alaska and St. Elmo, Colorado, which incidentally are reputed to be two of the most haunted towns in America, can't compare with this. It's like Mercy is suddenly flooded with the dead.'

'Are you sure?' Theo frowned.

'Of course I'm sure, my head is so full of their voices it feels like my skull is about to split open.' 'What did you do?' she turned to Olivia.

'Nothing,' she shrugged helplessly.

'Are you sure, you must've done something. Your spirit seems to be the catalyst, the gateway for all the others. She appeared and they all followed suit.'

'I swear I didn't do anything Fiona, she just appeared that's all I can tell you.'

She grunted slightly mollified.

'What have you managed to find out then?'

'Her name's Charlotte, she was my Grandmother's aunt. She drowned the night before her wedding to the Mayor's son. I haven't any proof yet but I get the uncomfortable feeling her death might not have been an accident.'

'You're probably right' Fiona conceded, 'restless spirits especially those locked in death cycles usually have died in violent circumstances. You still haven't been able to communicate with her?'

Olivia shook her head.

'I came close; she recognized her name when I called her, especially when I called her aunt. She seems to be aware of the familial connection between us.'

'Blood recognizes blood, that's probably why she showed herself to you.' Fiona paced the floor restlessly, 'we need to figure out what she's trying to tell you. Maybe then we can figure out why the other spirits have suddenly made an appearance.'

Fiona stopped pacing and scratched her chin thoughtfully.

'We've been lucky up until now, most of the sightings have been pretty harmless but with the rate the deceased are pouring into the town it's only a matter of time before we get some nasty ones.'

'That's the reason I'm here,' Olivia replied.

'What happened?'

'My friend Jackson who runs the pub, he seems to have an unhappy spirit. He has flickering lights, cold spots, nasty smells and knocking in vacant rooms. Then last night several of the glasses on the bar moved and then just exploded.'

'I see,' Fiona frowned as she yanked on her snow boots and pulled her coat down from the stand, 'we better go and take a look.'

'Um don't you want to get changed first?' Theo asked.

She stared at him, her eyes narrowing dangerously.

'Never mind,' he replied.

Grabbing her keys, she headed towards the door. 'We may as well take your car,' she told Olivia as they stepped out onto the porch.

Nodding in agreement she led the way down to where she'd parked. By the time they pulled into the parking lot around the back of the pub Theo had a pounding headache. Olivia headed towards the private entrance and knocked lightly.

Jackson opened the door, his usual carefree smile and laughing eyes were noticeably absent and instead his mouth was set in a grim determined line.

'Maybe I should've taken you up on your offer last night,' he told Olivia as she stepped into the pub.

'What offer,' Theo walked in behind her, nodding in greeting as he passed.

'To sleep in one of your spare rooms.'

'I take it you didn't get much sleep last night young man,' Fiona marched in behind Theo.

'To put it mildly,' Jackson held out his hand. 'You must be Fiona.'

'That's right,' she shook his hand briskly.

'Why don't we go on through to the bar area and take a seat,' he offered.

Fiona wandered off in the direction he indicated, followed by Theo.

'Are those her pajamas?' he whispered to Olivia as they followed.

'Just go with it,' she smiled.

'Theo you're looking a little green around the gills if you don't mind my saying, are you alright?'

'Theo decided to get up close and personal with Don Julio last night,' Olivia replied.

'Ah,' Jackson smiled, 'why don't you take a seat my friend. I'll make you something that'll fix you right up.'

'Thanks Jackson,' he took a seat at the bar and laid his head on the cool wood.

Jackson slipped behind the bar and grabbed a silver cocktail shaker and began adding various ingredients.

'What the hell's in that?' Olivia asked dubiously.

'Bit of this and that,' he laughed, 'some hair of the dog. It's an old family recipe, don't worry beautiful I'll have your man as right as rain in no time at all.'

'If you say so,' she shrugged.

'Mr. Murphy,' Fiona interrupted, 'if you don't mind perhaps you could fill us in on what happened last night.'

'Jackson,' he corrected her, 'well I'll tell you alright. Like I said to Olivia last night, up until now our house guest has been pretty benign. A few cold spots, some flickering lights, some strange knocking noises. I'm used to that sort of thing; you expect it with these old buildings as they all come with a past.'

'You don't seem bothered by that,' she lifted a brow questioningly.

'Darlin' I'm from Ireland, land of magic and myth. I was raised on tales of Red Mary of Leamaneh Castle in County Clare where I grew up. I'm certainly no stranger to ghost stories or the odd strange happenings but this is a whole new level for me. Last night I felt as if I was trapped in a William Friedkin movie. I almost expected Linda Blair to make an appearance.'

He poured a nasty dark pungent liquid into a glass and placed it onto a coaster, sliding it over to Theo who picked it up and eyed it suspiciously.

'Trust me Theo,' he nodded.

'I suppose if it kills me at least it'll stop the pounding in my skull.'

'It won't kill you,' he laughed, 'but it will cure you of the evils of a hangover.'

Shrugging Theo tipped his head back and gulped half of it down.

'That is of course if you can keep it down,' Jackson murmured.

Theo's stomach heaved in protest as he clamped his lips shut and swallowed convulsively.

'If I vomit I'm aiming for you,' he croaked as he dropped his head back down on the bar.

Jackson chuckled and turned back to Fiona and Olivia.

'As I was saying, up until now fairly benign, then last night it started getting more…active.'

'Explain,' Fiona replied absently as she began to wander around the bar area.

'It started at closing time with the glasses detonating on the bar like tiny bombs. After that there was a lot of banging about. When I came in to check, the furniture had all rearranged itself, some of it was even upside down. I finally went to bed and sometime during the night the bed started shaking, gave me quite a turn I can tell you. Didn't sleep much after that.'

'I can imagine,' Fiona murmured running her hand along the smooth wood of the bar and closing her eyes. 'He was wronged in some way. He isn't just restless he's angry, so very angry.

She opened her eyes and turned to face Jackson.

'With you, he's angry with you.'

'Why me specifically?' Jackson frowned.

Fiona shook her head. 'I get the feeling he's looking at you and seeing someone else,' she tried to explain. 'It's almost like you're the proxy, he can't have who he's really mad at so he's blaming you. It may be that you are related to the person who wronged him or it may be as simple as you physically resembling that person. Spirits can get confused and fixated on one person.'

'Well that's just grand,' Jackson muttered sourly.

'Judd,' she mused after a moment, 'his name is Judd. He's tied to this building somehow, I can't get much from him, just waves and waves of anger. I don't think there will be any reasoning with him. Some spirits can be appeased and laid to rest.'

'But not this one?' Jackson replied.

'No,' she shook her head, 'you need to trust me on this. Things will only get worse from this point. He's escalating, it's only a matter of time before someone gets hurt and as this is a public building, usually filled with people, you can't afford to take any chances.'

'What do you suggest I do?'

She rummaged in her jacket pocket and came up with a gum wrapper and the stub of a pencil. Leaning down on the bar she scribbled a number and handed it to him.

'That's the number for All Saints Church; you want to ask for Father Hubert.'

'Are you suggesting what I think you are?'

'Yes,' she nodded, 'I'm not a huge advocate for this solution usually but under these circumstances what you need is an exorcism.'

'Are you serious?'

Suddenly the screeching of wood broke the quiet as the chairs surrounding the individual circular tables fanned out simultaneously.

Theo's head snapped up as he looked at the new formation of the chairs. 'What the hell?' he frowned.

'Here we go again,' Jackson sighed.

The loud screeching of the chair legs grinding against the wooden floor rose in volume and each chair began to spin slowly in a circle getting faster and faster. Theo moved closer to Olivia putting her behind him protectively.

'Has it done this before?' Fiona yelled above the noise.

'Not like this,' Jackson yelled back.

Suddenly the furniture split straight down the centre of the room, parting like the Red Sea, as the tables and chairs were swept against the walls, piling up either side of the room. An ominous silence filled the air which was now thick with the stench of ozone.

A shattering sound split the silence as the glasses stacked neatly behind the bar began detonating one by one, spraying the area behind the bar with glass. The bottles of alcohol were next, fountains of colored liquid spilled to the floor like tiny multi colored waterfalls. Jackson jumped up over the bar, skidding along the wood to drop down on the same side as Olivia and the others.

They all turned as the doors and windows began to rattle and shake violently as if they were caught in the grip of an earthquake. A loud cracking noise forced them to turn back to the bar. For a fraction of a second Olivia thought she saw an older man, with a bald head and grey skin and wearing a plaid shirt, reflected in the mirrored wall behind the shattered bottles before the whole wall exploded outwards showering them with great shards of jagged glass.

Olivia felt Theo grab her and spin away from the bar, folding her into him protectively as he shielded her with his own body. The sheer force of the explosion knocked them to the ground and then all was silent.

The sudden stillness was eerie; the only sound was the creak and grind of the glass beneath them as they began to move.

'Are you alright?' Theo breathed as he checked her for injuries.

'I'm okay,' Olivia nodded wincing slightly at the sting in her left palm. Pulling a large splinter of glass from her skin she turned to Theo. 'Are you okay?'

He grimaced lightly and felt the back of his shoulder. When he pulled his hand away his fingertips were coated with blood.

'Let me see,' she pulled him closer.

He leaned forward and she could see a large jagged piece of glass protruding from his shoulder.

'Pull it out.'

'Are you sure,' she frowned.

He nodded, hissing slightly as she did as he asked.

Looking up she saw Jackson stirring, he looked as if he had a small laceration to the forehead but otherwise seemed to be unharmed.

'Fiona?' Olivia called, and as she turned towards the older woman her heart almost stopped. She could see Fiona lying on her back, gasping for breath, a huge shard of glass sticking awkwardly from her neck.

'Fiona!' Olivia pushed away from Theo and scrambled over the sharp debris to reach her.

Blood pumped from the wound at her neck, pooling on the wooden floor and when she tried to open her mouth to speak, blood bubbled from her lips coating her teeth and running down her chin.

'Hold on Fiona,' Olivia breathed heavily, 'we've got you.'

Theo reached for the shard at her neck.

'NO!,' Olivia snapped sharply as she peeled the collar of her jacket back to get a better look at the wound, 'it's too close to her carotid artery. If we remove the glass she'll bleed out.'

She grasped Fiona under the arms and hauled her into a sitting position so she was lying reclined against her chest.

'The wound is higher than the level of her heart. If we keep her upright her heart has to work harder to pump the blood up to the wound; it should slow the bleeding.'

'I'll call an ambulance,' Jackson reached for the phone.

'There's no time,' Olivia shook her head. 'The medical centre is only a few blocks from here, it's quicker if we take her ourselves.'

Theo nodded as he slid his arms underneath her knees and her back, lifting her easily and trying to keep her in a seated position. With hands slippery with blood Olivia pulled her keys from her pocket as they headed out the back towards her car. Theo climbed into the back with Fiona while Jackson and Olivia jumped in the front. She tore through nearly every red light between the pub and the medical centre, the only crazy illogical thought circling her brain was who the hell would look after all Fiona's weird cats if something happened to the sweet crazy old lady.

She screeched up to the centre and planted the car in the middle of the emergency entrance, flinging open the door.

'You two get Fiona inside I'll move the car,' Jackson told Olivia.

Nodding as she helped Theo lift the unconscious woman out of the car she tossed her keys to Jackson and raced in after Theo.

'HELP!' she called as they ran through the entrance.

The startled medical staff quickly pushed a gurney

towards them and Theo laid her down. They both watched helplessly as she disappeared through the double doors of the trauma room.

'What's happening?' Jackson rushed through the doors to join them.

'Nothing yet,' Olivia shook her head, 'they're working on her now.'

'Jesus,' he raked his hand through his hair.

A nurse pushed her way through the doors of the trauma room and headed for Olivia.

'Miss?'

'West,' Olivia told her, 'is she going to be okay?'

'It's a bit early to tell,' she told her gently. 'She has a very serious wound and she's lost a lot of blood. The doctor's trying to stabilize her now and then she'll be taken up to the OR. It would be really helpful if you could give me some details.'

Olivia nodded mutely.

'What's her name?'

'Fiona Caldwell, she lives over on Fairfield Avenue.'

'Okay,' the nurse nodded, 'do you know if she has any allergies to any medication?'

'I don't know; I don't know her that well.'

'It's okay,' she squeezed her arm reassuringly; 'we'll pull her medical files.'

The doors crashed open and the gurney Fiona was on was pushed out quickly, surrounded by a team of medical staff.

'It looks like they're taking her up to surgery now,' she nodded. 'I'll keep you updated on her condition.'

'Thank you,' Olivia murmured as she watched Fiona wheeled into the elevator.

'I guess now we wait,' Jackson breathed heavily.

The minutes dragged as they took it in unconscious turns to pace the hall waiting for news.

Mac and Jake stalked purposefully through the

doors, their gaze immediately falling on the blood stained trio standing by the trauma room, each looking slightly shell shocked.

'Olivia,' Mac nodded as they approached. 'Why are you always covered in blood every time I see you,' he sighed.

Mac,' Olivia greeted the new Chief of Police, 'it's not mine this time.'

'Do you want to explain what the hell happened?'

Olivia turned to Jackson. 'Do you want to take this one or shall I?'

'Er...'Jackson looked at the two police officers, trying to come up with an explanation that didn't sound completely insane.

Olivia shook her head and sighed.

'We need to talk in private,' she told them, gazing around at the staff who were trying not to stare.

'Why do I get the feeling I'm not going to like what you have to say,' he breathed heavily.

She stared at him expectantly.

'Fine,' he indicted towards the trauma room where Fiona had just been treated.

Olivia glanced around as they entered the room, trying to ignore the empty blood bags, used gloves and wadded up bloodied gauze strewn across the floor.

'Could you give us a minute?' Mac asked the tech cleaning the floor.

He nodded and slipped quietly out the door.

'So spit it out then,' Mac frowned as he threw a calculating look at Jackson. 'Does this have anything to do with Nathaniel?' he asked carefully.

Olivia shook her head ignoring Jackson's puzzled look.

'Who's Nathaniel?'

'No one you need to worry about right now,' she murmured.

'Is this related to what we saw last night?' Jake

asked.

'Yeah,' Olivia replied, 'it got completely out of hand and trashed the pub.'

'What got completely out of hand?' Mac interrupted.

'Jackson has a very violent spirit at the pub, it's very angry, apparently at Jackson and while we were there it went on a bit of a rampage. It threw all the furniture around and smashed pretty much every piece of glass in the bar.'

'A spirit?' Mac repeated.

'Yes,' she nodded, 'again I know we're kinda throwing you in the deep end here Mac, but I don't think this will be an isolated incident. Apparently the spirits of the dead have all decided to throw a party and Mercy is the venue of choice. We're still not sure why at the moment.'

'I see,' he replied thoughtfully.

'You seem to be taking this pretty calmly,' Jackson said curiously.

'Well,' Mac scratched his chin thoughtfully, 'I probably would have been a little more skeptical if I hadn't spent last night drinking scotch with my old partner who was shot and killed on the job fifteen years ago.'

'You've seen them too,' Olivia answered slowly.

'I thought I was going crazy at first but then again after what I saw at Mid Winter I'm learning to take everything at face value.'

'Probably for the best,' Theo finally spoke up.

'What about the woman who was hurt?'

'Her name's Fiona Caldwell, she's a medium. She was helping us try to find out who was haunting Jackson, when it all just went crazy. She was hurt when the glass behind the bar shattered.'

'I see, so what do we do now?'

'We still don't know what is pulling all the spirits into Mercy,' Olivia told him. 'We're trying to figure it out at the moment but first we need to deal with the spirit at the pub.'

'I take it you're going to be closing for a few days until you've got this under control,' Mac asked Jackson pointedly. 'I don't want anyone else getting hurt.'

Jackson nodded.

'We'll get this dealt with immediately but even if we manage to exorcise the spirit it's going to take a bit to get the bar repaired and back up and running. There's quite a lot of damage, although I don't know what the hell I'm gonna tell the insurance people.'

'Okay then well, let me know if you need anything and keep me apprised of the situation.'

'We will,' Olivia nodded, 'we should head back to the pub and deal with this before people start showing up for work. Can you have someone call me as soon as Fiona's out of surgery so we know she's okay?'

Mac nodded and watched silently as the three of them filed out of the room.

Olivia stepped out onto the street ignoring the stares cast her way as she was joined by Theo and Jackson.

'We'll have to make sure we stop by Fiona's later and feed her cats for her,' Olivia told Theo.

'God, do we have to,' he grimaced.

'What's wrong with cats?' Jackson asked.

'These things aren't cats,' Theo replied dryly, 'they're creepy and unnatural looking.'

'They're Sphinx cats,' she explained to Jackson, 'you know hairless cats.'

'Oh...urgh.'

'Exactly,' Theo nodded, 'besides we don't have her house keys... what are those?' He asked noting the keys dangling from Olivia's fingertips.

'Fiona's house keys,' she replied smugly. 'I knew the nurses probably wouldn't hand them over as I'm not her next of kin, but her personal effects were still in a plastic bag in the trauma room.'

'But when did you...'Theo began in confusion.

Jackson chuckled. 'You stole them right under the nose of the chief of police?'

Olivia shrugged. 'Mis-spent youth,' she pulled her phone from her pocket and began to dial the number on a piece of gum wrapper in her other hand.

'Hey!' Jackson checked his pockets for the wrapper Fiona had given him, 'you pick pockets too?'

'It's amazing the skill set you pick up when you grow up in foster care,' she smiled as the line began to ring at the other end.

'All Saints church, Father Simmons speaking.'

'Hi,' Olivia replied, 'could I speak to Father Hubert please.'

'I'm sorry he's not available right now, may I be of assistance?'

'I hope so,' she took a deep breath, 'this is going to sound a bit strange but I need an emergency exorcism.'

7.

Father Simmons pushed open the door of the pub with some difficulty, noticing the heap of wooden chairs piled up behind it like a barricade. Squeezing his way through the tiny gap his shiny shoes crunched against the rough broken glass crushing it further into dust.

'Hello?' he called out.

'Come on through Father,' a thick Irish accent echoed through the bar area.

'Mr Murphy?' Father Simmons stepped over yet more debris.

'Aye, watch yourself there Father we're in a bit of a mess at the moment.'

'My goodness,' he glanced around the bar at the destruction, 'what on earth happened here?'

'That would be the work of our ghost,' Jackson looked up from where he was sweeping.

The young priest glanced around dubiously.

'A spirit did this?'

'Aye,' Jackson's eyes narrowed suspiciously.

'Are you sure he's a priest?' Theo muttered to Olivia, who was perched on the edge of the bar taking a sip of whiskey from a cracked glass. 'He looks like he's about twelve years old.'

'I can assure you Mr…?'

'Beckett.'

'Mr Beckett, that although I may be young in years I am a fully ordained priest of the Roman Catholic Church,' he puffed out his chest and pushed his glasses back up his nose. 'I am more than capable of dealing with your little problem.'

'You think this is a little problem,' Olivia chuckled as she lifted her glass to the devastation in the room.

'You must be Miss West, we spoke on the phone.'

'Yes we did,' she replied. 'Let me ask you a question Father Simmons, do you believe in ghosts?'

'I believe in evil spirits, just as I believe they can be cast out with the word of God. Although in most cases it is more a question of the theological standpoint rather than the physical manifestation of those spirits.'

'So you believe in spirits because the church tells you that you have to, but you don't really believe in ghosts,' she laughed lightly and raised her glass to her lips. 'This should be interesting,' she muttered.

'Perhaps we should wait for Father Hubert as Fiona suggested,' Theo frowned.

'Mr Beckett,' Father Simmons replied tightly, 'Father Hubert is busy at the moment attending to the last rites of a cancer patient at the Terminal Care Facility on Rose-lake Lane and is unavailable.'

'I'm sure Theo didn't mean any offense,' Jackson replied easily, 'he simply meant given the nature of our 'little' problem it might be best if we had someone with a little more experience.'

'And as I said Mr Murphy,' he answered with irritation, 'I am more than capable of performing a…'

A picture which had been screwed to the wall suddenly flew across the room and shattered on the opposite wall.

'What was that?' he asked carefully.

'Here we go again,' Olivia sighed in resignation

and she jumped down from the bar and tucked herself underneath it with Theo beside her, 'you might want to duck Father,' she warned.

Several overturned chairs scrapped ominously against the wooden floor before being slung violently across the room missing the young priest by inches.

He threw himself forward and tucked himself under the ledge of the bar alongside the others as the lights flickered rapidly, the windows shook and trembled and furniture threw itself around the room.

A mournful wailing began somewhere in the building and seemed to echo all around them.

'That's new,' Theo took a sip from Olivia's glass as a table crashed to the floor in front of them.

'What is?' Father Simmons stared at them with wide eyes.

'The wailing,' Theo replied easily, 'he hasn't done that before.'

'He?'

'The ghost you don't believe in.'

After a few moments the room once again fell silent and the lights steadied themselves. One by one they all crawled out from under the bar.

'Perhaps I should call Father Hubert,' Father Simmons whispered, his ashen face sweating lightly in the dim light.

'Seems like a good idea,' Jackson clapped him on the shoulder, 'can I get you a whiskey Father, I'm sure I can still find a glass around here somewhere?'

Father Hubert stepped over the rubble much as his counterpart had done, surveying the destruction.

'Good heavens,' he chuckled, 'looks like someone had a good time and I'm guessing by the look of you three, it wasn't you.'

He took in their bloodstained clothes and superficial injuries, before glancing across to Father

111

Simmons. The young priest was sitting on a battered wooden chair, sipping an amber coloured liquid from a glass tumbler which had most of one side broken away.

'Father Hubert,' Jackson held out his hand.

He took his hand and shook firmly.

'Goodness got yourself a real angry spirit here haven't you,' he breathed in deeply looking around the room, 'I can smell it.'

'Had some experience then have you?'

'Some yes,' he chuckled.

'Would that be from a more theological standpoint then?' Olivia asked dryly.

'No dear,' he answered as he glanced down at his shaken colleague. 'I've seen and experienced the real deal, in fact I've seen things that would probably turn your hair white.'

'I doubt it,' she muttered.

'I'm sorry Father,' Jackson apologized, 'as you can imagine it's been quite a day and Father Simmons seemed slightly disinclined to believe we had an actual ghost problem.'

'I can imagine,' he sighed. 'Well I'm here now, so what say we get this show on the road.'

'What's that?' Theo asked curiously as he noticed the tattered black leather bound book in Father Hubert's hand. 'Is it the bible?'

'No,' he shook his head chuckling lightly, 'this is the Rituale Romanum. I like to think of it as a kind of religious 'how to' guide. Nowadays when we perform a major exorcism its generally on a person, but it can be on a place or an area as well and with any luck we'll be able to cast out your unwelcome visitor for good.'

'Amen,' Jackson breathed.

'Alec,' he called to the other priest, 'I know you've had a bit of a nasty shock lad but I'm going to need you to pull yourself together and help me out here.'

Nodding shakily, he rose to his feet placing the

broken glass on the bar and moving to stand next to Father Hubert.

'Look,' Jackson nudged Olivia, 'I've got an old priest and a young priest.'

She couldn't help the amused giggle which escaped her lips causing the two priests to stare at her.

'Sorry,' she mouthed silently.

Father Hubert removed a flask from his pocket as well as a purple stole. Handing the flask to Father Simmons he hung the stole around his neck and pulled a silver crucifix from beneath his dog collar.

He cleared his throat and began in a tremulous voice.

'Regna terrae, cantate Deo,'

'psallite Domino
qui fertis super caelum
caeli ad Orientem
Ecce dabit voci Suae
vocem virtutis
tribuite virtutem Deo.'

'What is he saying?' Theo whispered to Olivia.

'He said 'Kingdoms of the Earth, sing unto God. Praises to the Lord that carry above the sky of Heaven to the East. Behold, He sends forth his own voice, the voice of virtue. Attribute the virtue to God.'

Father Simmons began to flick the contents of the flask across the floor as he wandered around the room, after a moment Olivia realized the flask contained holy water.

'Exorcizamus te, omnis immundus spiritus
Omnis satanica potestas, omnis incursio
Infernalis adversarii, omnis legio,
Omnis congregatio et secta diabolica.'

The remnants of the furniture suddenly twitched and began to scrap slowly and chillingly across the floor.

> *'Ergo draco maledicte*
> *Et omnis legio diabolica adjuramus te.*
> *Cessa decipere humanas creaturas,*
> *Eisque aeternae Perditionis venenum propinare.'*

Father Hubert paused and looked up at the sudden movement.

'Keep going,' Olivia urged him.

> *'Vade, Satana, inventor et magister*
> *Omnis fallaciae, hostis humanae salutis.*
> *Humiliare sub potento manu dei,*
> *Contremisce et effuge, invocato a*
> *Nobis sancto et terribili nomine,*
> *Quem inferi tremunt.'*

Olivia flinched as one of the last remaining pictures on the wall was violently flung across the room smashing loudly. All the furniture was beginning to churn in a perpetual motion. The lights began to flicker rapidly as any remaining glass began to explode sending needle like shards skittering across the scarred floor. She felt Theo's hand sneak into hers and hold on tightly. He pulled her into his body to protect her, his eyes darting around cautiously as if not knowing from which direction the danger would come.

The whole room was filled with the pungent scent of ozone and charged with static electricity. She could almost feel the hairs on her arms and the back of her neck rising. The atmosphere was so thick with rage she felt like she was suffocating. Random pieces of wood from the broken furniture were suddenly fired across the room like missiles, embedding themselves deeply in the wooden paneling on the opposite wall.

> *'Ab insidiis diaboli, libera nos, Domine.*
> *Ut Ecclesiam Tuam secura tibi facias*
> *Libertate servire, te rogamus, audi nos.*
> *Ut inimicos sanctae Ecclesiae humiliare digneris,*
> *Te rogamus, audi nos.'*

Every so often Olivia would catch a flicker at the edge of her vision but when she turned to look it was gone. Theo grabbed her and forced her down to the ground as another severed chair leg shot across the room like an arrow, to land with a deep thud as it penetrated the wall with such force it left only a small stub protruding from the surface.

She turned as she felt a terrible wrenching and watched helplessly as Theo was torn from her grasp and flung across the room, skidding through the fragments of glass and dust to land in a sharp pyre of splintered wood. Before she could move to help him she felt herself being flung backwards like a rag doll and pinned to the wall by an invisible force. She couldn't move her body an inch, her wrists were pinned to the wall either side of her head. She could barely even curl her fingers against the force holding her immobile. Her chest felt heavy as if it were being crushed and slowly and inexorably she felt herself being dragged up against the wall, rising higher and higher until she was suspended three feet from the floor.

She glanced across to the two priests. Father Simmons was kneeling on the floor clutching his bible desperately, his eyes wild and fearful. Father Hubert on the other hand stood towering above the young priest implacably, his focus unwavering and his voice a boom above the howl and shriek of a violent wind which had come from nowhere. Glass and debris swirled around him in a tornado of fury. His hair whipped back from his face and the wind tore at clothes, yet in the midst of the chaos he stood like an ancient oak, immovable and determined.

Olivia blinked as she noticed the flickering again. This time she could see small glimmers of silver and she suddenly realized they were flames. She could see them darting around the room furiously, before finally turning towards Jackson. She watched helplessly as he was thrown against the broken glass wall behind the bar. The tiny flames coalesced in front of him, but he seemed unable to see it. As a wall of fire made up of pure silver flame roared up before him, Jackson wheezed and scratched at his neck, his eyes darting around frantically as if trying to see the invisible creature attacking him. His face was turning red as he fought for breath.

Olivia was barely aware of the old priest's voice as he built up to a crescendo, screeching above the roar of the wind. To her his voice seemed somehow distant, like an echo. Her mind was focused entirely on Jackson as the silver fire he seemed unable to see pulsed and rippled until it resembled the shape of a man and for a second she though she saw a pair of eyes flicker in her direction.

Her breathing slowed and her heartbeat evened out. Much as it had before in the woods, when she had conjured Hell fire for the first time, she seemed to detach from her physical self, from her emotions, as a strange kind of calm settled on her. Time slowed and she watched with curious detachment as the men in front of her seemed to freeze, almost trapped in one moment of time. The debris hung in the air like a strange kind of sculpture and the fragments of glass churned up by the wind tinkled in the air as they caught the light.

She looked across to the creature of flame and fire. Now she could see it clearly she picked apart the silver threads of the flames which made up its substance, to find the entity beneath it. It was a spirit, a very angry one. It stopped trying to choke the life from Jackson and twitched as if suddenly sensing her looking at him. It turned and for one moment she looked into its metallic silver eyes down into its soul. Its mouth opened in a slow cry of fury and it released Jackson, turning towards her.

Everything suddenly roared back into focus, too loud, too bright, too chaotic. It was heading straight for her and without even thinking her magic burst into flame, only instead of the familiar red and gold of her Earth fire or the deep, dark, blue-black of her Hell fire it roared to life in pure silver.

'Terribilis Deus de sanctuario suo.
Deus Israhel ipse truderit virtutem
Et fortitudinem plebi Suae.
Benedictus Deus. GLORIA PATRI!'

She vaguely heard Father Hubert shrieking behind her. The roaring in her ears drowned everything else out, her vision narrowed as she felt the power tear through her veins like wildfire. She could see the entity rush towards her. Her back arched against her bonds as her magic burst outwards. A bright white light blotted out everything and she suddenly felt herself falling.

A soft feather-like touch stroked her face. She could hear a familiar voice calling her name as she swam up through the heavy layers of consciousness. Opening her eyes she blinked a few times at the blurriness and tried to focus.

'Hey,' Theo breathed in relief as she opened her eyes. 'Are you alright?'

She lifted her head as he helped her into a sitting position and looked around the room.

'I'm okay,' she nodded meeting his concerned eyes. 'You?'

'Few scrapes,' his mouth curved, 'I'll survive.'

'What about Jackson and the others?'

'We're fine,' Father Hubert replied.

Olivia looked around Theo and noticed Father

Simmons helping the older priest to his feet. Father Hubert seemed to be slightly pale and perspiring heavily but other than that he seemed to be unharmed.

'Jackson?' she asked in concern.

'I'm here Olivia love,' the familiar lilting brogue spoke from behind them. 'Is that it then?' Jackson turned to the two priests, 'is it over?'

'The spirit has been cast out,' Father Hubert nodded. 'I can no longer feel it's presence.'

'Thank God,' Jackson breathed.

'That's the general idea,' Father Hubert smiled.

'You know,' Jackson answered, 'considering I'm Protestant I have never been so glad to see a Catholic priest in my whole life.'

'Well,' Father Hubert chuckled, 'I won't hold it against you. We're all children of the same God regardless of how we choose to serve.'

'Amen,' Jackson murmured.

'Now if you'll excuse me, I believe I'll have Father Simmons here help me home. I'm rather exhausted.'

'Of course Father,' Jackson stepped aside and allowed them to pass. 'You know,' he turned back to Olivia and Theo, 'I do believe that's one Catholic I could actually grow to like.'

'What the Hell?' a startled but familiar voice broke the air causing them to turn towards the door.

Shelley glanced around the absolute devastation of the pub before her gaze finally fell on the unholy trio of Theo, Olivia and Jackson, taking in their ripped and bloodstained clothes and their various injuries.

'Did you have a party and not invite me?'

Jackson grinned. 'Ah Shelley love 'tis a long and tall tale best told over two fingers of Jameson's.'

She glanced past him to the shattered remnants of the bar stock. 'Uh I don't think you have any left,' she frowned, 'or any glasses.'

'Do you want us to help you start cleaning up?'

Olivia glanced around the room.

Jackson shook his head.

'You've done more than enough, and it's grateful to you both that I am. My staff will be arriving for their shifts soon, they can help with the clean up. You should get on home and get cleaned up; you look as if you've just survived a zombie apocalypse.'

'What's a zombie?' Theo whispered to Olivia.

'Never mind,' she shook her head before turning back to Jackson and wrapping her arms around him, 'call us if you need anything.'

'That I will,' he nodded to Theo as they picked their way over glass and debris towards the door.

By the time Olivia and Theo stepped through their front door Beau was dancing around desperately.

'Hello baby,' Olivia kneeled down and stroked him as he jumped all over her. 'I'm sorry we took so long.'

Not only had they been gone pretty much all day but they'd had to stop off on their way home from the pub to take care of Fiona's legion of cats, a task Theo was extremely unhappy about. The hospital had finally contacted Olivia and although Fiona had pulled through and was out of any immediate danger she would still likely be in hospital for several days, leaving the felines as Olivia's responsibility.

Stretching tiredly as Beau headed for Theo she yawned.

'We should feed him; he's probably starving by now.'

'Why don't you go and take a hot shower and I'll see to Beau,' Theo stroked the length of her spine comfortingly.

'Are you sure you don't mind?'

'No,' he shook his head.

'Alright then,' she headed up the stairs.

Stepping into the bathroom she discarded her

clothes carelessly, it wasn't even worth putting them in the hamper, they were stained with blood and covered with tiny tears from all the glass and way beyond saving. Turning the water up as high as she could stand it she pulled her hair loose from its ponytail and stepped under the spray. Her skin felt tight and covered in something gruesome. Parts of her exposed skin were layered with Fiona's blood and her own and probably some of Theo's as well.

Sighing she closed her eyes, putting her face under the water as she raked her hands through her hair. Her life was just insane, it had been from the moment she'd driven back into Mercy. Pressing her hands against the cold tile she leaned forwards and allowed the hot water to cascade between her shoulder blades and down her back, soothing the scratches. Her gaze fell absently on the blood tinged water as it swirled down the drain at her feet.

Would she have had it any other way? A frown marred her brow as she turned the thought over in her mind. It was a question she'd asked herself a lot recently. What if she'd never come back to Mercy? Would she have been better off not knowing the truth about her parents? To go on living a lie, a mockery of her life, with Mags the one person in the world she'd thought she could trust unconditionally, who turned out to be just another person who'd been lying to her all along.

No, she sighed. Ignorance wasn't always bliss; she'd take truth any day even if it came with heartbreak, at least then you knew where you stood. So now she would just have to accept the fact her life was a crazy circus of demons, hell hounds, ghosts and people she thought were dead who turned out to be lying, cheating sociopaths.

She pressed her forehead against the cool tile and closed her eyes. The only thing in all of this mess she didn't regret was Theo. The deep need she had inside for him was something she wouldn't allow herself to take out and examine too closely. She'd just carried on like everything was normal, not dealing with any of the issues she knew they had. She'd been avoiding a conversation she needed to have with him for days, weeks even. There was just never a good time.

No, she thought to herself. It was more than that, she'd been deliberately avoiding having the conversation with him, which wasn't fair to him and she knew it. He needed to know that he wasn't obligated to stay with her, that he was free to choose his own path. The trouble was she was afraid; afraid that he was going to leave her, but more afraid that he was going to stay.

She was messed up, she needed her head examining. Why couldn't she just be normal? Why couldn't she give him the one thing he wanted but never asked for. She could see the hurt and rejection in his eyes every time he told her he loved her and she didn't say it back. It just got caught somewhere between her heart and her mouth and the words wouldn't come out.

He deserved better, someone who could love him the way he deserved to be loved. The problem was she just couldn't let him go, it actually gave her a sharp pain in her chest when she thought about him not being there in the house with her. She was stupid and selfish.

Her heart gave a helpless thud in her chest as she heard the shower door slide open and a gust of cool air waft over her wet skin. A moment later the door closed again and she felt familiar arms wrap around her, pulling her in against hard naked flesh.

Everything in her sighed and relaxed. The ball of tension she'd been carrying inside her all day, drained away and she leaned back against his chest, her eyes still closed.

'Livy...'

His breath gusted warm against her ear and she felt rather than heard his voice under the thunder of the water. Her heart did a long slow roll at the ache in his voice.

Turning her in his arms his mouth took hers, even

121

as his fingers tangled in the wet ropes of her hair. She was as lost to him as he was to her, helpless to deny him anything. In these moments between them the whole world ceased to exist. Her mind emptied until her only thought was the pleasure of his hands, his mouth and his body.

He tasted her slowly and surely as if they had all the time in the world, sucking her bottom lip into his mouth tugging gently. He trailed lower brushing her warm wet skin with his lips, down her throat to her collar bone. She arched helplessly in his arms as he took the tips of her breasts into his mouth first one then the other, tugging and teasing them into aching points as his fingers stroked between her thighs plunging into the warm wet velvet heat of her. Her breath caught in her throat on a gasp of intense pleasure.

'Theo please.'

He withdrew his fingers and turned her sharply pressing her hands up against the wall, his own larger hands covering hers. She could feel the cool hard tile against her sensitive breasts and his warm body pressed up against her back.

Her breath was forced from her lungs in small pants of anticipation, her whole body throbbing with the need to have him buried deep inside her. His lips once again resumed marking a trail down the side of her neck, his fingers locking with hers against the tile before sliding across the backs of her hands and down her forearms, tracing the curve of her elbows to her upper arms, leaving trails of fire scorching along her skin.

He was learning quickly. After they had become lovers, it had been so tentative and new at first, just raw passion and a race to satisfy each other as quickly as possible. Somewhere along the line though, it began to change. He was learning how to drive her up to the highest peak and hold her there, prolonging the delicious anticipation of intense pleasure. He knew her body so well now, perhaps better than she did. But there were moments like this when he simply took over; a small smile momentarily curved the corner of her mouth. Usually if she'd been anywhere near Jackson, it seemed to bring out a sharp possessive streak in Theo, which she was discovering she liked, gloried in even. She was his and he made sure she knew it.

His hands slid down the backs of her shoulders and underneath, grazing the curves of her breasts. One hand slid around her ribcage holding her in place while the other slid lower across her abdomen between her thighs slowly stroking. His talented fingertips found the tight bundle of nerves and began to circle.

Her hands fisted against the wall as she threw her head back against his shoulder. A loud gasp escaped her lips as she pressed back against the hard aroused length of him. She bucked against his hand, at war with her own traitorous body, trying to find some relief for the toe curling intensity and yet at the same time not wanting him to stop. But there was nowhere to go, trapped between his body and his extremely talented fingers she could do nothing but take the pleasure he gave her.

A cry tore from her lips as the tension in her body climbed higher, tightening to an almost painful acuity and when she thought she'd almost reached the peak she felt the thick hard length of him sliding into her, slowly inexorably until she could do nothing but climax so hard it felt like her legs were going to collapse.

Theo felt her body tighten around him and gritted his teeth, determined not to follow her release. Grasping her hips he pulled out and slid back in slowly as she leaned forwards and pressed her fevered forehead to the blessedly cold tile. He rocked in and out of her as her breath escaped in small pants and gasps.

'More,' she breathed heavily.

He pressed her up against the wall and quickened his pace; plunging deep with each stroke as she reached back over her shoulder and gripped his dark hair tightly.

'Harder.'

Helpless but to obey, a soft growl escaped his lips as he lost himself in her, pounding deeper and harder.

When his name tore from her lips in a desperate plea, he pulled away and spun her around lifting her and pressing her back against the wall as he slid back into her. Wrapping her arms around his neck and her legs around his waist she took his mouth swallowing his moans and gasps and this time when he felt her body tighten around him he followed her down into oblivion.

8.

Theo stared into the darkness absently stroking the smooth soft skin of Olivia's thigh. Once again he couldn't sleep. Glancing across at Olivia's sleeping form he lightly stroked his finger down her spine, tracing the slight indentations, vertebrae as he now knew they were called. He'd taken some time from reading up on world history to study modern medicine and it was fascinating. The human body and what it was capable of, so many of the illnesses and ailments they'd feared in his time had been no more than simple infections due to a lack of medical knowledge, poor hygiene and social hysteria. His brow folded unconsciously into a frown; so much death and destruction caused by ignorance. When he thought back to the minor things which had been blamed on witchcraft, and by extension on any poor woman unlucky enough to be accused of being a witch, the bile rose in his throat and he almost choked on the burning guilt.

Trying to shake away the dark thoughts he watched the shadows flicker across Olivia's naked skin which glowed in the pale moonlight. What would they have made of Olivia if she had been thrown back in time rather than him being pulled forwards? he thought randomly. Would they have known what she was?

Unfortunately he knew what would have happened. They wouldn't have seen the beauty of the things she could do, they would have known only fear and in their fear they would have destroyed her. She would have been led to her death as so many others had, swinging from a rope on Gallows' Hill.

He couldn't bear the thought and as he shut his eyes against the painful image of Olivia with a rope around her perfect throat, her face was suddenly replaced by another familiar one, it's icy blue eyes staring back at him from a pale face framed by golden hair. He shot bolt upright in bed and drew in a shaky breath, those cool accusing blue eyes still mocking him. Olivia murmured sleepily at the sudden movement of the bed and snuggled back into the rumpled sheets, her breathing once again resuming its slow measured pace.

Throwing his legs over the side of the bed he scrubbed his hand over his face, resisting the urge to curl back around Olivia's warm body and breathe in the familiar scent of her skin. Scooping his track pants off the floor he pulled them on and grabbed a t shirt as he moved silently on bare feet towards the door. Beau, woken from his sleep in front of the dying embers of the fire, got up and plodded sleepily over to him.

Smiling, Theo kneeled down in front of him stroking his soft head.

'Watch over her for me will you?' he whispered as his eyes once again found Olivia's sleeping form.

Beau licked his hand and trotted over to the bed. With a small leap and a lot of scrambling he finally managed to pull himself up onto the bed and after turning in a circle a few times he settled down with his head resting across Olivia's legs and closed his eyes.

Theo headed downstairs, his mind awake and his body unsettled. Wandering into his studio he flicked the lights on, intending to just scoop up one of his sketch pads and curl up in his chair. But his gaze snagged on the canvas in the corner of the room, propped up facing the wall so only the bare wooden frame at the back was exposed.

He stood there for a moment just staring at it. He hated it, he wished he'd never painted it even though it was one of his best, or rather it had been. The portrait of his wife was now buried under thick multi coloured layers of oil paint, obscuring any hint of what lay beneath. He should have just thrown it away but for some reason he couldn't explain he hadn't, just as he didn't know why he'd painted the damn thing in the first place.

His feet were moving before he even realized it. Reaching the corner of the room he grasped the painting and as he turned it around his heart stopped in his chest and his breath hissed out of his mouth. As his trembling fingers clutched the frame his heartbeat suddenly kicked up into overdrive. The painting was no longer covered in a Jackson Pollock -like maelstrom of colours but once again a pristine portrait of Mary stared back at him with cold eyes and a disapproving mouth. What the hell was going on?

Grabbing a sharp knife from one of the pots on the table he placed the portrait on the empty easel and stabbed the knife into the corner of the canvas. Following the line of the wooden frame he cut the canvas away, removing the entire portrait from the frame. Rolling it up he shoved it into the trash can and headed out into the kitchen. He grabbed a bottle of whiskey and a box of matches from the cupboard, stopping only long enough to pull on his boots and coat before he slipped out of the back door and down the steps into the yard area overlooking the lake.

Placing the trash can down in the snow he poured in a generous amount of whiskey and struck the match. He watched in satisfaction as the canvas caught alight, blackening and curling at the edges as the flames consumed it.

Breathing in the cold night air he glanced across the lake. Once again it was shrouded in a strange undulating mist, much as it had been for weeks now. A sudden cold chill danced down his spine making him shiver. Just for a second the mist seemed to appear not as a whole, but rather to be made up of thousands of writhing shapes rolling across the surface of the water. Suddenly uneasy he turned back to the trash can and watched as the painting finally burned itself down to ashes. Scooping aside some of the snow to reveal the hard ground underneath he tipped the ashes out and then covered it back over with snow.

Heading back up the steps to the door he took one last troubled look at the lake and stepped back inside, careful to ensure all the doors and windows were locked.

'No, no girl, the next channel,' Fiona scowled. 'Good God what on earth is this rubbish?'

'Why don't I just switch it off Ms Caldwell' the nurse replied, digging deep to find her patience.

'Why don't you let me go home,' she countered irritably.

'Now, Ms Caldwell you know the doctor won't allow it. You've just had very serious surgery and you need to recover before we discharge you. It would be different if you had someone living with you who could keep an eye on you.'

'Now you listen here, I've been taking care of myself for the last forty years. I don't need some twenty year old nurse telling me what I can and can't do. I demand to see the doctor right now.'

'She's busy at the moment, she'll be down to see you on rounds later,' she answered as she smoothed down Fiona's rumpled bed.

'Then go and get me the release forms, I'll discharge myself.'

'Ms Caldwell,' she sighed in exasperation.

'Still terrorizing the staff I see,' a familiar voice had them both turning towards the doorway.

'Their incompetence astounds me' Fiona grumbled, glaring mutinously at the nurse.

'She's all yours,' the young woman breathed a sigh of relief as she slipped from the room.

'How are you feeling?' Olivia smiled, stepping into the room holding a bunch of flowers and a bag.

'Why are you here?' she snapped. 'Why aren't you looking after my cats?'

'I have been looking after your cats,' her mouth curved in amusement as she put the bag down and pulled a plastic pitcher from the locker beside the bed before disappearing into the bathroom to fill it.

'So you say,' she huffed, 'they can't be left on their own for too long.'

'They're fine,' Olivia re-emerged from the bathroom and began to arrange the flowers.

'I want to go home.'

'Well you can't,' she replied pleasantly, 'they've only just pulled a six-inch shard of glass from your neck. I'm afraid you're stuck here until they decide you can go.'

'Traitor,' she hissed folding her arms. 'If you don't have anything more useful to say you can leave too.'

'And if you can't be more pleasant you won't get your surprise.'

'What surprise?' she asked suspiciously.

Olivia pulled a packet of cigarettes from her pocket.

Fiona let loose a delighted cackle. 'I knew there was a reason I liked you girl.' Fiona began to throw back the covers.

'Uh Uh' Olivia shook her head 'wheelchair.'

Fiona paused. 'Stuff and nonsense,' she replied indignantly, 'I don't need a bloody wheelchair.'

'Those are the terms,' Olivia waved the cigarette pack in front of her. 'I guess the question is, how bad do you want one of these?'

'Fine,' Fiona's gaze narrowed.

Olivia retrieved the bag and pulled out some fur-lined snow boots and a thick winter jacket, which she had retrieved from Fiona's house, knowing the ones she'd been wearing when she was brought in were torn and covered in blood. Within minutes she had her tucked up in a wheelchair and covered with a blanket.

'Shush,' Olivia chuckled as she stuck her head around the corner to check the coast was clear. Noting that the nurses station was empty she pushed the wheelchair quickly down the corridor towards the elevators, both of them giggling like school girls.

'Roof,' Fiona decided as the doors opened and Olivia wheeled her inside. 'They'll never think to look for us up there.'

They came out on the top floor heading for the exit onto the roof. Unable to hold back any longer Fiona pulled a cigarette from the pack and lit it taking a long drag and exhaling with a deeply pleasured sigh.

'You couldn't wait two more seconds?'

'Nope,' Fiona replied as she took another deep inhale before the door opened up and she found herself breathing cold air. 'God that's better,' she sighed in relief, 'it was beginning to feel as if the walls were closing in on me.'

'You're welcome,' Olivia smiled parking the chair by the ledge and putting the brakes on.

She dusted the snow off the bricks and sat down next to Fiona.

'This would go down a treat with a brandy.'

'Sorry,' Olivia laughed, 'but I draw the line at booze. I don't know what meds they've got you on but I'm pretty sure alcohol wouldn't mix well.'

Fiona shrugged and resumed puffing away at her cigarette. 'So what's been happening?'

'Not much since Father Hubert got rid of

Jackson's guest.'

'You haven't seen Charlotte again?'

Olivia shook her head. 'I'm at a bit of a standstill, I don't know what she's trying to tell me and in the meantime there seems to be more and more sightings. I spoke to Jake this morning and the phone has been ringing off the hook down at the station with people convinced they've seen ghosts. I can't figure it out, I've never heard of so many spirit sightings, so suddenly, and all in one town.'

Fiona watched Olivia silently as she absently tapped the ash from her cigarette.

'It's like you can feel them,' Olivia murmured thoughtfully. 'Like a flicker at the edge of your vision but when you turn your head there's nothing there. You walk down the street and the tiny hairs on the back of your neck begin to rise as if the air is filled with static electricity. They're everywhere; it's almost as if…'

'As if what?'

'As if someone has left a door open and they've all just wandered in,' her gaze locked on Fiona who was chewing on her lip pensively. 'What?'

'I think you've probably hit the nail on the head.'

'What?'

'Picture it in your mind,' Fiona replied quietly, 'all the different versions of the afterlife you've ever heard of, the Nether, the spirit world, the summer lands, the other world…all the realms of the dead. They're all real and they're all connected. Everything is connected, each with its own doorway leading to someplace else. What if one of those doorways was left open?'

'Let's just say for one moment you're right, shouldn't the doorways be locked or guarded?' Olivia frowned.

'Yes,' she nodded, 'which begs the question who would have the knowledge and power to open one and why?'

'Great, more questions,' Olivia sighed.

'I'm afraid so,' Fiona pulled another cigarette from the pack and lit it from the first before flicking the butt into the snow. 'But I believe it is the most important question; this is what we need to figure out the answer to and I'm afraid we don't have much time.'

'Why do I get a really bad feeling when you say that?'

'Like I said,' she took a drag of her fresh cigarette, 'everything is connected by a series of doors and gateways. We're all just parts of a whole, like one giant cosmic jigsaw puzzle. Just as all the spirit realms are attached to our world; other worlds are attached to them.'

'Such as?'

'The Underworld, Hell, Sheol, Tartarus, again all the most terrifying places of every faith and religion, where the sinners and monsters are cast down. They are all real. How long do you think it's going to take them to realize there is an open doorway to the human world? And how long before they realize they can use the spirit world as a corridor from their hell to our world.'

She took another pull and blew out a deep discontented breath.

'If that happens,' she shook her head, 'the last thing we'll have to worry about is a few ghosts. There are true horrors in the underworld, creatures who haven't seen the light of day in thousands of years. What the hell do you think they are going to do if they are suddenly set loose on earth?'

'So we need to find the doorway and close it?'

'The problem is the gateways exist outside of the human range of perception. We can't see them, even those of us who are gifted. There are very few creatures who can detect them; it's supposed to be a failsafe to stop them from being opened. Even if we could find this one I have no idea how it was opened in the first place therefore I have no idea how to close it.'

'We're screwed,' Olivia replied slowly.

'Bet that brandy sounds good right about now doesn't it?'

'You're not kidding.'

Suddenly the door to the roof banged open and Louisa emerged pulling her coat on over her scrubs.

'Thought I saw you escaping up here,' she dropped down on the wall next to Olivia and plucked Fiona's cigarette out of her hand and took a long drag.

'I didn't know you smoked,' Olivia frowned.

'I don't,' Louisa blew out a steady stream of smoke. 'I quit three years ago,' she glanced back and forth between Olivia and Fiona noting their serious expressions. 'You look like your day's been about as good as mine. What's the problem?'

'The end of the world,' Olivia breathed heavily, 'and you?'

'Lost a patient,' she answered quietly as she took another pull, 'and I seem to have misplaced my husband.'

'Oh,' Olivia clarified, 'Tommy's with Theo. He's teaching him how to drive, God help us. Although it is kinda cute, I think they have a little bit of a bromance going on.'

'Well at least he's still talking to someone,' she muttered.

'Is there a problem?'

'No,' Louisa sighed, 'I don't know, Tommy's just been...different since he came home this time.'

'Different how?'

'He doesn't sleep, when he does he has nightmares but he won't talk about it he just keeps snapping at me.'

Olivia put her arm around Louisa pulling her in close until their heads rested together.

'I'm sure it will be okay, I can't even begin to imagine the things he's seen. He's bound to have trouble re-adjusting to normal life.'

'That's just the problem, I think he's suffering from PTSD but I can't get him to talk to me about it.'

'Just give him time,' Olivia replied, 'that's all you can do.'

'I suppose,' she finished the cigarette and flicked it into a small snowdrift, 'but for now I'm afraid I'm going to have to take my patient back in before she catches Pneumonia and we're stuck with her for even longer.'

'It's not my fault your staff are incompetent morons,' Fiona shrugged as Louisa released the brakes and steered her back towards the door.

'You made one of the orderlys cry yesterday.'

Fiona cackled delightedly. 'He should grow a thicker skin then.'

'Maybe you should grow some manners,' her mouth curved in amusement.

Olivia followed behind them quietly, only half listening to them trade good natured insults. Her mind was still turning over what Fiona had told her about the gateways. If they didn't figure out a solution soon she had the uncomfortable feeling they were going to be in deep trouble.

After saying goodbye to them, Olivia headed back to her car. She barely even noticed the drive home until she pulled up in front of her house. Her mind was filled with the disturbing possibilities of an open portal left unchecked for any dark creature to be let loose on her world. Glancing down at her watch as she climbed the steps to the porch she realized Theo probably wouldn't be back for a while. She could spend the next few hours trawling through the Internet looking for any reference to gateways or doorways to the spirit world. Somewhere, someone must have encountered one before.

As she slid her key into the lock her brow folded into a frown, something didn't feel right. She opened the door slowly and stepped into the hallway, letting the door close behind her with a gentle click. She paused but the house was still and quiet and nothing seemed out of place. Pulling her jacket off and hanging it on the rack by the door she kicked her boots off.

Beau suddenly came scampering down the stairs wagging his tail enthusiastically.

'Hey baby,' she leaned down to stroke him, 'have you been napping on my bed again?'

He leaned into her hand, his whole body wagging with pleasure that she was home as he nipped at her hand and jumped up at her legs.

'Come on,' she smiled, 'we've got some work to do.'

She turned and headed for the library but as she reached the door she froze and her heart banged painfully in her chest.

'Hello Olivia,' her mother spoke coolly as she sat comfortably on the tatty couch. 'I see you haven't done much with the place,' she glanced around the room distastefully, 'still the same as I remember it.'

'What are you doing here?' Olivia whispered coldly.

'I came to see you.'

'That's funny because last time we were together you shot me.'

'If I'd wanted you dead Olivia,' she answered casually, 'you'd already be dead.'

'Like Nana?'

Something unreadable flickered behind Isabel's eyes. 'Unfortunate but unavoidable.'

'She was your mother,' Olivia whispered, 'how could you?'

'She was in my way,' Isabel rose slowly to her feet.

Olivia stood watching silently, unable to find any words, as Isabel moved until she was standing directly in front of her. Olivia's heart clenched painfully as she looked into her mother's eyes for the first time in twenty years. The child deep inside her wanted so desperately to put her arms out and be held by her mom, but the adult in her knew that she was a cold blooded murderer who could not be trusted.

'I never wanted you,' Isabel whispered.

'What?' Olivia gasped painfully.

'Pregnant at eighteen?' she replied calmly, 'you think that was what I wanted? I couldn't even have an abortion, my mother and my aunt knew just by looking at me that I had conceived. I had no choice but to have you,' her fingertips reached out and slowly toyed with a stray lock of Olivia's hair. 'I remember the first time I held you...so tiny...so fragile...it would have been so easy to smother you.'

'Then why didn't you,' she replied quietly.

'Because I saw something in you.'

'What?'

'Me,' she answered slowly.

'I am nothing like you,' Olivia responded bitterly.

'I've felt your power Olivia,' her hand dropped from Olivia's hair as she began to circle her like a hunter. 'Its raw...undisciplined...unfocused...I could teach you,' she moved back in front of Olivia and stopped. 'I could teach you how to harness your power, you have no idea yet what you are truly capable of.'

Olivia couldn't speak, couldn't form the words as yet again her world was torn apart.

'We could be together again,' she crooned softly, 'you could have your mother back, isn't that what you want? What you've always wanted.'

Tears burned in her eyes as her gaze fixed on Isabel's face. 'No,' she whispered defiantly, 'No!' she shoved her mother's hand away and stepped back. 'My mother is dead, she died twenty years ago.'

Isabel's mouth curved in amusement.

'Deny it all you want Olivia but I am your mother and you and I are not finished. We will never be finished whether you like it or not.'

The rage began to burn in her chest, smothering the pain as she felt for her magic, drew it down like armor and punched outwards with it. The invisible force hit Isabel and threw her back against a bookcase. Loose papers and books tumbled to the floor as Isabel straightened herself and smiled slowly.

'Like I said undisciplined,' she flicked her hand as if swatting away an errant fly and Olivia felt herself thrown backwards violently. The air was knocked out of her lungs as she landed on the desk, scattering more papers across the floor, followed by her laptop which cracked loudly as it hit the ground.

'Unfocused,' Isabel clenched her outstretched fist and threw it towards the opposite wall and Olivia was tossed like a rag doll. She felt her shoulder crack as she hit the other bookcase and dropped to the floor, books raining down on top of her.

Beau went mad, snapping at Isabel's ankles and growling loudly as he tried to protect his mistress. Isabel barely spared the puppy a glance, making a dismissive sweeping motion with her hand. Beau yelped as he skidded across the wooden floor out into the hallway before the door slammed shut in his face. Olivia could hear him barking and scratching frantically at the door trying to get back in. She tried to catch her breath while pushing herself up but her injured shoulder collapsed beneath her.

'You have so much to learn,' Isabel murmured as she kneeled down next to her daughter sweeping a dark lock of hair from her pale face and tucking it tenderly behind her ear. 'Think back Olivia...think back to the night at Boothe's Hollow to when I broke the devils trap and set Nathaniel free and ask yourself this...why did I use your blood when mine would have sufficed?'

Olivia stared in confusion as her mother stroked her cheek softly, then she saw her hand curl into a fist and darkness was the last thing she remembered.

She wasn't sure how long she'd been out but when she finally came around she was lying on the cold floor amidst the destruction of her library, with Beau desperately licking her face.

'Alright boy,' she murmured reaching out for him and stroking him soothingly, 'I'm okay.'

She pushed herself slowly into a sitting position wincing at the sharp pain in her shoulder. Glancing around the room she realized with a slow roll of dread in her stomach that this was far more destruction than that caused when her mother had thrown her across the room. This looked as if the room had been trashed deliberately, as if Isabel had been looking for something.

'No...no,' she shook her head in denial, her heart sinking as her gaze landed on the empty box where she had stored Hester's Grimoire. That's what her mother had wanted, she'd come looking for Hester's spell book. Messing with her daughter had probably just been an added bonus. Fighting back the tears she shuffled against the nearest bookcase and leaned back. Beau climbed across her lap and settled down with a sigh, looking up at her with dark eyes. She touched her jaw gingerly and hissed with pain.

Her mother obviously had a hell of a right hook, her jaw was badly bruised and the side of her mouth felt swollen but that was nothing compared to the pain of seeing her mother again, of being used yet again.

She heard the door open and close and Theo's voice call out to her. Beau leapt up and scrambled into the hallway barking frantically as if trying to tell him what had happened.

'Hey boy,' he reached down to stroke Beau, 'where's Olivia?'

Beau snagged Theo's sleeve with his teeth and tugged hard.

'What is it Beau?' Theo frowned.

Beau dragged him towards the library. He

straightened up as soon as he saw the devastation of Olivia's favorite room, his eyes tracking around until they fell on where she had curled up against the wall with her head resting on her knees.

'Olivia!' he breathed heavily as he dropped down beside her, 'what happened?'

She raised her head unable to hide the marks on her face, watching as Theo's gaze hardened.

'Who did this to you?'

Olivia sighed.

'My mom decided to drop by.'

'Your mom?'

Olivia's head snapped round to the voice in the doorway, wincing as she caught sight of Tommy standing open mouthed, staring at the mess in the room and the bruises on her face.

'I thought your mom was dead?'

'Oh shit,' she breathed.

9.

'So let me get this right,' Tommy frowned into his whiskey. 'Your mom is not dead, because your Father didn't kill her. But he did stab her because she killed her mother, your grandmother. Your dad was convicted of killing her which he didn't because she is still alive but escaped from a mental institution because your mom started murdering other people.'

'Yeah,' Olivia mumbled as Theo carefully pressed an icepack to her jaw.

'Olivia your family is fucked up.'

'Tell me about it,' she sighed. 'Look Tommy you can't say anything, it's not common knowledge that my mom is still alive and there are reasons for that, good reasons.'

'I don't know Olivia, 'your mom sounds like a psycho and she was here in your house.'

'I know but if she wanted me dead believe me I would already be dead.'

'That doesn't make me feel any better about this,' Tommy scowled. 'You need to tell the police.'

'They know,' Theo answered for her.

'What?'

'Mac, the new police chief and Jake already know

the truth.'

'And they haven't reported it?'

'Like Olivia said there are reasons.'

'But you're not going to tell me those reasons.'

'Look Tommy,' Olivia removed the icepack so she could speak more clearly although her words were still slightly slurred from the swelling, 'I know it's frustrating but it's kind of a need to know basis. Please just trust us on this, we'll tell you as much as we can but as for the rest of it you need to let it go.'

'Answer me one thing.'

Olivia nodded.

'Does Louisa know the truth; I mean all of it?'

Olivia hesitated, knowing that her answer was going to make a tense situation between Louisa and her husband even worse.

'That's what I thought,' Tommy interpreted her silence and stood, abruptly heading out of the room.

'Tommy!' Theo called after him as he heard the front door slam.

'Let him go,' Olivia caught Theo's sleeve. 'Louisa will deal with it; she knows him better than we do.'

'I wish we could tell him the truth,' Theo took the ice pack from her and pressed it back to her mouth gently. 'I hate having to lie to him, it feels wrong somehow. He's a good guy.'

'Yes he is,' she murmured, 'which is exactly why we're doing him a favor by not getting him involved with this mess. He's dealing with problems of his own right now; he doesn't need the added stress.'

'Maybe,' Theo conceded, 'but it still feels wrong.'

'I know,' she stroked his forearm as he softly held the icepack against her face.

'Why don't you tell me the rest of it now, whatever it was that you didn't want to say in front of Tommy.'

'My mom stole Hester's Grimoire.'

'Damn it,' he breathed. Then he looked into her eyes, realizing there was more. 'What is it?'

'She said something to me, right before she knocked me unconscious.'

'What?'

'She told me to ask myself why she used my blood to open the devil's trap instead of just hers.'

'And?'

'And I've been turning it over and over in my mind. She didn't just use my blood she used both of our blood to break the trap.'

'What does that mean?'

'There's only one reason I can think of; her blood gives her immunity from him.'

'I'm not sure I follow.'

'She built him a mortal body and forced him into it with her magic, sealed with her blood. While he is trapped in that body he can't harm her and because she used my blood too...'

'He can't harm you either,' Theo frowned in confusion. 'She was protecting you?'

'I keep going over that moment when she shot me. I was standing at almost point blank range and at that distance, even if she was a lousy shot, she couldn't miss me. If she'd wanted me dead she could've just put a bullet in my head but instead she shot me in the shoulder, incapacitating me and gaining access to my blood.'

'She was trying to save you,' he replied quietly. 'I know Nathaniel and the first thing he would have done was kill you, she knew it too.'

'What I don't understand is why?' her voice rose higher, revealing an underlying fragment of panic, as she fought back the tears threatening to spill over. 'It's all part of some manipulation, it has to be... I just can't figure out why'

'Olivia,' he spoke softly, 'maybe she saved you because you're her daughter, because deep down she loves you.'

'No,' she shook her head in denial, 'you don't know her. She does everything for her own selfish reasons. If she saved me it's not because she loves me it's because she wants something from me, I just need to figure out what it is.'

Knowing he wasn't going to get through to her while she was in this frame of mind, he kissed her forehead softly and gathered her up gently in his arms, rocking her slightly until he felt the tension and panic drain from her body.

'Why don't you go up and have a hot bath,' he stroked her hair back from her face. 'I'll make you something to eat and bring it up.'

'Theo,' she murmured, her mouth curving slightly; 'you're a lousy cook.'

He chuckled lightly.

'I can manage grilled cheese sandwiches and soup without needing to call out the fire department.'

'It sounds great,' she nodded as the first tear began to fall.

'Don't cry Livy love,' he murmured against her mouth brushing the tear away with the pad of his thumb. 'It rips me apart when you cry.'

'I have such a need for you inside me Theo,' she finally admitted, 'it scares me how much I need you.'

'I'm not going anywhere,' he kissed her gently, 'because I need you too.'

Unable to say anything she simply nodded and slid off the stool. Theo watched her silently as she slipped out of the kitchen and headed towards the stairs.

'Go with her and make sure she's okay,' he told Beau, who thumped his tail against the floor in reply and trotted out of the room obediently.

'You took your time,' Nathaniel spoke coldly as Isabel entered the cavernous room, his dark eyes glowering at the object she carried in her hands.

'You need to learn some patience,' she replied.

'I've waited nearly a thousand years witch,' he spat venomously.

'Then a few hours shouldn't make a difference.'

His lips peeled back in an angry snarl and he lunged for her but with a sudden shower of sparks he was pushed back two paces by an invisible barrier.

Isabel's mouth curved in an amused smile.

'You can't harm me demon, or have you forgotten that already? I always knew your race were ignorant. I didn't realize they were stupid as well.'

'Be very careful,' he said menacingly from between clenched teeth, his eyes filled with contempt. 'This filthy pig suit you have forced me into will not last forever and when I break free...' his gaze raked over her dangerously, 'the things I am going to do to you.'

'Don't bother threatening me Nathaniel you don't scare me,' she replied coolly as her gaze slid over to the half naked man chained up and suspended from the ceiling by his wrists. His head hung forward, his face mostly concealed by his dark matted hair. His torso bore vicious looking slash marks and was streaked with congealed blood and burn marks. The faint odor of blood and singed flesh lingered in the damp cold air.

'I see you've been amusing yourself with our guest.'

'He's remarkably resilient,' Nathaniel conceded grudgingly. 'I've pulled out his organs several times but they just grow back again.'

'The body of an immortal,' she stepped closer tracing the seared flesh of his ribcage with her fingertips. 'I wonder,' she murmured, her lips close to his ear, 'do you feel pain the way we do?' She dug her fingers viciously into the wound causing his head to lift and a gasp to escape his dry ragged lips. Her fingers, now coated with his blood, softened and she traced his skin lightly causing the tiny hairs on his body to rise, 'do you feel pleasure?'

'Stop playing with him,' Nathaniel growled, 'he's here for a purpose.'

Isabel stepped back smiling.

'Take him down from there.'

Nathaniel moved to the wall where the end of the chain was anchored and released it. The damaged man dropped to the floor, limp and exhausted, the heavy weight of the black metal collar he wore weighing him down. He didn't even bother to raise his head as the demon dragged a metal chair over the exposed floor with a sharp screeching sound. He felt himself being roughly lifted and thrown into the seat. He peered through the crack of one eye, the other swollen shut, watching silently as Nathaniel dragged a table over and placed it in front of him.

Isabel placed a rectangular object wrapped in black velvet on the table in front of him. Carefully folding back the heavy fabric he leaned forward in interest as a large leather bound book was revealed. A triple moon was etched into its face and underneath it was a depiction of the tree of life; he could feel the ripples of power laced through the pages even without touching it.

'This is a book of power' he slurred, his damaged jaw making speech difficult.

'Yes it is,' Isabel looked down at him. 'I want you to use it to locate her.'

'No,' he stared up at her defiantly.

'You don't have a choice,' she answered smoothly as she circled him slowly. 'Give me what I want and you have my word you will go free.'

'I don't believe you.'

She shrugged unconcernedly.

'I have no other interest in you or the gateway,' she leaned in closer. 'Can you feel them, unchecked and pouring into Mercy; they are everywhere.'

He could feel them. It was like standing in a smog composed entirely of souls, lost, wandering and trying to connect with the living. It went against everything he was; it wasn't supposed to be like this. He had to find a way to return them all to the other side but there was no way to achieve that whilst he was fettered by the damn collar. Even now he could feel his powers bound deep inside him, unable to reach them or to break free. He wanted to raise his head and howl in frustration. If only he could reach his master but that too was impossible. His master had not walked the earth in thousands of years and wouldn't go topside just because he'd been careless enough to get himself captured by the witch and her pet demon.

'You're running out of time you know' she smiled, her voice soft and cajoling. 'For now only human souls have escaped the gateway. How long do you think it's going to take for the others to realize the doorway is open? Are you really ready to let the Hell dimensions loose on earth?'

'You really would condemn your own people to that?' he looked up into her eyes.

'You have no idea the lengths I am willing to go to, to possess Infernum.'

'You're not the first to search for it and you won't be the last. It has been lost for millennia, far beyond the reach of a mortal witch and her delusions of grandeur.'

Her hand cracked sharply across his cheek. Pain exploded across the side of his face as she connected with his swollen flesh and damaged jaw.

'Find her,' she hissed, 'I know you can.'

'No,' he growled, a trail of blood and spittle trailing from his lip.

'Then watch as the earth is overrun, if you think the destruction of humanity is worth the price of one soul.'

'Go to Hell,' he spat.

'We may all do just that before this is over,' she whispered in contempt.

Picking up the book and folding it safely back into

her arms she turned to Nathaniel.

'See if you can make him slightly more co-operative.'

Nathaniel smiled, his black eyes burning eagerly. 'My pleasure.'

He removed his shirt, his mismatched torso, which resembled the scars of Frankenstein's monster, glowing in the dim light as he laid a roll of coarse fabric on top of the table with a metallic clank. He unrolled the material to reveal a gruesome assortment of metal hooks and knives. 'I'm going to look forward to this,' he picked up a cruel looking needle pointed knife which split halfway down the blade and curved away into a wicked looking hook. 'I haven't had the chance to use some of these since the fall of Constantinople.'

Isabel ignored the pain filled screams as Nathaniel began his grisly work and moved away, pausing to gaze out of the cracked window pane down at the lake below. She watched the sylph like apparitions gliding across the lake and disappearing as soon as they touched the shoreline, leaving strange tracks leading up towards the main road into town.

This was taking longer than she'd hoped but she was still confident he would give up the location of the soul she was searching for, sooner or later. Even an immortal couldn't hold out indefinitely and Nathaniel was nothing if not creative when it came to getting answers. She gazed down at the leather bound volume in her hands; she couldn't believe her mother and aunt had concealed this from her. Whenever she had asked she had been told it had been lost along with the location of Hester's grave but they'd lied to her. They'd hidden it from her all along and handed it over to her daughter. Her fingers tightened convulsively on the creaky leather and her jaw clenched in anger. So they'd suspected her, even back then. She should have known.

Her fingertips curved gently under the edge of the

cover and opened it. The parchment pages fanned open, releasing a strange dusty smell. She gazed down at the black inky letters on the page as they undulated and streamed across the pages, arranging and then rearranging themselves into nonsense words. She slammed the book shut again in frustration. No matter what she did she couldn't read it. Hester had obviously found some way to guard her secrets even from her own blood, but it was of no matter anyway. Soon they would have the answers they needed and nothing and no one was going to stand in her way.

Olivia tossed restlessly in bed before a sudden chiming had her eyes flying open. In the darkness a scream caught in her throat as she saw a familiar pale figure standing over her, staring with white lifeless eyes. Theo opened his eyes and jolted awake as he too focused on the apparition beside the bed.

'Don't move,' she clutched his wrist and hissed under her breath. 'Don't scare her away.'

He froze, watching silently as the girl continued to stare at Olivia.

'Charlotte?' Olivia whispered.

The girl raised her hand which was clenched tightly in a fist and as she opened it over the bed Olivia looked down at the handful of old coins dropping into her lap. She picked one up and turned in over in her hands, it was another Greek coin, they all were. She looked up at Charlotte and noticed she was holding something else. Her gaze narrowed in the darkness of the room until she realized what the girl was holding was the stick she'd pulled from the lake the first night she'd seen her. She must have led her down to the lake, Charlotte had wanted her to find the stick; it was important somehow.

She watched calmly as the girl held out the stick to her. Olivia reached out slowly, all her attention now on the strange object, ignoring the girl. It almost felt like the stick was calling to her, singing to her in the very depths of her soul. She felt a resounding vibration like a silvery chord strike inside her. Her trembling fingertips closed around the stick and its song roared to life inside her mind blocking out everything else. She didn't notice when Charlotte disappeared. If she had looked up she might have been convinced she saw a ghost of a smile curve the corner of the girl's mouth. But she was oblivious, unable to tear her gaze away from the stick in her hands as she rose from the bed.

The strange Greek lettering began to light up with a bright silver glow. At first she thought it was just a trick of the light but the stick seemed to be lengthening, elongating until it was no longer a stick but more like a staff. Strange silver flickers appeared at the edge of her vision much as it had the day they had been caught in the pub with the angry spirit. She could feel the atmosphere in the room change; it crackled with static electricity causing the hairs on the back of her neck to rise. Her whole body trembled but not in fear, more like she was being charged with energy. Somewhere in her consciousness she realized it was almost the same way she had felt after she had conjured Hell fire. As she made that connection, the staff roared to life bursting into bright silver flames which licked at her skin but didn't burn.

Theo's eyes widened in fear as Olivia was engulfed in silver flames. She stared, unseeing, as she clutched the staff tightly in her hands. Her eyes, instead of her usual warm aged whiskey colour or the molten gold shade that came with her power, were now a bright shimmering silver.

In his panic and without thinking he reached for her. As his fingers wrapped around her forearm he felt a sharp jolt and a searing pain. He let go and felt back against the bed, his back arching in agony as the fire raged unchecked through his veins. A high pitched buzzing filled his ears and a bright white light blinded him. His body felt like it was burning, being consumed from within as he felt the vast inescapable power and with it a sense of thousands upon thousands of souls.

Thin vines of pure silver snaked up his arm alongside the blue and black coils left seared into his flesh from Olivia's Hell fire. The silver fire coiled around his arm intertwining with the other lines and embedding itself deep into his skin, permanently etching itself into his arm.

Slowly the fire began to ebb; the high pitched buzzing subsided until he became aware of the frantic drumming of his own heartbeat hammering in his ears. His breath was rapid and ragged as he tried to calm his racing heart. He gingerly flexed his fingers and then his arm. The flesh was sore and swollen, branded by fire and magic. He sat up once again, his concerned gaze seeking out Olivia but she remained much as she had before, still clutching onto the staff her silver gaze unblinking as she watched something only she could see.

Olivia shivered as she stepped barefooted onto the sandy shore of the lake. Strange she thought to herself as she glanced back up at the bank and then across to the jetty, all the snow was gone and although the air was chilly it was nowhere near as cold as it should be for this time of year. She looked down to her bare feet and frowned, noticing for the first time that she wore an iridescent robe of an unusual delicate shimmering fabric and as she moved forward it whispered about her legs like the smooth gossamer wings of a butterfly. Realizing it was still dark she automatically reached down inside herself for her magic and with a small absent gesture two of her dragonflies burst into flame. They hovered over her shoulder dancing with silver flames rather than their usual warm fire.

Her fingers tightened on the strangely glowing staff; the flames had banked low so now only the old gnarled knot at the top of it burned like a pale torch in the blackness. She could hear the soothing lap of the water against the shore and looked out across the lake at the fine mist which hung over the water like a shroud. The mist undulated and shifted and suddenly she realized it wasn't mist at all, but souls, hundreds and hundreds of them all heading towards the shore.

'So now you finally understand,' a familiar voice spoke from behind her.

Olivia turned slowly until she was staring into the beautiful timeless face of the Goddess Diana.

'Mother,' Olivia breathed slowly.

'Beloved daughter,' she smiled stepping closer. Her gaze swept over to the staff Olivia carried and the silver dragonflies dancing enthusiastically at her shoulder.

Olivia looked towards the flaming staff and then held out her hand to the Goddess. As she unfolded her fingers silver flames danced merrily on her palm.

'What is it?'

'Spirit fire daughter,' her smooth voice washed over Olivia until she felt it right down to her bones. 'It is made from the very fabric of the other world, an element of the spirit realms and it can be used to harm or to heal.'

'But how do I know which?'

Because you are a Mistress of Fire; there has never been anyone like you and I suspect there never will be again.'

'I don't understand,' Olivia frowned.

'You will,' her mouth curved, 'eventually.'

Her gaze was drawn suddenly from the Goddess to a huge white stag who appeared at her side. Diana stroked his pale coat lovingly her eyes fixed on Olivia who watched entranced as he reared up onto his hind legs. His body elongated and slimmed, the pale white fur retreating into his body to reveal pale human-like skin. His white hair streamed down his back, almost to his buttocks, his face fair and unmarked by the centuries. The only tell tale sign that he wasn't human was the pale silver antlers protruding from his temples. He crossed the sand towards Olivia, completely at ease with his nakedness.

Olivia gasped as he neared her, her eyes widening.

'You're Herne aren't you?'

The God looked down on her in amusement.

'So you know who I am then do you, Olivia West.'

She couldn't find the words as she looked at the sheer perfection of the naked God before her.

He glanced at the staff much as Diana had done and then at the dragonflies, stretching out his hand so one of them landed on his fingers as he studied it curiously.

'Fascinating,' he spoke absently to Diana, 'the child has learned to conjure Spirit Fire.'

'The child is standing right here,' Olivia answered pertly before she could censor her words.

'She is a fiery one is she not,' he laughed in delight, 'yes she will do nicely.'

'Olivia,' Diana stepped closer, 'time is running out, you need to close the gateway.'

'But I don't know how, I don't even know where it is.'

'Are you sure about that?'

Olivia frowned, the protest dying on her lips as her gaze was once again drawn to the silent souls drifting over the water.

'The lake,' she breathed, 'it was right in front of me the whole time, the lake is the gateway.'

'The answers are before you, you have only to look.'

The shroud of souls parted momentarily and once more, just for a split second, she caught sight of a small wooden skiff drifting aimlessly on the current. Its lantern glinted off the oily looking water before the fog rolled in and it disappeared from view. Her mind was working furiously now; it was the same boat she'd seen the night she pulled the staff from the icy water of the lake. She glanced down to the glowing Greek letters on the staff and felt a sudden weight in her other palm. Opening her hand, she saw a small pile of coins nestled against her skin.

She gasped with sudden realization and as she blinked, the lake disappeared and her room swam back into focus until she was once again by her own bed with Theo staring at her in concern.

Her eyes once again burned a dark whiskey colour and when she spoke her voice was a breathy whisper.

'The Ferryman.'

10.

'So the Ferryman is missing?' Theo frowned as he stared absently into his empty coffee mug.

They both sat amidst the destruction of the library as the pale rays of morning crept through the frosted window pane. Theo sat comfortably on the sofa, his bare feet propped up on the coffee table while Beau curled up contentedly in his lap. Olivia sat at the desk trying to access her laptop, sullenly viewing the massive crack across the screen from when it had been swept violently to the floor.

'It's the only explanation for what's happening.'

'And this Ferryman is Greek,' he struggled with the idea, 'but he is not a spirit?'

'No he's an immortal.'

'A God?'

'No,' Olivia shook her head, 'not exactly, but he is extremely powerful.' She tapped a couple of keys absently, cursing softly when the screen stayed blank.

'I guess my laptop's dead,' she sighed in annoyance. 'Okay I'm going to have to try and do this from memory.' She sat back in her chair and picked up her cup of tea, taking a sip and grimacing at the barely lukewarm liquid.

'So, the Ferryman is part of Greek mythology. We're going back nearly three thousand years to the stories written by the Greek Poets Homer and Hesiod, although the actual myths themselves are much older. From what I remember the Ferryman's name is Charon; he is the servant of Hades, the God of the underworld.'

'Okay,' Theo didn't sound convinced.

'Charon would carry the souls of the deceased across the river Styx, which divided the world of the living from the world of the dead. People would leave a coin either in or on the mouth of the deceased so they could pay for the passage. Anyone who didn't have a coin to pay the Ferryman, would be left to wander the banks along the shore for a hundred years. Don't you see it all makes sense now; this is what Charlotte has been trying to tell me. The Greek coins are the ones used to pay the Ferryman. The Greek inscription on her grave and the Greek poppies that bloom in the middle of winter. She also led me to the lake, where twice now I've seen a boat lit by an old lantern drifting aimlessly on the water without its oarsman. The stick I pulled from the water, it's not a stick at all, it's the Ferryman's pole, the one he uses to steer the boat and carry the deceased to the underworld.'

'And the lake?' Theo replied.

'The lake is the gateway, but because he has disappeared the gateway remains open which is why all the souls are escaping and returning to the world of the living.'

'But I don't understand,' he rubbed his tired eyes, 'you said he ferries souls across the river Styx but isn't that in Greece?'

'No, I don't think so,' she shook her head, frowning as she tried to piece it together. 'The River Styx isn't an actual physical river it exists only as part of the myth. What if it's the word used to describe any waterway Charon uses,' a sudden understanding dawned in her mind. 'The river Styx is wherever it wants to be, it's anywhere and everywhere.'

155

'So,' Theo began reluctantly, 'this Charon is real? He serves a God named Hades?'

'Yes,' Olivia nodded.

'So you're saying there is another God.'

'I'm saying there are many,' she told him sympathetically. She knew how hard this must be for him to accept having been raised as a Puritan with a belief in one Christian God. 'Hades is the brother of Zeus, the father of the Greek Gods and also the brother of Poseidon but there are many Greek Gods, not to mention the ancient Egyptian Gods, the Roman Gods, the Peruvians, the Mesopotamians. Every different culture over the course of history has had their own pantheon, their own Gods and Goddesses. I always thought they were just stories, just myths but I think this is what Fiona was trying to tell me the other day. It's all real, all of them. The universe is so much bigger than we thought and our world and humans are such a small piece of it.'

'I suddenly feel very insignificant' Theo frowned.

A rush of sympathy and understanding had her up from the chair and dropping down onto the sofa, curling into him.

'Theo this doesn't change anything for you,' she ran her hand through his hair absently as she gazed into his dark eyes. 'Even if the other Gods exist, your God exists too. Just because there are others it doesn't take away what you feel for him, it doesn't change your faith.'

'It's just a lot to take in.'

'I know,' she murmured laying her head on his shoulder and watching the dancing gold and red flames in the fireplace, and suddenly feeling cold she let the warmth seep into her body.

'What are we going to do?' he wondered out loud, 'an exorcism is one thing but you're talking about immortal Gods and Goddesses.'

'I don't know,' she sighed as his fingers interlocked with hers and she gazed down at their entwined hands. 'I guess we need to find Charon, he must have the power to send all the souls back to the other side and close the gateway.'

'I wouldn't even know where to start.' Theo stated bluntly.

'Me neither.'

Theo wrapped his arm around her and pulled her in close. He sat in contemplative silence staring into the flames as Beau snuggled contentedly between them.

Olivia's glance fell on Theo's hand as it rested comfortably against her. Frowning as she noticed the red swollen skin., she turned and pushed the sleeve of his sweater up. Below the red irritated flesh a deep silver vein coiled around his arm, entwining with the blue and black of the metal sunk into his skin.

'What's this?' she frowned sitting up.

'It's nothing,' he pulled the sleeve back down.

'It's not nothing, what happened?'

'Last night,' he answered carefully, 'when you touched Charon's staff it lit up and so did you.'

'What?'

'Your eyes went silver and you were bathed in silver fire. Without thinking I reached for you, but when I touched you this happened. My arm started to burn and these markings just appeared.'

'I did this to you?' she whispered. 'I hurt you.'

'No,' he shifted abruptly to take her face in his hands, the action tipping a disgruntled Beau onto the floor. The pup yawned in displeasure before curling amongst the books in front of the fire and going back to sleep. 'This is not your fault,' he told her pointedly.

'Does it still hurt?'

'It's fine,' he replied.

She knew it wasn't; she could tell by the raised angry red skin it must have hurt like hell. She swallowed back the bitter taste of guilt and forced herself to think about it logically.

'Have you tried to use the knife?'

Theo shook his head.

'Call it now.'

Taking a breath Theo pushed his sleeve up and held out his hand. Olivia watched as the blue, black and silver coils slid down his arm like liquid, pooling in his palm and coalescing to form a blade. Theo turned the knife over in his hand and frowned. Before it had been the length and shape of a large hunting knife, the hilt had been a highly polished onyx and the blade itself had been a strange metallic blue black inscribed in a strange language neither himself, Olivia nor Jake had been able to read. When he turned the blade and it caught the light the lettering would normally glow a dim phosphorescent blue. Now the shiny black hilt of the knife was decorated with a thin vein of silver, woven with tiny little silver leaves. The blade was still the same metallic blue black but now it bore additional lettering which glowed silver alongside the pale blue of the original script.'

'It's changed,' Theo murmured studying the blade closely.

'It must be the Spirit fire,' Olivia leaned in closer.

'What's Spirit fire?'

'It's the silver coloured flames you saw,' she paused wondering if she could conjure it for him, 'watch.'

This time when she reached for her magic it felt different. Before there was just a place deep inside her, filled with heat and light. Now she could sense different colours and each colour felt different. The red and gold of her Earth fire was warm and rich, the blue and black of her Hell fire felt seductive and powerful but the silver of her Spirit fire felt cool and ageless as if it carried with it the sense of hundreds of thousands of souls. Grasping onto the feeling she unfolded her palm and once again one of her dragonflies burst into flame, dancing and hovering on the air, shimmering with pale silvery flames.

With a sudden bark and a frantic scramble of

claws on wood Beau leapt up and headed straight for the dragonfly which danced merrily out of reach. Olivia let loose an unexpected peal of laughter as she watched Beau madly chasing this new friend around the room creating more chaos, tipping over piles of books she'd begun to neatly stack ready to be placed back on the shelves and stirring up loose papers. The dragonfly seemed to be playing with Beau almost allowing him to catch it and then skipping out of his reach.

'Alright that's enough you two,' she laughed and held out her hand.

The dragonfly swooped down and landed smoothly in her palm, her skin glowed momentarily as it was reabsorbed into her body. Beau leapt up and nuzzled his soft furry face into her hands, sniffing rapidly as if to try and figure out where the sparkly creature had disappeared to.

'Crazy dog,' she smiled and wrapped her arms around his small body, pulling him into her lap and kissing his head affectionately.

'So Spirit fire is silver,' Theo clarified, watching them in amusement.

'Yes,' Olivia nodded, 'it's made up of the very fabric of the Spirit realms and apparently is incredibly powerful, although I must admit I don't really know what it does yet.'

'Maybe it's something we can use if we come across any more violent spirits.'

'Maybe,' she agreed.

Olivia looked up as the doorbell rang.

'I'll get it,' Theo pulled himself off the couch and disappeared into the hallway. Almost immediately he stuck his head back around the door. 'There's a delivery for you, are you expecting something from the museum?'

'Oh,' she suddenly remembered, 'yes I am. Renata called last week and said she had some items that were loaned to the museum by the West family. She was going to send them over.'

'Well they're here so where do you want them?'

'Um, just get them to stack it in the hallway, once we see what's there we can decide where to put it.'

He nodded and disappeared again.

Olivia slid off the sofa and started gathering up the piles of paper and books Beau had once again scattered around the room. Ignoring the banging and cursing coming from the hallway she began to sort the books into some sort of order. She hadn't realized just how many books had been collected by her family over the years. There were so many on the occult and magic, not to mention all the historical books and mythology and folklore. That was before she'd even started sorting through the hundreds of years' worth of journals the women in her family seemed obsessed with writing.

Pausing thoughtfully, with a small stack of books in each hand, she chewed her lip absently. Instead of just putting them all back on the shelves where they'd been she might as well make a project of it. Veronica had already offered to help her make some sense of her family history, she may as well sort through all the other books while she was at it and see what was actually there. Maybe also redecorate the room and give it a really good clean as she doubted it had been done in years.

'Olivia?' Theo's voice startled her out of her reverie.

'Yes,' she turned towards the doorway.

'You might want to come and take a look at this.'

Curious, she set the books down and stepped out into the hallway.

There was a large rectangular object standing against the wall, wrapped carefully in old moth eaten blankets and tied securely with thick string. She found a label suspended on the string, and turned it over in her hands trying to read the tiny elegant scrawl.

'Loaned to the Mercy museum May 1952 by the West

family. Piece commissioned circa 1920 craftsman unknown.'

Her curiosity piqued, her fingers fumbled with the knotted string until she managed to loosen it and pull it free. Theo stretched up and helped her to unwrap the blankets until they dropped to the floor in a cloud of dust.

Her breath caught in her throat, her mouth slightly open and yet unable to form words as she beheld the tall elegant grandfather clock in front of her. She recognized the wood, Olive wood native to Greece. She traced her fingertips reverently along the gorgeous patterning caused by the grain of the wood. Despite the clocks obvious age it was in a flawless condition and polished to a highly glossy finish.

Her fingers moved to the tiny golden key in the door and turned it gently. The lock released with a gentle click and the door swung open without any groan of protest, as if the hinges were freshly oiled. The inside mechanism also seemed to be in excellent condition and had not aged at all, the huge polished pendulums hung silent and still. She turned her gaze to the face of the clock itself, her eyes widening in surprise. The picture which had been painted directly into the clock face was of the lake, shimmering in the moonlight, and on it was a tiny little boat, a small wooden skiff with a post at one end from which hung an old fashioned lantern. In the boat stood a tall lean figure in a short linen tunic belted at the waist. In his hands he held a long pole with which he steered the boat. Around the circumference of the clock face was a tiny inscription in Greek lettering and underneath the clock was a small gold plaque which simply read *'for Charlotte.'*

'This was Charlotte's clock,' Olivia gazed up at Theo. 'She must have wanted us to know about it. This is the chiming we've been hearing ever since she appeared. Look at the picture.'

'It must be Charon,' Theo replied. 'I guess you were right, Charlotte is trying to tell you about the

Ferryman.'

Her gaze fell to the foot well of the clock beneath the pendulums and she noticed a design etched into the wood. Leaning down she squinted in an attempt to make out the design, but struggled in the shadow and poor light of the hallway. Kneeling down next to the clock she snapped her fingers softly and one of her dragonflies appeared, burning brightly with the warm gold and red of her Earth fire. It hovered over her shoulder before darting into the cavity of the clock, lighting the inside.

Now Olivia could see the design clearly on the bottom wooden plate. Etched deeply into the wood was a poppy. She traced her fingers lightly over the delicately designed flower and felt a tiny shift in the wood. She moved her fingers over the design again and once more she felt the almost infinitesimal movement. It was a false bottom and there was something underneath it. She felt the wood carefully, tracing along the edges until she reached the top left hand corner. She pressed down gently and the bottom right corner lifted just enough for her to curve her fingers underneath it and prise it loose.

There was a secret compartment and it looked as if something was hidden inside. She reached in and her fingers curled around something hard and rectangular, covered in cloth. Pulling it free she blew away the dust and turned in over in her hands.

'What is it?' Theo asked as she began to unwrap the cloth covering.

She dropped the material to the floor and found she held a leather bound book with *Charlotte Lilly West* etched into the cover in tidy gold lettering.

'I think it's Charlotte's journal,' Olivia answered as she opened the first page.

'Well the women in your family are nothing if not consistent,' Theo murmured. 'Do you keep a journal?' he asked curiously.

Olivia shook her head. 'No, I've never felt the

need to,' she replied, 'but over the last few hundred years it was fairly common for people to keep journals. Not so much now,' she smiled up at him in amusement, 'now that people have Facebook.'

A sudden banging at the door startled them both. Olivia looked up to see her dragonfly still hovering in the air and she held up her hand. Theo waited until it had safely disappeared before he answered the door.

'Hi,' the voice was familiar, 'you must be Theo. I'm Veronica from the museum. I was wondering if Olivia was in.'

'I'm here Veronica,' Olivia called from the floor, beckoning her in.

Veronica's gaze dropped to where Olivia, still in her pajamas, sat on the floor surrounded by boxes.

'Ah, I see you got your items back from the museum. They said they were going to deliver them today.'

'Well I certainly wasn't expecting it to be as much as this, but we're in the middle of sorting out some stuff in the house so I guess a few more boxes won't hurt,' Olivia climbed to her feet.

'What happened to your face?' Veronica frowned at the dark bruising along Olivia's jaw.

'That,' she pointed towards the mess in the library.

Veronica poked her head around the door and gasped. 'What on earth happened?'

'I was trying to sort through and rearrange the room and a load of books fell on me,' she lied easily. 'I really should have waited for Theo to help me get the ones down from the higher shelves but I was impatient and ended up dropping a load of stuff on me.'

'Goodness,' Veronica laughed, 'you're getting as clumsy as I am.'

'So how are the renovations going?'

'Good,' she nodded enthusiastically, 'we're almost done and should be able to reopen by next week.'

'That's great.'

'Actually the reason I popped by today was because of your...um...ghost problem' she whispered, looking around nervously.

'Oh?' Olivia replied in amusement.

'Yes, you know I told you that she had been engaged to the mayor's son.'

'I remember, Clayton Swilley wasn't it?'

'That's right. I told you he had a daughter and that she was still alive and living in Salem?'

Olivia nodded.

'Catherine Swilley isn't it?'

'It was,' Veronica replied, 'she changed her name after her mother remarried, took the stepfathers name. She prefers to be known as Ms Catherine Lindsey now. I contacted her and she is willing to meet with us this afternoon if you're free. Renata said I could take the rest of the day off so are you up for a drive to Salem?'

'Sure I'd love too,' she turned to Theo.

'I'm supposed to be meeting Tommy this afternoon,' he told her, 'but if you want me to go with you I can cancel.'

She looked at his forlorn expression and bit back a smile. She knew Tommy was giving Theo another driving lesson and knowing how much he was enjoying himself, didn't want to deprive him.

'It's fine,' she stretched up on tip toes and kissed him softly, 'you go play with your friend I'll be fine. Veronica and I will make a girls' day of it seeing as I had to cancel our shopping trip last week.'

'If you're sure?'

'I am,' she turned to Veronica, 'give me ten minutes to shower and dress and I'll be good to go.'

By early afternoon they'd pulled up at the address they'd had been provided with and as Olivia climbed out of Veronica's rather sensible Nissan Sentra, she looked up at the house and her mouth curved in amusement. It was a

Greek revival, decorated with smart pale blue grey clapboards and crisp white trims. Flat white pilasters decorated the corners of the house to give the appearance of Greek style columns, an architectural trend of the early to mid-1800s.

'Oh, what a pretty house,' Veronica locked the car and joined her on the sidewalk, staring up at the large well kept property.

'Yes it is,' Olivia murmured as they started towards the house.

They were greeted at the door by a tall willowy woman in her forties with pale red hair tied neatly back in a low ponytail.

'Yes,' she smiled politely, 'may I help you?'

My name is Veronica Mason and this is my companion Olivia West. Ms. Lindsey invited us to join her for tea this afternoon. I'm afraid we may be a little early.'

'Oh,' recognition dawned in her eyes, 'yes she did mention you would be visiting. You work at the museum in Mercy, isn't that right.'

'Yes I do,' Veronica smiled offering her hand.

'I'm Lucy Wainwright,' she shook each of their hands in turn and stepped back to allow them entrance. 'I'm Ms Lindsey's niece, please come in.'

They both stepped into a wide elegant foyer, a small circular table stood at the centre of the glossy floor and on it was a tall Waterford vase filled with elegant long stemmed lilies. The walls were painted a delicate biscuit colour with white trims. A slim staircase curved upwards to their left and to the right was a well-lit day room, its entrance an open archway flanked by two slender white columns.

A maid appeared at their side and efficiently whisked away their heavy winter coats.

'If you'd like to come with me I believe Aunt Kitty is in the parlor.'

Veronica and Olivia followed along obediently,

observing the house as they went. The whole place spoke of money and class. Towards the back of the house they entered a parlor decorated in a pale cool green and smelling of lilies of the valley.

A small tidy woman looked up from the book in her hands and removed her reading glasses, placing them down with her book on the low table in front of her. She smoothed back perfectly coiffed hair which looked as soft and silvery as a cloud.

'Miss Mason and Miss West I presume,' she stood slowly and offered her hand.

'Ms. Lindsey,' Veronica took her hand gently, 'it's very good of you to see us.'

She nodded as Veronica released her hand and Olivia stepped forward.

'Ms. Lindsey,' Olivia wrapped her hand around the old woman's tiny little hand. Much like her friend Renata, her delicate bones felt fragile and her skin felt like dry dusty paper. 'I'm very please to meet you,' she smiled softly.

Catherine Lindsey held onto Olivia's hand and for a brief moment studied her face curiously.

'Please take a seat,' she finally released her and indicated towards a high backed cream colour sofa opposite her. 'It's a little early but it's such a chilly day I think some tea would be nice.' She turned towards the tall red haired woman, 'if you would be a dear Lucy.'

'Of course Aunt Kitty,' she smiled fondly and disappeared.

'My niece,' she smiled at them. 'Lucy is the middle child of my younger half sister. She takes care of me and is a great comfort.'

'I'm sure she is,' Olivia replied, 'it's nice to have family.'

'You are here about your family if I am to understand Miss Mason's letter correctly.'

'I am,' Olivia nodded, 'I'm researching my family

history. I am interested most particularly in my Great Great Aunt, Charlotte Lilly West, who I understand was engaged briefly to your father.'

'Hmmm,' she folded her hands neatly in her lap, 'I know about Charlotte.'

'You do?'

'I never met her obviously, she died ten years before I was even born but on occasion my father would speak of her.'

'Did he?' Olivia's brow rose in surprise.

'Miss West,' she sighed, 'my father was a difficult and complicated man. He had many personal demons and I believe Charlotte West was one of them.'

She looked up as Lucy re-entered the room. She was pushing a small trolley which held a delicate porcelain tea service of white china edged in gold and decorated with pink roses. She served each of them in turn but as Veronica took hers the china tinkled merrily as her hand shook.

'Oh my goodness' Veronica breathed, nervously examining the cup more closely. 'Is this Meissen?'

'Yes it is,' Ms. Lindsey replied, 'is something wrong?'

'No, I,' she gulped nervously, 'I'm just a little clumsy I'm afraid I might damage it.'

'Perhaps you would prefer to use my Great Grandnephew's sippy cup,' her mouth curved in amusement 'or maybe a nice plastic beaker?'

Veronica's face flushed at the old woman's' teasing tone.

'Stop worrying so much child,' she told her gently, 'good china is meant to be enjoyed. If it gets broken, it gets broken. It's not the end of the world.'

Veronica took a sip of her tea, managing a small smile before she placed the cup very carefully down on the coffee table.

'Now where were we?' Ms Lindsey straightened in

her chair and sipped her tea thoughtfully. Finally, she looked back at Olivia with a sigh. 'The truth is Miss West my father was not a well man. Growing up with him was like being trapped on a disturbing merry go round and unable to get off. One moment he was attentive and overly affectionate and the next…he could be so cruel. My mother suffered through the worst of his episodes; unable to help him, unable to leave him. It may be an unchristian thing to say but the day he died was a blessing for us all. My stepfather was a lovely man and very good to my mother and I. She met him about a year after my father's death and they were married within six months. They gave me a half brother and sister. We were so happy, my stepfather never treated me any differently to his own children. We were a real family, and mother and I tried our best to put our life with my father behind us, But some things remain with you and his obsession with Charlotte West was one of those things I've never been able to forget.'

'His obsession?' Olivia frowned.

'What I know of her and their relationship I have built from fragments of many conversations with my father and when I say conversations I am being polite. Most of the time when he spoke of Charlotte he would be ranting, either drunk or caught in the middle of one of his episodes.'

Olivia sat quietly, patiently waiting for the old woman to organize her thoughts.

'I think he did love her,' she began again, 'but it was a possessive unhealthy love.'

'How so?'

'I think he believed she was in love with someone else. During the worst of his rants he would shout and scream that she was his and his alone; that he was rather see her dead than with another man.'

'Ms. Lindsey,' Olivia asked carefully, 'I don't wish to cause offense but do you think he was capable of hurting Charlotte?'

'You want to know if he was responsible for her death?'

'The thought had crossed my mind.'

'I did wonder about that for a very long time and it weighed on me but the truth is I simply don't know. I think he was capable of it but whether or not he actually killed her I can't say. The only two people who know the truth are dead, but if she did come to harm at the hands of my father she wasn't the only one.'

'What do you mean?'

'My mother told me that he had been married previously to a woman named Madeline.'

'We found their marriage certificate,' Veronica spoke up, 'but were unable to find out what happened to her.'

'She died,' she told them. 'According to my mother, Madeline was rather reliant on Laudanum and I don't blame her after being married to my father. From what I understand eighteen months into the marriage she was found dead in her bath. The official cause of death I believe was accidental drowning due to acute Laudanum intoxication.'

Veronica and Olivia threw each other a speculative look.

'Like I said,' Ms. Lindsey continued, 'I can't tell you with any degree of certainty what my father might or might not have done. All I can tell you is the sort of man he was and allow you to draw your own conclusions.'

'I appreciate that Ms. Lindsey,' Olivia answered as she watched Lucy hand the old woman a slightly battered looking box.

'Lucy dear could you retrieve the small square gift box from my room and some tissue paper,' she spoke softly to her niece before turning back to Olivia.

'I want you to have this.'

Olivia took the box curiously. It was an old

wooden cigar box with the words Rocky Ford branded into the top and Monarch etched into the side. Opening it up there was a faded illustration of a native American on the inside of the lid, but she barely glanced at it as her gaze was already caught on the box's intriguing contents. She lifted out delicate newspaper clippings browned with age and falling apart at the folds as if they had been handled too often. She unfolded them carefully, revealing a clipping of Clayton and Charlotte's engagement announcement and another of Charlotte's death announcement. Underneath it was a faded hymn card from her funeral and beneath that a photograph. Olivia lifted it out with trembling fingers as she beheld Charlotte's face for the first time. Not the pale bruised dirty skin and white lifeless eyes she had experienced but Charlotte as she should have looked. Her eyes dark, her face young and unmarred at eighteen and her hair falling dark and glossy to her shoulders.

'You look like her,' Ms. Lindsey startled her from her thoughts.

'The family resemblance runs strong with the Wests,' Olivia murmured.

Reaching back into the box her fingers closed around a small circular locket. She pulled it out and turned it over in her hand. The chain was broken but the locket itself was still intact, although a little tarnished. The face of the locket was engraved with the depiction of a coin surrounded by a wreath of olives. She clicked it open and inside was one word written in Greek.

'Agapitós'

'Beloved,' Olivia whispered as she traced the word with the pad of her thumb.

She looked up as Lucy re-entered the room with a small square gift box and handed it to the old lady, watching with interest as she lifted the empty teacup and saucer Veronica had been using. Taking care she wrapped each item individually in a soft white tissue paper and slid them into the box before handing it to Veronica.

'I would like you to have this Miss Mason.'

'Pardon?' Veronica stared back at her holding the box awkwardly. 'I can't accept this, it's Meissen and its part of a set.'

The old lady chuckled in delight.

'When you get to my age you will realize just how unimportant things like that truly are.'

'Then why?' she frowned in confusion.

'It is a statement,' she told her. 'I want you to take that teacup home with you and I want you to use it every day to remind yourself.'

'Remind myself?'

'Things break Miss Mason, it's the way of the world. But you cannot let fear of what may happen hold you back. That's not the way life works. Take a risk every now and then, it's good for you.'

She accepted the box from the little old lady and stared at it. 'I don't know what to say.'

'Probably best not to say anything then,' she smiled as she held her arm out to her niece. 'Now as much as I have enjoyed your company ladies I'm afraid I must retire as I am a little tired.'

'Of course,' Olivia replied as they both stood, 'thank you so much for taking the time to speak with us.'

'You're welcome,' she nodded.

'Thank you,' Veronica spoke quietly, 'for the teacup. I'll take good care of it.'

'I know you will dear.'

Olivia and Veronica watched quietly as the old woman walked slowly and painfully from the room, leaning heavily on her niece. The maid suddenly materialized by their side and ushered them out of the room, and before they knew it they had their coats on and were once again standing outside in the brisk air.

'Are you alright Veronica?' Olivia asked in concern.

Veronica stood frozen in thought, staring down at

the box in her hands.

'Veronica?'

Veronica looked up suddenly as if Olivia's voice had only just registered.

'What is it?'

Veronica took a deep breath and pursed her lips thoughtfully. 'It's still quite early are you in a rush to get back to Mercy?'

Olivia shook her head.

'No, why what have you got in mind?'

'I think I want to take a risk,' she looked up at Olivia, 'I want to cut my hair.'

'Cut your hair?' she repeated slowly.

'I don't want to be a clone of my mother anymore, I want something different' she answered. 'Maybe some new clothes too.'

'Well,' Olivia's face broke into a smile, 'you've come to the right girl. Get in the car Veronica, by the time I've finished with you your credit card might be wheezing a bit but you'll feel like a completely new woman.'

Veronica laughed nervously and climbed back into her car.

11.

Beau twitched and made squeaky little yipping noises as he slept on the rug in front of the inviting fire in Olivia's bedroom. Olivia smiled at him in amusement before she turned her attention back to her toenails which were now a murderous red and decorated with little sparkles. She lay back against the cushions on her bed and relaxed, wriggling her toes in pleasure. While Veronica had been having a complete overhaul in the intimate little salon they'd found in Salem she'd treated herself to a pedicure. She couldn't ever remember spending any real time in a salon before but there was something gloriously decadent and deliciously feminine about relaxing and having someone pamper her. She'd needed it; she hadn't realized how tense she'd been over the past several months. Just taking a few hours out with a friend to do something as simple as shopping and visiting a beauty salon had made a huge difference. Sighing in contentment she slid further down the bed and picked up Charlotte's small leather bound journal and began to read.

Theo wandered out of the bathroom absently rubbing his wet hair with a towel, the tiny rivulets of water clinging to his bare chest glistening in the firelight and his sweatpants riding low exposing the v shape of his hips. He absently tossed the towel into the hamper and raked his fingers through his hair, pulling out the worst of the tangles. His gaze locked on Olivia who was now lying sprawled on her stomach wearing nothing but one of his t-shirts, swinging her legs absently back and forth as she lost herself in the book in her hands.

Olivia felt the bed dip next to her and looked up. Smiling at Theo she rolled over onto her back giving him space to stretch out next to her, his head propped absently on one hand as she turned her attention back to the book.

'Is that Charlotte's journal?' he asked although his gaze had snagged on her brightly coloured toenails; he loved it when she painted them different colours.

'Yes it is,' she chewed her lip thoughtfully.

Theo pulled his gaze from her fascinating toes and trailed his eyes appreciatively along her long golden legs. Unable to resist he traced her skin lightly with his fingers marveling at the softness of her skin. He loved the smoothness too, completely hairless, unlike the women from his time. He wanted to press his face into her skin and breathe her in, she always smelled so good. Sliding down the bed he trailed his lips across her skin following his fingers along the length of her legs. When he reached her thighs, unable to help himself, he nipped her skin playfully before soothing it with his tongue.

'Stop distracting me,' she chuckled.

'I can't help it,' he propped his chin on her legs and looked up at her.

'Listen to this,' she turned back to the journal and began to read.

December 16th, 1919.

'I conjured fire today. It was really rather frustrating. I finally managed a weak flame but it spluttered out as quickly as it had appeared. I don't think I'll ever be able to master the elements, not like Beth, it comes so easily to her. Fire is her greatest skill. I cannot even master the simplest of spells. I am beginning to think I

may not have my family's magical gift at all.

I wish Mother was here. It has been a year since we lost her, perhaps if Beth or I had our grandmother's gift for healing we may have saved her. Father says it was just what was meant to be and we shouldn't question it. Despite our magic, we cannot interfere with the natural order of things. We have no control over life and death but I miss her so terribly.

It feels like I have a hole inside me that nothing will ever be able to fill. I love my father and I love Beth but I feel as if a part of me is missing. I'm not like the others, I have no talent for the magic which runs so strongly in our family. I feel as if I don't belong, like I'm waiting for something or someone. Maybe when I am older I will fall in love with a kind man and have a family of my own and perhaps then it will soothe the ache in my heart.

Tomorrow Beth is going to help me try to conjure wind, although honestly I don't know why she bothers. She has been able to master the elements since we were five years old. I am fourteen now, surely if I haven't mastered it by now I never will.'

'She sounds so sad,' Olivia looked down at Theo who was toying absently with the hem of the shirt she was wearing.

'Who is Beth?'

'Her sister Elizabeth I would imagine.'

'So her sister was a master of fire like you.'

'So it would seem, but then again I'm directly descended from Elizabeth, she was my Great Grandmother and quite often strong magical gifts are inherited. I would imagine if I ever have a daughter of my own she may inherit my gift for fire too.'

Theo watched her thoughtfully as her gaze dropped back to the journal and she once again began to leaf through the pages. Her words echoed in his mind and he found himself picturing her holding a tiny dark haired child, with her whiskey coloured eyes and his dark curls. He could imagine her now, with her belly swollen with his child and the thought was arousing. He wanted that more than anything; he wanted her and the beautiful children they would make together.

Deep down he knew if they had any chance of a future together he had to tell her the truth about his wife. Fiona was right he had to tell her everything. He would just have to trust her and hope that somehow she would understand and forgive him.

'Listen to this,' her voice jolted him out of his thoughts, 'her journal entries jump from 1919 to 1923. That would have made her just turned eighteen years old. It seems she didn't keep any records during her teen years.'

He listened as she began to read aloud once again.

May 29th, 1923.

'I saw him again, through the window, the boatman. It was late, the moon had risen and was glittering upon the water as if it reflected a thousand stars. I was looking from my window and there he was in a small wooden boat lit by a lantern. He looked up and our eyes locked for the barest moment before I hid behind the drapes, my heart thundering in my chest...'

'She could see him?' Theo interrupted in surprise, 'do you think she knew he wasn't human?'

'I don't know,' she murmured as she moved to the next entry.

June 2nd, 1923.

'I spoke with him; I can scarcely believe I had it in me to be so daring. I waited until papa and Beth slept and I crept from the house down to the lake. He was sitting on the dock with his boat moored. He looked up at me and smiled as if he had been waiting for me and when he spoke his voice was so familiar, like a voice in a dream I cannot recall and yet it felt like I had been waiting too. His name is Charon and I know he is not of my world; I can feel it but I don't care. All I know is that when I am near him the empty place inside of me doesn't exist.'

July 23rd, 1923.

'I watch for him every night, waiting for him. I know who he is now and why he cannot be with me all the time. He comes to me when he can. I yearn for him when we are not together and I find myself wondering if he feels the same. I can see the gateway now; it is as if my eyes have been opened. I now understand why I could not master the magic that came so easily to my sister, because it was not my path. I have the sight, I can see into the otherworld, into the spirit realms. Charon has been teaching me to use my gift so that even when we are not together I can still see him.'

August 19th, 1923.

'He came back to me tonight, he brought me a poppy. He says it comes from his homeland, brought into creation by the Goddess Aphrodite. He says she created it from the blood of her lover Adonis when he was slain by a wild boar and into it she poured all of her love and longing for him. He took my hand and at the touch of his skin I knew. I knew I'd been waiting for him all along; my soul has been waiting for him for such a long time.'

October 21st, 1923.

'We made love tonight, under the stars upon the banks of the lake. I didn't feel the cold, only him. He was every breath I took, every beat of my heart and I know now I belong to him. I will always belong to him.'

'They were in love,' Theo breathed slowly.

'I guess so,' Olivia frowned, 'this can't have ended well.'

'What do you mean?'

'Well I know somehow she ended up engaged to be married to Clayton Swilley, the mayor's son. But putting that aside, Charon is an immortal, a servant of Hades the God of the underworld. I can't imagine his boss being pleased he was involved with a human.'

'What else does her journal say?'

Olivia skimmed over the entries until she neared

the end and began to read.

July 18th, 1924.
'I have not seen him in months, he is beyond my sight now.
I cannot even see him in any of the spirit realms. It can only mean
Hades is angry with him, if he is in the underworld it is beyond my
power to reach him. I tried to forget him but I can't. No one else
knew about us, not even my sister. My father, only wanting the best
for me convinced me to marry Mr Swilley. He seems a nice enough
man, he certainly is handsome. We are supposed to be married
tomorrow afternoon. I thought I could do it, I wanted to make my
father happy but it feels like a betrayal. I belong to Charon and I
cannot promise myself to another man. Even if Hades keeps us apart
forever it will not change my heart. I will wait for him until the end of
days if I have to and even beyond that. I am meeting Clayton this
evening and I will have to tell him I cannot marry him. I can only
hope that he will understand.'

'That was her last entry,' Olivia breathed heavily, 'it was made the night she died.'

'Do you think Clayton Swilley killed her?' Theo frowned.

'It's beginning to look that way.'

'What is it?' he asked noting her puzzled expression.

'I just wonder what is was about her that was so special,' her eyes locked with Theo. 'I don't mean that in a detrimental way at all. She was just a normal human girl, not even with any phenomenal magic powers and yet an immortal fell in love with her and was willing to risk the wrath of a God to be with her.'

'I think you underestimate the power you West women hold,' he took the journal from her fingers and closed it, placing it carefully on her nightstand. He moved up her body and settled himself between her thighs. Reaching out he wrapped a wayward curl of her hair around his finger gently, 'if she was anything like you he would probably have risked everything for her.'

'Theo,' she breathed slowly as he leaned in closer.

Her heart was pounding in her chest as she traced his lower lip with the pad of her thumb down, to the tiny indentation at his chin. His eyes were so dark they almost seemed to go on forever, drawing her in. She could feel his breath against her mouth as he held her on the delicious edge of anticipation. She ran her fingers through his damp hair and clutching gently gave a slight tug as she rocked her hips, pressing him closer.

His lips grazed against hers before the soft slow glide of his tongue traced the seam of her lips. She could feel him harden between her thighs and as he rolled his hips slowly she felt him press against her. She gave an involuntary gasp and then his mouth closed over hers. It was like drowning in pure pleasure, a mix of heat and warmth and contentment. His tongue met hers with slow lazy strokes that she felt all the way down to her core and without realizing it her eyes drifted closed, shutting out everything but the man who had become as necessary to her as the air she breathed.

His hands stroked feather light down her sides, gripping the hem of her shirt and inching it up and over her head. Beneath it she was naked and now she was pinned beneath his hard body. She moaned against his mouth as the light dusting of hair on his chest teased her sensitive breasts.

'Livy,' he breathed, unconsciously rocking into her, desperate to be inside her.

She arched up into him as his hand found her breast and the other wrapped around the back of her neck squeezing gently as he nipped her mouth with single minded intensity.

Her fingers ran the length of his spine causing him to shiver against her body. When she reached the waistband of his sweatpants she hooked her fingers in and peeled them slowly over his hips. Unable to take it any

ger he sank slowly into her, inch by torturous inch, until
e wrapped her long lean legs around his hips forcing him
o plunge in. When he thought he could go no further he
tensed up and sank deeper.

'God,' he gasped, closing his eyes and burying his
face in her neck. He took deep ragged breaths as he felt
her tighten around him, squeezing him deliciously.

She wrapped her arms around his neck as she had
wrapped her legs around his hips until he was surrounded
by her. He could do nothing but breathe in the scent of his
woman. Slowly he began to move, rolling his hips, sinking
into her deeply, saying a thousand things with his body
that he simply couldn't find the words for and she
answered him in kind. In that moment consumed by each
other there were no doubts, no insecurities, no lies, they
existed only for each other. The tiny carriage clock on the
mantle ticked away the moments and the fire began to die
down, leaving the room bathed in long flickering shadows.

She could feel the tension in her body climbing as
she hooked her leg around his and rolled until she was
laying over him. He wrapped his arms around her tightly,
brushing her hair back from her face to kiss, unable to tear
his lips from hers as she rolled her hips against his. He
watched through heavy lidded eyes as she sat up straddling
his legs, with him still buried inside her. Her back arched
and as he watched the light and shadow play across her
naked skin he knew he was lost to her; she owned him
mind, body and soul.

Her pace increased and he gasped out a ragged
breath as he gripped her hips, thrusting up into her body,
helplessly as they both cried out in their release. Olivia
slumped forwards against him and he wrapped his arms
around her, pulling her in and tucking her against his heart,
knowing that there were no words for the intensity of what
they had just experienced. He closed his eyes and content
he fell into a deep restful sleep still inside her.

The moon rose high above the lake in the dark crystal clear sky. The strange silvery ghostlike mist which had shrouded the lake for weeks began to dissolve and thin out. A strange eerie light appeared beneath the dark churning waters and black wraith-like shadows began to bob and weave across the waves. Several strange shapes began to undulate just beneath the surface of the water, every now and then offering a tantalizing glimpse of pale human-like flesh as they headed towards the shoreline.

Renata yawned at her desk and stretched out her aching neck and back. Her thin fragile fingers closed over her watch as she tried to make out the time through exhausted eyes. She hadn't realized it was so late. Her driver was used to her keeping unsociable hours but she'd never stayed this late before. She was a little surprised he hadn't called but then again over the last few weeks she'd been working late with Veronica while she trained her and in return she had given her a ride back to her little apartment. No doubt her driver had assumed Veronica had taken her home again. Sighing, she began to straighten up the paperwork on her desk. She hoped Veronica and Olivia had enjoyed themselves in Salem. She had high hopes for their friendship, it would do them both the world of good to spend some time together. They didn't know it but they both had wounded souls and there was nothing like surrounding yourself with dear friends when you had very little family left.

At the thought of family Renata opened her desk drawer and rummaged around until her fingers caught on the small brass frame she was looking for. She pulled the picture out and stared at it. It was very small and somewhat battered. She'd managed to hide it from the Nazis and it was all she had left of her family. She traced the picture with loving fingers as she took in the face of her mother and father. Beside them she stood with her hair tied in a pale pink ribbon; although you couldn't see the colour on the grey photograph she could remember it

. it were yesterday. If she closed her eyes she could
.1ost feel her mother's fingers against her hair as she
.1lled the soft bristles of her brush through her thick wavy
.1air. It had been thick and wavy back then and a deep
chestnut brown colour.

Her gaze moved back to the picture to the
handsome little boy sitting on her mother's lap. Schaja had
been such a good boy, so sweet and loving. He would curl
up in her bed after their parents had gone to sleep and
make her read him stories. She could still recall the smell
of his hair, the faint scent of the lemon soap her mother
would use on him as she scrubbed his neck and behind his
ears with a rough washcloth, despite his complaining.

A small smile graced her lips; she remembered the
day this photograph had been taken. It had been a bright
and pleasant day when they had worn their best clothes
and walked down to Mr Zimmermann's photographic
studio. She had felt so grown up standing alongside her
parents while Schaja sat in her mother's lap. They looked
so happy together, a moment frozen in time unaware of
the horror that would await them in a mere four months'
time.

She had spent years trying to repress the images of
the death camp in her mind, the helpless terrified screams,
the uncomfortable horror of having to witness the press of
naked bodies herded through the mud and rain, regardless
of age or gender with no thought given to dignity and then
the silence, the awful silence after they had been sent to
the showers.

Tears filled Renata's eyes as the image of her
mother, her head shaved with a few tiny clumps of missed
hair as she clutched her tiny petrified brother to her skin,
flashed in front of her eyes and she felt the same helpless
rage she had all those years ago. She sighed bitterly,
sometimes she wondered if she shouldn't have lied about
her age. If she'd told them the truth she would have been
sent to the gas chamber with them, at least then they

would have all been together.

She pressed the aching bones of her hands together trying to find some relief from the pain. It hadn't all been bad, her life. She'd spent many happy years in Mercy; it had saved her in a way no other place could. But still deep down in her soul some of her scars had never fully healed.

She glanced down again at the picture and shivered. All of a sudden the room had gotten so cold, but then again no one was supposed to be in the museum at this time so the heating had probably shut off. Her breath was expelled as a fine mist and as she looked up her mouth fell open in a gasp of shock. She felt her heart jolt violently and for a moment she froze even as her breath seemed to stop.

Her mother stood in front of her smiling warmly. She was wearing her favorite blue dress and the jeweled peacock brooch her father had given her for her birthday. Her thick chestnut hair was elegantly styled in soft waves, just the way Renata remembered. Standing beside her mother was her father, tall and robust, with his rounded belly and slicked back salt and pepper hair. His mouth curved into a smile beneath his thick bushy moustache, no longer the broken emaciated man she had last seen but seemingly whole and happy. Lastly her gaze was drawn to the little dark haired boy between them, in his short trousers and shirt and vest. His hair was parted neatly to the side as he grinned up at her with a perfect little set of white teeth.

'Mutter?' Renata gasped, her hand resting against her heart as she unconsciously lapsed into the language of her homeland, a language she had not spoken in years. 'Vater?'

Her little brother held his arms up to her.

'Rena! Rena!'

She was on her feet and around her desk without even thinking about it, scooping the precious boy into her arms and holding him tightly.

'Schaja!' tears filled her eyes and caught in her throat as she inhaled deeply, smelling little boy and lemon soap.

She looked up at her parents.

'Ich habe dich so sehr vermisst,' she whispered.

'Wir haben auf dich gewartet,' her mother smiled.

Renata looked down at her arm, the markings tattooed on her forearm were no longer there. Her skin was no longer wrinkled and loose but smooth and soft. She turned her hand over and the age spots and skin discoloration was also gone. Reaching up to her hair she found it was thicker and softer and when she pulled it over her shoulder it was no longer white but deep chestnut brown.

'It's time to come home Rena,' her father wrapped his arm around her shoulders, 'are you ready?'

She nodded as her face broke into a smile.

'Rena?' Schaja cupped her face, 'will you tell me a story.'

She pulled him in closer and tucked his head under her chin and she rocked him softly, 'I have a whole lifetime's worth of stories to tell you.'

Her parents watched on, smiling contentedly as the little boy continued to chatter away and as the four of them faded from view Renata did not look back nor did she see her old fragile body, cold and lifeless, slumped across her desk.

12.

Olivia rolled over, reaching blindly for her insistently ringing phone which had woken her.

'Lo,' she murmured pressing her face back into her warm soft pillow. 'Veronica?'

She listened to the muffled voice at the other end of the line for a moment.

'What?' she sat up abruptly, waking Theo.

'Oh God' she breathed, rubbing her hand over her face before swinging her legs over the side of the bed. 'No, of course I don't mind. I'll be right there.'

She hung up the phone and tossed it on the bed as she searched out some clean underwear and then dragged on her jeans.

'What's wrong?' Theo murmured as he propped himself up on his elbow scrubbing his hand through his disordered hair.

'That was Veronica,' she paused and took a deep breath. It was then that Theo heard the slight tremor in her voice and saw the tears brimming in her eyes.

He hauled himself out of bed and took her in his arms.

'What's wrong?'

'Renata died last night.'

'Christ,' he muttered pulling her in closer, 'what happened?'

'I don't know exactly, Veronica arrived for work this morning and found her slumped over her desk.' She pulled back slightly and wiped a stray tear before smiling sadly, 'she always said she was going to die at her desk, I guess she got her wish.'

'I'm sorry Livy' he stroked her back comfortingly, 'I know how fond of her you were.'

Another tear rolled down her cheek and he leaned forward brushing it away with the pad of his thumb.

'Are you heading to the museum now?'

She nodded mutely.

'I'll get dressed and come with you.'

She couldn't say anything, a hot tight ball of sadness ached at the back of her throat as she wrapped her arms around Theo and buried her face in his chest. He held her gently while she cried, murmuring soft soothing words into her ear and smoothing her hair back from her face until she was ready to let go.

They dressed in silence and left, and by the time they pulled up in front of the museum it was a frantic bustle of activity. Police tape cordoned off the entrance and this had attracted a small crowd of onlookers. Olivia climbed out of the car and headed directly for the front door. As they approached the entrance she recognized the police officer guarding it.

'Olivia,' Deputy Hanson nodded.

Olivia took in the tall blonde police officer unsure of how to address her. It had been a few months since the last time they'd seen each other. That had been the night Olivia had been shot by her own mother. Coincidentally it had also been the night she found out that Officer Hanson was actually her father's younger half-sister, which technically made the enigmatic blonde woman her aunt. She also knew her real name wasn't Helga Hanson at all but Danae Connell. However only a few people actually knew the truth so Olivia decided just to go with the name she'd known her by and bull headedly ignore the fact that they were related.

'Officer Hanson,' she returned the brief nod.

'I'm afraid you can't cross the tape Olivia,' she told her, 'got the coroner in there at the moment and until he's satisfied this was a death of natural causes it has to be treated as a crime scene.'

'I got a call from my friend Veronica Mason. She's the assistant curator here and the one who found Renata, she asked me to come.' She looked up at her entreatingly, her tone softened 'please, she's only been here a few months, she doesn't know many people. She shouldn't have to go through this on her own.'

Helga studied her silently for a moment before relenting and nodding slowly. She lifted the tape and allowed Olivia and Theo to slip underneath and head up the steps to the front door.

'Officer Gilbert?' Veronica spoke softly as she approached Jake.

'Veronica?' he replied in surprise as his gaze swept over her.

'They said you have some questions for me?'

'Some questions...right,' he murmured as his eyes continued to study her. Last time he had seen Olivia's friend, her thick bushy brown hair had been pulled back into an unflattering ponytail at the nape of her neck and she'd been wearing frumpy clothes and really ugly low heeled shoes which would have been more suited to a middle aged woman. He wasn't sure exactly what she'd done to her hair but it now hung glossy and smooth in a sassy bob which fell just past her chin and was slightly shorter at the back. Every time she tilted her head it swung like a curtain of silk with new glints of honey and gold, making his fingers involuntarily twitch with the urge to find out if it was as soft as it looked.

His gaze slid down to the silk blouse she wore which clung flatteringly to her breasts. It was tucked into the impossibly small waistband of a tight pencil skirt which fell to below her knees. He had no idea she'd been hiding a body like that. His eyes slid scandalously down her shapely legs to land on the killer heels she was wearing giving her nearly an extra five inches in height. He almost smiled, given how endearingly clumsy she was he briefly wondered if she had her personal liability insurance paid up.

'Um Officer Gilbert?' she prompted him, 'questions?'

He cleared his throat and shook his head frowning; it was unlike him to lose his trail of thought like this.

'You came in at approximately 8.45 this morning?'

'Yes,' she nodded, 'I start work at 9.00am. I'm usually in a lot earlier but I was running late this morning.'

She wasn't about to admit she'd been late because she couldn't remember how to use the stupid straightening irons she'd bought in Salem the day before.

'And you discovered Ms. Gershon?'

'About ten minutes after I entered the building,' she blew out a deep breath remembering the details too well. 'I was opening up this morning as Renata wasn't supposed to be in until later. The doors were locked, as they should be, but I remember thinking it was strange that the alarm hadn't been set. That had me worried so I headed straight into Renata's office and that's when I found her.'

'When was the last time you saw her before that?'

'Yesterday late morning, I took a half day and went into Salem with Olivia. Renata was supposed to lock up last night; it wasn't unusual for her to be in the building on her own until late.'

'I see,' he frowned, looking down at his notes.

'Veronica!'

She looked up and saw Olivia hurrying over to her. Theo was by her side, holding her hand as if to provide comfort. She didn't realize how choked up she was until Olivia threw her arms around her. At the sweetness of the gesture something in her chest clenched tightly, making swallowing almost impossible.

'Thank you for coming,' she managed.

'Of course we came,' Olivia pulled back and looked into her eyes. 'You're not on your own, always remember that.'

Veronica nodded but her gaze tracked sideways to a gurney being pushed through the lobby, a black body bag strapped to it. At the terrible sight her eyes filled with tears. Olivia wrapped her arm around her shoulders and pulled her in close. Together they watched Renata's body leaving her precious museum for the very last time.

'She looks so tiny,' Veronica whispered.

'I know,' Olivia tilted her head so that it pressed against Veronica's.

A tall man with black hair and a pleasant appearance stepped away from the trolley nodding to his assistants to keep moving. He approached their small group and turned to Jake. Olivia judged him to be in his thirties. His skin was a deep pleasing brown, his black eyes hidden under high winged brows and when he spoke his voice betrayed a subtle accent.

'Officer Gilbert,' he nodded.

'Doc,' he inclined his head in greeting. 'This is Dr Sachiv Achari,' he introduced him to the others, 'he's our new Coroner.'

They all murmured greetings.

'So can you tell us anything yet?' Jake asked.

'I'm afraid nothing conclusive until I've

performed the autopsy but from my preliminary examination I suspect it was probably a heart attack.'

'Did she suffer?' Veronica asked.

'It's unlikely,' he told her sympathetically, 'the chances are it was very quick. She would probably have been barely aware of it.'

She nodded mutely as more tears slid down her cheeks but she managed a weak smile of thanks as Jake handed her a tissue.

'I guess I'd better go deal with all the workmen,' she sniffed, 'they're nearly finished with the last of the renovations. Then I guess I'll start getting all Renata's paperwork up to date for the next curator.'

'What do you mean the next curator?' Olivia frowned. 'The whole reason Renata gave you the job was because she intended you to take over from her.'

'I know that was what she originally intended,' Veronica blew out a heavy breath, 'but she hadn't even finished training me yet. I imagine the town council will want someone with more experience, especially after all the funding they've just sunk into this place. I expect the Mayor will appoint someone else. Hopefully they will want to keep me on in my current position but if not,' she shrugged in defeat, 'I guess I'll have to go home to Boston.'

'That's not going to happen,' Olivia took her hand and squeezed. 'It took you long enough to run away from home, you're not going back. We'll sort it out I promise.'

'I hope so,' she sighed as she looked across at the workmen huddled together near one of the cordoned off exhibits. 'I'd better go deal with them,' she turned back to Olivia, 'are you sticking around for a while?'

'Sure,' she nodded.

She watched thoughtfully as Veronica walked away, an idea forming in her mind.

'Theo,' she turned to him, 'do me a favor.'

'What?'

'Can you keep an eye on Veronica for me, I've got something I need to do. I'll be back in a while.'

'Sure,' his eyes narrowed suspiciously, 'but where exactly are you going?'

'To speak with the Mayor.'

'I knew you wouldn't be able to resist interfering.'

'Then I don't have to explain myself do I,' she smiled as she stretched up on her toes and dropped a kiss on his mouth.

'Just bring me a coffee when you come back,' he sighed.

She watched as he turned and disappeared in the direction Veronica had gone.

'Olive,' Jake spoke softly as she turned to face him, 'I'm glad I ran into you. Do you remember you asked me to look through the police archives for any reports on Charlotte West?'

'Did you find something?'

'Yes,' he answered, 'I'm quite surprised I did actually, I almost stumbled on it completely by accident.'

'So what did you find out?'

As he opened his mouth to speak one of his colleagues called to him.

'I don't have time to explain it now,' he apologized.

'Why don't you come by the house this evening after you've finished your shift?'

'Okay,' he nodded as he reached out and caught her face gently in his hand, his thumb tracing the bruise on her jaw, 'and I want to have a conversation with you about your mother,' he told her quietly.

'What's the point Jake,' she pushed his hand away in irritation. 'You won't find her unless she wants to be found, there's nothing we can do at the moment.'

'We'll see,' he replied.

He knew she didn't want to talk about her mom, she just kept pushing it away pretending the problem didn't exist, but Jake didn't trust Isabel West's motives at all when it came to her daughter and he was going to do whatever it took to make sure his oldest friend was safe.

'Look I have to go,' she squeezed his hand gently, 'I'll see you at the house later okay?'

'Okay,' he conceded.

She watched him join his colleagues before disappearing back through the main entrance. Ducking under the tape she averted her eyes, not wanting to see Renata's body being loaded into the large dark Coroner's van and headed down the street towards the council offices.

Hoping that the Mayor was in and that by some miracle she would be able to get in and see her, Olivia entered the building and headed up the stairs towards her office. It had been some months since she'd last been to the council offices but she remembered where she was going, although she didn't recognize the Mayor's new assistant. She cast her mind back to when Erica had brought her to see the Mayor, at the end of the previous year when she was being harassed by the former Chief of Police. She seemed to recall the Mayor's last assistant had been pregnant at the time; she must be on maternity leave now. Cursing lightly she headed towards the desk; she had been counting on the previous assistant remembering her. Now she had to convince the new assistant to let her in to see the Mayor.

Plastering on her most affable smile she wandered up to the desk and waited for the assistant to acknowledge her.

'Can I help you?' she looked up from her computer screen.

'I'd like to see Mayor Burnett please.'

'Do you have an appointment?'

'No, I don't but I do know the Mayor and she told me to stop by if I needed anything so I was hoping you'd be able to squeeze me in. It will only take ten minutes.'

'The Mayor is busy all day,' she replied in a flat unfriendly voice. 'You'll have to make an appointment for another day.'

'But this can't wait.'

'I'm sure it can't but you'll still have to wait for another day,' she tapped a few keys and peered at her screen. 'I can fit you in on the 27th.'

The 27th?' Olivia replied incredulously, 'that's two weeks away.'

'Of March,' the gloating assistant added.

'Next month?' Olivia answered, 'are you kidding?'

'No, I'm not,' she smirked, 'the Mayor is very busy.' She looked Olivia up and down as if she considered her beneath the Mayor's notice.

'Look,' Olivia leaned forward placing either hand carefully on the desk and when she spoke her voice was low and dangerous. 'I am getting in to see Mayor Burnett today and no secretary on a power trip is going to stop me.'

'I'll call security,' she threatened.

'You do that,' Olivia smiled pleasantly, 'I'll be waiting for them in the Mayor's office.'

She rounded the desk and headed for the door intending to just knock. She probably wouldn't have been so forward but the self-righteous jumped up secretary had pissed her off and she was spoiling for a fight.

The assistant jumped up from her desk and moved to block Olivia just before she got to the door.

'You can't go in,' her voice jumped up an octave.

'Get out of my way,' Olivia warned her, eyes flashing 'or I will make you get out of my way.'

'I'll have you arrested for this.'

'Be my guest,' Olivia invited.

'Security,' she shouted.

The door was suddenly wrenched open from behind her.

'What on earth is all the shouting about?' Tammy

Burnett stood with Erica by her side.

'Mayor Burnett,' the assistant replied, 'I'm so sorry for the interruption but this woman was insisting on seeing you and was about to barge into your office despite being told she would have to wait for an appointment. I was just about to call security.'

Tammy looked around her assistant and as she caught sight of Olivia her face broke into a warm smile.

'Olivia dear, how nice to see you. It's quite alright Andrea,' she brushed the woman aside briskly, 'I always have time for Olivia.'

She knew it was childish but Olivia couldn't quite resist throwing a smug look in the assistant's direction.

'Hey Olivia,' Erica greeted her in amusement as she watched Andrea's face flush red with anger.

'Erica,' Olivia returned her smile.

'Olivia,' Tammy interrupted, 'I just need to make a quick phone call, could you give me a few minutes?'

'Sure.'

'Andrea,' Tammy turned towards her, 'be a dear and see if Olivia would like some refreshment?'

As the door closed with a quiet click Andrea turned to Olivia.

'Would you like a drink or something?' she asked from between clenched teeth.

'A cup of tea would be lovely thank you,' she smiled widely.

She watched as the assistant stalked away. There was no way in hell she was going to drink anything that woman made her but she didn't want to spend the next five minutes while she waited for the Mayor with the snooty bitch of a secretary shooting poison daggers at her.

'Charming isn't she?' Erica smiled.

'How on earth does Mayor Burnett put up with her?'

'She's sickeningly polite to Tammy,' Erica laughed, 'besides she was the most qualified for the job. Thankfully its only until Audrey comes back from maternity leave. I'm glad I caught you actually, I wanted to have a word with you.'

'Oh?'

Erica took her arm gently and steered her away from the door to the couch in the waiting area.

'I know this isn't really the place for it but I wanted to tell you I'm leaving Mercy.'

'What?'

'I've been offered a job with a large and extremely prestigious law firm in Boston, so I'm leaving. I'm afraid I won't be able to be your lawyer anymore but if you have no objections you'll be added to my colleague Jason's books. He's very good, I'm sure you'll get on well.'

'I don't really have any objections,' Olivia frowned, 'but I just can't believe you're leaving Mercy.'

'I know it's going to be strange but I don't want to spend the rest of my life in a small town. I want a career; I want to be a high court judge someday. I'm not the 'marriage and kids' kind of woman. I may even branch out into politics. Congresswoman Kelly,' she laughed, 'it has a ring to it doesn't it or how about Senator Kelly.'

'What about you and Jake though?' Olivia asked.

'Jake and I,' she sighed, 'it wouldn't work. We were never really a couple you know, despite what everyone assumed. What we had was casual, we were both married to our careers. We wanted the same thing, or I thought we did.'

'What do you mean?' Olivia frowned.

'I care a great deal about Jake and I hope we can remain friends but he'll never leave Mercy and despite him saying he doesn't want to settle down, that he's not the 'marriage and kids' type, it's exactly the opposite. You can't be a lawyer without learning to read people and I'm telling you now, Jake will make some lucky woman an amazing husband and he will be a great father. He just hasn't figured that out yet. I on the other hand mean it when I say I don't want to settle down.'

'Have you told him yet?'

'Yes I have,' she sighed. 'His pride is a little bruised, that I was the one to call it a day, but he'll get over it. It's not like we were in love.'

'Well then,' Olivia blew out a breath, 'I guess all that's left to say is congratulations?'

'Thanks,' she smiled.

The door to the office opened again and Tammy beckoned Olivia in.

'Take care Olivia,' Erica hugged her.

'You too,' she nodded as she watched the tall elegant redhead disappear down the hallway.

'Come in Olivia,' Tammy smiled.

'Thanks for seeing me Mayor Burnett,' Olivia walked past her into her spacious office.

'It's no problem, as I said I always have time for you. I'll make sure Andrea knows that if you decide to drop by again.' She indicated for Olivia to take a seat.

'Now what can I do for you?'

'It's about Renata Gershon.'

'Yes,' Tammy sighed, 'I did hear about Renata, poor dear.'

'Well I've actually come to speak with you about Veronica Mason.'

'Oh?'

'She's under the impression you are going to hire someone else to take over from Renata.'

'To be honest I haven't had time to think about it, I only heard about Renata an hour ago.'

'But Veronica should be the one taking over the museum, it was what Renata wanted.'

'Olivia I'm sure Veronica appreciates your loyalty but Renata hadn't even finished training Veronica. We're not talking about a smooth transition here, the museum is right in the middle of phase one of a very expensive expansion project. The revenue that the museum and its research facility will generate is important to our local economy, especially considering the current economic climate. We simply can't afford to get it wrong.'

'I know and believe me I understand that but Renata loved that museum, it was her whole life. She spent years searching for the right person to replace her and she believed that Veronica was that person. All that I'm asking is for you to give her a chance to prove herself, for Renata.'

Tammy leaned back in her chair as she regarded Olivia thoughtfully.

'Very well,' she replied after a moment. 'I'm prepared to give her a trial period of three months to prove herself and if at the end of those three months she hasn't impressed me I will replace her, is that fair enough?'

'Yes,' Olivia smiled, 'yes that's more than fair, thank you so much Mayor Burnett.'

'Don't thank me just yet, your friend has a lot of work ahead of her. I am a notoriously hard woman to please.'

'Still thank you anyway,' Olivia rose from her seat, 'and thank you for seeing me on such short notice.'

'You're welcome,' she smiled as Olivia turned to leave. 'Olivia?'

She turned back.

'I hope Veronica knows how lucky she is to have you as a friend.'

Olivia smiled and stepped through the door.

Veronica sighed and rubbed her tired eyes, it had been a hell of a day. Olivia and Theo had been a great comfort to her, helping deal with the workmen, while the police had finally finished documenting everything. It had put the renovations behind but she was confident it would still get finished up more or less on schedule. A wave of sadness washed over her at the thought that Renata had not lived to see it finished. She'd dedicated most of her life to the museum, Veronica could only hope she lived up to the faith she had shown in her. Not only that she now also had Olivia to thank for speaking with the Mayor on her behalf.

There was still so much to sort out, she only had three months to prove to the Mayor she was up to the job because she sure as hell didn't want to go crawling back home to her family. It would only confirm in their eyes that she couldn't do anything for herself. Renata had never made her feel that way, she'd always treated her as if she was special, talented even. Although that had always baffled her, she hadn't realized how much she'd come to appreciate and respond to Renata's belief in her.

Another tear slid slowly down her cheek and she absently wiped it away. She'd done nothing but cry all day long; she was surprised there was any moisture left in her whole body. She missed the old lady already. She knew Renata didn't have any family left and she had many casual acquaintances but not a lot of close friends. A sudden thought made her frown. Who was going to arrange Renata's funeral? She made a note to speak with the police in the morning to find out when the body would be released. If no one else was going to step up, she was going to make sure she had the best possible funeral. Maybe she could speak to Olivia and see if she wanted to help, she had after all been extremely fond of Renata.

Looking up at the clock she realized how late it was. Her stomach growled loudly as she stretched out the kink in her neck. Shuffling all the paperwork back into some semblance of order she rose from her desk and flicked off the lamp. Scooping her heels off the floor where she'd kicked them earlier she tucked them neatly into her bag and pulled her on thick fur lined snow boots. Zipping herself into her thick coat and slipping her bag over her shoulder she flicked of the main lights and closed up her office. It didn't take long to check through the museum seeing everything was as it should be, before she set the alarm code and slipped out of the front door locking it behind her.

The sky was black although sprinkled with dozens of tiny pinpricks of light. The air had once again dropped below freezing causing her to shiver and snuggle further down into her jacket. She trotted briskly down the steps to the sidewalk and headed towards the parking bays where she'd left her car. At first nothing seemed out of place, the streets were quiet due to the late hour and the cold weather but as she travelled further along the street she felt the curious sensation of being watched.

She stopped and looked back, unable to see anything but the empty street behind her. Frowning slightly, she turned and resumed her pace. The air around her felt different, almost heavier and this time when she looked up the stars had disappeared, the sky now covered with thick clouds. She stopped in awe, she'd never seen a cloud formation like it before. It was strangely thick and textured, as if someone had smeared butter cream across the sky leaving it in thick tide marks and peaks.

Something cold and fragile grazed her frozen cheek and she brushed it away absently. Then it came again landing on her eyelashes as she tried to blink it away. Holding out the palm of her hand a thick white snowflake landed on her glove, so big it was almost the size of an egg. She looked back to the sky now filled with huge white flakes, swirling and billowing on the cold eddies of air.

Clutching her coat tighter around her she began to move again, she needed to get to her car but the snow flurry was now coming down so thick she could barely see anything in front of her. She fought her way through the sudden and bizarre snowstorm, holding her hand up in an effort to shield her eyes from the driving snow. She suddenly felt icy cold fingers dancing down her spine and an uncomfortable weight settle between her shoulders.

Something was stalking her.

Her head bowed down against the howl and

..riek of the wind she pressed on trying to move quicker. She was aware that her boots were beginning to slip on the freshly fallen snow which was now so deep it was pushing over the tops of her boots against her stockinged legs and she cursed herself for wearing a skirt. She made it to the end of the block and as she turned the corner the sense of urgency returned full force. She fought the urge to flat out run, knowing it would be impossible in the treacherous conditions, although she knew something was behind her. She crossed the road but the depth of the new snow made her misjudge her step up at the other side. Missing her footing she stumbled and fell forwards. She felt her knee crack against the edge of the sidewalk and gasping in pain she risked a glance back over her shoulder. The snow flurry was so wild she could barely make out a thing but suddenly she saw a flash of something white, something tall and slim almost like a person but it moved too quick for her to see.

Hauling herself to her feet she gingerly put her weight on her injured knee. Although it throbbed unmercifully and she could feel the warm trickle of blood, she could still move on it. Hobbling forward she knew she was close to her car. She fumbled in her pocket for her keys and saw another strange flash of white sweep past her. She froze in fear, her heart pounding in her chest so hard she could almost hear it.

The shape rushed past her again and she spun around trying to make it out. Suddenly the figure stilled; it was a woman tall and willowy with long limbs and pale ivory skin. Her hair was white and fell to her hips. She was incredibly beautiful and also completely naked. Veronica couldn't believe what she was seeing, her startled gaze swept over the woman, seemingly unaffected by the cold or the storm despite her naked body. The snow flurry spun around her as if somehow she was the epicenter of the strange weather. Veronica's eyes were finally drawn to the woman's face. Her eyes were slitted like a snake, black and

filled with a terrible hunger.
Veronica's mouth fell open and the only sound she heard
was her own terrified scream.

13.

'Thanks Olive,' Jake smiled gratefully as she popped the top and handed him a beer. 'It's been a hell of a day.'

'I know,' she watched him as he absently leaned down and scratched Beau's ears. 'Has the Coroner finished the autopsy yet?'

'It's still too soon,' Jake shook his head as Theo wandered into the kitchen and took a seat next to him. 'Dr Achari says it'll be a couple of days before he can get to her but it looks like it was natural causes.'

'I still can't believe she's gone,' Olivia sighed.

Theo reached out and stroked the back of her neck comfortingly.

'So what were you going to tell me earlier?' She switched subjects not wanting to dwell on Renata's death, 'you said you found out something to do with Charlotte?'

Jake nodded. 'You said she had been engaged to Clayton Swilley at the time of her death?'

'That's right.'

'Well, I came across the report of Charlotte's death, it was sketchy at best even for back then. It seems the first Officer on the scene was someone named David Haverhill. He questioned Clayton who told him they had been out for a late night sail on the lake, but that Charlotte had fallen in and because it was dark he couldn't see her in time to save her.'

'You don't seem convinced,' Theo tilted his head as he studied Jake's expression.

'The notes were almost illegible, there were large sections of the report crossed out and too many unanswered questions so I dug a little further. It seems two days after Charlotte's death Clayton Swilley's father Augustus, who was the Mayor at the time, made a sizable donation to the Mercy police dept. and not too long after that Officer Haverhill was promoted suddenly.'

'You think he was buying their silence.'

'The whole thing reeks of a cover up,' Jake shook his head in disgust as he took a swig of his beer.

'I guess that would explain why she's so angry,' Theo pointed out.

'and locked in a death cycle,' Olivia replied quietly. 'If Clayton murdered her and it's looking more and more likely, then it means her killer was never brought to justice. The whole thing was just brushed under the carpet and covered up.'

'I don't blame her for being pissed,' Jake agreed.

Olivia looked up at the sudden banging at the front door. Beau leapt up and hurtled down the hall in a mad scramble of claws, with Olivia following closely along behind him. She peered curiously through the peephole before pulling open the door.

'Veronica?' she frowned in confusion, 'are you alright?'

Veronica stood trembling on her doorstep, her hair wet and plastered to her pale face. Her blue eyes were wide and as Olivia's gaze dropped she noticed a streak of dried blood running from her knee down her leg to the top of her boot.

'You're hurt?' Olivia grabbed her hand and pulled her inside. 'Good God Veronica, you're frozen.'

As soon as she stepped through the door into the safety of the house, her body was wracked with deep shudders.

'I...the snow...storm...and I fell...the woman...'

Olivia listened in worry as her friend's voice got higher and higher, hysteria lapping at the edges as her breath came in great gasps. Her eyes were wide with fear and the more she tried to speak the less she made any sense.

Grabbing her hand firmly she dragged Veronica into the warm kitchen where Jake and Theo were looking on curiously.

'What happened?' Olivia frowned as she pulled off Veronica's wet coat and handed it to Theo to hang up to dry.

'The storm came out of nowhere, there was snow everywhere and the woman, she was following me...'

'What woman?' Jake interrupted, frowning.

'She was naked and her eyes...her eyes were...' Veronica was now taking such great big lungful's of air her vision started to grey at the edges and swirling spots appeared before her eyes.

'Okay,' Olivia pushed her into a chair, and seeing she was hyperventilating she pushed her head between her knees. 'Calm down Roni, just breathe,' she turned to Theo who was watching in concern. 'Theo grab a paper bag out of that drawer will you?'

Taking the bag from him she opened it and handed it to Veronica.

'Here try this.'

Veronica took the bag and breathed in and out of it, trying to slow her racing heart.

Folding up the hem of her skirt she took a look at

her rapidly swelling knee and the grazes which had mostly stopped bleeding.

'Here,' Theo handed her a first aid box.

'You do it,' she shook her head, 'I'll get some ice.'

Theo dropped to his knees in front of the traumatized woman and taking out an antiseptic wipe began to clean the wounds. Olivia glanced across at Jake as she pulled a bag of peas from the freezer and handed them to Theo to press against the swelling. Jake poured a glass of whiskey and handed it to Veronica.

'It'll help settle you,' he told her gently as she looked up at him with glassy eyes.

His brows rose in surprise as she removed the paper bag and chugged the whole glass back in one go.

'Thank you,' she breathed handing back the empty glass.

'Can you tell us what happened?' Olivia moved back to her side rubbing circles on her back soothingly.

'I was leaving the museum,' she took a deep breath, 'I had just stepped outside when it began snowing again. Only it was like no snow storm I had ever seen. The snowflakes were as big as my hand and coming down so fast I could barely see in front of me. I felt really uneasy like I was being watched so I headed towards my car. I knew I needed to get home and out of the storm as soon as possible but the snow just kept getting worse. I tripped and smacked my knee because I couldn't see where I was going. I'd almost made it to my car and that's when I saw, I mean I thought I saw...'

'What did you see?'

'You're going to think I'm crazy,' she whispered.

'Trust me we won't,' Olivia smiled.

'There was a woman standing in front of me, she was incredibly beautiful and..um'

'And?'

'She was naked.'

'Naked?' Jake repeated slowly.

Veronica nodded.

'It was like she didn't even feel the cold. She had long white hair which reached past her waist almost to the backs of her thighs and the snow, it's strange, it was kind of swirling around her like she was the center of the storm and that's not even the really weird part.'

'It gets weirder than naked snow lady?' Jake asked.

'It was her eyes,' Veronica frowned, 'they were slitted like a snake. I don't know how to describe it, it's like she wasn't even human.'

'What happened next?'

'I'm not sure, that's when it gets a little blurry,' Veronica shook her head. 'I screamed and the next thing I remember I was in my car driving out of town towards your house.'

Olivia glanced towards the window. Although it was dark out she couldn't see any significant snowfall around her property.

'Once I left the town itself the snow let up' Veronica told her, almost as if she'd read her mind. 'It's like the storm was concentrated right in the centre of town and once you got past the outer edge the weather returned to normal.'

'What the hell is going on?' Jake muttered casting a glance at Olivia's worried face.

'And you definitely don't remember what happened between seeing the woman and being in your car driving?'

'No,' Veronica breathed, 'it's one big blank. I don't even know how I got in the car.'

'Maybe it's just shock?' Jake replied, 'that could account for the memory loss.'

'Maybe,' Olivia murmured thoughtfully as she watched her friend.

Suddenly the windows started rattling and the kitchen light flickered with a metallic buzzing.

'Oh God,' Veronica breathed, 'it's not your ghost

is it?'

'I don't think so,' Olivia frowned, 'it doesn't feel like her.'

Olivia's eyes widened in shock as a man appeared in front of her, battered and bloody.

'Olivia,' he whispered.

'Sam!' Olivia rushed forward as Theo caught him and eased him to the floor.

'What the hell?' Jake gasped at his sudden appearance.

Olivia risked a quick look at Veronica who was once again breathing rapidly into the paper bag, her eyes wide with disbelief.

'Sam,' Theo called to him urgently.

Olivia looked over his torn and bloodied clothes noticing the expanding blood stain at his side which was saturating his shirt. Yanking the shirt out of the way she gasped at the ragged wound torn deeply into his flesh.

'Damn it,' she pressed her hands to the wound to stop the bleeding as she gazed down at the man she hadn't seen in months, the same mysterious man who had pulled Theo through time and helped her set up his new identity. 'We need to get him to the hospital.'

'No,' Sam gasped weakly trying to raise his head and panting hard with the exertion. 'No hospitals, no one can know I'm here.'

Growling in frustration she looked up at Theo.

'Theo go and get the medical supplies Louisa left here just before Christmas.' She turned to Jake, 'call Louisa and tell her we have an emergency, we need her here now.'

Jake nodded and pulled out his phone. Theo dropped down next to her and rummaged around until he came up with several packs of sterile dressings. Ripping them open Olivia took the thick pads and pressed them into Sam's side, hoping it would slow the bleeding.

'She's on her way,' Jake told them, 'so this is Sam?'

'That's right,' Olivia nodded, 'Jake go and get a

pillow and blanket for him before he goes into shock.'

Jake nodded and disappeared from the room.

'Veronica,' she called, 'are you okay?'

'He appeared out of thin air,' she replied incredulously.

'Yep, welcome to Mercy,' Olivia muttered. 'Your life will never be the same.'

Sam groaned as he swam back into consciousness.

'Sam,' Olivia spoke softly as his eye rolled trying to focus. The other eyes was swollen shut and his face was decorated with varying colours of bruises. Some of them obviously days old, whilst others were fresh. 'What happened to you, who did this?'

'It doesn't matter,' he swallowed painfully.

'Of course it matters,' she frowned.

'I can't tell you,' he whispered as he faded out of consciousness again, 'can't contaminate the time line…'

'What's he talking about?' Veronica frowned.

'Nothing,' Olivia replied dismissively.

Veronica had now dropped the paper bag into her lap and was watching them curiously.

'No, I heard him, he said he couldn't contaminate the time line. What did he mean?'

'Look at the state of him,' Olivia explained, 'he's probably delirious.'

Veronica didn't have a chance to say anything else as Jake rushed into the room with a blanket and cushion. She simply sat back and watched suspiciously. Theo tucked the cushion under Sam's head and looked up at Jake as he laid the blanket over Olivia's hands while she continued to keep the pressure on his wound.

'How long is Louisa going to be?'

'Not long,' Jake muttered, 'knowing the way she drives.'

Beau whined and curled up into Sam's side, laying his furry face on his legs and watching him with huge dark eyes. It felt like an eternity as they sat on that kitchen floor waiting for Louisa but in reality it hadn't actually been that long before she burst through the door with Tommy following close behind her.

'Alright I'm here who is it this time?' She spoke rapidly as she stepped into the kitchen and shed her coat. 'Her gaze fell to the unconscious man bleeding on the floor, 'who's he?'

'Sam,' Theo answered.

'That's Sam?' her gaze snapped to Theo's face, 'as in 'Sam' Sam?'

'The Sam who knows Theo,' Olivia replied carefully as she noticed Tommy hovering at the edge of the kitchen taking in the scene before him. She hoped he wasn't going to freak out. They had to be careful what they said now as neither Veronica nor Tommy knew the truth about how Theo had landed up in Mercy.

'Okay then,' Louisa briskly pushed up the sleeves of the shirt she wore beneath her scrubs, 'let's get him off the floor.'

She moved the fruit bowl, whiskey bottle and empty glasses off the island in the centre of the kitchen as Theo and Jake lifted Sam off the floor and laid him down carefully.

'This is getting to be a habit,' Louisa pulled her stethoscope from her pocket as her eyes locked with Olivia's over Sam's body.

'At least it's not me this time,' Olivia murmured quietly enough for only Louisa to hear.

'All right everyone out,' Louisa ordered. 'Olivia as you're already covered in blood you can stay and help.'

Theo ushered everyone out and into the library while Jake scooped up the whiskey bottle and nodded to them on the way out.

'Call if you need help.'

'We will,' she answered absently as she checked Sam's airway.

'Okay, now it's just the two of us why don't you

tell me what the hell is going on?' Louisa demanded even as she began to check his various injuries.

'I have no idea,' Olivia shook her head. 'I haven't seen Sam in months and he just appeared in the kitchen and collapsed.'

'Who's the woman who was here?'

'That's Veronica, she's not long moved to Mercy from Boston. She works at the museum.'

'Does she know the truth about all of this?'

'No,' Olivia sighed, 'and now I have to figure out what the hell to tell her as Sam appeared right in front of her.'

'Good luck with that,' Louisa answered, 'do you think she'll freak out?'

'Well she hasn't so far,' Olivia frowned. 'I don't know,' she shrugged and let out a weary breath, 'it's certainly never dull since I came back to Mercy.'

'This is one wicked mess you've got on your hands Olivia,' Louisa frowned as she moved her hands and peeled back the gauze at Sam's side. 'For God's sake Olivia, he needs to be at the hospital.'

'I know, but he made me promise not to. I didn't know what else to do.'

Louisa scowled as she pulled on her gloves and pressed two fingers deep inside of Sam's wound. He groaned and moved.

'Hold him down will you?'

Olivia did as she was told.

'His kidney seems to be intact, the wound looks like it was made by a knife, quite a large one with a serrated edge. His organs appear to be okay but I can't be sure.'

'There is one way you can be sure,' Olivia told her seriously.

'Liv, I haven't done that since we were kids and nothing on this scale. This isn't a game; we're talking about a man's life here.'

'I know and I wouldn't ask if it wasn't important,'

she replied softly, 'please Louisa.'

She sighed heavily. 'I can't even guarantee it will still work.'

'Just try, that's all I'm asking.'

'Fine,' she conceded.

Louisa placed her hands over the wound and closed her eyes. She concentrated on taking deep slow breaths, feeling her heartbeat as her body began to relax and she felt the old familiar sensation of sinking. Reaching deep within herself for that secret place where her own magical ability lay dormant, she gave it a little nudge and felt it awaken and unfurl like a flower stretching towards the warm rays of the sun. A surge of pleasure and adrenalin rippled through her, just as it had when she was a child and she found she'd missed this feeling. She knew she had deliberately closed down that part of herself when she believed Olivia was gone, too hurt to have anything that reminded her of her best friend. Over the years she'd learned to live without it but now it was awake and far more potent than she remembered.

Her own heartbeat began to fade into the background as she became more aware of Sam's body. She could hear the whoosh of his blood pumping through his veins loudly in her ears and she could feel his heart pumping so strongly, as if she cradled the pulsing organ in her hands. She allowed her thoughts to spread throughout his body checking for injuries.

Olivia watched in fascination as Sam's skin beneath Louisa's hands began to glow with a faint blue light. His labored breathing evened out and his body relaxed.

'What the hell?'

Louisa's eyes flew open at the startled exclamation and both she and Olivia turned towards the doorway to see Tommy staring at Louisa's glowing hands.

'Shit,' Olivia cursed under her breath.

'Which one of you wants to tell me what the hell I

just saw?' he crossed his arms and glared at both of them.

'Not now Tommy,' Louisa turned back to Sam.

'Not now?'

'Yes,' she snapped irritably, 'not now. I need to take care of Sam and stitch up his wound, after that we'll talk.'

He turned on his heel and stalked angrily from the room.

'I take it things still aren't better between you two?'

Louisa sighed. 'We seem to only open our mouths these days to yell at each other,' she shook her head, 'but I meant what I said. I need to deal with my patient before we start in on what is going to be a very long complicated conversation. It was hard enough talking my way out of the fact I knew your mom was still alive.'

'What did you tell him about that?'

'The bare minimum,' she pulled out a suture tray and peeled it open carefully. 'I told him that your mom survived the fire and that Chief Macallister and Jake are still looking for her.'

Olivia nodded.

'I hate to say it Louisa, but with everything that's going on at the moment we may have to tell them the truth.'

'And you think that's a good idea?'

'I don't know,' Olivia frowned as she watched Louisa clean the wound and start carefully stitching the ragged edges together. 'I'd rather not but we're just going to keep running into these situations. There's only so much you can hide from your husband and I hate knowing that it's just adding to the friction between you.'

'I guess it's time for some honesty between us,' Louisa frowned. 'We've ignored it for too long, pretending we have the perfect marriage when the truth is between my job and his we really don't know each other that well at all. He shipped out almost as soon as we were married and I spent all my time training to become a doctor.'

'Do you still love him?'

'Yes,' she sighed, 'I'll love him until the day I die but sometimes love isn't enough.'

Olivia sat quietly and watched as Louisa patiently stitched Sam's wound and dressed it.

'So what's the prognosis Doc?'

Louisa looked up at Olivia and stretched the kink out of her spine.

'He's got a couple of broken ribs, but as far as I was able to sense he had no major internal injuries. However, someone sure took the time to work him over, he had a lot of internal bruising as well as the external ones. The orbital bone is cracked and there's a lot of swelling to his face. Also all of his fingers are broken so I'm going to have to go back to the hospital and get some splints and make sure the bones are set straight before they start to heal. He has lost a fair amount of blood but its borderline. He could do with a transfusion to be on the safe side but I don't have any here and I don't know his blood type so I'll set him up on an IV with a saline solution. I'll take blood samples back to the lab with me so I can type and cross match just in case he takes a turn for the worse.'

'Thanks Louisa,' Olivia replied quietly, 'I appreciate it.'

'Just be careful what you're getting yourself into,' she told her seriously.

'What is that supposed to mean?'

'I've seen injuries like this before and let's just say he didn't get them falling down a ladder. Just be careful that there isn't someone who's going to come looking for him and end up on your doorstep.'

'I'll be careful I promise.'

'Good,' Louisa nodded, 'let's get him settled in one of your spare rooms. You'll need to watch him when I head back to the hospital to get the splints.'

It was getting late by the time they had Sam settled safely in one of the spare rooms close to Olivia's and Theo's, but everyone was still in the library and showing no signs of moving.

'We're going to have to talk to Tommy and Veronica before you head back to the hospital,' Olivia told Louisa as they headed down the stairs and paused by the library door.

'I guess,' Louisa grimaced, but how much do we actually tell them?'

'As much as we can without them freaking out,' Olivia replied.

'I suppose we should get this over with then.'

Olivia followed Louisa into the room and watched in amusement as every eye in the room turned to them questioningly.

'Are you redecorating or something?' Louisa frowned as she caught sight of the mess.

'Don't ask,' Olivia shook her head.

Louisa dropped down tiredly into one of the chairs, watching as Tommy paced the floor and Veronica sat numbly on the sofa clutching the bottle of whiskey.

'So are you going to tell us what is going on?' Tommy asked.

'Louisa, Jake and Theo already know the truth, all of it,' Olivia told him, 'it's only you and Veronica.'

'Fine,' he stopped pacing and crossed his arms, 'so start talking. I want to know how the hell your mom is still alive, yet nobody seems bothered by that at all or the fact that she attacked you and trashed your room.'

'That was your mom?' Louisa asked accusingly.

'I thought you said your mom was murdered by your father?' Veronica frowned in confusion.

Tommy carried on as if they hadn't spoken.

'And how did that guy end up in your house being treated by my wife when he should have been taken to a hospital. I've seen war and I've seen men who have been tortured. You can't tell me that guy isn't caught up in something bad and what the hell was that weird glowing thing Louisa was doing?'

'Weird glowing thing?' Jake turned to Louisa, 'you used your gift? in front of him?'

'I didn't know he was there,' Louisa snapped, 'and in my defense I wasn't going to use it at all, Olivia talked me into it.'

'Necessary,' Olivia shrugged.

'What do you mean gifts?' Veronica frowned. 'I have to admit I'm so confused, I don't understand any of this. How did that man appear out of thin air?'

'He appeared out of thin air?' Tommy turned to Veronica, his eyes narrowing suspiciously 'How much of that whiskey have you had?'

'Not enough obviously,' she muttered.

'Alright enough,' Olivia held up her hands. 'That's enough; you want the truth?'

She cast a glance at Jake and then Theo who both nodded in agreement.

'Yes I do,' Tommy replied stubbornly, 'I want to know exactly what you've got my family tangled up in.'

'I appreciate that you are going through a lot at the moment Tommy. I also get that you are frustrated and worried but lose the attitude while you're under my roof,' Olivia warned. 'I didn't drag Louisa and Jake into anything, they are involved simply because they lived through it the same as Theo and I. There's no blame to go around and no one at fault, we are all in this together because we care about each other and we have each other's backs.'

Tommy stared at Olivia as he mulled over her words.

'Sorry,' he replied sullenly.

'Veronica,' Olivia's voice softened as she turned to her new friend. 'Do you want to know the truth? If you want to walk away now, it's fine, Jake can drive you home and you can forget tonight ever happened.'

Veronica also took a moment to study Olivia before drawing in a deep breath and shaking her head.

'No, I want to know the truth.'

'Be very sure you two,' Olivia told them seriously, 'once you know the truth there is no way back to your safe ordinary lives. From this moment on you will always look at the world through different eyes.'

Tommy looked to Veronica who nodded mutely back at him, her large blue eyes vivid against her white face.

'We want to know,' he answered for both of them, 'regardless of the consequences.'

Olivia drew in a breath and held out her hands. Her eyes flashed gold and her hands burst into flame.

'Holy shit,' Tommy stumbled backwards and dropped down on the sofa next to Veronica whose eyes were wide, her mouth hanging open in disbelief.

The flames in Olivia's hands separated and flickered around her. Her hair was drawn back from her face by an invisible wind and her skin glowed with power. After a moment Veronica and Tommy realized that the flames dancing merrily around Olivia were in actual fact dragonflies, composed entirely of flames.

'Wow,' Veronica whispered unable to tear her gaze from the sight before her. She held up the bottle to Tommy who took it without looking and took a deep swig of whiskey.

Olivia allowed the dragonflies to dance around for a moment longer and then one by one they disappeared back into her cupped hands.

'Not to state the obvious here,' Olivia smiled at them softly, 'but I'm a witch. I come from an extremely long and powerful line of witches. Both my mother and father possess powers too. My family for some reason had always wielded very strong magical gifts. I am a direct descendant from Hester West who escaped Salem with her sister Bridget and settled here. Slowly one by one they came, survivors of the witch trials, not just Salem but all over Europe and the Americas. After a while whole groups of them would arrive, drawn to this place and the undercurrent of power that runs beneath its surface and the town of Mercy was born. Almost everyone in town has some form of magical blood in them, but some are so weak they are barely even aware of it. Others more so.'

'So you have powers too?' Tommy turned to look at his wife.

'We both do,' Jake answered for her. 'Nothing like Olivia, but we do have our own gifts.'

'Which are?' Veronica asked curiously, 'that is if you don't mind me asking.'

Jake looked to his sister who nodded for him to continue.

'I have always been able to tell when someone is lying or being untruthful and Louisa has always been able to tell when someone is ill or injured.'

'Are you witches then?' Tommy asked.

'No,' Louisa shook her head. 'We were raised as Christians and that's what we decided to live our lives as. We don't really use our gifts, well not consciously. Today was the first time I've actively used my ability since I was a kid, that's how I was able to tell what injuries Sam has.'

'And you?' Tommy turned to Theo, 'are you a witch?'

'No,' Theo smiled in amusement. 'I was raised a Puritan but I do have abilities of my own. I have visions.'

'Seriously?'

'Puritan?' Veronica interrupted, 'that's…unusual.'

'Veronica,' Olivia shook her head 'we haven't even scraped the surface yet. The reason I am telling you about our abilities is so that you can accept the premise that magic is real.'

'So this Sam guy who appeared in the kitchen, I'm assuming he has abilities too.'

'Yes,' she replied. 'I don't know the extent of his

gifts but I do know that he is able to travel from one place to another instantaneously and not just across distances but across time as well.'

'Time?' Tommy snorted, 'now I know you're messing with me, there's no such thing as time travel.'

'That's where you're wrong,' Olivia answered as she turned to Theo. 'Do you want to tell them?'

'Tell us what?' Tommy frowned.

'My name is Theodore Beckett,' he told them quietly, 'and I was born in Salem in the year 1664. Sam pulled me through time to Mercy last year around Halloween.'

Tommy was staring suspiciously at Theo as if he couldn't quite figure out why he would make up such an outrageous lie.

'That's why you don't know how to drive, even though you have a driver's license?' he asked.

'Sam provided me with identification in case anyone started looking into my background.'

'This is insane.'

'I know it's a lot to take in Tommy,' Jake interrupted, 'but it's true.'

'Just listen to yourselves,' he shook his head, 'it's not possible.'

'I would probably be skeptical too if I were in your position,' Theo told him, 'but I give you my word that I am telling the truth.'

'What really happened to your brother?' Tommy asked suddenly as he thought back to their conversation a few weeks before.'

'He was a witchfinder,' Theo replied as his face flushed with shame, 'as was I.'

'You were a witchfinder?' Veronica gasped as she turned to look at Olivia, 'but you're a witch?'

'It's a bit complicated,' Olivia told her, 'but trust me I'm in no danger from Theo.'

'This is crazy,' she replied.

'Tip of the iceberg, sweetheart,' Jake answered ruefully. 'You might as well tell them the rest Olive; we've come this far.'

'There's more?' Veronica breathed heavily, swiping the bottle back from Tommy and taking a large gulp of the fiery liquid.

'Okay, you've had a lot to take in this evening so I'm going to give you the highlights of the last few months and then when you've had time to take it in you can ask any one of us any questions you like.'

'Alright,' she nodded.

'My dad didn't kill my mom, he injured her but she escaped the fire and survived. She returned to Mercy the same time as I did last year and she is responsible for the murders that took place.'

'What?' Tommy gasped.

'This is where it gets really sticky,' Olivia replied apologetically. 'I won't go into details now but basically she was killing those men as sacrifices to raise a demon.'

'Oh come on,' Tommy laughed, 'this is getting ridiculous, a demon?'

'I've seen it,' Jake told him seriously. 'I was there when Isabel West raised it; I wouldn't have believed it unless I'd seen it with my own eyes.'

'After that night my mom and the demon disappeared and we don't know exactly where they are or what they want. To be honest we haven't really had time to look for them because as you are already aware, Veronica,' she addressed the pale quiet woman, 'Mercy was suddenly overrun with the spirits of the dead and that became our main priority.'

'You know why they're here though, don't you?'

'Yes we do,' she looked back at Tommy, 'and just try to run with it okay?'

He indicated for her to continue.

'In order for me to explain what is going on you need to understand one thing... everything's real.'

'I don't understand,' Veronica frowned.

'Magic, spirits, demons, Gods, Goddesses, every myth and folk tale that has ever been told came from a real supernatural creature that actually existed.'

'Okay,' Veronica answered slowly.

'Charon, the Ferryman from Greek mythology is not only real but he is missing.'

'Who the hell is Charon?' Tommy frowned. 'Sorry but I'm not up to date on my Greek mythology' he added sarcastically.

'Charon ferried the souls of the dead to the underworld,' Veronica explained.

'Exactly,' Olivia nodded in approval. 'Because Charon is missing the doorway to the spirit world has been left open and spirits have been returning to the world of the living. The problem is, it's only a matter of time before other creatures from the underworld figure out there is a doorway to the human world open and they start filtering through.'

'This is nuts,' Tommy suddenly stood. 'I'm sorry but you guys are just letting your imagination run away with you. I'm prepared to accept the whole witchcraft thing but time travel? Gods and Goddesses? It's not real, seriously you guys need help.'

He stalked angrily towards the door, half convinced he was the butt of a really weird joke.

'Sorry,' Louisa sighed, 'I'll talk to him.'

Olivia watched as they both headed out of the room and after a few moments she heard the front door slam.

'Well that went well,' Olivia replied dryly, 'Veronica?'

'I...' she stared at the label on the bottle she was still holding, 'I...want to go home if you don't mind.'

'I'll take you,' Jake told her gently.

'Thank you,' she murmured absently.

Olivia watched silently as she too disappeared out

of the room followed by Jake.

She sighed heavily as Theo wrapped his arms around her.

'Did we do the right thing by telling them the truth?'

'There's no right or wrong answer to that,' he kissed her softly, 'we did what we thought was for the best. It wasn't fair to ask Louisa to keep lying to her husband and as Veronica seemed to be caught up in the middle of all of this she deserved to know what she was getting involved in.'

'I suppose,' she relaxed into his body. 'I don't think she'll want to speak to me after this and Tommy will want to have us all committed.'

'Don't be so sure,' he murmured, 'maybe she'll come around…maybe they both will.'

14.

Theo rolled over and stretched out but instead of finding his soft warm woman he encountered a very enthusiastic fur ball. Happy that Theo was now awake Beau jumped up and clambered all over him with soft paws, nuzzling his face and licking him.

'Cut it out Beau,' Theo pushed him back and sat up, looking around. 'Where's Olivia?'

Beau gave a joyful bark as if in answer to Theo's question and jumping down off the bed he scrambled out of the room. Theo stretched then reached down and grabbed his sweatpants off the floor and pulled them on. As he trotted down the stairs pulling his t-shirt over his head he realized the house was silent. Rubbing his face sleepily he headed towards the kitchen where Beau was dancing expectantly in front of the back door.

'Hey Boy,' he reached down and petted him before unlocking the door and watching him scramble down the steps.

He turned towards the smell of coffee and poured himself a cup. Picking up the note Olivia had left propped against the coffee machine he smiled in amusement.

'Running out of coffee, gone shopping, back soon xxx.'

Filling up Beau's food bowl and letting him back into the kitchen he turned and headed towards his makeshift studio. He'd found that for the last few days he had a painting turning over and over in his mind. He still wasn't sure exactly what it was yet, it felt like a dream that he'd forgotten and couldn't quite piece together. But he usually found that if he picked up a paintbrush whatever was subconsciously bothering him would end up on the canvas sooner or later.

Dropping his coffee down on the table he moved over to the canvases stacked against the wall, intending to find either a clean one or something he could paint over. He flicked through them idly until he reached one that made his blood run cold. Pulling it out he set it on the easel and stared at it in disbelief.

The portrait of Mary Alcott Beckett stared back at him with cold hard accusing eyes as he felt his heart thump wildly in his chest. He'd burned this portrait, he'd taken it outside and burned it, burying the ashes beneath the snow. There was no way it could be back here amongst his things and yet there it was, pristine and whole as if it had only been painted the day before.

'She's not going to be ignored.'

Theo jumped at the familiar voice behind him and spun around. Sam sat comfortably in Theo's favorite shabby chair beneath the curved window looking at Theo with sympathy.

'What are you talking about?'

'Your wife Theo, she is not going to be ignored and she is not going to let you destroy that painting. You are going to have to face the truth and deal with her.'

'What are you doing down here anyway?' Theo scowled irritably. 'Shouldn't you be in bed resting?'

Sam grinned, his face a kaleidoscope of varying shades of bruising. The swelling in and around his eye had mostly subsided and he was at least able to see out of it once again. His fingers were still bound together in splints and one arm was bandaged across his ribs but otherwise he appeared to be on the mend.

'I'll be back in bed before Olivia returns,' he chuckled. 'I wouldn't want to deprive her of the opportunity to fuss over me.'

Theo retrieved a hammer and turning the painting over he used the claw to yank out the nails holding the painting to the frame.

'Are you feeling better?' Theo asked as he dropped the discarded nails onto the table.

'I've had worse,' he shrugged.

'I don't suppose you are going to tell us what happened to you?'

'No,' Sam replied. 'I can't, but I am grateful to you both for taking care of me.'

Theo peeled the painting from the frame and rolled it up.

'I'll be leaving soon,' Sam told him.

Theo slotted the rolled up painting into a leather tube and set it in the corner of the room, before turning back to face Sam and studying him intently. He'd been with them for days and he'd healed a lot quicker than any normal person would have. That in itself raised a lot of questions but the truth was he owed Sam, he'd saved him and brought him to Olivia. If he needed to keep his secrets Theo would respect that and help him, with no questions asked.

'Olivia won't be pleased.'

'Olivia likes to mother everyone, whether she realizes it or not,' Sam smiled. 'She'll get over it, besides pretty soon you both are going to have your hands full.'

'You know you're really annoying when you do that' Theo frowned, 'giving us cryptic little comments but not actually helping.'

'I know,' Sam sighed, 'I get that it must be very frustrating for you. I wish I could do more but I can't risk changing anything and by helping you there is a risk I could inadvertently influence decisions you will have to make, which may ultimately change the time line. Everything that happens from now on will lead up to a fixed point in time. That event has to happen and I cannot interfere no matter how much I want to. I know it's frustrating but eventually you will understand.'

'This event, does it have to do with the Ferryman? Can you at least tell me that?'

'He is the catalyst; it all begins with him and snowballs from there. You have to find him.'

'I know,' Theo replied, 'but we don't know where to start and I'm guessing that's one of the things you can't help us with.'

Sam simply smiled at him.

'I will give you one hint,' Sam answered carefully after a moment. 'Everything is connected, just think of everything that is going on at the moment in your lives as threads of a much larger tapestry. Once they are all woven together they will form a larger picture.'

'That doesn't really help,' Theo frowned.

'It's the best I can do,' he smiled apologetically, 'and she is one of the threads you need to deal with.'

'Who?'

Sam indicated the easel behind him and as Theo turned he swore silently. The canvas he had just taken so much care to remove and store away in the leather tube was now once more firmly attached to the frame and staring back at him.

'She's not going to be ignored,' Sam told him, 'so tell Olivia about her.'

'If I do will Mary stop plaguing me?'

'That I honestly don't know,' he shook his head. 'If she escaped through the doorway with the other spirits it's possible she has her own agenda regarding you but it will affect Olivia too. She needs to know that Charlotte is not the only spirit loose in her home.'

'That's easier said than done,' Theo replied.

'Now's your chance,' Sam grinned and disappeared as Theo heard the front door open.

Theo took the painting down from the easel and tucked it back against the wall behind several other canvases, just as Olivia wandered into the room with a bag of groceries.

'Hey,' she smiled.

'Hey,' he turned back towards her.

'Did you check on Sam?'

'Yes,' Theo smiled, 'he's fine. He's doing a lot better than I expected considering it's only been a few days.'

'I know' she nodded, 'it's incredible the rate at which he's healing. Louisa said she'd drop by later and remove his stitches and the splints on his fingers.'

'Is Tommy coming over with her?'

Olivia shook her head slowly.

'I'm sorry Theo,' she felt really bad for him. He and Tommy had started to cultivate a really good friendship and she felt almost as if she had come between them. 'I think he's struggling to believe the things we told him.'

'I'm guessing you haven't heard from Veronica either? Theo asked.

'No,' she sighed, dropping the heavy bag down on the table. 'There's really not much more I can do but leave her alone. She knows where to find me if she wants to talk.'

Theo turned to look thoughtfully out of the window. She could see something was troubling him but again he seemed disinclined to share it with her. There were just too many secrets between them, too much left unsaid and she hadn't helped matters by avoiding things she should have discussed with him months ago.

'Theo,' she sighed, 'are you happy here with me?'

He turned back to her with a puzzled expression.

'Of course I am.'

'It's just that, we were kind of thrown together into a really intense situation and naturally a relationship developed between us but I want you to know you have a choice. You don't have to stay here with me because you feel as though you should or because I am familiar. You can choose any life you want; it doesn't necessarily have to be with me.'

'You still don't believe that I love you, do you?'

'It's not that,' she frowned shaking her head. 'I do know that you care about me but when all is said and done we really don't know each other that well.'

'You tell everyone your favorite colour is blue,' he said softly, 'but it's really pink, you just don't want people to know because you don't want them to see you as girly and vulnerable. You love spaghetti and you only ever drink half a cup of tea. You like to read romance novels when you think no one is looking. You cry at the happy parts in movies. You love the ocean but don't like being on boats. On stormy nights you like to stand outside in the dark and close your eyes so that you can listen to the wind in the trees. You love *San Giorgio at Dusk* by Monet and *Starry Night* by Van Gogh. You're stubborn but kind.' He stepped closer to her, his voice low and hypnotic, 'you love me but you won't admit it to yourself because you are afraid that I'll betray you...' he reached out to her and pulled her closer with gentle hands. 'You want me to stay but you'll push me away because you're expecting me to leave.'

'Theo...' the words caught in her throat as she looked up into his dark eyes.

'I love you Olivia,' he traced her jaw lightly with his fingertips, 'I want to stay here with you for the rest of my life proving it to you. I know you and I know exactly what I want, the question is…what is it that you want?'

She drew in a shaky breath, her body felt soft and fragile as if he held her bare soul in his hands. He saw her the way no one else ever had or ever could.

'I want you to stay with me,' she whispered.

'Always,' he breathed as his lips closed over hers, and cradling her face gently in his hands he took her under, deep into a place where only she existed. That was her magic; the spell she wove over him and his heart without even realizing she was doing it and he was helpless to resist.

'Livy,' he broke away breathing hard with the need for her, his gaze flicking across the room to the stack of canvases against the wall, 'there is something I need to tell you…'

The silence of the room was suddenly broken by the blare of her ring tone.

Pulling back she slid her phone from her pocket, frowning when she saw the caller ID.

'Jackson?' she answered with a puzzled expression, 'are you okay?'

She listened to him for a moment and then cursed lightly under her breath.

'What?' Theo mouthed.

She held up her hand as she tried to listen to Jackson.

'Okay we'll be right there.'

She hung up the phone and turned to Theo.

'We have a problem,' she frowned. 'It seems the exorcism didn't work, the spirit is back and apparently angrier than before.'

'Damn it,' Theo swore, 'I'll go finish getting dressed.'

She nodded as he darted out of the room. She dropped the grocery bag in the kitchen without even bothering to unpack it and headed into the library. First she scooped a small silver framed mirror off the mantelpiece and stuffed it into her bag, then turning to the desk she rifled through the drawers until she came up with a length of cord which she also thrust into her bag.

'What's that?' Theo asked as he hurried back into the library, already in jeans and boots and pulling a sweater over his t-shirt.

'Supplies,' she headed past him into the hallway and handed him his coat. 'Given the level of the spirit problem we have in Mercy I've spent some time looking up ways to keep them under control. We can't call a priest every time a bad one starts playing up and apparently that didn't work anyway.'

'Do you know what you're doing?'

'No,' she smiled, 'we're going to do what we do best.'

'And that is?'

'Wing it,' she sighed, 'and hope for the best.'

'I'm not exactly sure what you mean by that,' Theo frowned, 'but it doesn't exactly fill me with confidence.'

He followed her out of the door moving quickly down the steps to the car.

'Here.'

He looked up at her just in time to see her toss something in his direction. He reached up and caught the small object easily and when he opened his palm his face creased into a puzzled frown as he recognized her car keys.

'You drive,' she smiled.

'Really?' he looked up at her as she opened the passenger door.

'Yeah, just be gentle with her,' she replied, 'my car is a little old lady compared to Tommy's beast of a four wheel drive.'

Theo grinned as he jogged around to the driver's side and slid into the seat folding in his long legs so they were almost under his chin.

'You adjust the seat here,' she showed him the

little lever and waited for him to adjust his mirrors. 'We're probably going to have to get you your own car,' she mused thoughtfully.

Theo turned to her and smiled joyfully, like a little boy with a new toy. She shook her head and smiled as they slowly pulled out and headed down the driveway but by the time they pulled up in the parking lot outside The Salted Bone, Theo was frowning.

'I don't like your car.'

'That's because you've been spoiled learning to drive in a brand new truck,' she laughed as she climbed out. 'Don't be such a snob or Dolly will get offended.'

'Dolly?'

'My car.'

'You named your car Dolly?'

Before she could answer Jackson opened the back door, hovering anxiously.

'Are you alright Jackson?' Theo asked as they headed in.

'No, I'm pretty damn far from alright,' he scowled as he headed towards the main bar area with both of them following in his wake.

As the corridor opened up into the main space, they could see the repairs were well underway. The bar had been sanded down, repaired and re-varnished. The mirrors and lighting behind the bar had all been replaced along with all the glass shelving. The walls all had new drywall which was just waiting for a coat of paint and all the dark wood paneling had been replaced and was once again glossy and unblemished. In the centre of the room brand new wooden tables, chairs and bar stool were stacked neatly, all covered in plastic.

'The repair work seems to be going well,' Olivia noted.

'Aye,' Jackson sighed, 'problem is the insurance wouldn't pay out as I couldn't adequately explain how the damage had occurred in the first place.'

'You've had to pay for all this yourself?' Olivia turned to him in surprise.

'That's right,' he frowned. 'I've got damn near every cent I own sunk into this place. If that bloody bastard tears it apart again I can't afford to fix it. I'll have to close the pub, I'll lose everything.'

'That won't happen Jackson,' Olivia told him gently.

'Why don't you tell us what happened?' Theo asked.

'I came in about ten minutes before I called you,' he shook his head. 'I knew something was off the second I walked through the door, there was that same unpleasant smell and the air felt heavy and cold. As I walked into the kitchen area there was a rattling and a knife flew straight at me; I barely ducked in time.'

Olivia looked up and noticed the thin knick at the edge of his jaw.

'I ran outside and called you. I figured it would cause less damage if I wasn't in here for it to take pot-shots at.'

'And there is definitely no one else in here except us?' Olivia frowned as she turned and scanned the room.

'No, none of the staff are due in this afternoon and I cancelled the contractors who were supposed to be working later, why?'

'I just thought I heard something,' she murmured continuing to look around the room.

The silence was suddenly split by a scream.

'I thought you said there was no one else here?' she spun back towards Jackson.

'No one is meant to be,' he turned towards the bar area.

The scream came again.

'Where is it coming from?' Theo asked urgently.

'The beer cellar.'

Jackson took off, pulling up the hinged section of

the bar that led to the area behind. He ran to the far end and wrenched open a heavy wooden door, moving quickly down the steep stone steps into the cold alcohol scented air. Huddled in the corner was Jackson's red-haired waitress Kaitlin.

'Katy love,' Jackson breathed heavily, 'what on earth are you doing here?'

'I was taking inventory,' she panted.

'But that was supposed to be yesterday.'

'I had an appointment yesterday afternoon, I figured it would be okay if I came in early this morning to do it instead.'

'You've been here all this time on your own?'

Olivia focused on Kaitlin's pale face. Despite the cold air of the cellar her face was coated in a thin sheen of perspiration and her breathing was labored, but not in fear Olivia realized. The scream they had heard had not been one of fear but one of pain. Olivia's gaze slid down Kaitlin's swollen belly to the leggings she wore underneath her smock style dress. Although the leggings were dark she noticed an even darker wet stain down the inner thighs. She dropped down to her knees as Kaitlin's wide green eyes focused on her.

'Kaitlin,' Olivia said softly, 'how far apart are your contractions?'

'What?' Jackson asked in panic.

'I don't know,' Kaitlin shook her head, they're too close I keep losing count.'

She grasped her belly and cried out again as Olivia took her hand and allowed her to squeeze hard.

'It's okay,' she soothed her calmly, 'just breath through it Kaitlin, just concentrate on the sound of my voice and breathe.'

As the vicious contraction passed she let out a deep hiss of breath.

'They started so suddenly,' she breathed heavily, looking at Olivia, 'I felt my waters break and it came on so quickly. I couldn't get back up the stairs to call for help and my phone is in my purse in the bar.'

'It's alright,' Olivia soothed her, 'you're not alone anymore.'

'It's too early,' she shook her head her eyes wide with fear. 'It's too early the baby isn't due for another eight weeks.'

'You're thirty two weeks?'

Kaitlin nodded.

'It'll be alright,' Olivia assured her, 'it is a little early but your baby still has a chance of survival if we can get you straight to the hospital, okay?'

'Okay,' she gasped as another contraction gripped her womb ruthlessly.

'Theo, I doubt we'll get a signal down here, can you go up to the bar and call for an ambulance?'

He nodded and headed up the steps.

'I'm so sorry Katy love,' Jackson dropped down next to her and took her hand. 'If I'd known you were down here I'd never have left you on your own.'

'I know that Jackson,' she growled through the pain, 'it's not your fault.'

As Theo made it to the top of the steps the door slammed shut violently. Olivia and Jackson turned to look as Theo braced his shoulder against the wood and shoved it hard. After a few moments he headed back down the steps.

'It won't open,' he shook his head.

Olivia opened her mouth to speak but paused as her breath was expelled as a phantom-like mist. The hair on the back of her neck started to prickle and her nostrils were suddenly filled with the pungent stench of ozone.

'Dammit, not now,' she breathed as Kaitlin let loose another cry of pain.

She stood and turned to Theo who was looking anxiously around the small room.

'Livy, there's no way we can get her out,' he

whispered, 'it's trapped us in here.'

Olivia looked up into Theo's eyes. 'You and Jackson need to take care of Kaitlin.'

'And what about you?' he gripped her arm as she turned away.

'I'll be fine,' she replied, 'I'll keep him away from you for as long as possible but you need to help her. That baby is about to be born whether we like it or not.'

'I don't know anything about child-birthing.'

'And you think I do?' She breathed heavily, 'look we just have to do the best we can. Childbirth is the most natural thing in the world, just let it happen. All you need to do is keep her calm and make her feel safe okay?'

'What are you going to do?' he asked.

She stepped back from him and smiled as her hands burst into silver flames.

'I'm about to see if my Spirit fire will work.'

Jackson's eyes widened in awe as he caught sight of Olivia. Her skin rippled with power as her magic flooded the small cellar, and he angled his body in front of Kaitlin so she couldn't see what Olivia was doing.

Theo stood watching silently as she let her fire loose. It fanned out and spun around them until it blurred into a thin silvery shield encasing them protectively.

'What's that light?' Kaitlin gasped through the pain.

'Nothing Katy love,' Jackson soothed her.

Theo turned back to them both and dropped to his knees in front of Kaitlin.

'Oh God,' she cried out, 'I feel like I want to push.'

'Okay just hold on Katy love, we've got you,' Jackson smoothed her sweaty hair back from her face. 'Kaitlin?'

Her green eyes locked on Theo's as she let out another deep groan.

'This baby is not going to wait,' he told her gently.

'I'm going to remove your leggings and we're going to make you more comfortable okay?'

She nodded as her breath came out in short pants.

'Jackson, are those towels behind you?'

Jackson looked behind and noticed the three big plastic wrapped bales of brand new bar towels.

'They are, but they're a bit small.'

'It's all we've got, tuck one of them behind her like a pillow and open up one of the others, we'll spread them out on the floor.'

Jackson nodded and set to work as Theo carefully removed Kaitlin's boots and leggings.

Kaitlin let out another cry as Theo laid his hand on her stomach and felt it tightening viciously.

'Okay just breathe through the pain.'

'I need to push,' she panted.

'Okay,' he nodded, 'with the next contraction I want you to push okay?'

She nodded and pushed herself up onto her elbows as Jackson wrapped his arm around her to hold her up.

'Have you done this before?' Jackson whispered.

'A couple of times,' Theo replied carefully...'with cows.'

'Cows?'

'I grew up on a farm,' he answered.

He turned his attention back to Kaitlin as he felt her stomach harden beneath his hand once more.

'Alright here we go Kaitlin, are you ready to push.'

She nodded, unable to catch her breath enough to speak through the pain.

'Okay then, on the count of three I want you to push, ready?'

She nodded again desperately.

'One...two...three...push'

She let out a scream and she bore down as hard as she could.'

Olivia watched from the other side of the silver dome she'd placed over them. No matter what happened they would be safe in there. She shivered as the temperature plummeted again. She stepped further into the small room, her gaze trailing over the barrels and plastic tubes which fed the alcohol up into the bar taps. He was here she could feel him, the same roiling rage and anger from the last time she'd been in the pub. She felt a nudge against the shield and turned back to look. The shield rippled but held fast. She felt a surge of anger and the invisible force pushed harder against the shield. Again it held, this time the presence hurled itself against the shield shrieking in impotent fury when it held strong.

She watched calmly as the presence flickered and coalesced into a form and when it turned to look at her with silvery hate-filled eyes she saw the same pale skinned man who had hurt Fiona.

She widened her stance and her hands burst into silver flames. When she looked at him her mouth curved slightly and her eyes flashed.

'If you want them you son of a bitch...you're going to have to go through me first.'

15.

Olivia felt a curious detachment from her emotions, just as she had that day in the woods when she'd conjured Hell fire to stop the Hell Hounds. No longer aware of the cold she focused on the malevolent spirit in front of her, pleased that she seemed to be drawing his attention away from Theo and the others. His cold furious eyes locked on her as he turned in her direction. Unlike Charlotte, who always seemed to move with jerky movements, he drifted away from her shield slowly and smoothly, circling the room as if he were stalking her.

She felt him lash out at her, knocking her back a few paces. For a second she skidded along the cold stone floor of the cellar but still she drew down her power like armor and punched out. The spirit's head snapped back as if it had been struck and its eerie silver eyes widened in surprise. Seizing the advantage, she felt her fire flow down her arms like liquid. Her hand flexed and gripped instinctively as she felt her fingers wrap around a handle.

Looking down she found she held a long lean whip which glowed brightly with silver flames. A strange calmness washed over her as she watched the vicious spirit stalk her warily.

He lashed out and as her head snapped to the side she tasted the metallic tang of blood in her mouth. Her eyes flashed dangerously and she began to circle the whip, slowly gaining in speed. When she lashed it in his direction the spirit howled in pain as a great tear appeared in the flesh of his torso. She lashed out again and this time a slash mark appeared down the side of his face.

He bared his teeth in fury and rushed her. This time when she flicked the whip out it wrapped around him, winding round and round his body until his arms were pinned to his sides and he was held captive. Olivia reached quickly into her bag and removed the mirror. He shrieked as she held up the small glass and tried to advert his face, but it was too late. His pale ghostly flesh seemed to stretch and pull as if it were being sucked into the mirror. He howled and pulled back as much as he could but the silver flames of her magic held him fast. Olivia moved closer, resolutely holding the mirror up and watched as he was dragged into the glass, shrieking in fury.

Olivia glanced down at the reflection but instead of her own face, it was his reflected back, beating against the glass. Pulling the cord from her bag she began to wind it carefully around the mirror muttering quietly as she did so.

With magic I bind you spirit of the deep,
Within the glass your anger keep,
Now be still and no harm to cause,
Time be still and give you pause,
With magic I bind you,
With power I hold you,
Sleep now and wait,
An eternity to forge your fate,
As I will so mote it be.'

She finished wrapping the cord around the glass, making sure to bind it tightly. It was the best she could do under the circumstances. It might not hold him forever and she would probably need to take extra precautions to prevent him from escaping. It was beyond her power or experience to banish him completely but perhaps when they found Charon she could hand the spirit over and he could send him back to the afterlife for her. She slipped the mirror into her bag and as she looked up at the silvery shield in front of her it began to pulse and fade.

Kaitlin let out another ear piercing scream and Theo felt a warm rush of blood gush over his hands. He looked up in concern and met Jackson's equally worried eyes.

'What is it?' Kaitlin gasped, 'what's wrong.'

'Nothing Katy love, everything's just fine,' Jackson soothed her.

'Okay Kaitlin I can see the head, on the next contraction push hard.'

She nodded as she felt the muscles in her abdomen lock viciously. Screaming in pain she pushed.

'Okay the head's out, on the next contraction just one more push.'

'I can't,' she panted as she fell back against Jackson.

'Yes you can,' Theo shook her face lightly as he felt the pain and exhaustion taking her under. 'Kaitlin look at me, just one more push okay.'

She felt an agonizing pain lance through her womb and as a scream tore from her lips the tiny infant was expelled from her body in a thick rush of blood and fluids. She fell back against Jackson, her eyes closed and her breathing shallow.

Kaitlin?' he shook her lightly but couldn't rouse her. Laying her back gently against the towel bale he looked up at Theo who was cradling a tiny perfectly formed child. The umbilical cord was still attached and the

239

baby, barely the length of Theo's hand as he held it carefully in his palms, was unmoving.

'He's not breathing,' Theo massaged his chest gently.

'Isn't there anything you can do?'

Theo looked up, his sad eyes meeting Jackson's and shook his head slowly.

Olivia watched silently, her heart squeezing painfully in her chest when she suddenly felt a warm familiar presence standing at her shoulder. The calming fragrance of woodlands and spring flowers washed over her.

'Isn't there anything you can do?' Olivia whispered.

The presence did not answer but simply moved towards Theo. He looked up, his face etched in sorrow, and his breath caught in his throat as he beheld the Goddess Diana. Jackson's mouth fell open at the sight of the incredibly beautiful woman who had suddenly appeared in the cold dingy cellar. She almost seemed to carry her own light with her and it reminded him of sun dappled trees. The scent of her wrapped around his throat and filled his nostrils making him think of summer meadows and wildflowers. He noticed with a start that wherever she walked a thick carpet of grass and flowers grew under her sandaled feet.

'Give me the child, Theodore,' her voice was soft and musical but carried a hint of command.

Silently he held out the tiny lifeless body to her. She plucked a long blade of grass from beneath her feet. It shimmered in the light as she wrapped it around the cord close to the baby's belly and tied it off. Withdrawing her hunting knife from her wide leather belt she severed the cord easily and dropped the knife back into its sheath. Taking the tiny little boy with gentle hands she cradled him lovingly. Leaning closer she pressed her lips to his tiny perfect little mouth and for a second Theo could have sworn he saw her breath, warm and golden, pass from her mouth to his.

'Wake up little one," she whispered.

His tiny chest heaved once and then again as he drew in his first breath and let out a weak cry.

Instead of passing the baby back to Theo she turned to Jackson and handed the child to him. He pulled off his sweater and wrapped it around the boy, cradling him gently against his chest.

'This child is very important,' she told him softly. 'Make sure he is well cared for.'

'I will, I swear,' he whispered in awe.

'What about Kaitlin?' Theo asked as he looked down at her pale unconscious form.

Diana leaned forward and placed her hand on Kaitlin's stomach. The blood which had still been oozing between her thighs, slowed to almost nothing.

'She will live,' Diana told him. 'Her womb will never again bear life but she will have her own path to walk.'

'Thank you,' Olivia nodded.

Diana turned, her eyes locked on Olivia's and then with a small inclination of her head she disappeared.

Theo pulled off his coat and laid it over Kaitlin as she slept.

'I'll go call an ambulance,' he climbed to his feet and headed up the stairs to the stout door which was now open a crack.

'Jesus, Mary and Joseph,' Jackson breathed.

'Wrong religion,' Olivia smiled.

'Who was that?'

'That was the Goddess Diana,' she told him softly.

'Does this happen to you regularly then?'

'She's been known to drop in on me from time to time,' she smiled.

He looked at her intensely as if he were seeing her through new eyes, still with the same affection but now mixed with a profound respect.

'Thank you Olivia.'

'For what?'

For everything,' he replied simply.

'You're welcome,' she touched his arm gently as she leaned over to get a good look at the baby. 'He's a sweetheart isn't he.'

'Aye,' Jackson nodded, 'I reckon Adam would be real proud.'

'I think he would,' she agreed.

'Ambulance is on its way,' Theo headed back down the steps.

'Good,' she nodded.

'What happened to the spirit?'

'Got him locked up tight,' she patted her bag. 'I have a few ideas of what to do with him when we get home.'

'He won't come back will he?' Jackson asked.

Olivia shook her head. 'No,' she promised, 'we'll make sure he doesn't this time, I swear.'

He nodded gratefully as they heard sirens drawing near.

Olivia and Theo disappeared up into the bar to pour themselves a well-deserved drink and to keep out from under the feet of the paramedics as they filled the cramped cellar.

'God,' Olivia took a sip of her whiskey and blew out a deep breath. 'I feel exhausted.'

Theo downed the contents of his glass and dropped it onto the bar.

'I know,' he agreed, 'me too.'

'I need a vacation,' she sighed longingly.

'A vacation?' he gave her a puzzled look.

'Yes, you and me on a beach sipping Mai Tai's and watching the sun go down.'

'I don't understand any of what you just said.'

She laughed in delight. 'A vacation is when you go

242

to a different place, preferably another country and relax; basically do nothing for a couple of weeks.'

'That doesn't sound like fun,' Theo frowned.

'That's because you can't picture it,' she smiled. 'Just imagine you and me on a tiny little island surrounded by a turquoise blue Indian ocean and white glittering sands. You in a pair of board shorts, me in a bikini, curled into each other on a hammock strung between two palm trees.' She sighed in pleasure lost in her own little fantasy, 'our feet trailing in the warm water as the tide comes in…heaven.'

'I'm still not sure what you're talking about.'

'Here,' she beckoned him closer as she pulled out her phone, connected to the internet and began searching. The picture she finally showed him was almost exactly what she had been imagining with white sands, palm trees and clear ocean.

'Is this a real place?' his eyebrows rose.

'Yes,' she smiled, 'this is the Maldives just southwest of India and Sri Lanka.'

'And we can go here?'

'I don't see why not,' she shrugged. 'After we've dealt with the Charon problem why shouldn't we disappear for a couple of weeks?'

'What was the other thing you mentioned you'd be wearing?'

'A bikini?'

'Yes,' he nodded, 'what's one of those?'

Grinning to herself she scrolled back through her phone and brought up another image.

'That's a bikini.'

Theo's eyes widened as he took in the scandalous image.

'Do you own one of these?' his eyes swept over her hungrily.

'Actually I own several,' her mouth curved.

He grabbed her and pulled her in close, his face

nuzzling into her neck as he breathed in the scent of her.

'I believe I would enjoy a vacation,' he murmured

She laughed lightly. 'I thought you might say that.'

They looked up as two paramedics wheeled Kaitlin through on a stretcher, followed by a third who cradled the baby gently in a blanket. Jackson followed behind hovering nervously over both of them. Handing Theo his coat as he passed them he shrugged into his own.

'I'm going to head to the hospital with them both and make sure they're okay.'

'You do that,' Olivia leaned over and kissed Jackson's cheek softly, 'you're a good man Jackson.'

'So people keep telling me,' he shook his head in amusement. 'I don't suppose you'd mind locking up the pub for me?'

'We'll take care of it,' Theo assured him.

By the time they returned to the house they were both tired and hungry but Theo wanted a shower, to wash away the dirt and blood from the morning's unexpected events. Olivia headed for the kitchen to make sandwiches and leaving Theo's on a plate on the side, she took one upstairs for Sam.

Knocking lightly, she stuck her head around the door but instead of finding him in bed she saw he was standing by the window fully dressed and gazing pensively down at the lake.

'Hey,' Olivia spoke softly.

'Hello Olivia,' he turned and smiled.

'I guess you're feeling better.'

'I am,' he replied. 'Louisa stopped by while you were out and removed the stitches and splints. I'm a little sore but other than that there seems to be no lingering injuries.'

He took the sandwich she offered and bit into it.

'Sam,' she sighed shaking her head, 'I'm worried about you.'

'Are you now,' he sat down on the side of the bed regarding her thoughtfully as he ate.

'I know you can't tell me what happened to you but I know almost nothing about you.'

'I know it's not fair and I know I'm asking a lot, that I'm asking you to trust me without giving much in return but all that is about to change.'

'What do you mean?'

He finished his sandwich and brushed the crumbs from his fingers.

'I have to go,' he murmured, his eyes distant. 'I've already been gone for too long.'

'Gone from where?'

'Nice try,' he chuckled before sighing. He wandered to the window and once again gazed out down to the lake as if watching something only he could see.

Knowing he couldn't tell her much, that he had strict rules he had to abide by she hadn't expected him to answer. So when he quietly started speaking, she held her breath, afraid to break the spell.

'In my time we are at war,' he murmured. 'Heaven went up like a tinderbox, chaos spread to earth; the Hell dimensions rose up and everyone in between was caught up in it. The humans barely notice what is going on right before their eyes, that every day is a fight to survive, to save their world, to save their families…and ours.'

'Do you have a family?' Olivia whispered.

When he turned back to her his eyes flashed with pain.

'I have to go now,' he crossed the room to stand close to her. Wrapping his arms around her he hugged her close and dropped a sweet brotherly kiss on her forehead. 'Thank you for taking care of me.'

She nodded silently as he pulled back and looked down into her eyes.

'Stay close to Theo no matter what happens' he told her ominously, 'and find Charon.'

Before she could answer he disappeared leaving her standing in an empty room with the faint scent of him lingering in the air.

With a sigh of frustration she turned and walked out of the room heading towards the attic. There was one thing she needed to do before anything else and that was to deal with the haunted mirror she currently had stashed in her purse. She hurried up the stairs to the third floor and opened the door to the attic, flicking on the light as she went. Shivering in the cold air she headed further into the room, carefully avoiding piles of all sorts of strange items. She remembered vividly as a child playing in the attic with Jake and Louisa. It had been a place of wonder, an Aladdin's cave, or a Turkish Bazaar, and even a smugglers cave. They had spent hours playing amongst hundreds of years' worth of her family history, dressing up in vintage clothes that today were probably worth a lot of money.

But there was one item she remembered, something they used to play with all the time, that she was specifically looking for. She pushed an old rusted birdcage out of the way propping it next to a broken lamp with the shade missing. Shoving aside a couple of stacked boxes her eyes landed on a small black rectangular box, heavy and made from iron. She dragged it across the floor and sat down in front of it. It was not much bigger than a shoe box, but slightly deeper. The whole box was decorated with deeply etched circular symbols and on the lid there was a heavy black metal key inserted into the lock. She grasped the key with curious fingers and turned and the lock released with a barely audible click, allowing Olivia to open the lid.

When she spied the contents she sat back and smiled. A childish treasure map was rolled up inside along with her grandmother's pearls and brooch, and also there was a handful of dimes and quarters. She scooped them out and turned them over in her hands remembering that the last time they'd used this box they'd been playing pirates. She took the map out and unrolled it, laughing lightly at Jake's seven-year-old version of a skull and crossbones which looked more like a pumpkin on skis. He'd always insisted on drawing the maps she smiled fondly.

'Hey,' Theo's voice interrupted her thoughts, 'what are you doing?'

'Looking for this,' she smiled.

'A picture of a turnip sitting on chopsticks?' he looked over her shoulder at the drawing.

'No,' she laughed, 'the box.'

'Why?'

'Help me take it downstairs and I'll explain.'

He grabbed her hands and hauled her to her feet before bending and easily lifting the box. She followed him down the stairs, closing the door to the draughty attic and locking it before they headed towards the library. Theo set the box down on the desk amidst piles of books and papers and as Olivia glanced across at the fire it burst joyfully into flames.

'That's better,' she murmured as warmth began to spread through the room, 'it's getting cold again; I think we've got more snow heading our way.'

'Probably,' Theo agreed, 'so what's this box?'

'It was a box we used to play with as kids, something that's always stuck in my head,' she moved closer and ran her hands over the markings. 'To me it was just a really cool box we used to play with but it was only the other day when I was thinking about it I realized it's true purpose.'

'Which is?'

'I'm pretty certain it's a Maledictionem chest.'

'A what?'

'Maledictionem chest, it's Latin. It roughly translates to curse box. It's designed to hold or trap supernatural objects.'

'What sort of objects?'

'All sorts of things I guess, theoretically it's supposed to contain cursed objects, possessed objects and hopefully spirit traps.'

'Are you sure?' he frowned looking closer, 'it just looks like an ordinary chest.'

'Well it's made of iron to start with, which is supposed to affect spirits and some supernatural creatures and do you see these markings on the outside?'

Theo nodded.

'They're sigils. Sigil comes from the Latin word *sigillum* which means seal. They are basically seals that keep whatever is in the box trapped in there.'

She shook her head, laughing lightly under her breath as a thought occurred to her.

'What?'

'These boxes are extremely rare and very powerful and Nana used to let us use it for pirate treasure.'

'She sounds like a nice woman.'

'Yeah, she was,' Olivia murmured as she turned to retrieve the bound mirror from her purse.

Theo watched quietly as she placed the mirror carefully inside the chest and locked it, removing the key and dropping it into the desk drawer.

'Can you put it up there, on the top shelf.'

Theo nodded and placed it up high.

'That should stop anyone inadvertently stumbling across it.'

'Do you think it will hold him?'

'Yes, it should do,' she replied. 'Between the binding spell I used and the box it should keep him contained at least temporarily.'

'Temporarily?'

'I'm hoping that when we find Charon he'll know how to banish him back to the spirit world.'

'I hope you're right,' Theo frowned, 'I don't like the thought of having him trapped in the house.'

'I don't much care for the idea either,' Olivia shrugged, 'but better here than in the pub which will soon be full of walking, talking targets.'

'I guess so,' Theo mused, 'maybe we could ask Sam if he can take it someplace safer.

'Sam's gone,' Olivia told him.

'Already?'

'Yeah,' she nodded, 'but the last thing he said to me was that we need to find Charon.'

'He said pretty much the same thing to me the other day.'

'You know I love that everyone just keeps stating the obvious but no one is actually offering to help look for him.'

'I guess it's up to us then,' he frowned.

'Yes it is,' she picked up a heavy book from a stack near the fireplace and handed it to Theo. 'You start here.'

He turned it over in his hands and looked at the spine; it was a book on Greek mythology.

'We need to go right back to the beginning,' she told him, 'and find every single scrap of information or reference to Charon. If we can understand exactly what he is and how or why he might have disappeared, then we can start figuring out where to look.'

'That's very vague,' Theo replied doubtfully, 'how are we going to know if some kind of harm has befallen him or whether or not he just decided to take a vacation.'

Olivia smiled.

'Let's think about this logically. He has been the Ferryman for thousands of years, it's obviously a duty he takes very seriously. I can't see him just deciding to disappear for no reason and not only that I don't think Hades would allow it.'

'Then something obviously happened to make him abandon his post.'

'Maybe not abandon,' she murmured thoughtfully

249

as her gaze landed on the staff propped in the corner of the room. 'What if someone took him?'

'Kidnapped?'

'Possibly,' she replied, 'I mean if it were me and I knew I needed to disappear for a while I'd make sure all my affairs were in order before I left. Not only was the doorway to the otherworld left open so that the spirits could escape, but his boat was left drifting on the lake and his staff was found floating in the water. The whole thing suggests his departure was so abrupt it may not have been voluntary.'

'It does make sense,' Theo nodded, 'then I guess the question is who would want to kidnap the Ferryman?'

'I think if we work out the how, we may figure out the who.'

'So if we find out what his weaknesses are we may know how they were able to take him?'

That narrows down the list of suspects doesn't it? Olivia answered. 'Then if we figure out the who, we may figure out the where.'

'I guess we better get reading then,' he picked up another couple of books and settled himself on the sofa, while Olivia booted up her new laptop and began trawling through the internet hoping that somehow, between them, they would find something helpful.

Showered and changed, Jackson walked back into the hospital and headed straight for the NICU. The hour was fairly late but as he had accompanied Kaitlin and her son to the hospital earlier the staff seemed happy to let him through. He suspected that they had assumed he was the father; an assumption he didn't bother to correct as it would just make it more difficult to get in to see them both.

He stepped quietly into the NICU. The lighting was on low and the room was filled with what looked like giant baby fish tanks, big rectangular clear plastic incubators each occupied with a premature or sick child fighting for their lives. It made him feel strangely humbled and a little sad as he made his way quietly through to one in particular. He recognized the shock of red hair as Kaitlin sat in a wheelchair wrapped in a thick blue robe, staring down into the incubator.

'There you are now,' he whispered as he sat down next to her, 'how are you feeling darlin'?'

'Better,' she replied absently, 'tired and sore but it will pass soon, so they tell me.'

'Of course it will,' Jackson peered down into the tank, 'and how is your little man doing?'

'They tell me he's doing really well actually, for a baby born at thirty-two weeks on a dirty cellar floor.'

He turned to her as he caught the bitter edge of her tone.

'Well he's a fighter isn't he, like his father.'

'Didn't do Adam a lot of good either did it?' she turned accusing eyes on him, 'he's still dead.'

'Aye,' Jackson replied, 'but I know he'd be right pleased with his son. Have you named him yet?'

'No,' she turned back to the tank and stared again.

'What is it Katy love?'

She glanced at his piercing blue eyes, shifting uncomfortably.

'Whatever is going on in your mind, you can talk to me you know.'

She sighed. 'I don't think I'll make a very good mother, Jackson.'

'Of course you will,' he soothed her, 'you only feel this way as everything happened all of a sudden, it's a lot to take in. But your little man here, all he needs is love and someone to look up to.'

She blew out a slow breath.

'I didn't want to be pregnant, I didn't want a baby. After Adam died I felt like I should keep the baby because it's what he would've wanted but,' she paused shaking her head, 'I don't know how to do this Jackson. I don't know how to be someone's mom.'

'You'll learn just like every other new mother does,' he told her gently. 'You don't have to go through this alone, I'll be right there for anything you and the baby need.'

'You're a good man Jackson do you know that?' she replied quietly.

'Aye I may have heard it said a time or two,' he grinned, 'but it's always nice to be told.'

He patted her hand gently. 'Don't fret so Katy, you've had a very traumatic day, you don't have to decide your whole life tonight. Get some rest then tomorrow give the boy a name and you'll feel better for it.'

She nodded slowly as she beckoned one of the nurses over.

'I want to go back to my room now,' she murmured.

The nurse nodding sympathetically took hold of the handles and steered her wheelchair away from the baby.

Jackson watched her wheeled from the room before he turned back to the sleeping baby, marveling at his tiny toes and perfect nose. His diaper was so big it reached almost up to his armpits, his skinny little legs poking out either side covered with wrinkly skin, like a little old man. The little woolly hat covered most of his head and he was attached to several tubes but he seemed quite content. His skin had warmed up to a nice pink colour, unlike the sickly blue-tinged white he'd been when Theo had held the boy in his hands. The Goddess's words echoed in his head as he looked down at the child. She was right he was special.

The nurse returned to the room and headed towards Jackson.

'Is it alright if I stay a while, I won't be any trouble I promise,' he threw her his trademark smile.

'Sure,' she replied slightly dazed, charmed by his lilting brogue. 'You can touch him if you like. He's doing very well despite being so small; he's actually got very strong vitals. If you slip your hand through the hole there you can let him know you're close, they respond well to the contact.'

'Thank you.'

'No problem,' she smiled as she moved away to check on another incubator.

Jackson slipped his hand through the circular hole and reached out with trembling fingers to stroke his fragile hand. At his touch the baby's fingers instinctively flexed and grasped onto Jackson's fingertip.

'I know you don't know who I am yet,' Jackson whispered, 'but I knew your daddy. He was a good man too and I know he wishes he could be here with you but he can't because he had to go to heaven. But I don't want you to worry because I'll be watching out for you, for him.' The baby's fingers flexed again, squeezing feather light, almost as if he'd understood. Unable to look away Jackson sat watching over the tiny little boy knowing from this moment on his life had irrevocably changed and that he would do whatever he could to make sure Adam Miller's son was taken care of.

16.

Olivia slammed her new laptop shut with a growl of frustration. They'd been at it for nearly two days now and they'd barely found any useful information on Charon except the basics. Every resource and reference they found simply regurgitated the same few facts, Ferryman of the dead, coins to pay passage, blah blah blah.

She leaned back in her chair and rubbed her tired eyes. She had no idea how he appeared, if people could summon him or even if they could see him. Did they have to be dead to see him? It felt like she'd been banging her head against a wall for 48 hours straight and she was still none the wiser, only now she had a wicked headache brewing. With a sigh of defeat she slid out of her seat and headed to the kitchen for some aspirin.

As she grabbed a couple of pills from the bottle in the cupboard, a playful bark drew her attention. Turning towards the window over the sink she saw Theo out in the back yard throwing a stick for Beau. The puppy was joyfully diving face first into the deep snow to retrieve it. Smiling at the sight she absently took a clean glass from the drainer and turned the faucet on. Beau's antics could not distract her for long and as she downed the pills and placed the glass down on the side, her thoughts were once again drawn back to the problem of locating Charon. For a while Charlotte had been kind of steering them in the right direction, whilst scaring the crap out of them at the same time, but Olivia was forced to admit there was no way they would have worked out the spirit infestation was down to a three-thousand-year old Greek myth going missing. She frowned as she thought of Charlotte who, since the clock had been delivered to the house and they'd found her journal, seemed to have gone silent.

'If you're listening Charlotte,' Olivia murmured into the empty kitchen, 'I could really use some help finding Charon.'

The temperature in the kitchen suddenly plummeted and she watched as the faucet turned itself back on. Hot water gushed out and a great cloud of steam rose up, fogging up the window in front of the sink. Once it was completely misted over the faucet turned itself off again. The silence of the room was suddenly split by the squeaking sound of an invisible finger being dragged along the window, as letters began to appear on the cold pane of glass ......namtaod

'What the hell?' Olivia frowned, 'what on earth was namtaod?'

She stood for a moment, head tilted in concentration as she tried to decipher the strange cryptic message until Theo stomped back up the steps. He kicked the snow off his boots before stepping back into the kitchen, closely followed by Beau whose fur was now thoroughly soaked.

'Go dry off by the fire boy,' Theo told him and he scampered off towards the fire in the library as if he'd understood every word out of Theo's mouth. 'Hey,' he wandered over and dropped a kiss on Olivia's mouth, 'why did you write 'boatman' on the window.'

'What?'

She turned back to the window and realized that he was right, the letters were backwards. From the outside it would read boatman.

'I didn't write it,' she replied, 'Charlotte did.'

'Why did she do that?'

'I asked for her help,' Olivia shook her head. 'It doesn't really help though does it? She's just kind of stating the obvious, we already know it's the Ferryman.'

'Are you sure that's what she means?' Theo replied as he pulled his coat off.

'Ferryman, Boatman, it is basically the same thing. Fiona said once that spirits get confused; she probably just used the wrong word.'

'I guess so,' Theo shrugged. 'So did you find anything else?'

'No,' she sighed, 'we're still back at square one.'

'Why don't we take a break?'

'And do what?'

'Let's get out of the house for a while. We could go to the hospital and visit Kaitlin and her baby. I know you want to see how they're doing.'

'I do,' Olivia replied softly, 'but I don't know if Kaitlin will want to see me. After all she doesn't actually like me very much. I think she's still half convinced I had something to do with Adam Miller's death.'

'She was alright with you the other day.'

'That was because she was panicking and trying to give birth.'

'Well you'll never know unless you try will you?' Theo turned her around as he grabbed his coat once again. 'You need to get out of the house for a while whether you like it or not, so go get your boots on.'

'Alright,' she sighed, 'but only because I'm getting cabin fever.'

Jackson headed towards Kaitlin's room with a big bouquet of flowers and blue balloons. That girl needed cheering up; over the last few days she had become more and more withdrawn. She'd barely seen the babe more than twice and she still hadn't given him a name. She was supposed to be seeing her doctor today and if Jackson was able to, he was determined to have a word in private with the man. He had a sneaking suspicion Kaitlin might be suffering from post natal depression.

Finding the door wide open he walked into her room but came to an abrupt halt. His eyes momentarily swung back to the number on the door to check he had the right room, as the room was empty and stripped bare, apart from a small heap of used sheets and blankets on the floor. A small blonde nurse looked up as she changed the sheets.

'Can I help you?' she smiled.

'Sorry love,' he smiled back, 'I'm looking for Kaitlin Moore. Has she changed rooms then?'

'Oh,' she dropped the sheet and straightened up. 'Miss Moore checked herself out this morning. Are you Jackson Murphy?'

'I am.'

'She left this for you,' the woman dug in the pocket of her scrubs and came up with a thick white envelope.

Jackson took the letter, frowning as he stared at it.

'Why don't I give you a minute,' she smiled sympathetically.

Leaving the bed half made, she went out of the room leaving him alone. He placed the bouquet of flowers down on the bed and absently let go of the balloons which drifted up to the ceiling to bob there silently. Turning the envelope over in his hands he dropped down to sit on the edge of the bed and tore open the letter.

Dear Jackson,

I'm sorry to leave this way, but it's for the best. I really appreciate your kindness and support but I'm not ready to be a mother. In some ways I don't think I'll ever be. I'm too selfish to be anyone's mom and I can admit it. I wouldn't be any good for him, he's better off without me. I'm leaving Mercy, there's nothing else keeping me here and I feel like I'm slowly suffocating. I saw the way you looked at the baby, with love and awe and that's something that I don't feel; maybe I'm not capable of feeling it. I would like it very much if you would raise him as your own, again I know it's selfish of me to leave this all on you. But you once told me that all a child needs is someone to love him, someone he can look up to and I know that person is you. Attached to this letter I have written a note, which the doctor co-signed, stating that I am of sound mind and that I am fully aware of the consequences of giving up my rights as his mother. I have named you as his legal guardian giving my permission should you wish to adopt him as your own. If you don't want to I won't hold it against you, it is after all a lot to ask of someone. In that case may I ask one more favor and that is that you make sure he goes to a good and loving family who will give him all the things I never could. Thank you Jackson.

Kaitlin.

'What the hell?'

Jackson read the letter through three times before it actually began to sink in what she was asking of him. He read through the attachment and found that she had indeed signed away her maternal rights to the child, naming him as guardian. Did he want the boy? Was he ready to dedicate his life to raising someone else's child? He thought back to that precious little boy in the incubator and his heart almost broke for him. He had no parents now; one hadn't known about him and the other hadn't wanted him. He'd never grow up in a rowdy loving home as he had, but was he really ready to step into those shoes and become someone's father? Shoving the letter into his pocket he walked out of the room, leaving the crushed flowers strewn across the unmade bed.

Olivia walked through the main entrance and immediately spotted a familiar face.

'Fiona!' she called out feeling a slight pang of guilt that she hadn't been by to see the woman recently. After she'd snuck Fiona outside for a cigarette that day the woman had indeed come down with a chill as Louisa had predicted. That had indirectly caused complications to her neck wound as every time she sneezed or coughed too violently, she would split her stitches. So, much to Fiona's utter disgust, she had been kept in the hospital even longer. After the first few days of feeding Fiona's legion of cats, the neighbor had returned from visiting a relative and Olivia had gladly handed over that particular chore.

'Olivia,' Fiona hobbled over with her suitcase in one hand and leaning on a cane with the other, 'thought you'd forgotten about me.'

'Not at all, just been busy.'

'So I hear,' she nodded. 'Jackson Murphy stopped by to visit me a few days ago, brought me flowers too.'

'That was nice of him.'

'Heard what happened in the pub,' she replied briskly. 'I'd like to hear your side of it, stop by for a cup of tea when you have the time.'

'I will,' Olivia replied.

'Still, I expect I'll probably see you at Renata Gershon's funeral anyway.'

'Renata's funeral?'

'Yes,' Fiona nodded, 'it's on Friday.'

'Is it?'

Fiona nodded. 'That girl from the museum, Veronica something, she's been organizing it.'

'Has she,' Olivia replied slowly. She knew what she had told Veronica had been a lot for the girl to take in and Olivia had been more than prepared to give her some space, but she had to admit that Veronica not telling her about Renata's funeral or even asking her to help, stung a little.

'Should be interesting,' Fiona mumbled, 'never been to a Jewish funeral before.'

'I expect I'll see you at the funeral then,' Olivia frowned. 'Are you heading home now?'

'Yes,' she huffed, 'been away too long. I want to see my cats.'

'Do you need a ride?'

'No I have a cab waiting out front.'

'Can I take your bags for you Fiona?' Theo offered.

'Thank you Theodore,' she dropped the case into his hand, 'appreciate it.'

His arm suddenly jolted as she let go, unprepared for the sheer weight of such a small suitcase.

'Have you got bricks in here?' he murmured.

She cackled in delight. 'Books my boy, lots of books, been bored out of my mind trapped in here...anyway,' she turned back to Olivia, 'don't be a stranger, things aren't over yet.'

'Believe me I know,' Olivia muttered.

'Come on then Theodore,' she rapped her cane against the floor to get his attention and strode purposefully towards the doors, leaving him to trail along behind her, hauling the heavy case.

'Olivia!'

She turned at the sound of her name being called and saw Louisa making her way over.

'I'm glad I caught you on your own; there's something I need to tell you.' Olivia looked at her friend curiously as she drew her aside into a corner where no one could overhear them.

'What is it?'

'I ran Sam's blood to type and cross match it just in case he needed a blood transfusion in the future;

something about that man tells me he's no stranger to life threatening injuries.'

'You know, boys will be boys,' Olivia shrugged.

'That's just the problem Olivia' she frowned, 'I wouldn't describe him as a boy in fact...' her voice dropped to a whisper, 'I don't think he is human.'

'Sorry what?' Olivia's brow rose questioningly.

'There were significant anomalies in his blood work,' she clarified. 'His blood isn't human, it had a lot in common with human blood but when I started to get suspicious I ran some extra testing. That's why it's taken me so long to get the results. His DNA has way too many base pairs.'

'Alright I don't understand the significance of that.'

'Trust me, he isn't like us.'

'I'm beginning to get that,' Olivia frowned thoughtfully. 'Louisa listen you can't tell anyone about this, and I need you to destroy all your samples and notes.'

'I already did,' she replied.

'Have you told anyone else about this?'

'No,' she shook her head, 'only you and I know.'

'Okay,' Olivia breathed out slowly, 'let's keep it that way for now.'

She looked over and saw Theo making his way back towards them, jostled in every direction by a crowd of people. Now she thought about it, she'd never seen the hospital so busy.

'Hi Louisa,' Theo greeted her.

'Hey Theo.'

'It's very busy in here today.'

'I know,' she sighed, 'we've had a bit of an influx of patients.'

'Dr Linden,' a lightly accented voice called out.

Olivia looked across as the tall dark haired Indian doctor, an impeccable suit under his white lab coat, strode purposefully towards them.

'Dr Linden,' he stopped in front of them, slightly breathless, as if he'd been rushing. 'We had another 12 patients admitted in the last half an hour.'

'Are they all displaying the same symptoms?'

He shook his head as he caught sight of Olivia and Theo.

'Miss West, Mr Beckett,' he held out his hand in greeting, 'how nice to see you again.'

'Dr Achari isn't it,' Olivia replied thoughtfully, 'we met at the museum. Aren't you the coroner?'

'I am, but it's all hands on deck today as it were.'

'What do you mean?'

'We've been inundated with patients and we're understaffed as half the staff also called in sick,' Louisa told her.

'Sounds almost like you've got an epidemic going on,' Olivia frowned.

'I thought that too at first but the weird thing is none of their symptoms match. People are being admitted to the hospital at an alarming rate but they all have different diseases. We've had cases of Flu, Spanish Flu, Bird Flu, stomach Flu, E-coli, Chicken Pox, Measles, even Polio, and that's practically nonexistent anymore.'

'Then we get on to the really unusual ailments' Dr Achari added, 'Cholera, Dysentery, Lyme's disease, Dengue fever and even West Nile Virus.'

'How is that even possible?' Olivia frowned.

'I just don't know,' he shrugged. 'If I was superstitious like my mother I would say you had a Raksasha on the loose,' he laughed in amusement.

'I'm sorry what's a Raksasha?' Olivia asked curiously.

'Sorry, poor attempt at a joke. We are Hindu and as my mother is a very superstitious woman, we were raised on folklore. A Raksasha is an evil spirit led by the demon Ravana, and they can look like animals or humans. They are said to be powerful creatures whose strength increases at night. During the hours of the night they cause sickness and death to humans.' He shook his head lightly, 'they don't exist of course, but as most of the sick people were either admitted at night or fell ill during the night, it just made me think of my mother's tales.'

Dr Achari turned back to Louisa.

'I'll see if the staff can free up some beds but if this continues we may have to call in the CDC.'

'Alright do what you can,' Louisa nodded. 'If it gets too bad we'll see if we can call in some additional staff from Georgetown or Salem.'

Olivia watched as he disappeared back into the throng of people with his clipboard tucked neatly under one arm.

'Didn't you say it was only a matter of time before other creatures start coming through the gateway?' Louisa asked.

'It's possible,' Olivia murmured thoughtfully. 'If Raksasha's are real then I guess one of them on the loose would certainly explain all the sick people.'

'Great,' Louisa rubbed her face tiredly. 'Look I have to go; I'll catch up with you later.'

Olivia nodded as Louisa also disappeared into the ever thickening crowd of people.

Jackson stared down into the incubator lost in thought. Every now and then the baby's limbs would twitch slightly but otherwise he slept peacefully, his tiny little chest rising and falling in a good strong rhythm. He was making a mental list of all the reasons why becoming the baby's legal guardian was a bad idea. He was single, he ran a pub, he kept unsociable hours, he knew nothing about raising a child, he didn't even know how to change a diaper. Surely the boy would be better off in a more stable family environment with a mother and a father?

The problem was the more he tried to convince himself what a bad idea it was, the more his mind drifted to the small spare room in his apartment and what colours would look good for a nursery. That led his thoughts towards the pub. Not only was he in the middle of fixing up all the damage ready to re-open as soon as possible, he worked long late hours. What the hell was he going to do with a baby? Even as he tried to talk himself out of the guardianship idea, the thought occurred to him that Shelley was his most trusted member of staff and he could promote her to manager and have her run the place during the day. He lived in the apartment above the pub, but if he could find a nanny to sit with the boy while he worked the evening shift....

'You look like you're deep in thought,' a familiar voice interrupted from behind him.

'Aye,' he looked up into Olivia's smiling face, 'where's Theo?'

'He's waiting outside the NICU,' she replied. 'They're really strict on how many visitors are allowed in.'

'Oh,' he answered absently as he turned once again to gaze down into the incubator.

'How's he doing?' she glanced down at the baby.

'Really well,' Jackson replied, 'in fact they're quite surprised at how well he's doing.'

'And how's Kaitlin? I wasn't sure whether to visit her or not, given how she feels about me.'

Jackson let out a weary sigh. 'She's gone Olivia.'

'Gone? What the hell do you mean gone?'

'She took off early this morning, checked herself out of the hospital. I called her place but her landlady says she gave notice on her apartment, packed her bags and left.'

'Why would she do that?' Olivia frowned in confusion, 'why would she leave her son? Did she say anything to you?'

Jackson reached into his pocket and withdrew the crumpled letter, wordlessly handing it to her. Olivia took it from him and read through it silently, her face hardening as she reached the end.

'She just left him?'

'Apparently so,'

'That selfish bitch,' Olivia scowled.

'Olivia,' he chided.

'No,' she shook her head, 'you don't get to defend her, not this time Jackson. I don't have any respect for someone who would just abandon their own child.'

She looked down into the incubator at the baby's precious face and his minute fingers and toes.

'Look at him Jackson,' she said softly, 'he's just so tiny and all alone in the world.'

'I know,' he whispered.

'You know, Kaitlin's right about one thing, he does deserve better than her.'

Jackson sighed and continued to watch the baby, with a confused expression on his face.

'What are you going to do?' she asked softly as she handed the letter back to him.

'I don't know,' he shrugged helplessly, 'what the hell do I know about raising a child?'

'What does anyone ever know? Nobody is born knowing how to be a good parent. You just put your children first, love them unconditionally and hope for the best. It's a learning curve for everyone. The question is; are you prepared to accept the responsibility?' Olivia stepped aside allowing the nurse to check the baby's monitors.

'Is something wrong?' Jackson asked, hovering anxiously.

'No,' she smiled at him softly. 'Actually he's doing so well, sometime later today we're going to take him off the intravenous feeding tube and try him with a bottle.'

'Good,' Jackson murmured, 'that's good then.

'Would you like to hold him?'

'What?'

'Would you like to hold him?' she smiled gently, 'it's good for him to have the contact.'

'I...I don't know,' he replied nervously, 'he's so small.'

'You'll be fine,' she lifted up the side of the incubator and detached a couple of the tubes and monitors before lifting him out carefully and placing him in Jackson's trembling arms.

'Such a tiny little man,' he murmured as he gazed down into the baby's face.

At the sound of Jackson's raspy voice the baby opened his eyes and stared up into his face, blinking and opening his mouth in a yawn. Jackson's mouth curved and without even realizing he was doing it he rocked the baby gently.

'Hello little man,' he whispered, stroking his hand and allowing the baby's fingers to grip his gently.

Olivia watched them both, smiling to herself. Anyone with eyes could see it was love at first sight for both of them. Something inside her relaxed, they would be good for each other, of that she was sure.

'If you decide to do this Jackson, you won't be alone,' she assured him. 'Theo and I will help you any way we can. In fact I think you'll be surprised how many people will be lining up to help.'

'Is that so,' he smiled in amusement.

'You're a good man Jackson.'

'Oh Aye,' he rolled his eyes as he continued to rock the baby, talking softly as if he were speaking to him. 'You can just have that engraved on my headstone. Here lies Jackson Murphy, he died sad and alone but he was a good man.'

'I don't think you'll ever be alone again,' she smiled. 'You have a son now, and maybe one day even grandchildren, who'll sit on your knee and call you 'pops', begging you to tell them tales of Ireland.'

'You think?' he looked up smiling, his eyes glittering.

'Yes I do,' she reached out and traced a finger

gently along the baby's head, 'and I'll be his crazy Aunt Olivia, the witch who lives by the lake.'

'Thank you Olivia,' he replied seriously.

'Some things are just meant to be Jackson,' she told him. 'Think back to the cellar, just after he was born and Diana appeared. What did she do?'

'She saved him.'

'After that?'

He looked at her blankly.

'She didn't hand him back to Theo,' she replied softly, 'she gave him to you and she told you to make sure he was cared for.'

'You think she wanted me to have him?'

'Like I said, everything happens for a reason.'

'I guess I should get a lawyer then,' he replied.

Olivia continued to smile as she watched Jackson lovingly swaying with him in his arms.

'What are you going to call him?'

Jackson thought for a moment before answering.

'Miller, I'm going to call him Miller after his father.'

'Miller Murphy?'

'Aye,' Jackson's smile was brilliant, 'Miller Murphy.'

17.

'So is Jackson really going to raise the boy as his own?' Theo looked up from the couch as Olivia handed him a mug of coffee.

'Looks that way,' she replied dropping down next to him and putting her feet up on the coffee table. 'I still can't believe Kaitlin just skipped out on her baby.'

'At least he will have Jackson,' Theo stroked her leg comfortingly, 'he'll be well cared for.'

At the sudden knock at the door Olivia laid her head back against the couch and sighed.

'I'm just too damn tired to deal with any more drama tonight,' she yawned.

'I'll get it' he smiled, dropping his coffee down on the table.

She murmured something unintelligible as she closed her eyes and felt him climb over her legs. She was vaguely aware of the door opening and of hushed voices but her mind refused to focus as she slid towards sleep.

'Olivia?' she felt Theo brush against her cheek.

'Mmmmn,' she mumbled as she tried to rouse herself but the bone-deep exhaustion of the past couple of days was catching up with her and she drifted off again.

'She looks exhausted,' a soft female voice fluttered around the edges of her mind.

'She is,' she felt Theo's fingertips once again, lightly tracing the skin of her cheek.

'Let her sleep, I'll come by in the morning.'

'Thanks,' Theo replied quietly, 'I'll show you out.'

'No need,' the familiar voice came again, 'I know my way, you take care of her.'

Vaguely aware of the door opening and closing she felt Theo's arms slide around her and lift her gently. Releasing a slow breath, she relaxed into his arms and let go.

When she woke the next morning she rolled over and reached out but found the bed empty. Lifting her head and yawning sleepily she glanced towards the window. It was light out which meant she must have slept late. Groaning, she blindly fumbled for her phone which was laid on her nightstand and looked at the time. Wow, she thought to herself, it really was late. She'd slept nearly fourteen hours straight, which wasn't really a surprise. She'd been running on empty for days now and the constant stress and worry hadn't helped either.

Peeling the warm covers from her body she swung her legs over the side of the bed and stretched out the kinks in her spine. Yawning again she padded silently into the bathroom and turned the shower on. Dropping her clothes from the night before haphazardly on the floor, she stepped under the hot spray and sighed in contentment.

She felt wrung out, it seemed like she hadn't stopped since the moment she stepped back into Mercy and she found herself wishing it would all just stop, just for a minute, so she could catch her breath. The only peace and quiet she'd had was after that night at Boothe's Hollow while she was recovering from her bullet wound. She and Theo had holed up in her house, just the two of them, and looking back now it had been bliss. For a while the outside world hadn't existed. Once her shoulder had begun to heal they'd spent long lazy days curled up in the warmth, making love or watching the snow fall silently outside the windows, covering the outside of her property in a thick undisturbed blanket of white. They'd talked endlessly about history and watched silly movies. She almost wished she could go back to that time and stay there. She sighed and tipped her head back, allowing the water to soak her hair and sluice down her body, washing away the last remnants of fatigue.

She was so frustrated; everyone seemed to be looking to her to figure everything out and she found herself on more than one occasion with the words 'why me' hovering on her lips. If she could just figure out the mystery of the Ferryman maybe they could find him and get him to send all the spirits back to the other side and close the gateway, but the truth was she didn't have a clue how to locate Charon or even if he wanted to be found. She couldn't actually discount the possibility he had simply left rather than being forcibly abducted.

The problem was there was now a distinct possibility that other creatures were coming through the gateway and she could only imagine it was going to get worse. How the hell were they supposed to deal with that? She had no idea what half the creatures were, let alone how to stop them from harming anyone and since when was it her job anyway? She was a historian and an author for God's sake. She hadn't even started a new project in months and although she had some tidy little royalties rolling in from her various publications and also had money set aside for a rainy day, she would have to start working again soon.

Feeling the water start to run cooler she washed

quickly and shut off the water, stepping out of the shower and shivering in the cold air as she grabbed for a towel. Throwing her discarded clothes absently into the hamper she headed back into her room but found herself drawn towards the window. It was snowing again, big fat flakes coming down fast. At this rate her poor little car was going to be useless, the snow would be too deep. As quickly as they were ploughing the roads it was simply getting covered up again. Shaking her head and sighing she turned from the window and pulled out clean warm clothes. She was going to have to run to the store and stock up on food and emergency supplies in case they got snowed in.

Once dressed she ran the dryer quickly through her hair and scraped it back into a messy ponytail. Trotting down the stairs she headed for Theo's studio, which was usually where she found him, but he wasn't there. She paused for a moment hearing the low murmur of voices coming from the kitchen.

She stepped into the warm well lit room and her eyes widened slightly in surprise as they fell on Veronica who was sitting at the island with Theo, chatting comfortably as she sipped her coffee.

'Good Morning,' Theo smiled, 'I thought you were going to sleep the day away.'

'Not quite,' she replied.

'Hello Olivia,' Veronica gazed directly at her with clear blue eyes.

Olivia was about to reply when the quietness was split by a roll of thunder so loud it shook the cold frozen windows.

'What the hell?' she frowned. She moved towards the window and looked up into the sky, but all she could see was the blizzard. 'Thundersnow?'

'Thundersnow? Theo repeated, 'what's that?'

'Basically the same as a regular thunderstorm,' she replied thoughtfully, 'only the main precipitation takes the form of snow rather than rain.'

'I didn't know that was possible,' Veronica murmured.

'It is,' Olivia gazed out of the window, 'it's just really rare. They're more likely to happen over or near large bodies of water because of the lake effect but I've never seen one before.'

'What are you thinking?' Theo asked seeing her puzzled expression.

'I'm just wondering what is driving this extreme weather' she answered, turning back towards them., 'even the snow itself. At this time of year, it should start to let up a bit as we head towards Spring, but if nothing else the snow seems to be getting heavier and the temperature is getting colder.'

'I think I may have an explanation for you,' Veronica spoke up nervously.

Olivia slid onto the seat next to Veronica as Theo threw her a reassuring look and rose to make Olivia a cup of tea.

'First I'd like to apologize for not contacting you sooner. I don't want you to think I was avoiding you after the other night. I keep losing the signal on my cell phone because of the weather and I've been busy trying to sort out the final renovations at the Museum, which are finally finished. I did stop by last night after work.'

'That was you?'

Veronica nodded. 'You were exhausted and I didn't want to disturb you,' she replied. 'After the other night, after everything you told me, I kept running over and over it in my mind. Although I'm finding some of it hard to believe, I know that the spirit problem is very real which got me thinking about what you said about there being a gateway and about other creatures coming through. Do you remember what I told you that night about the woman I saw in the snow?'

'The naked one with eyes like a snake?'

'That's it,' Veronica nodded as she rummaged in

her bag and came up with a large flat reference book. The tips of post-it notes peeked from the top of the pages where she'd obviously tagged the ones that were of interest to her. 'Well I started to wonder if she was one of the other creatures that had come through the gateway so I started doing some research.'

'Of course you did,' her mouth curved in amusement as Veronica opened the book at one of the bookmarks and slid the open book across the surface so Olivia could get a better look.

When she looked down at the illustration she saw a picture of a beautiful woman with slitted serpentine eyes. She was naked and surrounded by what looked like a sandstorm.

'This is what I saw the other day, only she was surrounded by snow instead of sand' Veronica told her.

Olivia's eyes slid over to the text accompanying the drawing.

'Janns, a class of evil spirits from Islamic tradition. They can transform into animals or humans but as humans they appear as beautiful women with slit eyes like a snake. They are savage, causing storms and bringing death,' she read out loud. 'Are you sure this is what you saw?'

Veronica nodded. 'I didn't want to believe what you told me, I mean it's crazy. Things like this don't happen outside of books and movies, but...'

'But?' Olivia prompted.

'I can't reason away the things I've seen, the things I've felt,' she sighed. 'I saw one of these creatures, I know I did.'

'I believe you,' Olivia told her softly, 'it's not the only creature on the loose.'

'What do you mean?' Veronica frowned as she watched Theo place a cup of tea down in front of Olivia.

'We think there's another creature who has come through the gateway, a Raksasha.'

'I've never heard of one of those before,' she

pulled the book back towards her and started leafing through the pages.

'It's Hindu in origin I believe' Olivia told her, 'they cause disease and death amongst humans.'

'We were at the hospital yesterday,' Theo spoke up, 'and there were many sick people being admitted. Apparently many more than are usual, showing symptoms of diseases and illnesses that are also not commonplace.'

'God,' Veronica breathed heavily, 'what a mess.'

'Tell me about it' Olivia shook her head, 'and it's only going to get worse. At the moment people are getting sick but it's only a matter of time before people start dying.'

'What can we do about it?'

'Find the Ferryman,' Olivia replied bluntly. 'These creatures are way above my skill level. The only way to send them back from where they came from is to find Charon and hope to whatever God you believe in, that he has the ability to send them back and close the doorway.'

'Still having no luck with that?'

'No,' Olivia shook her head in frustration, 'we've hit a dead end. I can't find any more information on him and at this point we're not even sure if he's left on purpose or if he's been abducted, although we're leaning more heavily towards the latter.'

'I'll see if I can find any information for you' Veronica told her, but to be honest if you can't find any then I'm not sure I'll be able to do much better.'

'Thanks anyway,' Olivia sighed, 'at this point we need all the help we can get.'

'There was another reason I stopped by to see you.'

'Renata's funeral?'

Veronica nodded.

'With no surviving family there really wasn't anyone else to arrange the funeral and Jewish tradition dictates that the body be interred as soon as possible, as anything else is considered a humiliation of the deceased. Not only that but Jewish law forbids cremation or any kind of embalming. She also doesn't have any surviving family to sit Shiva for her.'

'Shiva?'

'It means 'in mourning' for her. Shiva can last anything up to seven days but as none of us are Jewish I found a compromise. I have arranged a Rabbi and a Jewish service for her but afterwards the Mayor has given permission for us to hold a small wake at the museum for her. I think she would have like that.'

'Of course she would,' Olivia smiled. 'It's a perfect way to say goodbye, she loved that place.'

'Anyway, it's all been a bit of a nightmare trying to organize it in such a short amount of time and this weather hasn't helped much' Veronica told her. 'The last I heard, at the cemetery they were having trouble actually digging the grave for tomorrow as the ground is frozen so solid. Also the phone lines keep going down so I'm heading out that way after I leave here, to double check everything is ready for tomorrow.'

'If you don't mind, I might tag along' Olivia replied. 'I need to go into town to stock up on some supplies anyway and I'd quite like to see Jed, he's the custodian of the cemetery.'

'Not at all,' Veronica smiled, 'I'll be glad of the company. Usually cemeteries don't bother me but after everything that has happened recently….'

'That's understandable,' Olivia turned to Theo, 'do you want to come?'

He shook his head. 'Not unless you specifically want me to, I have a painting I want to finish.'

'Okay.'

'You don't mind do you?'

Olivia smiled. 'Of course not, I told you, you don't need to tag around after me all the time, you should have your own interests. You don't need to feel guilty if you want some time to yourself.'

Without saying a word, he simply rose and dropped a kiss on her upturned lips. Her eyes followed him in silence as he smiled at Veronica and wandered out of the kitchen with Beau trailing along on his heels.

'God, he's gorgeous,' Veronica sighed, 'you're so lucky.'

'Yes I am,' she murmured thoughtfully, still watching the doorway he'd disappeared through.

'Olivia?'

'What?' she was startled out of her thoughts, 'oh right, the cemetery.'

Veronica glanced out of the window. 'The snow seems to have stopped for the moment, we should probably get going before it starts up again.'

Olivia slid off her seat 'okay I'll just get my boots and coat on'.

Veronica finished her coffee and politely rinsed the cup out, before picking up Olivia's cup and realizing with a smile that it was still half full. She didn't know what it was about Olivia but she never finished a cup of tea. Dumping the cold contents into the sink she rinsed that cup out too and set them both in the drainer. She was just tucking her book back in her purse when Olivia reappeared, all warmly wrapped up.

'Let's get going then,' Olivia grabbed her own purse.

With a quick goodbye to Theo and Beau, they were heading down the steps of her front porch when Olivia noticed that instead of her car, Veronica was driving a shiny new truck. Not only that she realized with a small jolt, it was one she recognized.

'Isn't that Jake's truck?'

'Yes,' she climbed into the driver's side.

'Did something happen to your car?' Olivia asked curiously.

'No,' Veronica frowned.

'Why are you driving Jake's truck then?'

'Because he stole my keys.'

'He stole your keys,' Olivia replied slowly, her eyes narrowing suspiciously. 'What's going on?'

Veronica sighed heavily. 'He seems to think I'm clumsy and accident prone. He said he'd feel better if I was driving his truck instead of my car in this weather.'

'That was sweet of him,' she answered in amusement.

'No it wasn't, it was bossy and controlling,' Veronica scowled. 'He seems to forget I grew up in Boston, I'm used to winters like this. I'm perfectly capable of driving in the snow.'

'Does he look out for you often?' Olivia asked innocently.

'He drops by most days, says he's just checking I'm okay, but he probably thinks I'm going to accidentally burn my apartment down.'

'No, he probably is just checking up on you to make sure you're okay. He was there the other night when you told us about the Janns you encountered outside the museum. He knows what's going on and he knows there are more and more creatures coming through the doorway, that's why he's checking up on you.'

'Oh,' Veronica frowned, 'I guess that is kind of sweet.'

'It is, so maybe you should cut the guy some slack,' she smiled.

'Hmmm we'll see…' Veronica replied as she pulled away from Olivia's house and headed down the driveway.

Theo watched from the window as they disappeared from view before turning back to the picture he had covered on the easel. It was something he'd been working on for Olivia.

Beau curled up on his cushion in the corner and with a sigh laid his head down, content to watch Theo as he pushed up his sleeves and started to pull out various tubes of colour and squeeze them out onto a pallet. He took his time sorting through the masses of brushes he'd accumulated, checking them meticulously and discarding the ones he didn't want to use. With everything set up the way he wanted he turned to the easel and pulled the sheet off. His heart jolted and then sank as he saw the picture in front of him. No longer the painting of Olivia's Stick House under a stormy sky, the picture of his wife once again stared back at him. Turning in frustration to the finished paintings he had stacked facing the wall, he began to turn them round one by one, searching for Olivia's painting but now every single one of them bore the same cold unforgiving face staring back at him. Abandoning the paintings, he picked up his sketchbook flipping through page after page of the same thing. All his pencil sketches were gone, replaced by picture after picture of Mary Alcott Beckett.

He picked up the next one and the next, but all the sketch pads contained exactly the same thing. Throwing them back onto the pile in frustration he turned back to face the room and froze. All of the paintings which had been neatly stacked against one wall were spaced around the room facing him, dozens of pictures of Mary's face all staring back at him.

Sighing in defeat, he pulled out the bottle of Jack he had stacked behind a pile of art supplies and poured himself a generous glass. He dropped down heavily into his favorite chair and mockingly toasted the portrait of Mary. A door slammed violently somewhere in the house as Theo threw his head back and drank deeply.

'Okay then Mary,' he spoke into the still room, 'now you have my attention.'

Olivia and Veronica pulled up to the cemetery and the first thing they noticed were the two police cruisers parked just inside the entrance, alongside the Coroner's van.

'Oh for God's sake' Olivia muttered, 'what now?'

They both climbed out of the truck and waded through the deep snow to a plot that was cordoned off with police tape. The gravestone seemed to have been knocked off kilter and set at a strange angle and the pristine white snow was streaked with mud and wooden splinters. They watched in morbid curiosity as the coffin was winched up out of the earth and set alongside the exhumed grave. Veronica's breath caught in her throat as they saw the top of the coffin, the wood split and caved in. Rather than something trying to break out it looked as if something had tried to break in. Olivia shivered, not knowing which reality was worse as both scenario belonged in a horror movie.

Dr Achari stepped forward as the men prized the remains of the lid off, and peered into the coffin. He reached in with gloved hands, briefly examining whatever corpse was in there. After a brief scrutiny he turned to Jake and the two began a hushed conversation. Jake nodded after a moment and Dr Achari beckoned his two assistants forward. Noticing Olivia and Veronica, Jake broke away and stalked through the snow towards them.

'Hey Jake,' Olivia greeted him.

'You two seem to make a habit of showing up at the wrong place and time,' he frowned. 'What are you doing here?'

'I came to speak with Jed about Renata's funeral tomorrow,' Veronica told him.

'What's going on Jake?' Olivia asked.

He sighed and readjusted his hat. 'It looks as if we've got some nut job on the loose, who's been disturbing graves.'

'And when you say disturbing graves, you mean?'

'Digging them up and cracking the coffins open.'

Veronica grimaced. 'Why would anyone want to do that?'

Jake hesitated, his gaze tracking over to where they were loading up the corpse and damaged coffin to be taken in for examination.

'You might as well tell us the truth Jake,' Olivia interrupted his thoughts.

'There is some evidence to suggest something has been…'

'Oh for heaven's sake Jake will you just spit it out.'

'Feeding on the corpses,' he finished in distaste.

'Are you joking?' Veronica's mouth fell open.

'I wish I was,' he shook his head.

'Do you think it's some sort of animal then?' she asked hopefully.

'Could be,' he replied.

'But not likely, given the look on your face Jake,' Olivia frowned. 'You might as well tell us all of it, I expect we'll find out about it sooner or later.'

'Dr Achari seems to think the bite marks resemble human teeth marks.'

'Eeew,' Veronica swallowed convulsively, 'I think I may be sick.'

'Just breathe through it Roni,' Olivia shook her head and turned back to Jake. 'You said corpses as in plural, are there more?'

'We've discovered two this morning, it's hard to tell though as it keeps snowing. Any evidence or disturbed graves are getting covered up quicker than we can discover them, but the two we have found are very recent. This one was buried just three days ago and the other one about a week and a half ago.'

'Fresh meat?' Olivia stated.

'Please Olivia,' Veronica paled.

'That,' Jake replied, 'and loosely packed soil, easier to dig up.'

'God damn it,' Olivia muttered under her breath.

'This is getting out of hand now Olive,' he frowned, 'a few ghosts are one thing, but the thing

Veronica saw in the snow the other night, all the sick people in the hospital and now this? We've got a very serious problem.'

'I know,' Olivia let out a frustrated breath.

She looked out across the Cemetery and noticed Chief Macallister breaking away from the other cops and heading in their direction.

'Olivia,' he nodded as he joined them.

'Mac,' she answered, 'this is Veronica Mason, she's taking over from Renata at the Museum.'

'Temporarily,' Veronica replied holding out her hand, 'it's nice to meet you Chief Macallister.'

'Miss Mason,' he nodded again as he shook her hand politely, before fixing his attention on Olivia. 'We seem to have a bit of a problem here.'

'That's an understatement.'

'Jake's filled me in on everything that's been going on, including Miss Mason's involvement,' Mac told Olivia, 'so what are you doing about finding the Ferryman and how can we help?'

'I just don't know Mac,' she shrugged helplessly. 'I think he's been abducted but I can't be a hundred percent certain. I don't know who'd have the power to take him or why.'

'Do you think your mother has anything to do with it?' he asked carefully, 'after all she does have a pet demon. I'm willing to bet a demon has enough juice to capture the Ferryman.'

'Possibly,' Olivia frowned, 'I certainly wouldn't put it past her to cause this much chaos but what I can't figure out is why she would want him, what could she possibly have to gain?'

'Why don't we get together at your place when we're not freezing our asses off in a cemetery and go over everything you have so far. If it is an abduction, we'll work it like any other case and hopefully between us we can generate some useful leads or at least a working theory.'

'Sounds good,' Olivia replied in relief. 'Let's deal with Renata's funeral first but why don't you and Jake come by the day after tomorrow.'

'Sounds like a plan,' he answered. 'I have to get back to work now, Jake you coming?'

'I'll be right there,' he nodded as Mac disappeared back towards the crime scene, 'You two need to be careful.'

'We're fine,' Veronica retorted, 'we can take care of ourselves thank you.'

'Veronica,' Jake scowled, 'you can't even keep yourself upright half the time.'

'Just because I trip up every now and then doesn't mean I'm going to go trawling through a graveyard in the middle of the night looking for some creature so it can chew on me. I'm not stupid.'

'I didn't say you were,' his eyes flashed angrily, 'I just asked you to be careful.'

'Well fortunately for you I'm not your responsibility,' she turned and stormed off.

'Veronica,' he growled and moved to follow her until Olivia stopped him.

'Just let her go Jake,' she smiled sympathetically. 'In this argument I don't think there are any winners.'

'Look I'm just worried about you both. With the rate creatures are pouring into Mercy it's only a matter of time before one of us comes up against something we won't be able to handle.'

'I know,' she soothed him, 'we'll be careful I promise. Are you coming to Renata's funeral tomorrow?'

Jake shook his head. 'I'm working.'

'Then I'll see you at my place the day after,' she reached up on tiptoes and pressed an affectionate kiss to his cold lips. 'Stop pouting, I'll watch Veronica.'

'Yeah but who's going to watch you?' he grumbled.

She smiled and walked away leaving him shaking

his head in exasperation.

Olivia headed for Veronica who was standing talking to Jed as he watched the exhumation in disgust.

'What is the world coming to,' he shook his head, 'folks aren't even safe in their own graves. Vandals!'

Assuming Jake hadn't shared the part about the bite marks Olivia wisely chose not to respond. 'So are we having a funeral tomorrow or not?' she asked carefully.

'We are,' Veronica breathed in relief, 'Jed says everything's ready to go.'

'Had a bit of trouble breaking ground for the plot as it's so damn cold, dirt was frozen solid,' he replied scratching his chin thoughtfully, 'had to get a digger in. I wonder how the vandals were able to dig up Mrs. Peabody so easily.'

Olivia didn't want to try and explain that supernatural creatures probably wouldn't let something as mundane as frozen dirt stop them from digging up a fresh corpse if that was what they wanted, so she steered the conversation to safer ground.

'Did you know Renata then Jed?'

'Might've nodded in passing a few times over the years, was a fine looking woman that one.'

'Jed,' she smiled, 'did you have a bit of a thing for Renata?'

'Now, I didn't say no such thing,' but his cheeks pinked up, which Olivia suspected had nothing to do with the cold.

Veronica glanced at Olivia and smiled at the sweet old guy.

'Go on,' he blushed again, 'get on with you, some of us have work to do.'

He shooed them away and headed towards his cabin down the hill.

Veronica laughed as Olivia wrapped her arm through hers and they walked companionably back up the hill together.

'So what was all that business with Jake earlier?'

'Nothing.'

'Roni?'

Veronica shrugged. 'I just don't appreciate it when he gets all male and bossy, it's condescending.'

'No it's not,' Olivia replied, 'he's genuinely worried.'

'Well I'm not his to worry about.'

'I thought you two were friends?'

Veronica sighed, it wasn't because she didn't like Jake. The problem was she liked him a little too much, something she couldn't admit to Olivia who'd been one of his best friends since they were kids. The guy was insanely good looking with all that blonde hair and blue eyes and his face sure was nice to look at. She had been genuinely touched when he had first starting stopping by her place to check on her. She'd looked forward to seeing him, in fact it had fast become the best part of her day. She'd half convinced herself he was interested in her but that was just a stupid fantasy; she was sick of people treating her like a clumsy child who couldn't look after herself. She'd had enough of that from her family, just for once she'd wanted someone to see her as a woman. What she wouldn't give to be as confident and carelessly sexy as Olivia was. It was one of the things she both admired and envied about her friend. But that wasn't who she was and now every time she was around Jake she would end up being snippy and defensive because she felt like a stupid nerdy kid with a pathetic crush on the high school Quarterback.

'Roni?' Olivia nudged her gently.

'I'm okay, we are friends, sort of,' she conceded, 'he's just annoying.'

'Okay,' Olivia replied carefully.

'Why don't we head into town,' Veronica changed the subject. 'You can do your shopping and, did you hear Liddy Mayberry has just opened up her own bakery and tea room?'

'No,' she replied in surprise.

'I've heard she makes a wicked cup of cocoa, my treat.'

'You had me at Liddy Mayberry,' Olivia laughed. 'Anything that woman has had a hand in always ends up tasting phenomenal.'

It's a date then,' she smiled as they wandered back along the path.

Suddenly Olivia stopped, her smile disappearing as she looked around the cemetery. Snowflakes were once again drifting down from the sky, pale and ghostlike on the silent air.

'What is it?'

'I don't know,' Olivia frowned, 'it just felt like we were being watched.'

'Come on,' Veronica tugged on Olivia's sleeve, 'this place is starting to give me the creeps.'

Turning back to her friend and nodding in agreement they hurried back to the truck.

Nathaniel pulled back into the shadow of the Mausoleum, the fresh blanket of snow concealing him even further as he watched the West girl and the other human who accompanied her. That one was of no importance, it was the West girl who held his interest. He had seen her that night at the hollow. She'd wielded Hell fire; he was certain of it. He'd watched her pull a bow and arrow of sapphire and black flame and although she held back she'd conjured the ancient and powerful fire, something no human had ever been able to do. What made her so special?

Isabel West had gone to a great deal of trouble to make sure he couldn't harm the girl. He looked down at his hands, turning them over and studying them in the pale light. As long as he was trapped in this filthy rotting prison of human flesh, he couldn't do anything. Although the fact she had trapped him made his fists clench tightly in silent fury, he knew patience was the key. She could not keep him trapped forever, the witch was so arrogant she thought she had the upper hand, but he was simply biding his time. Her single-minded obsession to find Infernum blinded her to all else. He was not so narrow minded. He had spent thousands of years searching for Infernum; he knew its allure, just as he knew it was supposed to be his. So he would use the witch for now and once he broke free from the pig flesh body she had trapped him into he would take Infernum and with it he would raise up his brother Seth from the darkest and deepest level of Hell. The Hell gate would burst open and all their brethren would be freed. They would rule as kings, and all the mortals would know true suffering.

He glanced down as something caught at his wrist. At first he thought it was a snowflake, but as he grasped its edge and tugged a sliver of human flesh peeled away. Nathaniel smiled, it would not be long, the fleshy prison could not hold his true form for ever, it was already starting to break down. Once he was free he would make sure that Isabel West suffered for what she had dared to do to him. He would peel the flesh slowly from her body then he would tear her slowly limb from limb before boiling her in oils, after the time he spent during the Crusades and then later in Constantinople he had learned some truly exquisite torture methods, it was almost amusing the inventive ways these humans came up with to cause each other untold amounts of pain. He would be happy to take his time with the witch making sure she got to fully experience every single moment of it, her daughter on the other hand was an entirely different matter as for Olivia West...well he had plans for her.

18.

Olivia glanced around the room, nursing what would turn out to be her only glass of wine. The funeral had been as perfect as Veronica could have made it and Renata had been laid to rest in Mercy cemetery as she'd wanted. Any evidence of the unpleasantness from the day before had been removed. Besides it wasn't much of a crime scene as it kept snowing and covering everything up. They probably wouldn't know until Spring how many graves had actually been disturbed. But Jed, bless his heart, had made sure the police tape and anything else was removed so as not to alarm anyone at the funeral. Veronica had been especially worried about burying Renata, knowing there was some sort of horrible creature on the loose digging up fresh graves and feeding on the corpses. Still, Olivia had managed to find a way around that with a simple charm and hex bag. She dropped it into the grave disguised in a handful of soil, right under the nose of the Rabbi, to ensure her grave would be protected.

Renata had a good turnout, all things considered. The snow had still not let up much with the temperature hovering at a bone-jarring level below freezing, and besides half of the town were sick with various ailments. But everyone who could make it did and for that Olivia was pleased. Renata may not have known it, being the intensely private person that she'd been, but she'd been well liked and respected and frankly she would be sorely missed by so many people, herself included. She was glad Veronica was being given the opportunity to run the museum but it still didn't feel right, knowing that every time she walked through the door Renata would no longer be there to greet her. Noticing Veronica was beckoning her over, she glanced around the room once more wondering where on earth Theo had got to, before moving through the mourners to join her friend.

Theo leaned his head back against the wall and tipped his beer up, taking a deep pull. He was leaning casually against a wall in a quiet corner of the room, one hand tucked in his pocket, his tie loosened and his top button undone. It was the first time he'd had to wear a suit and although he had enjoyed the way Olivia's eyes had lit up with appreciation at the sight of him, the damn tie felt like a noose, making him very nervous for some reason.

His gaze automatically sought out Olivia as she crossed the room towards Veronica. He doubted she could see him from where he was standing but that just allowed him to watch her freely. He tilted his beer back again and took another swig. She was so damn beautiful it hurt to look at her sometimes, especially knowing that there was a big part of himself he was hiding from her. The day before he'd sat in his studio staring at the paintings of his former wife. He'd almost expected her to appear in person, but she didn't. It was like she was tormenting him, letting him know she hadn't forgotten what had happened to her nor the part he had played in it. She wouldn't let him forget it either and it seemed she wouldn't let him move past it.

He frowned absently as he looked down at the beer bottle in his hand, wanting to be free of the guilt and the pain. Every time he thought of Mary it was like a vice gripping his heart. They'd been friends once, before they married and even for a while after. He hadn't loved her, Olivia was the only one to ever hold his heart, even back then when he hadn't known she was real. But he had cared for Mary in his own way. Part of the problem had been Mary had loved him desperately and when he couldn't love her in return, the way she deserved or wanted, that was when things had started to turn bad. From that point onwards they had gone from bad to worse.

He had decided to tell Olivia the truth, making his decision while he'd been sitting staring at the portraits of Mary the day before. She deserved to know the truth and to be honest the guilt was beginning to suffocate him; he simply couldn't keep it from her any longer. He'd intended to tell her when she returned home, but the words just wouldn't come. So he'd changed the subject and listened to her talk about her afternoon, while eating one of Liddy Mayberry's strawberry tarts that she'd brought home for him.

He began to scratch absently at the label with his thumbnail, glancing back up at Olivia as she tilted her head and laughed at something Veronica had said. Her smile caught him every time, and he wasn't even aware of the small smile gracing his own lips as he watched her.

'Don't you ever get tired of watching her?' a familiar voice broke into his musings.

He turned towards Tommy, who now leaned against the wall next to him. He was almost a mirror image of Theo with his tie loosened, his top button undone and a beer in one hand, the other hand tucked in his pocket.

'No,' Theo's mouth curved in amusement.

'Do you know you get this really dopey look on your face when you're looking at her.'

'Do I?

'Yeah it's practically nauseating.'

Theo laughed lightly. 'How are things between you and Louisa?'

Tommy took a pull of his beer then sighed as his head dropped back against the wall.

'Good days and bad days, I guess we've had problems for a long time but we've just papered over the cracks.'

Just as Theo had done, Tommy stared down at his bottle and absently began to peel the label off. 'I still love her and I know she loves me, I guess now that I'm back for good we need to find a way to live with each other.'

'Nothing's ever simple is it?'

'You got that right,' Tommy took another sip of his beer before changing the subject. He glanced back at Theo with a wry smile. 'So you're what, three hundred and forty something year's old then?'

Theo snorted lightly. 'No, I'm 31. I just happen to have been born in a different place and time.'

'You do know that's crazy, right?'

'I take it you still don't believe me then?'

'Hell no,' Tommy laughed, 'there's no such thing as time travel or three-thousand-year-old Greek guys who ferry souls across a lake in the middle of a small town in Massachusetts. I think you're all crazy or having some sort of mass hallucination. However, that being said I can't deny that there is some sort of weird shit going on in Mercy. So for the moment I'm prepared to agree to disagree.'

Theo shrugged. There really was no way he could convince Tommy he was telling the truth so there was nothing else to do but let it go. Tommy would either come around to the truth in his own time, or he wouldn't. Either way Theo was just glad to have his friend back.

'You know Ms Gershon well?' Tommy asked after a moment.

'No, I hardly knew her at all, but Olivia was a

friend of hers.'

'You want to get out of here? I doubt they'd notice.'

'And do what?'

'We could go shoot some pool?'

'Shoot some pool?' Theo frowned. 'Do I need my gun?'

Tommy let out a sincere laugh. 'Come on' he said, still chuckling in amusement, 'we'll text Lou and Olivia once we're out of here. That way they can't stop us.'

'Do you think they'll mind?'

'Theo, there's one thing you'll need to learn about being in a long term relationship or a marriage' Tommy slapped Theo gregariously on the shoulder as he steered him towards the exit.

'What's that?'

'That it's easier to apologize after the fact than to get them to agree in the first place.'

'Isn't that somehow dishonest?'

'Ask Olivia how much money she spent on her last pair of shoes and then we'll talk about honesty in a relationship' Tommy laughed. 'It's all about meeting somewhere in the middle.'

'I really have no idea what you are talking about,' Theo frowned and Tommy let loose another laugh.

Veronica had moved off to circulate amongst the guests as Olivia, once again on her own, sipped her wine. She was absently scanning the room, lost in thought, when Louisa appeared next to her.

'Hey,' Olivia smiled, 'I thought you were working?'

'I am technically,' Louisa stifled a yawn. 'We managed to borrow some staff from Salem so I've got someone covering me for a couple of hours. I wanted to come, I was very fond of Ms Gershon. She always seemed like such a permanent fixture in Mercy and I can't believe she's gone.'

They were quiet for a moment, a comfortable silence that friends enjoy, until Olivia spoke out.

'Hey, has Jake said anything to you about Veronica?'

'No,' Louisa frowned, 'why? Is something going on between them?'

'No,' Olivia replied quickly, 'well not exactly, but I get the impression something's brewing.'

'Really?' Louisa replied slowly her mouth curving into a wicked smile. 'I might have to spend some time getting to know Veronica a little better.'

'Well you're about to get the chance,' Olivia finished up her wine. 'Meeting, my place tomorrow; Jake and Mac are coming over. It's up to you whether you bring Tommy or not.'

She nodded as she sipped her coke.

'I wonder where he's disappeared to?'

'Tommy?'

'Yes, he said he was going to get a beer and I haven't seen him since.'

'Theo seems to have disappeared too.'

Just then Olivia's phone chirped with a message alert. Scrolling through the screens she was about to read the message when Louisa's phone went off.

'Theo says he's gone to shoot some pool and have a beer,' Olivia frowned.

'Same as Tommy,' Louisa laughed. 'I guess they've kissed and made up.'

'He could've told me first.'

'Oh honey,' Louisa smiled, 'in the grand scheme of things it's not the worst thing he could have done and it's certainly not the worst thing Tommy could've dragged him into. Be grateful it's just beer and pool.'

'I guess,' Olivia replied sulkily.

Louisa's message alert went off again. Sighing as she read the message she dropped her phone back into her pocket and handed her drink to Olivia.

'Sorry I've got to go; I'm needed back at the hospital. I'll see you at your place tomorrow.'

Olivia nodded as she watched her friend disappear through the throng of people. As she turned back, out of the corner of her eye she caught a glimpse of someone familiar. Dropping her empty wine glass with Louisa's half full one onto a nearby table, she pushed her way gently through the crowd of people. She lost her target for a moment but then spotted the familiar flash disappearing down one of the museum corridors. Throwing one last glance around the room to make sure no one was watching, she slipped down the deserted corridor.

The further away from the gathering she got, the more the noise of chatter faded into the background. Here the lighting was dimmer casting long shadows across the exhibits as she passed by. Her heels clicked quietly against the floor as she rounded a corner and ahead saw a door left slightly ajar allowing soft light to spill out into the hallway.

Checking to make sure she wasn't being followed she slipped through the door and shut it behind her with a soft click. Turning to face the person waiting in the room she scowled.

'Are you mad?' she hissed quietly, 'you're a wanted criminal. Why the hell would you walk into such a large gathering; half the town council are out there?'

'Hello Olivia,' Charles replied calmly from his seat. 'It's nice to see you too.'

'I want an answer,' she glared at him.

'Well it's not always about what you want Olivia,' he replied bluntly. 'I let you have things the way you wanted, and look what's happened. Mercy is being overrun with creatures escaping through the doorway.'

'Are you saying that mess is my fault?'

'No, that's not what I'm saying,' her father replied with infinite patience, 'but by refusing to listen to what I had to say about your mother, you have certainly contributed towards it.'

'How dare you?' she whispered.

His patience finally snapped and he came abruptly to his feet. 'No Olivia, how dare you. Stop being as stubborn as your mother.'

'Don't you compare me to her, I am nothing like her,' Olivia muttered.

'You don't want to be but you are' he sighed, 'stubborn, willful, and full of pride. That was Isabel's undoing Olivia, don't let it be yours.'

She stared at him, unable to find the right words to say.

'This should have been dealt with months ago. If you'd just listened to me, to what I had to say, maybe we could have figured this out together sooner. But instead I've spent the last several weeks running around with Davis and Danae, trying to clean up this mess.'

'What do you mean?' Olivia frowned.

'You've just started noticing the creatures coming through? The Raksasha, the Janns, the Jikininki?'

'The Jikin...what?'

'In the graveyard?'

'Oh,' she shook her head, 'we didn't know what it was. I figured it was probably a Ghoul.'

'Close,' they're more or less the same thing.'

He sat back down, his voice taking on the teacher's tone she remembered from her childhood and for a brief second she almost smiled. 'A Jikininki is from Japan. It's a priest who lived a selfish and opulent life, and in death is sentenced to live as a pathetic creature who must feed on corpses.'

'Nice,' she swallowed dryly.

'That's beside the point' Charles shook his head, 'the fact is these creatures and a lot more besides, have been coming through the doorway for weeks. Davis, Danae and I have been dealing with them, killing them if we can or sending them back, although that's only a temporary fix as they'll just end up coming back through the doorway now they know it's open. The problem is they're coming through thick and fast now, there's no way to track and deal with all of them with just the three of us. I'm supposed to be finding your mother but this is far more pressing.'

'I had no idea,' Olivia perched on the edge of a nearby table.

'No but you would have, if you'd just picked up the damn phone. I understand that you're mad at me Olivia and you have every right to be, but until we've found your mother we don't have the luxury of ignoring each other.'

'I guess not,' she murmured thoughtfully, 'a temporary truce then? Until we find mom and deal with her.'

'That would be nice' Charles smiled. It was the first genuine smile she'd seen grace his features since the first moment she'd seen him, months ago in the cabin in the woods, when she'd been held captive by the former chief Walcott.

'How's your friend Veronica after her run-in the other night outside the museum?'

'She's fine, shook her up some and she banged up her knee…' Olivia broke off as her gaze narrowed in comprehension. 'That was you wasn't it? You were the one who saved her from the Janns?'

He smiled quietly.

'But she doesn't remember what happened?'

'A simple memory charm,' he shrugged. 'Danae has quite a gift with them. Your friend was very shaken up, in fact nearly hysterical at the time so it was the best way to calm her down. I wanted to make sure the Janns didn't have time to circle back around and follow her home to her apartment before we could get to it and deal with it, so I 'suggested' to her that she go to your house. She was unaware of the suggestion but I knew she'd be safe with you.'

'Why did you save her?'

'Olivia,' he sighed tiredly, 'I know I've made a lot of mistakes but I'm not a monster. I saved your friend because I don't want anyone else to get hurt. I should have known the truth about your mother. I ignored the signs because I didn't want to believe the woman I loved was capable of murder, but every life she takes directly or indirectly are all on me. I should have stopped her when I had the chance. Now everything she does is on me.'

'You really think mom is behind the Ferryman's disappearance?'

'Why don't I start at the beginning and let you figure that out for yourself.'

'Fine,' she slid off the table and settled herself comfortably into a chair next to him. 'Where do we begin.'

'With what it is she's after, what she has been searching for all these years…Infernum.'

'Infernum?' Olivia frowned, 'Theo's mentioned that name a couple of times before. He said the Nathaniel from his time killed Hester West's mother and kidnapped her and her sister Bridget back in Salem, because he believed she knew where it was. But we don't know what Infernum actually is?'

'It's a book.'

'A book?' Olivia replied dryly, 'are you fucking kidding me. All of this is over a book?'

'Not just any book' Charles shook his head, 'no one knows it's exact origins. It's always been a myth, a kind of supernatural holy grail for demons. The book is called Infernum; do you know why?'

'Infernum is the Latin word for Hell.'

'Exactly, it's actually called Infernum Liber, and it literally translates to The Hell Book. It is the most powerful object in history. It contains within its pages all the power and magic of all the Hell dimensions. It means ultimate power to anyone who possesses it. The demons all want it, so do the humans and every supernatural creature in between. Whoever gains possession of the book will become the most powerful being in existence.'

'And this is what mom wants? To find the book?'

'She believes it's her birthright.'

'But I don't understand why? Why would she think that?'

'I asked myself that same question, right up until a year and a half ago' he told her. 'I was incarcerated at Morley Ridge when I had a visitor.'

'Who was it?' Olivia asked suspiciously.

'Your Aunt Evie,' he sighed sadly. 'She knew she was dying and she needed to pass on some information to you, a secret that has been passed down your family for generation after generation, for more than five thousand years.'

'What the hell are you talking about?' she frowned in confusion.

'I don't know all the details; it was a secret that was never supposed to leave the West family but with Isabel's betrayal everything changed. As I said no one actually knows the origins of the book. All I do know is that at some point the book was passed to a little girl and she was to become its first keeper, to prevent it from falling into the hands of a demon. From that point on her descendants were a single unbroken line of females, each generation becoming the new keeper of the book and each sworn to secrecy. They made a pledge never to use its power; they understood they were its keepers only and their role was to protect it. Did you never wonder why the magic in your family is so strong? It's because their destiny and the Hell Book are so deeply entwined, one feeds the other. With each generation that the book and the secret were passed down, the stronger the West women became. So the book continued to pass from mother to daughter to granddaughter, down the line until it reached Hester West.'

'Hester?' Olivia breathed, 'so she did know about Infernum. She told Theo she didn't know what it was.'

'As I said she was sworn to secrecy; she would never have told anyone about it other than her own child.'

'So where is the book now?'

'We don't know,' he shook his head and neither does your mother. The last person known to have had possession of it was Hester and after her death all knowledge of it simply disappeared. It was not passed on to her daughter as it should have been.'

'I wonder why?' Olivia frowned.

'We can only guess' he shrugged helplessly, 'but from what I understand Hester became an extremely powerful seer. It's possible she foresaw all of this. She would have known after Nathaniel killed her mother and kidnapped her and her sister, that he had made the connection between the Book and the Wests. She would have known it was no longer safe to pass it on down the line of her family. If she was able to see far enough into the future to witness Isabel's betrayal, she would have made sure it was not passed on to her. One thing you should know about Isabel is that, although make no mistake she is incredibly dangerous, the simple fact is for some reason she is nowhere nearly as powerful as the other women in your family. She has always carried a chip on her shoulder about that; her pride made her hate anyone she perceived as more powerful than she was. That is why she is so obsessed with the book, and she doesn't wish to simply be its caretaker.'

'She wants to use its power?'

'Yes she does, that's what drives her.'

'Nathaniel knows that the West Women are tied to the fate of the book?'

'Yes.'

'What if he allowed himself to be trapped by mom?' her brow folded into a thoughtful frown as an idea began to form in her mind. 'Clever little demon,' she murmured, 'he's rolled over and he's playing dead.'

'Explain?'

'How old would you say Nathaniel is?'

'I don't know' Charles frowned, 'but I would guess thousands of years old.'

'Exactly,' she replied. 'When we were trying to figure out the serpent seal on the murder victims we did some research on the demon Nathaniel and his brother Seth. This was before we made the connection between the demon Nathaniel and Nathaniel Boothe from 17th century Salem; before we knew they were one and the same.'

'Where are you going with this?'

'Hear me out,' she continued. 'Legend has it that his brother Seth is still trapped in the underworld, but Nathaniel was free to wander the earth. He was never summoned, he walked the earth in his true form for centuries until he ended up in Salem Massachusetts. Yet there is no mention of him in history nor the part he played in the witch hunts. Theo once told me that Nathanial always remained in the background manipulating others.'

'So?'

'Most of the colonists were afraid of their own shadows back then, he whipped them up into a dangerous cocktail of fear and righteousness and set them loose. He caused the witch hunts.'

'Demons like death and chaos, they love nothing more than to cause pain and suffering.'

'Yes but this was very specific,' she answered, 'and I'm willing to bet he stirred up the witch hunts in Salem to flush out the Wests. He'd already made the connection and he knew if he could get to them, he could get to the book. That's what he had been after all along.'

'That's a fair assumption,' her father agreed.

'He didn't just accidentally stumble across the connection with Hester, he had to have been tracking the book for a very long time to trace it back to my family and do you really think a demon that old and intelligent would just allow himself to be imprisoned in a body of flesh by a second rate witch?'

Charles's eyes narrowed as he considered her words.

'I felt him,' she said quietly, 'it wasn't just that Aunt Evie had left me the house. The moment she was gone, I could feel something calling to me, calling me home, calling to my blood. I didn't realize it but it was him and if I felt it, you can bet mom felt it too. He was luring her in. I'll bet he's been doing it all along, whispering in her ear, manipulating her and using her most desperate desire against her.'

'And because she's so obsessed she can't see that she doesn't have the upper hand at all,' Charles replied thoughtfully.

'Exactly,' Olivia answered. 'If Hester hid the book, it means he needs a West to find it. He's using her.'

'My God,' Charles breathed, 'once he's done with her and gets loose, God help us all. Even Hester with all her power didn't have enough strength to kill him in his true form, that's why she trapped him instead.'

'Where does the Ferryman fit into all this?' Olivia rose from her seat and began to pace the room restlessly.

'Well ask yourself this,' her father replied. 'What does the Ferryman deal in?'

'Money, Greek coins to pay passage for the…oh,' she replied slowly as the pieces began to fall into place, 'souls…he deals in souls and not just any soul.'

Charles sat back a small smile playing on his lips.

'Oh Hester you clever, clever girl,' Olivia shook her head smiling. 'I remember Nana Alice always telling me that Hester was the only one in our family to be buried in the woods rather than Mercy Cemetery. She left strict instructions that her body was to be buried in the woods with no marker, only a tree to be planted over her bones.

She made sure no one would be able to find her remains. If mom had Hester's remains she could perform a summoning ritual and call her soul back from the afterlife, compelling her to reveal where she hid the book. But by hiding her body she ensured no one would be able to recall her soul. That's why they went after Charon, they are trying to use him to locate Hester's soul.'

She turned back to study her father's face and found him staring at her with something that looked suspiciously like pride.

'You knew mom was after Hester's soul?'

'I know how your mom thinks,' he answered. 'If Hester was the last person to have the book, it stands to reason that is the first place Isabel would look. As Hester is dead the only way would be to summon her spirit back. As they can't do that because they don't have her remains, she would look for another way to bring back a soul. Who better than an entity that ferries souls to and from the underworld? Although I had worked out the bare bones of it I have to admit you filled in a lot of the blanks. I was so focused on Isabel' he frowned, 'I fear I may have underestimated Nathaniel and his part in this.'

'So,' she rubbed her forehead tiredly, 'we need to find mom? Find her and we find Charon.'

'And Nathaniel,' Charles added. 'Now we suspect he may be a major player I won't underestimate him again.'

'Okay.'

'There is one more thing you should know,' her father warned. 'We've really run out of time, something needs to be done now. The sheer amount of creatures pouring into Mercy through the doorway can no longer be contained by Danae, Davis and I. I estimate at the rate they're coming through we've got a day or two at the most before Mercy is overrun.'

'What can we do?' Olivia frowned, 'what do you need?'

'I have an idea, but I need more people. Will some

of your friends help?'

Olivia nodded. 'Everyone is meeting at my house tomorrow.'

'Alright then tomorrow,' he replied.

'I should get back before I'm missed,' she told him as she headed for the door.

'Olivia?'

She turned back to face him.

'I only ever wanted the best for you and if I could change things and give you back everything you lost I would.'

She sighed tiredly. 'I know, but you're right about one thing, 'what's past is past. It can't be changed and I can't allow it to keep ruling me. I'm not saying I forgive you exactly but in some ways you were as much a victim in this mess as anyone. If anyone's to blame, it's mom for putting us in this situation.'

'Thank you for that.'

She shrugged and headed for the door. Impulsively she stopped and turned back, looking her father in the eye.

'And for what it's worth, I missed you,' she admitted quietly, 'even when I hated you I still missed you.'

Charles's mouth tightened as he watched her turn and disappear from the room, his eyes dark and his expression unreadable.

19.

Theo lined up the shot, closing one eye and squinting as he tried to clear his blurred vision. He hit the cue ball and hoped for the best and with a small clang of colliding balls, his target rolled ponderously to the edge and dropped into the pocket.

'I did it!' he smiled, a big wide smile of the inebriated.

'Good job,' Tommy patted his shoulder, 'except for one problem. That was my ball you just sunk.'

'Oh,' Theo frowned as Tommy handed him a glass.

'Don't worry, you're doing okay for an old guy,' he grinned.

'I'm practically the same age as you.'

'Yeah,' Tommy laughed, 'give or take a couple of centuries.'

Theo knew Tommy didn't really believe he'd come from 17th Century Salem, but as it seemed to amuse him Theo didn't bother to argue.

'So what's going on?' Tommy leaned over the table. Wobbling slightly, he corrected himself and lined up his next shot, smacking it straight into the corner pocket. He took the glass back from Theo and downed the contents, eyeing his friend speculatively.

'Nothing's going on.'

'I've spent enough time with you Theo to know when you've got something brewing in that brain of yours.'

Theo sighed and glanced over to Jake who sat drinking a beer while he watched them try to play pool.

'Will this stay between the three of us?'

'Of course old man,' Tommy slapped him amiably on the back, 'Bro's before Ho's.'

'I have no idea what you just said,' Theo frowned.

'You'd better hope my sister doesn't hear you saying things like that,' Jake chuckled and Tommy looked around nervously, just in case.

'It's alright Theo,' Jake assured him, 'whatever you say to us is in confidence.'

'I have something I need to tell Olivia and it's…well it's complicated and I don't know how she'll take it. Things are good between us at the moment and I don't want that to change.'

'All relationships change,' Jake told him sagely as Tommy rounded the pool table to line up another shot. 'That's how they grow and get stronger. You have to be honest with her because without trust and honesty in a relationship it won't go anywhere; it will always be just something superficial.'

'Oh my God,' Tommy laughed, 'Do you want me to hold your uterus for you there, while you take a piss?'

'You know Tommy,' Jake took a swig of his beer, 'I liked you a lot better before you joined the army and came back with that smart mouth of yours.'

'I'll bet,' Tommy laughed. He turned back to Theo who was leaning against the pool table, propped up on his pool stick.

'Ignore the relationship guru over there, who has never had a relationship that lasted longer than three months. Theo what is it exactly you think you need to tell Olivia?'

Theo sighed and frowned. 'I need to tell her about my wife.'

Jake spewed his beer across the floor and started coughing violently.

'Seriously?'

'Seriously,' Theo repeated.

'You're married?'

'Yes, well no, I was...it's complicated.'

'No shit Sherlock,' Tommy shook his head. 'This we need more drinks for.'

He beckoned to the waitress nearby and she nodded and headed back to the bar.

'Okay start explaining,' Jake frowned.

'When I was younger I was married. My father insisted,' Theo added ruefully, 'but it wasn't a good marriage.'

'What happened?'

'She died.'

'Okay,' Jake pinched the bridge of his nose, trying to focus through the haze of alcohol. 'So did she die before Sam dropped you into the middle of Mercy; you didn't actually leave a wife back in Salem and take up with Olivia?'

'God no!' Theo shook his head, 'that would have made her my mistress. I would never do something like that to Olivia, no matter how I feel about her. It would have been disrespectful to Mary, to Olivia and to God. Adultery is a sin.'

'Okay, shove your Puritan back in his cave' Jake chuckled, 'I was just asking to clarify things. So this Mary was already dead when you came here?'

'Yes,' he nodded.

'So you're a widower?'

'Technically.'

'There's no technically about it,' Tommy interrupted. 'You have the best excuse ever for not telling her. It's like, honey it happened over three hundred years ago, it totally slipped my mind.'

Theo let out a small laugh, unable to help himself. 'I wish it were that simple.'

'It is that simple,' Tommy told him seriously, 'if you want it to be.'

'As much as it pains me to say it.' Jake added, 'Tommy's right.'

'Could I get that in writing?'

'Shut up,' Jake mouth curved in amusement. 'The fact is it happened over a lifetime ago, at least four lifetimes in fact. The past is the past, maybe it should be left there. Being in Mercy with Olivia is a fresh start for you. You're not still married; that life no longer exists. So why not just enjoy what you have with Olivia.'

'Well, that's the complicated part,' Theo grimaced. 'You know we have a bit of a spirit problem in Mercy at the moment?'

'Shit,' Jake shook his head in disbelief. 'I take it your ex-wife has put in an appearance.'

'You could say that.'

'Aw man,' Tommy shook his head, 'that just fucking sucks.'

'That's why I have to tell Olivia. At first I wasn't sure if it actually was Mary but there is no doubt about it. She's becoming more and more insistent about showing herself. Sooner or later Olivia is going to find out and I'd rather it came from me and not from my very angry and very dead former wife.'

'Well you're right about that,' Jake sighed. 'Good luck man.'

'Thanks,' Theo muttered dryly.

The waitress reappeared with three shot glasses.

'Thanks Shirl.' Tommy nodded handing the glasses to the other two as she moved away.

'To psycho ex-wives, may they rest in peace,' Tommy lifted his glass.

Theo sighed and raised his glass as the three of them tipped their heads back and downed the contents.

'So what about you?' Tommy propped himself against the side of the pool table next to Theo and stared at Jake. 'What happened to the hot red-head you were seeing?'

'Erica?' Jake replied. 'It's over, we don't want the same things.'

'Ah,' he nodded knowingly, 'started making noises about marriage and kids did she?'

Jake didn't answer, he simply took a long pull on his beer but Tommy didn't miss the fleeting look on Jake's face.

'Oh,' he drawled slowly, 'I see. It wasn't her wanting marriage and kids was it...?' He laughed in delight, 'how the mighty have fallen. Well Jake, seems you're just as human as the rest of us.'

'Shut up,' Jake picked up a chip from a nearby bowl and threw it at his brother in law.

'I'm sorry man,' Tommy was still laughing as he held up his hands in mock surrender, 'what happened?'

'She got offered a job in Boston, she's leaving,' Jake shrugged.

'You pissed because she's leaving, or because she broke it off?'

'Bit of both I guess,' Jake stared at his bottle toying with the edges of the label before he shrugged and looked up. 'Whatever, it's not like I was in love with her or anything.'

'Uh-huh,' Tommy replied staring at him meaningfully.

'I'm not,' Jake insisted. 'We had fun together, it was never serious and I'm not looking for marriage and babies. It's just lately,' he shrugged, 'I don't know I just figure sometimes it would be nice to come home to someone instead of a fridge full of beer, ESPN and an empty apartment.'

'Jeez, you got breasts to go with that uterus?'

'Shut up,' Jake laughed, 'I'm just saying is all.'

'Yeah yeah,' Tommy smiled, 'get a dog. It's less trouble and will spend less on shoes, trust me.'

'I'll tell my sister you said that.'

Tommy snorted in laughter and launched himself at Jake. They wrestled around and rolled out of the chair, landing on the floor in a tangle of elbows and knees as they scrambled to get each other in a neck lock.

'Is that all you got, NYPD Blue?' Tommy laughed breathlessly as he elbowed Jake in the kidney.

'Shut up G.I Joe,' he rolled over and yanked Tommy's arms behind his back. 'Your ass is mine now.'

'Said your sister last night,' Tommy replied in a muffled voice as his face was pressed into the floor.

With a war-like whoop Jake wrapped his arm around Tommy's neck and pinned him against his ribs and with the other hand scrubbed his knuckles against Tommy's scalp.

Theo was watching in amusement as the waitress wandered over and looked down at the two over-sized kids on the floor.

'What's he doing?' Theo asked.

'Ain't you never seen a noogie before?'

Theo looked blankly at her.

'Anyways, you boys want anything else to drink.'

'I wouldn't mind another one of these?' Theo held up his shot glass.

'Just bring us the bottle Shirley,' Tommy gasped as he tried to loosen Jake's hold on his neck.

'You got it,' she smiled and walked away.

'You know what?' Tommy panted.

'What?' Jake growled.

'We're missing a golden opportunity here.'

'What?' he relaxed his grip on Tommy marginally.

'Well if what you guys say about Theo is true and he really is like five hundred years old……'

'I'm only 31,' Theo interrupted in exasperation.

'That means he's never been noogied before.'

'Ah,' Jake turned to look at Theo with a wicked glint in his eyes, 'that's true.'

'Now just you wait a minute,' Theo held up his hands as Jake released Tommy and they slowly climbed to their feet.

'Too late,' they both laughed as they jumped him and wrestled him to the ground.

Olivia walked into the bar and scanned the room. It was fairly quiet but there again, between the weather and the epidemic that seemed to be sweeping through the town, she wasn't really surprised. Her gazed finally landed on the unholy trio she'd been searching for. Shaking her head and laughing lightly she headed over towards them.

Jake, Tommy and Theo were all sitting on the floor, propped up against the wall, passing a bottle of Johnnie Walker Double Black between them.

'Hey,' she greeted them and was greeted by three sets of bleary eyes blinking up at her.

Theo's face broke into a heart wrenching smile as he saw her, before looking at her like she was the most precious thing in the world.

'Time to go Theo,' she placed her hands on her hips and looked down at them in amusement.

'I gotta go home now,' Theo slurred as he turned to face his friends.

'Awww,' the other two protested, 'can't we have another hour?'

Olivia laughed delightedly, it was like dealing with a trio of 11 year olds.

'No, it's bedtime,' she smiled as she glanced at

Jake, 'and as for you deputy, shouldn't you be setting a better example for your community?'

'I am setting a good example,' he hiccupped.

'Oh really?' she raised a brow questioningly, 'and what's that?'

'If you're gonna get drunk use the good stuff,' he smiled beatifically as he waggled the almost empty bottle at her.

She chuckled and leaned down to grasp Theo's hands.

'Come on baby, let's get you home.' She hauled him to his feet, 'you can play with your friends tomorrow.'

He stumbled into her as he stood, wrapping his arms around her as he got his balance. He pulled her in tight against his body and her breath caught in her throat.

'Damn you're beautiful,' he murmured as his lips found hers.

Unlike most drunks this was not some sloppy drunken smooch as Olivia discovered. His kiss was devastating and she felt it right down to her toes. She could taste the Johnnie Walker on his lips but it wasn't unpleasant. He tilted her head and before she realized what she was doing her hands snaked into his hair and she opened her mouth, letting him taste her. He was even more potent like this she thought. She bit back a groan and pulled away reluctantly before she set an example for the community of an entirely different nature.

'Come on Romeo,' she chuckled, 'let's go home.'

He took her hand and gave a half assed drunken wave to the other two still planted on the floor.

'My house tomorrow Jake, don't forget,' Olivia reminded him.

'What's going on?' Tommy slurred, 'we having a séance or something?'

'Bring Mr doubty-pants with you too,' she rolled her eyes.

Jake saluted her with the bottle before taking

another pull.

They almost made it to the door when Theo stopped, trying to connect the two ends of the zip on his jacket. Olivia watched in amusement as he struggled with it, and finally taking pity on him she moved his hands away, hooking the ends together easily and zipping him into his jacket like he was a child. With a contented smile he leaned forward and buried his face in the crook of her neck, breathing in deeply.

'Theo?' she asked after a moment, 'are you …sniffing me?'

He mumbled something unintelligible into the collar of her coat.

'What?' she replied as she pulled back.

'I said,' he repeated slowly, 'you always smell so good.'

She laughed and shook her head. 'Come on let's go.'

She took his hand and headed out of the bar, amused that he was barely able to keep his hands off her as she steered him back to her car. No point now in telling him about her conversation with her father, she thought. Given how drunk he was he probably wouldn't even remember it in the morning. She got him into the car and as the snow seemed to be holding off, the drive home was mercifully easy and fairly quick. Theo smiled at her the whole way and she had to admit he was really cute when he was drunk.

By the time they stumbled into the hallway, slamming the door behind them, Theo was already tugging her coat off and discarding it on the floor alongside his own. Kicking off his boots he pressed her up against the wall.

'I want to be inside you,' he breathed against her lips as he tugged her shirt loose and stroked the bare flesh of her sides and her back.

'Bed,' she panted, 'it's too cold down here.'

He picked her up as she wrapped her legs around his waist and her arms round his neck. He stumbled up the stairs and into their room, dropping her down on the bed before stripped off his shirt. She watched him as the rest of his clothes followed, until he stood at the foot of the bed unabashedly naked. She sat up and let him unbutton her shirt and slip it from her shoulders. Her pants were next which he unhooked and peeled slowly down her legs leaving her in nothing but her silvery grey lace bra and panties.

'God, Livy,' his eyes roamed over her appreciatively, his fingertips tracing the curve of her breast through the see-through lace. 'I love what goes on under your clothes.'

He took her mouth, tasting her with long slow luxurious sweeps of his tongue. She involuntarily arched her hips curving against the hard press of his naked body, instinctively reaching out to find some relief from the low throbbing ache in her core. Theo knew he was lost; through the haze of alcohol he was drowning in the scent and feel of her, her soft skin beneath his hands, her body curving sweetly into his, seeking him out, seeking the pleasure only he could provide.

His lips trailed fire down her throat and across her collar bone and he slid his hands under her back and unclipped her bra. Peeling it from her body he tossed it to the ground as he filled his hands with her soft warm breasts.

'Theo,' she breathed heavily as she arched her back pressing herself more firmly into his hands. He continued to trail hot open mouthed kisses down her torso towards her belly.

There was only one thought in his mind, something he'd seen in one of the books hidden at the back of a shelf down in the library. A scandalous book filled with erotic and salacious images, something so sinful and foreign looking he'd been shocked when he stumbled across it. He'd turned from it, embarrassed to have seen such illustrations, but found he could not forget it. It was a book no decent God fearing person would ever have had in their possession. He'd reminded himself that things were not the same as they had been in his time and that such things were more accepted now. Even so, it still went against everything he believed in. But there was one particular image in it that thrilled him, filling him with a dark longing and fuelling his arousal. Something he wanted to do to her desperately.

His tongue toyed at the edge of the lace of her panties as she arched helplessly into his hands impatient and flushed. Unable to resist any longer he buried his face between her thighs breathing in the scent of her. His tongue pressed through the lace, slowly and tentatively at first until he heard her moan and reach down to grasp his hair. He licked and suckled her through the flimsy fabric as she writhed beneath him and he felt powerful.

The sound of tearing fabric filled the air as he stripped her panties from her body. She cried out in her need as he pressed back between her thighs with nothing separating him from her naked flesh. He had now crossed a line and inhibitions were gone as he licked the length of her before suckling the tight little bundle of nerves into his mouth. Sliding his hands under her buttocks he pulled her hips closer to his face. She was like a drug, one taste and he was hopelessly addicted to her.

She bucked beneath him at the sheer intensity of feelings he was creating with his mouth and as the pressure began to build towards her climax he acted on instinct, slipping a finger inside her, followed by another and stroked deep. Curling his fingers, he hit that place inside her that made her go blind. She gripped his hair tightly in her fist, trying to push him away yet at the same time trying to pull him closer. It was too much, too intense, not just for her but for him too. He ground his hips into the bed trying to find some relief from the intense arousal of doing something so forbidden.

She tried to pull away from the intensity but he pinned her hips keeping her in place, forcing her to take the pleasure he gave. A scream tore from her throat as she let go and crested wave after wave of acute pleasure. When she finally came down her body was trembling with the sheer force of her orgasm and Theo almost lost control. To give Olivia so much pleasure, to arouse her to such a pitch that he felt it as intensely as if it were his own, was like nothing he'd ever known.

He crawled up her body and thrust inside her as she wrapped her legs tightly around his hips pulling him deeper. She wrapped her arms around his neck pressing him against her, and he covered her mouth with his, swallowing every sound she made as he owned her body. Now driven by some deep seated instinct he pulled away and flipped her over onto her stomach. Spreading her legs, he grasped her hands interlocking her fingers with his as he slipped inside her again. Moaning in delight she curved her spine, lifting her hips so he could plunge deeper. When he bit down gently on the back of her neck a shiver shot straight to her nipples making them harden painfully. Disentangling her hands from his she reached back over her shoulder and grasped his hair tugging almost painfully.

'Harder,' she demanded.

He obliged her, grasping her hips to raise her to her knees, pounding into her as she moaned in pleasure, pressing her face into the covers of the bed. Another climax hit her hard and she reared up pressing her back to his chest reaching behind her to wrap her arms around his neck. He pressed his face into her neck, breathing in the scent of his beloved woman, licking the salty moisture from her soft skin. His hands skimmed her breasts, down her torso past her flat stomach stroking through the wetness between her thighs where they were still joined.

Breathing hard, with her heart pounding in her

chest, she turned her head to look at him and his lips found hers in a soft slow deeply intimate kiss.

'Theo,' she breathed against his mouth.

His movements slowed with her change in mood and he thrust slower, deeper until they dropped back down to the bed. She pulled away and pushed him gently down onto his back. He watched her with dark intense eyes as she stretched out over him, then he slipped back inside her slowly as she rocked against him, savoring each sound he made. She sat back on her heels taking him deep. He threw his head back and thrust up into her body, helplessly enslaved by her. He could feel her long dark hair brush against his thighs as she arched her back, her breasts thrusting upwards, and he knew he'd never seen anything so beautiful in his life.

She was so close, and with one final deep rock of her hips her orgasm exploded as she clamped down on Theo so hard he had no choice but to follow. He growled as he reared up wrapping his arms around her tightly and thrusting up into her body as he too crested the peak until they both collapsed back down onto the bed breathing heavily.

'God,' Theo covered his eyes with one hand as he tried to steady his pounding heart. 'Dizzy.'

'I'll bet,' Olivia smiled against his skin. 'I've taken terrible advantage of you in your delicate condition.'

He grabbed her and rolled her under him, tickling her ribs.

'Delicate?'

'Stop it,' she giggled trying to squirm away from him.

'Delicate,' he continued to tickle her mercilessly.

'Stop stop,' she laughed loudly, 'I take it back.'

He rolled onto his back, pulling her into his side and tucking her safely in his arms.

They lay in silence for a moment until Olivia finally scooted up his body and propped her face on her hand so she could look down at him.

'What's wrong?' she asked, 'you've gone quiet.'

The truth was, now the alcohol induced fog of lust had passed, he was feeling slightly ashamed of the way he'd lost control and the things he'd done to her. He hadn't made love to her the way she deserved, he'd been rough and demanding.

'I'm sorry if I was too rough with you,' he murmured watching her with dark eyes.

'Did it look like I was complaining?'

'No, but...'

She could see he was struggling with something, a faint blush spread across his cheekbones and he looked up at the ceiling as if he couldn't quite find the right words. If she had to guess, she would imagine he was probably feeling a little raw and exposed. He'd stepped outside of his comfort zone when he made love to her tonight. The alcohol had masked his inhibitions and he'd taken her hard and furiously and she had loved every second of it. But it was also the first time he'd pleasured her with his mouth and he was probably feeling pretty conflicted about that.

She knew that where he came from marriage and sex existed for one reason and one reason alone, for the procreation of children. Then he was suddenly thrust into a world where sexual liberation and sex outside of marriage were not only accepted but pretty common. Now, for the first time in his life, he was having to balance his own sexuality with the strict and moral religion he was raised with.

'Are you ashamed of what we did tonight?' she asked softly.

'No,' he shook his head.

'But you are embarrassed?'

He sighed as she stroked his cheek gently, turning his face so he was forced to look at her.

'Don't ever be embarrassed of what we do. If your God hadn't wanted you to enjoy sex he wouldn't have made it so pleasurable. It's not wrong and it's not a sin. It's how we are able to show each other how we feel.'

He stared at her silently as he struggled with the concept.

'Do you know how I felt with your mouth on me?'

He shook his head.

'Desired, powerful, pleasured,' her lips brushed his slowly. 'I felt close to you. I could feel how much you wanted me, how desperate you were for me and it made me want you even more. Now tell me is that wrong?'

'No,' he whispered as he toyed with a lock of her hair.

She smiled as she dropped a kiss on his lips.

'I need to use the bathroom, I'll be right back.'

She climbed out of bed and headed towards the bathroom. As she glanced at the fireplace it burst back into flames, filling the room with its warmth and soft light. By the time she'd finished and climbed back into bed, Theo's eyes were closed and his breathing was regular and even.

Smiling to herself she pulled the covers up over him and tucked them around him to keep him warm. She studied his face in the dim light; he was so sweet and loving and hot as hell in bed. But more than that there was something so uniquely appealing about him, it was as if he had been created just for her. He'd crossed time for her, he'd fought a demon for her, he was breaking every rule he'd ever been raised with and all for her.

God damn it, she sighed. She'd done the one thing she promised herself she wouldn't, she'd gone and fallen in love with him.

She dropped a ghost of a kiss on his parted lips, barely even brushing them with her own.

'Olivia,' he turned to her even in his sleep.

'I love you,' she whispered, but the words were lost as the sound of his soft snore filled the room.

20.

Theo stared up at the building which was shrouded by thick snow covered branches. It was high up on a small cliff overhanging the water's edge. Concealed at the base of the rock were steep narrow steps leading upward. He shivered and turned back towards the lake which was now completed frozen over, some of its surface thick with fresh snowfall and the rest flat sheet ice which reflected back the bright moon. Heavy white clouds streaked across the sky and the air was so cold it was like breathing in thousands of tiny needles.

Suddenly a great cracking sound split the icy air. Theo watched, taking an involuntary step back, as the lake burst open ominously at the center and massive shards of jagged ice began to rise through the breached surface, clawing their way towards the sky. A sense of urgency gripped him by the throat and he spun around to face the path, laying one foot on the first step. His hand grasped the rusted metal guardrail and he began to climb quickly, the steps creaking and groaning ominously beneath his feet. Branches blocked his path, scratching at his exposed skin with vicious needle-like claws.

He could see glimpses of a building at the pinnacle as he scrambled up the steps, feeling the guardrail sway dangerously. Pushing the branches out of his way he reached the top and the building came into view. It was huge, much bigger than he'd expected and once upon a time it would have been a grand sight to behold, with its curved corners and sharp arches. Parts of it were now shrouded with moss but in the moonlight he could still make out the ghostly creamy coloured walls and the cracked peeling blue grey of the columns and arches.

A sign hung above the entrance in huge elegant letters but several were missing and he could not make out the name in the dim light. He stepped forward and felt the ground tremble and shake violently beneath his feet. Turning back towards the churning icy mass of the lake he saw a great archway of ice and from it spilled masses of writhing smoky creatures. At this distance he couldn't make them out but as they scuttled across the broken uneven ice like a horde of giant insects his breath caught in his throat as he saw them swarm towards the shore in all directions.

His heart jolted in his chest as he felt the ground heave once again. He stumbled back and for a moment it seemed as though he was frozen in time, and everything around him had paused. He felt weightless, but as the ground beneath him broke away with a violent grinding sound it crashed down towards the lake edge, smashing through the ice, and suddenly he was falling.

With a sharp intake of breath Theo opened his eyes and blinked several times to clear his blurred vision. Slowly he became aware he was no longer in bed beside Olivia. He found he was crouched on the floor of his studio wearing nothing but his jeans, although he had no recollection of getting up and putting them on. They were now streaked with paint and as he glanced down at his bare chest and his hands he realized his skin was also smeared with paint. Shaking his head in confusion he looked up and saw Olivia kneeling on the floor in front of him, wearing his shirt and watching him carefully.

'Theo?'

'What's happening,' he asked, his voice rough and uncertain. 'Why am I down here?'

'You tell me?' she looked down at the floor beneath him.

He followed her line of sight and drew in a deep breath. A large part of the floor was covered in paint, not just random drips and splotches but a detailed painting of the building on the cliff. He must have painted it whilst in the grip of his dream.

'What is this place Theo?' Olivia asked quietly.

'I don't know' he frowned, trying to remember, but even now the last vestiges of the dream were fading from his memory.

'Theo?'

He looked at Olivia and for the first time noticed there was something not right about the way she was looking at him. He couldn't pinpoint it exactly but it was a mixture of puzzlement and hurt.

'What is it?'

'Who is she?' she whispered quietly.

For a moment Theo didn't know to whom she was referring until he looked up and his gaze scanned the room. He cursed softly; once again the room was covered in pictures of Mary's portrait. Not just the canvases which were spaced around the room but all of the pencil sketches which were pinned to the walls so there was barely any space left.

'Olivia,' he rose to his feet slowly as did she.

'Who is she?' she repeated more firmly.

He hesitated, aware of how the words coming

from his lips would sound. This was the moment he had been dreading for months and now there was no avoiding it.

'At first I thought it might be your sister Temperance, but I've seen your drawings of her. She looks just like you and she died when she was nine years old. But that woman,' she glanced back at the blonde woman in the portrait, 'she's at least in her twenties…so who is she?'

Theo let out a slow reluctant breath.

Her name was Mary Alcott…Beckett.'

'Beckett?' Olivia repeated questioningly, a feeling of dread sat like lead in her stomach.

'She was my wife.'

'Your wife,' the hurt coiled around her chest squeezing hard and when she spoke her voice was barely more than a whisper. 'You're married?'

'No,' he shook his head, 'not anymore. Look Olivia, I can explain.'

'I think you'd better,' she locked her arms across her chest like a barrier across her heart.

'We were very young when we married,' he sighed, 'I didn't want to be married but my father insisted. Although my brother Logan loved both me and Temperance, he always hated the farm, hated being at home, hated anything that reminded him of our mother. So he always found excuses to be absent which largely left the running of the farm to me. My father lived at the bottom of a bottle and was next to useless when he wasn't being violent. Then he insisted it was time for me to take a wife. I was barely more than nineteen years old at the time and I wasn't strong enough to stand up to him. He said Temperance needed a female in the house to teach her how to run a home and when her time came, how to be a good wife. I had let her run wild, I had given her more freedom than was acceptable for a girl child and it was beginning to show. Whilst I was more than happy to indulge her I did feel she would benefit from having a woman in her life that she could be close to, so in the end I agreed to marriage. My father already had a prospective bride in mind and had spoken with her father. Her name was Mary Alcott. She was only seventeen years old herself and she was a sweet, pretty little thing. Quiet but always smiled shyly when she saw me at church. I didn't think it would be so bad being married to her and at least it would give me someone else my age to talk to.'

'What happened to her?' Olivia asked quietly, not sure if she wanted to hear the answer. 'Did you leave her when Sam brought you to Mercy?'

'No,' Theo sighed, 'she died. Are you sure you want to know, it's a long story.'

'I have to know the truth Theo.'

He nodded in resignation and continued.

'For a while our marriage was good, we became friends and it was nice to have company. Although Temperance seemed happy to have another female in the house I noticed she always held back with Mary; she never quite warmed to her. Mary loved me, I knew she did. I'm not surprised she felt that way about me as I allowed her the same freedoms as I did Tempy. Coming from the home she did, with a Preacher father and a strict mother she suddenly felt valued. I listened to her when she spoke and let her form her own opinions, never chastising her for speaking her mind. I was very fond of her.'

'You didn't love her?' Olivia frowned as she tried to understand.

'I couldn't.'

'Why?'

'Because she wasn't you,' he whispered. 'I'd seen your face every night in my dreams for as long as I could remember, looked through a window into your world. Even though I didn't know at the time that you were real, it was your face I saw every time I looked at her. I knew I wasn't being fair to her but I couldn't help the way I felt, any more than she could change her love for me.'

'So what happened?'

'About a year into the marriage she began to change, it was so strange. She began sleeping a lot and she would forget things. At first I just dismissed it but then she stopped bathing and taking care of herself, her hair would often become dirty and matted and Tempy would sit with her for hours trying to comb out the snarls. After a while she started to become suspicious, she said I was watching her all the time and that she knew I wanted to hurt her. I didn't, I swear I would never have harmed her, but she seemed convinced I was going to kill her in our bed while she slept, so she stopped sleeping.'

'Go on,' Olivia urged him, frowning thoughtfully.

'Quite often she would start ranting suddenly but her words didn't make sense, her mind seemed so disorganized I couldn't keep up with her. She would switch randomly between subjects and from that point on it just got worse and worse. She started to hear voices, she said the voices told her I wanted to harm her and I would catch her looking at things that weren't there.'

'Hallucinations?'

'I don't know what that is?'

'It's when a person sees things that aren't real but they are convinced that they are.'

'Yes' he nodded, 'that is what she was like. She was convinced the house and the farm were crawling with mangy half-starved cats, which of course it wasn't. We had a couple of big toms to keep the mice out but that was it. My father's health deteriorated as did Mary's condition. Tempy and I tried to hide it from most people but it was getting harder and harder and people were beginning to talk. Mary had an outburst at church and began screaming at the congregation that they were all sinners and murderers and that they were all going to burn in Hell. After that we tried to keep her hidden at home as much as we could but it made her worse because now she believed we were trying to imprison her. But it wasn't safe to turn her loose, whispers of witchcraft had already begun. It was only a matter of time before the arrests would start. Fortunately, we were fairly isolated at the farm as it was on the outskirts of Salem village and a fair distance from Salem town itself.'

'If they'd seen her they would have assumed she was in league with the devil, she would have been accused,' Olivia surmised.

'Exactly,' Theo answered. 'Logan was already in Nathaniel's thrall at this point. He was almost at the point of taking vows and becoming a witch finder himself.'

'I don't understand' Olivia frowned, 'I've seen the court records and they state that you and your brother Logan were named witch finders by the court at the same time.'

'The records are incorrect,' he told her. 'It is my understanding that Logan went back and had the official records adjusted.'

'Why would he do that?'

'To change our family history' Theo shrugged. 'He wanted our name to be as feared as Hopkins or Searne. He wanted to promote the image of us a one fierce unified family of witch finders, which couldn't have been further from the truth. Our family was broken and damaged beyond repair at that point. Our father was dying and my wife was touched by madness. Tempy and I were having visions which would have condemned either one of us as witches, something we were both desperately trying to hide, not just from the fanatics but from my own wife and brother.'

'Surely Logan would not have allowed anything to happen to you both? he was your brother, he loved you.'

'Maybe,' Theo frowned shaking his head, 'I honestly don't know what he would have done if he'd found out. He was changing, it had started with the death of our mother. It was like something inside him was broken. As the years passed he became more and more bitter. We stayed at the farm, with Tempy and I nursing father and trying to keep Mary as calm as we could. When Tempy died I think it just pushed him over the edge.'

He broke off, breathing heavily as the painful memories washed over him.

'What happened Theo?' Olivia asked gently.

'Tempy was sick, she had a cough and she was starting to show signs of a fever. I begged her to rest but she insisted on helping me with Mary and father. The next day I needed to leave for a while as we had to sell our produce at market two towns over. There was no way around it, we had to survive. I didn't want to leave her alone with Mary and father but there was no other choice. I knew I could make the trip in three days, two if I didn't stay at the inn and but kept travelling, dozing in the cart.

I convinced Logan to accompany me, I couldn't take the chance of him going back to the farm while I wasn't there and discovering Mary's condition. I was also afraid because Tempy's fever seemed to be disrupting her gift; the sicker she got the less control she had over her visions. I couldn't risk Logan finding out about that either so we left as planned but on the way back we got caught in a storm. By the time I managed to return home a week had passed. Tempy was gone, her fever had worsened in our absence and with only Mary by her side, she died. Mary was ranting about a man appearing and disappearing and cats everywhere eating the corpses. It seemed that in her sickness she'd burned Tempy's body instead of having her buried, because she thought the cats infesting the farm would dig up the body and consume it.'

'Oh God Theo' Olivia breathed, shutting her eyes against his pain and shaking her head. 'I'm so sorry.'

'I tried to keep Logan from seeing Mary's state of mind but it was too late. Driven mad with grief for our little sister and infuriated that Mary had burned her body instead of allowing her to receive the benefit of a Christian burial, he denounced Mary in her madness for a witch. I tried to stop them but by this point I too had succumbed to the fever which had taken Tempy. I was laid abed for days, drifting in and out of consciousness. By the time the fever broke and I had the strength to stand I crawled out of bed and headed for Salem where they'd taken Mary. Weak from my illness and lack of food it was a long and hard ride but when I finally got there I was informed Mary had already stood trial and had been found guilty. I climbed back on my horse and headed for Gallows Hill but I was too late.'

'Theo you don't have to finish.'

'No,' he breathed past the hard lump in his throat, 'you need to know. I did everything I could to save her but I was betrayed by my own weak body. As I approached I could see Logan reading the list of charges against her as she stood on a stool with a noose around her neck. I dismounted but my legs collapsed beneath me. Pushing myself up with everything I had, I forced my way through the jeering crowd but before I could reach her Nathaniel kicked the stool out from under her. Two of the men from the crowd held me back as I tried to reach her, but I had no strength left to fight them. They forced me to watch her die, kicking and struggling for breath.'

'Theo,' Olivia whispered sadly.

'I fell to the ground in the dirt and mud as the rain came down in torrents. The witnesses drifted away one by one, leaving me alone in my grief, watching as her lifeless body swayed in the wind and dangled helplessly at the end of a rope.'

He looked up at Olivia his eyes dark and filled with centuries old grief and pain.

'Logan came to me, the way he looked at me,' Theo shook his head. 'Just for a moment there was a brief glimpse of the man he had been, the man I had loved and as he put his arms around me for a brief time he was my brother again. I should have saved Mary and I should never have left Tempy alone with her.'

'Theo,' Olivia took a step towards him, 'it wasn't your fault, you didn't drive Mary to madness. From what you've described to me I think there was something very wrong with her.'

'What do you mean?'

'There's no way to prove it now but I suspect from the symptoms you described that Mary was suffering from Schizophrenia.'

'I don't understand this word?'

'Schizophrenia is a mental disorder and quite often doesn't present with symptoms until late adolescence or early adulthood. I had a friend at college who was diagnosed with it in our second year. The people who suffer from it display a range of different symptoms, depression, lack of personal hygiene, disorganized speech, paranoia and hallucinations. There was no way you could have helped her, not without modern medicine and in the grip of witch fever you could only have hidden her condition for so long. It was always going to end badly.'

'Still I should have been able to do something.'

'Theo you have to stop blaming yourself. You can't change what happened and this?' she encompassed the room with a sweep of her arms, 'it's not healthy, you need to stop carrying your grief with you and let her go.'

'I didn't paint all these.'

'What?' she asked slowly.

'I painted the original one, I don't really know why, but all these other paintings and sketches were of different things. I tried destroying the original painting; I painted over it, I burned it, I cut it up but it just keeps reappearing back in its frame. Now all the other pictures have changed and they are exact copies of the original, except for one thing. The painting's expression keeps changing.'

'What do you mean?' she whispered.

'I painted her as I remembered her, a young carefree, happy girl but when she started looking back at me her expression gradually got colder and angrier.'

'Theo,' she breathed heavily, 'are you trying to tell me Mary's spirit came through the doorway and she is haunting the painting?'

'I don't think she's in the painting anymore' he replied quietly.

Suddenly the silence was interrupted by a door slamming somewhere in the house, followed by another. Beau shot into the room and hid under Theo's chair, whimpering loudly. The windows started rattling, just like they had at the pub, the lights flickering on and off erratically. The pencil and brush pots Theo kept neatly lined up shook and skidded across the table scattering brushes everywhere.

'We need to get these out of here now,' Olivia started tearing down the pictures from the walls but as she turned to yank the original canvas off the easel, the tray in which Theo kept all of his sharper tools began to shake violently. An enraged ghostly scream ripped through the house as the box upturned and the instruments were hurled in Olivia's direction.

Theo grabbed her and turned, throwing her to the floor but as he did one of the sharp pallet knives caught her, slicing along the bare flesh of her thigh. She cried out in pain as they both hit the floor, slamming her elbow and knocking the breath from her. She looked up as the paintings began to rattle and sway and one by one they burst into flames.

That was the last straw and Olivia saw red. Having a spirit trapped in her house was one thing but it would not use fire against her, that was her gift. Olivia climbed to her feet ignoring Theo as her eyes flashed pure gold. She felt her power flash through her body, fuelled by her rage. She reached for the fire, felt the flames and gloried in the heat and power. This was hers and no crazed ghost was going to use it against her. She pulled the fire from the paintings, smothering the flames before they could catch and spread through the house.

A howl of inhuman rage swept through the room churning up the papers which ended up strewn across the floor. Theo was thrown violently across the room, cracking his head against the corner of the window and splitting the skin open. Olivia felt her head being flung backwards as if some unseen hand had cracked her across the mouth. She licked her lip and tasted the metallic tang of blood but held her ground. Debris was flying around the room now and Olivia watched in smoldering anger as a woman appeared in front of her. Her clothes were torn and dirty and her matted blonde hair hung down in a tangled mess. Her eyes were red and filled with madness and fury as she bared her dirty teeth. Olivia's eyes drifted to her neck and she saw the deep agonizing welts of rope burn. Mary faced her, her dirty fingers curved into claws as she let out another wail.

Olivia tried to find some sympathy but she couldn't, she was so damn angry. Everything collapsed in on her, the pain of knowing Theo had been married and that he had kept it from her, the demon, the spirits, the fact that everyone seemed to be looking towards her to deal with it all when all she wanted was a normal quiet safe life. God dammit she'd earned it, it was so unfair, no one had asked her what she wanted and she was sick to death of people hurting her. The rage and unfairness all coalesced into a hot hard ball in her chest and she thrust her hands up into the air reaching for her spirit fire.

This time, unlike when she'd called it before, it was huge, vast, almost the same as when she'd called the Hell fire against the Hell Hounds. The power was immense and she held it in her bare hands with all the raw energy of a freight train. It was like riding a lightning bolt. Her heart hammered in her chest and her breath came in heaving gasps. Her skin felt like it was alive, prickling with thousands of pinpricks of electricity, even her hair felt like it was standing on end. This time when she looked at

Mary, growling at her like a rabid dog, she embraced the power. Her fists gripped until her knuckles turned white and she pulled the power down.

'GET OUT OF MY HOUSE!' Olivia screamed furiously and punched out.

The power exploded out of Olivia's chest like a blast of silver white light flung violently outwards like a shock wave. When the light hit Mary it flung her through the wall of the house until she appeared on the other side. Olivia rushed into the hallway and yanked open the front door, rushing onto the frozen porch in bare feet, not even aware of the freezing cold. She watched the ring of silver light continue to expand, carrying a struggling Mary as if she were snared in a fisherman's net. Once it reached the glowing and pulsing blue protective ring of Olivia's wards, Mary was shoved to the other side.

Olivia strode down the steps angrily and out onto the snowy path. She speared her hands up to the churning sky and pulled more silver fire down. Great bolts of silver lightening rained down, lighting up the protective circle which suddenly flared up, roaring to life in great silver flames. Olivia rode the whip of power, embracing the fire as it burned higher and higher and suddenly exploded outwards with such force it made the ancient thick trunked trees tremble, knocking the snow from their branches so it fell to the ground it giant heaps.

When the light and fire died down she stood trembling, her breath heavy and uneven. She watched as the sky which had been alive with purple and pink began to lighten and the sun slowly began its ascent. As the sky began to fill with early morning light she gazed out across the water the lake was almost frozen solid and covered in places with a thick dusting of snow.

Her body began to come down from its high and as the adrenalin drained away leaving her exhausted, she felt as if she'd been hit by a truck. Her feet were frozen and she began to shake violently. She was aware of a blanket being wrapped around her and she felt Theo lift her gently into his arms. Burying her face into his neck, unable to find any words, she breathed in the beloved familiar scent of him and for the first time it brought her no comfort but only a sharp pain in her heart.

She said nothing as he carried her back inside and shut the door. Nor did she utter a word when he carried her up the stairs and sat her on the side of the bed. She watched him slowly as he kneeled in front of her his eyes filled with pain and remorse.

'I'm so sorry Livy,' he whispered.

Words were still lost to her as she dropped the blanket he had wrapped her in, rose and silently walked past him to the bathroom and slammed the door shut. Turning the water on as hot as she could stand it she stripped off Theo's shirt and stepped into the shower. Blood covered most of her thigh and ran down her leg, turning the water a pale rose colour. She slowly slid down the wall until she was sitting crouched in the corner and with the water cascading over her, drenching her hair, she pressed her face into her knees and sobbed.

21.

Olivia stared numbly out of the window. Her fingers were wrapped around a mug of steaming tea and she was snuggled in her favorite thick chenille sweater but she still felt cold right down to her bones. She gazed out at the lake which was now completely frozen and covered with snow. Her eyes tracked across to the edge of her protective wards, her body still tingling with residual energy from wielding such an ancient and powerful magic as Spirit Fire. She could feel the pressure against the wards as Mary pushed at it, trying to get back in. She wouldn't be able to, Olivia knew that much. Her wards had been seared with both Hell fire and Spirit fire now, and as protective shields went hers was pretty hardcore. That said, she wasn't stupid and she wasn't careless. They were safe enough for now but she knew they would have to be extra careful every time they left the protective circle of the house, at least until they could get to Charon and banish the spirits back to the Otherworld.

She looked down as a big truck rumbled across the edge of the circle and drove up to the house, parking by the steps leading up to her front porch. She watched as Danae and Davis climbed out, followed by her father. Both her aunt and uncle skirted the edge of the truck and began hauling huge bags and supplies out of the back. Charles stopped and turned, glancing back down the drive towards her shield as if he too could sense the angry spirit trapped on the other side. He continued to watch for a moment, then turning back to the house his gaze lifted to the window where she stood and their eyes locked. For one brief heart rending moment she was seven years old again and was swamped with the overwhelming urge to run to him and let him fold her safely in his arms, but she couldn't, she wouldn't. She saw Davis turn and speak to her father, drawing his attention away from her and he nodded to his half-brother following him up the porch steps.

Olivia looked back at the wards as she felt the pressure again, felt the wave of anger as Mary continued to test it, circling it like a predator. Even from this distance Olivia could see sections of the shield fog up as hand prints appeared then disappeared again. She deliberately turned her back on the window and stepped back into the room, heading towards the stairs. By the time she made it downstairs Theo had already opened the door and the others were stamping the snow off their boots and heading into the house. Theo looked up at her silently as she paused on the bottom step. He looked pretty worse for wear. Not only was he probably sporting a pretty bad hangover from the night before, he also had a nasty cut and bruise at his hairline where Mary had thrown him into the corner of the window. Ignoring him she turned as her father came through the door and stopped abruptly. He sniffed and his eyes narrowed suspiciously.

'What happened?' he asked bluntly, 'this place reeks of magic.'

'Nothing that concerns you,' Olivia replied coldly, 'it's been dealt with.'

'Is that so?' his response was equally cool.

'You're here because you need help,' Olivia told him curtly, 'not to concern yourself with my private affairs.'

'I see,' he watched her speculatively.

'Olivia?' Davis interrupted holding a big brown packing box, 'where do you want this?'

'It depends,' she frowned. 'What is it?'

'Supplies, we'll explain in more detail when the others arrive.'

'Put it in the kitchen then.'

He nodded and headed back, she didn't want to ask how he knew where her kitchen was; she had a feeling she wasn't going to like the answer much. Danae nodded in greeting, following behind her brother with two big olive green military looking canvas bags, which clanged and rattled slightly.

'Theodore,' Charles turned to face Theo, studying his harried appearance and the large painful welt at his forehead. 'I don't suppose you'd care to explain as my daughter seems so reluctant.'

Theo's jaw clenched and his eyes narrowed a fraction.

'Like Olivia said it's private.'

'This wouldn't have anything to do with the rather angry dead woman stalking your perimeter?'

'Private and off limits,' Olivia repeated as Charles lifted one brow questioningly.

The doorbell rang again and Theo turned to answer it, stepping back to allow Veronica in. She stomped the snow off her boots and held up a huge bakery box.

'I brought pastries, is everyone here yet?' she asked, looking up curiously at Charles.

'Not yet, Roni,' Olivia replied quietly. 'This is my father, Charles Connell.'

'Your father?' her voice came out as a small squeak and her eyes widened.

She couldn't blame Veronica for being slightly nervous, despite the fact her dad hadn't actually murdered her mom, it wasn't for lack of trying and after all he was still a wanted fugitive.

'Hello, you must be Miss Mason,' he smiled at her charmingly his voice low and smooth as he took her hand gently. 'It's nice to meet you, I hear you are doing great things with the Museum. I am a professor of history myself. I taught at the High School and I was very fond of Renata and the Museum. I'm pleased to see it has been passed into such capable hands.'

'Uh-huh,' she seemed mesmerised by him.

'Perhaps when there is more time you could fill me in on your plans for the research suite expansion. I must confess I do find the idea intriguing.'

'For God's sake Charles,' Davis laughed as he reappeared, 'stop charming the poor girl. Can't you see you're confusing her.'

Charles laughed lightly and tucked Veronica's arm companionably through his.

'This is my younger half-brother Davis and his twin sister Danae.'

Veronica's eyes narrowed as they turned to Danae.

'I know you,' she frowned. 'You were at the Museum the morning I found Renata's body, you work with Jake. Deputy...Hanson, Helga Hanson?'

'That was my brother's idea of a joke and now I'm kind of stuck with it,' she scowled. 'My name is Danae, but as you can appreciate I would prefer to keep my relationship to Charles a secret and besides, the rest of the town knows me as Helga. I'd be grateful if you could keep my real name to yourself.'

'Of course,' Veronica replied nervously, wondering and not for the first time exactly what she'd got herself tangled up in.

Charles moved into the library with Veronica still on his arm, and his siblings followed. The doorbell rang again; this time it was Chief Macallister followed by Jake who was looking as delicate as Theo. Olivia wasn't surprised given the amount they'd drunk the night before.

'Olivia' Mac smiled, dropping an affectionate kiss on her cheek.

'Hey Mac,' she replied, 'go on through they're in the library.'

He nodded and disappeared, as Jake yawned. 'Olive, I'd murder for a cup of coffee.'

'I'll go put a pot on.'

'Olivia,' Theo stepped towards her. She glanced back at him in silence before turning towards the kitchen.

'I guess you told her then,' Jake murmured to Theo, picking up on the strained silence between them.

Olivia froze halfway down the hallway and turned slowly back to Jake. She stared at him for what seemed like a painfully awkward eternity before she turned her gaze on Theo.

'He knew?'

Theo sighed and nodded, knowing that he was done lying to her. No matter what, he had to come clean or there was no hope of her ever forgiving him.

'And Tommy?'

Theo nodded again and silently cursed himself for opening his mouth the night before. He should never have told his friends before he told Olivia.

She stared at him in silence for a moment, then without saying a word she turned and walked towards the kitchen.

'Olivia,' he started towards her but Jake caught his arm and held him back. 'Best give her some space Theo.'

'It's killing me,' Theo breathed quietly, 'she won't talk to me. She hasn't shouted, screamed, called me names, set me on fire, nothing. It's like she's just shut down. I did that to her.'

'Just give her time,' he told him. 'You hurt her, but she'll come around, she cares about you too much not to.'

'Do you think so?' he asked hopefully.

'Theo if she didn't care, trust me she'd have torn you a new one and thrown you out of her house, but you're still here aren't you?'

'For the moment.'

'It's been a big shock for her and the last few weeks have been really stressful for everyone, her in particular. She needs time to process everything, just like she did when she found out about her mom. When Olivia's hurting she shuts down and wants to be left alone while she figures things out.'

He knew Jake was right, when Olivia was hurting she retreated into her own private bubble until she was ready to face everyone again. She'd done it before with her mom but he'd been right there with her. He was the only one she'd kept close and at the time he hadn't appreciated the significance of that. It was only now that he was on the other side he realised just how much he'd screwed up.

The doorbell went again and this time Louisa trudged through followed by Tommy, who was also looking pale and hungover.

'Hey,' Louisa greeted them, 'I brought more medical supplies. Something tells me we're going to need them. So where's the party at?'

'Library,' Theo and Jake answered together.

'I'll take that and put it with the rest,' Theo took the box from Tommy.

'Thanks man,' Tommy swallowed, 'got coffee?'

'Olive's just bringing it,' Jake reassured him.

'Wicked,' he replied following his wife into the library.

'Oh hey Mr Connell,' Louisa nodded as she headed into the room. 'You're looking better than the last time I saw you.'

'That's because you're not sticking needles in me.'

'The day is young,' she replied brightly taking a seat by Olivia's desk.

'Indeed,' he smiled in amusement, turning his gaze on Tommy who'd stopped dead in his tracks when he realised who Louisa was talking to. 'Tommy Linden,' Charles spoke slowly, 'I remember you, I hope your parents are well.'

'Uh yeah they are,' he replied.

'I realise I'm a few years late but congratulations on your marriage to Louisa.'

'Um thanks,' he moved to stand next to his wife, eyeing Charles suspiciously.

Theo headed back into the room after stashing away the medical supplies, followed a few minutes later by Olivia who set a tray down on the coffee table, next to the box of doughnuts and pastries Veronica had brought from Liddy Mayberry's.

'Okay help yourselves,' Olivia told them as she moved across to the other side of the room from Theo and perched on the edge of the couch opposite her father.

Shivering slightly at the cold she glanced over at the fireplace, watching with satisfaction as it burst joyfully into flames. Her gaze caught her father's as she turned back to the room.

'What?' she frowned.

'Nothing,' he murmured as he looked at the fire and then back to her, regarding her thoughtfully. 'Do we have everyone now?'

Olivia glanced around the room and nodded.

'All right let's get this show on the road,' Charles began. 'All of you are aware of the current situation. We have creatures coming through the doorway and they need to be stopped. I have an idea of what to do about that, which we'll get to shortly but even my solution will only be a temporary measure. The main objective is to find the Ferryman so he can close the doorway. Olivia and I are pretty sure Isabel and Nathaniel are behind his kidnapping, so where are we on locating them?'

'Hang on a minute,' Jake frowned, 'are you sure it's them?'

'As sure as we can be,' Charles replied calmly. 'I'm sure Olivia will fill you in on the details later but it's definitely the most likely scenario and Nathaniel is the only creature around here with enough power to take a supernatural being of Charon's age and ability.'

'Okay,' Jake conceded.

'Now,' Charles continued, 'where are we on location?'

'Not very far,' Olivia replied quietly. 'We've hit a dead end.'

'What about Charlotte?' Veronica asked softly. 'She was helping you, trying to tell you about Charon in the first place.'

'She's getting confused I think,' Olivia shook her head. 'She has tried to tell me something several times, each time she keeps giving me just one word. The first time she wrote it on the fogged up window in the kitchen. Last night as I got out of the shower she wrote it on the steamed up mirror.'

'What is the word?' her father asked her curiously.

'Boatman, which isn't really that helpful. We already know that it's the Ferryman, she just keeps repeating herself.'

'Boatman? What like the hotel?' Louisa asked absently as she scrolled through the message she'd received from the hospital.

'What hotel?' Olivia asked.

Louisa glanced up from her phone.

'Don't you remember the project we did in school? Oh no, wait a minute...' she frowned as she thought back. 'No that was in High School, you'd already left Mercy by then, my bad. We had to do a project on local landmarks and I chose the Boatman, it's the old abandoned hotel on the cliff above the lake.' She looked around the room at the blank faces. 'Is this not ringing any bells?'

They all shook their heads.

'Okay,' she set her phone down. 'A couple of miles from here, past the woods as the ground slopes uphill, there is a cliff overhanging the lake. A wealthy businessman from Salem decided to build a hotel there back in the twenties. He saw the lake and fell in love with it, story goes he wanted to build a luxurious and very exclusive hotel retreat overlooking the lake. Given that it was at the height of prohibition you can imagine exactly what kind of retreat he wanted to build there. Anyway they finished construction in '29 but unfortunately about two months before, the Wall Street crash had hit. The Boatman never got the chance to open its doors. The owner lost everything and the hotel was abandoned. By the fifties the economy had finally recovered and the hotel was sold to a chain of hotels. I forget which one, however they were set to renovate it but the company was then bought out by a larger chain and they didn't want the Boatman. They didn't see the financial viability for a hotel that size in such a small town, so it was sold on again to a private owner, but he was caught out on a tax audit and ended up in prison for tax evasion.'

'That's a hell of a lot of bad luck for one hotel,' Mac spoke up.

'You're not kidding, it changed hands a couple more times back in the seventies and eighties but the same thing kept happening. Whoever owned it ended up losing their fortunes which led to the rumour that the hotel was cursed,' she laughed shaking her head. 'Anyway I don't know who owns it these days, last I heard it was bought by some company called Black Orchid, but it's still abandoned. You used to be able to access it by road but back in the nineties we had all of those really violent storms. They brought down a load of trees on the road that led up to the hotel and as that road was privately owned and never used, the town council didn't bother to clear it. Nowadays its only accessible by boat, I'm not even sure if the jetty is still there, but it has a small stretch of private beach at the foot of the cliff and steps leading up.'

Olivia suddenly stood up and grasped Louisa's hand.

'Come with me,' she pulled her from the room and headed into Theo's studio. She flung the door open, ignoring the chaos from the previous night and dropped down to the ground brushing pieces of charred paper and brushes out of the way, until the picture Theo had seen in his vision, and painted directly onto the floor, was revealed.

'Is this it?' she asked.

Louisa dropped down to the floor and moved more pieces of paper out of the way.

'Yes it is,' she whispered looking up at Olivia. 'I mean its older and more overgrown than the pictures I've seen, but that's definitely The Boatman.'

'God,' Olivia breathed as she closed her eyes and shook her head. 'She's been trying to tell us all along where they are.'

She looked up as the others gathered in the doorway.

'All this time, they've been right under our noses just a couple of miles up the road.'

'Okay this changes things,' Charles frowned. 'Everyone back in the other room, we need a change of plan.'

They all filed back into the library and resumed their places.

'Now we know where they're keeping him we need to get him back, but at the same time we need to do something about the lake. It's the full moon tonight and as soon as the sun goes down creatures are going to start pouring out of that doorway. So we're going to temporarily block it and rescue Charon and we're going to have to do it all tonight.'

'How are you planning to block the gateway?' Olivia asked curiously.

'Magic,' he replied, 'we're going to cast a net over the entire lake trapping everything inside it.'

'A net that size?' Olivia shook her head, 'even between us we don't have that kind of power.'

'As I said it's only temporary,' he told her. 'We're going to borrow the power.'

'You're going to call the corners,' she whispered. 'That's why you needed more people.'

'Yes,' he replied his eyes locked on hers, 'we don't have a coven at our disposal so we're going to have to make do with what we've got. It's been a while and whilst they're not as powerful as I'd like and will be a bit rusty, Jake and Louisa have the gift, they'll do.'

'No,' Olivia shook her head, 'we only need four, that's you, me, Davis and Danae. You can't put them in danger like this. The second those creatures figure out what we are trying to do they'll try to stop us.'

'Excuse me,' Jake frowned, 'does anyone else have a clue what they're going on about?'

'Shut up Jake,' both Olivia and her father replied.

'We need them,' Charles answered firmly. 'There's eight of us, four teams of two, one to call the corner and one to protect the other.'

'Is math not your strong suit?' Olivia snapped, 'there's ten of us.'

'You and Theo have to go to The Boatman; you have to retrieve Charon.'

'Why us?' she frowned.

'Because your mother gave you protection. She made sure Nathaniel can't harm you and I'm willing to bet that she won't either. I'll get to you as soon as I can, but we have to stop the creatures coming through the doorway. Once they get through and scatter I doubt even Charon will be able to stop them. Spirits are one thing but these are creatures of the underworld, they are beyond his power. We have to hold them, you have to get Charon and bring him to the lake.'

She sighed knowing he was right. Nathaniel couldn't harm her and as a West she was one of the only people who actually stood a chance against him, but there was one thing she wasn't going to agree to.

'Fine I'll go but Theo stays with you.'

'WHAT?' Theo stood abruptly. 'No way. There is no way I am letting you go after Nathaniel alone, forget it.'

'You don't have any protection from him,' she hissed, 'he can't hurt me but he can hurt you.'

'I don't care,' he replied, you are not going without me.'

'Theo,' she sighed tiredly, aware that everyone was staring at them. 'Can we talk about this later?'

'You can talk all you want,' he replied stubbornly. 'You're still not going up to that hotel alone. Wherever you go, I go and that's not negotiable.'

'I may just like him after all,' Charles murmured.

Olivia threw him a dangerous look.

'Get angry all you like Olivia,' her father told her, 'but the man's right. You're not going alone and we simply don't have time to argue about it. We have about seven hours until sunset and we still have to teach them how to call the corners.'

'Fine,' she grated through clenched teeth. She stood and faced the rest of the room, taking a deep breath.

'Alright here's the deal people. As you may have gathered from all of that, we are going to cast a kind of supernatural net over the lake to stop anything from escaping. That kind of spell work requires a great deal of power, even an entire coven of witches would struggle to call forth that kind of power so we are going to call the corners. This is a ritual to call the four watchtowers of the North, South, East and West. Each watchtower is ruled by an element, fire, air, earth and water and each tower is protected by a guardian. We are going to call to each of them and entreat them to lend us enough power to cast the net.'

'What? like when the fairy godmother in Cinderella borrows magic for her to go to the ball but it must be returned at midnight?' Veronica frowned.

'Actually that's a pretty accurate analogy,' Olivia nodded, 'except we have until sunrise, after that we're pretty much screwed.'

'So am I to understand that you need Louisa and I to call a corner?'

'Each,' Charles replied, 'we'll need you to call a corner each. Danae and Davis have to stay together because they are going to call the corner where there is the heaviest concentration of creatures, Davis will call a corner and Danae will protect him, because she is trained for this. You have to understand the second they figure out what we're doing they'll try to stop us. So each one of us calling a corner will have a partner to watch our backs. Louisa and Jake, we'll put you on the furthest side of the lake where there will be the fewest concentration of creatures but I am not going to lie to you, there will be considerable risk involved.'

Tommy stood up abruptly.

'Okay, you've all had your fun now, but really this has gone far enough. It's been very amusing but listen to yourselves, you're crazy. This shit doesn't exist.'

'Tommy sit down,' Charles spoke calmly.

Tommy sat down as abruptly as he'd stood, his eyes widened in surprise as if he was not quite sure what had happened. He opened his mouth to speak again.

'Be quiet Tommy,' Charles told him and Tommy shut his mouth.

'What the hell?' Jake frowned, 'how did you do that?'

'Simple power of suggestion,' Charles shrugged. 'It doesn't work on everyone and I really don't like to use it much. I'm generally against anything that interferes with anyone's free will.'

He turned to Tommy apologetically, 'I truly am sorry Tommy but like I told Olivia we really don't have time to argue about this.'

'It's not permanent is it?' Louisa asked, looking at her husband worriedly.

'No,' Charles answered, 'it'll wear off soon enough.'

'Anyway,' Olivia continued, 'I don't want any of you to feel pressured. You can walk away right now if you want to. This has to be your choice.'

She glanced at them in turn as they nodded their silent consent, all except Tommy who was glaring furiously at them. She wasn't too concerned though. Louisa had agreed to go and whether Tommy believed or not, as a fully trained soldier there was no way he would let his wife go into the woods on her own, without him protecting her.

'Okay Davis,' she turned to her uncle. 'Why don't you go and get the supplies you brought and we'll start working out the details.'

He nodded and disappeared into the kitchen re-emerging moments later carrying the box and one bag slung over each shoulder.

'For the sake of time we're going to split you guys up,' Davis told them as he unzipped one of the bags and began to pull out several shotguns and boxes of cartridges. Jake and Louisa you go with Charles so you can start learning the spell, the rest of you, you're with me.'

'Oh my,' Veronica's eyes widened as she picked up a crossbow.

'Welcome to our world,' Davis grinned.

22.

'Okay,' Charles began as he unpacked items from the box, 'so Jake, you are going to be positioned at the northern most point of the Lake. You will be calling Uriel, Guardian of Earth.'

He handed him several thick stumpy green candles and a glass bell jar filled with dark damp earth. When Jake curiously unscrewed the top and sniffed, his nostrils were filled with a rich peaty smell.

'Do you know how to cast a circle?' Charles asked?

'Nope,' Jake replied, and as Charles turned to Louisa she shook her head too.

'If we pull this off it will be a miracle' he muttered, shaking his head. 'Okay listen, the spell we are going to be working with is partly traditional and partly tailor made as I seriously doubt anyone has been in this position before. Each of you need to cast a basic circle and once that is done you are going to summon the Guardians, which is unusual I admit. Normally they would just be called upon to watch over and protect the circle and the magic you are conjuring, however we are going to be entreating them to actually let us borrow more power. So Jake, for God's sake be respectful.'

'You know me,' he grinned.

'That's what worries me,' Charles grimaced. 'Just try not to offend them, we need their help. Once we've summoned the Guardians and if they agree to help…....'

'Wait a minute they have to agree to help?' Jake interrupted. 'What if they say no?'

'You'd better pray to whatever God you believe in that they don't, otherwise we're in serious trouble' Charles replied. 'If they agree to help' he continued, 'then we will move on to the main body of the spell to cast the net, which is what you'll need these for.'

He pulled out two big ball shapes, wrapped in heavy burlap and tied tightly with twine, each vaguely resembling the root ball of a large plant. When Jake picked one up it felt gross; squelchy and damp and smelled like road kill.

'Er… what the hell is in that?' he asked.

Charles shrugged 'herbs, bird bones, graveyard dirt and some other things you really don't want to know about.'

'What are they for?' Louisa asked.

'They need to be buried in the ground at the centre of your circle; these are the most important part of the spell. This is what is going to form the net to trap the creatures.'

'Okay' she nodded, 'so where am I going to be?'

'West' Charles replied. 'You'll be on the West bank of the lake and you'll be calling to Gabriel, the Guardian of water. It's very important you get as close to the lake as possible, but the bags have to be buried in soil not sand.'

'Gabriel?' Louisa frowned, 'and Jake will be calling

to Uriel? Who are the other two?'

'Davis will be calling to the East, to Raphael the Guardian of the air and I will be on the South bank calling to Michael the Guardian of fire.'

'Michael and Raphael, Gabriel and Uriel, but they are the names of the archangels,' Louisa replied in confusion.

Charles's mouth curved in amusement. 'Christianity, Islam, Judaism, Hinduism, Sikhism, Paganism, it's all just semantics. Magic all comes from the same place; you'll find they cross over more often than you think. We as humans seem to want to segregate everything, put it in its proper place. If you believe in one you can't believe in the others, but the truth is they are more closely tied than you can imagine. Nothing is ever black and white, everything in this world and every other, are just varying shades of grey.'

'Somehow that makes me feel a little better' Louisa replied, 'like we're not so alone in the world.'

'Existence is a bigger place than you can possibly imagine Louisa,' Charles told her gently, 'you just need to open your eyes and look.'

'So what else do we need?' Jake asked.

Charles resumed searching through the box and handed Louisa five short stumpy blue candles, similar to Jake's green ones. He also had a glass bell jar for her, this one containing slightly cloudy water.

'What's this?' she asked.

'Sea water' he answered absently as he also handed them both a carton of salt and five fat white candles. 'You're going to need an Athame each too' he murmured thoughtfully.

'What's an Athame?'

'It's a ceremonial knife.'

'Will this do?' Jake asked as he pulled from his belt the dagger Olivia had created for him.

'Where did you get this?' Charles took a sharp

intake of breath as he took the blade in his hands, turning it over to examine it. He could feel the intense power thrumming through the blue black blade. The strange lettering glowed lightly with a muted blue light and waves of a vast ancient power emanated from it.

'Olivia made them for us when we were going up against Nathaniel.'

'Them?'

'She made two; I have one and Theo has the other.'

'And she created them?'

'Sort of' Jake frowned, trying to find a way to explain. 'They were originally just ordinary hunting knives I got from the local store, she altered them with a kind of blue and black fire.'

Charles's head snapped up from his inspection of the blade and he looked at Jake intently.

'Blue fire? Edged in black?' he wanted exact clarification.

'Yeah that's the stuff, Olivia says it's called Hell Fire. You should see her pull a bow and arrow out of thin air and made entirely from Hell fire, it's really cool. She took out like eight Hell Hounds with that thing.'

'Olivia can conjure Hell Fire?' he repeated slowly as he turned a puzzled gaze on his daughter, across the room talking to Danae.

'Sure she can' Jake replied, a bit confused at Charles's reaction. 'I'm sure it's not a big deal, she can call up Spirit fire too now. You know, the silver stuff.'

'What?' Charles turned his penetrating gaze back to Jake, making him squirm uncomfortably.

'Look maybe you should talk to Olivia about this.'

'Maybe I should,' he replied thoughtfully. 'Alright this knife will be fine; I have one that Louisa can use.'

He shook his head and sighed, 'so, let's start with how to cast a circle.'

'As we don't know what kind of creatures you are likely to encounter' Davis told them, 'it's really difficult to know which weapons will be most effective. There isn't really a 'one size fits all'. Some creatures are susceptible to lead, others to silver. Some can be harmed with something as simple as salt. So we've come up with some weapons which will be effective against most creatures but not all. Your job is to keep them off the others long enough for them to cast the circle and complete the spell. Once that's done you should be safe within the circle, just don't step out of it.'

'Okay we're going to start with something fairly basic, Danae stepped forward holding a shotgun. 'Obviously Tommy and Mac are able to shoot, what about you princess?'

'I can shoot,' Veronica replied dryly.

'I'm not talking about BB guns at a carnival.'

'Neither am I,' she replied coolly. 'I can shoot most guns but I'm most comfortable with a .45 or a 9mm.'

Mac raised his brows in surprise at her admission.

'I also know my way around a shotgun but I don't see how they're going to help much if I've got a Hell Hound coming at me. I don't think he's going to be deterred by a bit of buckshot.'

Danae smiled and picked up one of the boxes of cartridges. Opening it up she pulled one out.

'Usually I would agree but this is something a little special Davis and I have cooked up.' She broke it open and poured the contents into her palm. Instead of your usual steel or bismuth we've filled them with a mixture of lead, silver and salt. It probably won't kill or even seriously wound anything you come up against, but it should slow them down some.'

'Now these are tactical shotguns rather than hunting shotguns. May sound flashy but it really isn't all that different from your standard 12 gauge,' Davis told them, 'except it looks cooler.'

'You're such a child,' Danae sighed shaking her head, 'the reason we chose these is simple because it holds more rounds. In the situation you're going to be in, your life and that of your wingman, or woman, is going to depend on how long your ammo lasts and how quickly you can reload. This is what we're going to be practicing in a moment. I'm not too worried about your aim, something tells me you're going to have plenty of close range targets. Aim for the face or the legs, try to disable them in any way you can. Remember your main objective is to buy time, once you're within the completed circle you'll be safe.'

Veronica swallowed convulsively, suddenly feeling a bit nauseous.

'In addition we have a selection of hand guns. There are regular bullets and we also have some silver bullets too, but please go easy on them as they're real hard to come by. There are the crossbows and you'll each have a knife, but you better pray they don't get that close.'

'Great,' Veronica murmured.

Danae glanced down at her watch.

'Okay time's getting on so we need to step it up a little. Who knows how to use a crossbow?'

Olivia frowned as she studied the map in front of her. As a shadow fell over it she looked up and saw Theo.

'We can drive as far as here,' she pointed to a section on the map. 'From there we'll be on foot but as the lake is frozen solid it should be safe enough to walk on, so we can skirt around this section of the woods and head straight for the private beach below the cliff face. Hopefully the stairs are still intact but it depends what they were made from.'

'If they are anything like my dream they are actually carved out of the rock itself, but the guardrail is metal so it may be in pretty poor condition after all this time.'

Olivia nodded.

'The next problem is what do we do once we get there. I managed to download the blueprints for the building from the internet, but to be honest they could be holed up in any of the rooms. We're literally going to have to search room by room.'

'Maybe not,' Theo frowned. I know Nathaniel, remember I spent a fair bit of time with him in Salem. He has very specific tastes and he doesn't like being closed in. That rules out all of the smaller private bedrooms and suites. He's probably been amusing himself by torturing Charon so he'd want a nice big open space to work in, probably with a view out over the lake so he could watch the doorway.'

'Okay,' Olivia switched to her laptop and brought up the blueprints for the hotel. 'The back of the hotel overlooks the lake so that rules out the dining room and the grand foyer. At the back, facing out to the lake, we have the ballroom and the swimming pool and Turkish baths.'

'We'll start with those three first,' Theo nodded.

'Of course if we actually manage to find them how do we deal with Nathaniel and my mom?' Olivia frowned. 'I suppose it's too much to hope for that we can just sneak in, find Charon and sneak back out.'

'I don't think our luck's that good,' Theo murmured. 'The chances are we're going to run into one of them if not both.'

'I know' she sighed, 'at least you still have the knife I gave you, that should come in handy.'

'What about your Hell fire?' Theo asked. 'It worked on the Hell Hounds, do you think it'll work on a Demon?'

'I have no idea,' Olivia frowned. 'If I can get a clear shot I can try to take him out with my bow, but what am I supposed to do about my mom?'

'Here,' Davis appeared next to her and handed her a gun.

The Ferryman

'You want me to shoot my mom?' she asked quietly.

'It's a tranq gun Olivia' he explained. 'One dart should do the job but if you can get two darts in her just to be sure, but only if the opportunity presents itself. Don't take unnecessary risks. Your priority is to get in there, get Charon and get out alive. We'll deal with Isabel after, but restoring Charon to the lake is our main aim.'

Olivia nodded.

'It's pretty simple,' he took the gun from her and turned it over, 'safety…aim, pull the trigger, okay?'

She nodded again and flicked the safety a couple of times before tucking the gun into the back of the waistband of her jeans.

'How are the others doing?'

'Pretty good all things considered,' he replied. 'The compulsion has worn off Tommy; he's not happy but he's agreed to go with Louisa. They'll have to leave soon to get to the West side of the lake in time. Charles will have to leave soon as well, as he's got the furthest to go to reach the South end.'

'Okay,' she breathed. She closed her laptop and headed towards the door.

'Olivia?' Theo called her name softly.

She turned back to him tiredly. 'I just need a minute.'

He watched in silence as she disappeared from the room.

Olivia headed back towards the kitchen. Here the bustle and noise of the library faded somewhat, although not completely. She bypassed the kitchen and headed into the small mud room attached to it, that she hardly ever used. Stepping into the small darkened room she pushed the door to and took a deep breath. With her back to the wall she slid down to the ground and laid her head against her knees.

After a moment she felt a soft furry face nuzzling

353

her hands. She looked up and Beau sniffed her face and licked her chin.

'Hey boy,' she whispered dropping her knees so he could climb up into her lap.

He padded over her thighs with soft paws and rubbed his face against her chest and neck, nuzzling her lovingly as if he knew she need the contact.

'Hey baby,' she wrapped her arms around him stroking his soft body.

Her eyes filled with tears as he rubbed his face against her cheek. She stayed there for a few moments just absorbing the simple uncomplicated love of her dog. She looked up as the door opened slowly and Mac appeared in the doorway. He pulled the door to behind him and sat down on the cold floor next to her.

'Was wondering where you got to.'

Olivia loved the sound of his voice, the low gravelly quality of it that just washed over her.

'Needed some space,' she explained quietly.

'You and Theo have a fight?'

'Something like that,' she shrugged.

'It's more than that though isn't it?'

Olivia sighed and laid her head back against the wall as Beau circled and settled comfortably in her lap.

'What is it Olivia?'

'Everything and nothing,' she sighed and 'everything in between.'

He sat silently, waiting for her to organise her thoughts.

'I didn't want this, I didn't want any of it. All I wanted was a quiet life. I wanted to settle down and maybe one day have a family of my own. But my life since I've come back to Mercy has been some horrific, never ending nightmare of murders, bodies, ghosts and demons and don't even get me started on the issues with my parents. Everyone looks to me as if I'm supposed to solve all these problems, but why me?' she muttered, 'I'm no one special.'

'I think you're wrong about that Olivia,' his voice was low and soothing. 'I've seen the things you can do, but putting that aside, people naturally gravitate to you because you just have this quality. It's like you're the calm at the eye of the storm. You exude strength and courage and that's what people reach towards.'

'I don't feel very strong, I feel like I'm flying apart at the seams and nothing is going to be able to hold me together.'

'I think you're wrong about that too,' Mac smiled.

'It's so unfair Mac,' she frowned, 'this is not what I want my life to be.'

'When destiny comes calling we rarely have a choice Olivia.'

'Destiny?' she scoffed.

'You don't believe in destiny?'

'If I believed in destiny that means are lives are already planned for us, there is no such thing as free will and nothing we do matters.'

'Everything we do matters,' Mac looked at her with piercing dark blue eyes. 'Okay let's simplify, sometimes bad stuff happens and someone needs to deal with it, so ask yourself this.'

'What?'

'Would you trust anyone else to do it?'

She frowned thoughtfully and then sighed. 'I guess not,' she replied wearily.

'We can't always have what we think it is that we want,' he told her softly, 'but sometimes...just sometimes, we end up with something better.'

She sighed and laid her head on his shoulder, there was something about Mac that she found so soothing. It was like everything in her calmed and she felt safe. Maybe it was because he had been the one to hold her, back in Philly, after she thought her mom was dead and her father had just been arrested. Ever since then she'd unconsciously equated him with being saved.

'I'm glad you're here Mac,' she whispered.

'I'm glad I'm here too.'

The door opened once again spilling a bright light across the pair of them. Charles stood in the doorway looking down at them, his expression unreadable.

'Louisa and Tommy are getting ready to leave,' he told them.

Mac stood, slowly pulling Olivia up with him as Beau leapt from her lap.

Olivia nodded and passed her father, following Beau out of the kitchen and back towards the library.

As Mac moved to do the same Charles stopped him.

'Problem?' Mac asked coolly.

'Not at all,' Charles responded. 'I just thought I'd let you know you'll be partnered with me at the South end of the lake.'

'Why?' Mac replied as he studied Charles's guarded expression, 'why me?'

'Tommy will be protecting Louisa and Danae will be with Davis, that leaves you and Miss Mason. She is better off with Jake at the North end, as it should be one of the quieter spots.'

'Maybe, but there's more to it than that, isn't there?' his eyes narrowed suspiciously. 'The South end of the lake is closest to the Boatman isn't it? You need someone to protect the circle once it's cast.' 'God damn it' he realised, 'you're going after her aren't you? You're going after Isabel?'

'That's not your concern,' his gaze hardened.

'The hell it's not,' Mac growled. 'She's a murderer and in case you haven't noticed I'm still a cop. If anyone is going to be dealing with her it's me.'

'She's my wife, my concern, my problem.'

'No way,' Mac shook his head. 'You said, once the circle is cast it's protected?'

Charles's jaw clenched but he remained silent.

'I thought so,' he replied. 'Once the circle is cast we both go after her and we take her alive. You may be pissed as Hell and I don't blame you, but taking her alive and letting her stand trial for what she's done is the only way to clear your name. We go together or we don't go at all.'

'Fine,' Charles answered coldly.

'I mean it Charles, you try to double cross me or leave without me and I'll put a bullet in you. Nothing you won't recover from of course,' he smiled nonchalantly.

Charles turned abruptly on his heel and headed out of the kitchen.

'What do you mean you're my partner?' Jake frowned.

'Charles said I'm to partner up with you and cover the North bank,' Veronica told him.

'No way in Hell.'

Her eyes flashed dangerously.

'You're not going,' Jake insisted stubbornly, 'it's too dangerous.'

'Louisa's going and you're not having a hissy fit about that.'

'I am not having a hissy fit,' he replied indignantly, 'and that's different. She is going to be inside the circle and she has Tommy to protect her. I'm going to be trying to cast a goddamn spell which I have never done before in my life. I'm not going to be able to protect you.'

'That's why I'll be there, to protect you.'

'Are you kidding? Roni you trip over your own feet half the time.'

'Well then,' her eyes narrowed, 'if I trip I'll be sure to take some of them with me.'

'You think this is a joke?' he shouted.

'Do you see me laughing?' she snapped, stepping closer to get right up in his face, despite the fact she only stood as high as his chest and had to tilt her head up to look at him.

'You're not going and that's final,' he crossed his arms stubbornly. 'I'll be just fine on my own.'

'Well that's not going to happen; I'm going whether you like it or.'

'She's a fiery little thing isn't she?' Danae murmured to her brother.

'He's right though, she is clumsy and inexperienced. She probably wouldn't last two seconds out there. You saw her when she came across the Janns,' he replied quietly.

'That's because she wasn't prepared and it was a shock; my money's on her.'

'Twenty says he wins this one,' Davis murmured under his breath.

'Done,' they slapped palms lightly.

'No you're not,' Jake hissed, 'I'll handcuff you to the damn chair if I have to.'

'As fun as that'd be,' she returned sarcastically, 'I'd just get Charles to let me back out again. Four teams of two, one to cast the circle, one to protect. You think Charles is going to risk one of the corners not being called while a Hell hound is busy using you as a chew toy?'

Jake's eyes flashed dangerously and his jaw ticked in anger but he remained silent.

'You think I'm not scared?' Veronica told him 'well I am, I'm terrified. Right now I think I would actually prefer being struck by lightning then face those creatures. But I'm still going and you know why? Because it's the right thing to do, because if they get loose everyone suffers. So I'm going to take my shotgun and I am going to march out there and protect the people I care about, protect the town I've chosen to call my home and god damn it I'm going to protect you too, even though you're thick-headed, stubborn and a royal pain in my ass. If they want to hurt you they'll have to go through me first, whether you like it or not.'

She finished up, her eyes blazing with anger and flounced out of the room in righteous fury.

'Oh I like her,' Louisa murmured.

'Jake,' Tommy slapped him on the shoulder, 'you need to marry that girl, she's a keeper.'

Davis rolled his eyes and sighed, silently handing his gloating sister a folded up twenty.

'What's all the shouting about?' Charles walked into the room and picked up his bag of supplies.

'The children were playing,' Davis replied dryly.

Charles turned to look at Jake, raising his eyebrows questioningly.

'Don't ask,' he muttered.

'Alright does everyone know what they're doing?' he asked and a murmur ran around the room followed by nodding heads. 'Alright then, Mac and I are leaving now as are Louisa and Tommy, next its Olivia and Theo, then Jake and Veronica, Danae and Davis will leave last. Any questions ask now.'

The room remained silent as Charles picked up a two-way radio and tucked it into his bag.

'Davis has radios for all of you, make sure you take one before you leave and stay in touch.'

He picked up his bag and headed out into the hallway to where Olivia was talking quietly with Mac.

'We'll take Mac's truck.' He pulled his keys from his pocket, 'you take mine, your car will never make it through the snow. Be careful once you leave the perimeter; that spirit is still out there and she's none too happy.'

'We'll be careful,' she took his keys, watching silently as both he and Mac slipped out of the front door.

Louisa and Tommy headed into the hallway.

'Be careful,' Olivia wrapped her arms around Louisa.

'I will,' she grinned, 'besides you need me. I'm still the only doctor in this little Scooby gang.'

'You be careful too Tommy' Olivia told him,

'Theo will be real mad if anything happens to you.'

'Please,' he scoffed, 'what's going to happen? I'm gonna bag me a couple of deer while you guys play make-believe.'

Louisa rolled her eyes and dragged him out the door.

'He's in for a bit of a shock,' Davis smirked from the doorway to the library.

'Yes he is,' Olivia murmured as she walked past him into the library where Theo was talking to Jake. She retrieved her bag, shoving a small first aid kit, a couple of flashlights and a bottle of water into it.

'Theo can you get down the Maledictionem chest?'

He raised an eyebrow questioningly but did as she asked anyway. He reached up and brought it down from the top shelf, laying it carefully on her desk. She turned the key with a quiet click and felt rather than heard a hiss as she opened the lid and retrieved the mirror she had placed in there. Carefully so as not to disturb the cords wrapped around it she placed it in her bag.

'What are you going to do with that?' he asked.

'Hopefully give it to Charon to deal with,' she answered. Finally, she grabbed Charon's staff which had once again folded in on itself and shrunk to a third of its length. Tucking it into her bag she zipped it closed, and although part of the staff still extended beyond the zip, most of it was covered.

'Okay then,' she pulled her coat on zipping it up and hooking her arms through her backpack. Yanking a dark coloured wool hat over her ponytail she turned to the others.

'Take this,' Davis handed her a two-way, 'and be careful.'

'We will,' she nodded and with one last glance she and Theo headed out into the dying light.

23.

'Lou this is ridiculous' Tommy complained, dragging a shovel behind him as they trudged through the woods towards the West bank of the lake. 'I'm freezing and my head is pounding, all I want is to curl up in front of the TV with a beer. Why the hell are you playing along with the others?'

'Tommy shut up,' Louisa snapped. 'You want to leave fine, go ahead, just don't complain when you find my mangled corpse in the morning.'

'Do you hear yourself, this stuff isn't real. You've just let your imagination run wild. Those things that Olivia said attacked them in the woods just before Christmas were probably just wolves or a pack of stray dogs.'

'I think Olivia would know a wolf if she saw one,' Louisa breathed out heavily as the tree line opened up and the frozen lake came into view. 'This should do I think, any further and we're going to hit sand instead of soil. Louisa.'

'Get digging soldier,' she smiled.

Letting out a deep sigh of resignation he dropped the bag containing his weapons and ammo and began to clear away a large circular patch of snow so that they could get to the ground beneath.

Her eyes softened as she watched him, cursing yet still digging. Even though he didn't believe a damn word they'd been trying to tell him for the past several weeks, he was still here indulging her in what he liked to call their 'mass hallucination'. He was a good guy and she knew it. He'd have her back right up to the bitter end, even if he didn't agree with her.

'I love you,' she said impulsively.

He looked up at her and his expression softened. 'You always say that when you're getting your own way,' he smiled.

'It also happens to be true.'

He went back to his digging, 'well I'm sure you can think of an appropriate way to thank me later, when all my appendages are frozen.' He glanced up and wiggled his eyebrows suggestively.

'I'm sure that I can,' she laughed as she began to pull the various items out of her bag. 'Don't forget to dig a hole at the centre for this thing,' she wrinkled her nose as she pulled the smelly damp burlap ball from her bag.

He nodded and continued to dig, and after a few back breaking minutes he stood up.

'Okay done; should we build a small fort next?'

'Very funny,' she rolled her eyes, 'widen it a bit more. I'll use that as a guide to cast the circle and no matter what happens do not step outside the circle.'

'I love it when you get all bossy and domineering,' he smirked.

'Tommy I'm serious' she looked up at him, her eyes losing their light-hearted playfulness. 'No matter what, do not step outside the circle. I didn't worry through two tours of Afghanistan for you to get hurt now.'

'Hey,' he dropped to his knees and took her face in his hands, realising that she was genuinely concerned. 'Nothing's going to happen to me.'

'I wish that were true,' she sighed shaking her head. 'I really am sorry about this Tommy. If I could keep you out of this I would, but you're in for a very serious shock tonight.'

He frowned at her expression and the tone of her voice and for the first time he began to have doubts.

Louisa glanced up at the sky.

'It will be sundown soon we're running out of time,' she pulled the rest of the items from her bag. 'You'd better get prepared, I'm almost ready to start.'

He nodded and began to pull the weapons from his bag, laying them out on the hard ground.

Louisa grabbed her Athame and scraped out a circle surrounding the hole Tommy had just dug, then she plunged her knife in and drew a pentagram into the frozen earth. Placing one of the five white candles at each of the five points she lit them, murmuring words Tommy couldn't quite make out. She placed the five blue candles in between each of the white ones but left them unlit. Placing the burlap bag within reach she also placed the jar of seawater within the confines of the pentagram. Taking the salt, she poured it around the edge of the outer circle making sure it overlapped and encased them both in the smaller spell circle.

The still air was suddenly split by a deep wet growling.

'What the hell was that?' Tommy's eyes widened as he picked up the shotgun.

'Get ready they're coming,' Louisa breathing nervously she stood as close to centre as she could and spread her arms.

'I call upon the old gods, upon Hecate and Herne to be with us, to watch over us, to guard, guide and protect us, during these rites.'

She crossed her arms over her chest.

'Blessed be.'

The snarling was getting closer. Tommy raised his weapon, training it on the tree line. His gaze sharpened, his protective instincts in overdrive as his training kicked in. The light was dying, the sky was ablaze with pink and purple, and as the sun slid inexorably towards the horizon a curtain of blackness followed in its wake.

Several pairs of white eyes appeared between the trees, the accompanying sound like no dog or wolf he'd ever heard. It was deeper, louder and somehow wetter than it should be. He glanced down to the ground, mentally taking stock of how much ammo he had and how many of them were appearing in the woods.

'You'd better hurry Louisa.'

Trying to calm her pounding heart Louisa focused on the circle. Extending her hand she started at the North East and began to turn clockwise. As she did an electric blue light seared the ground around them.

'I conjure this circle as a place between worlds, as a time out of time, a place of containment and protection.'

She made sure the edges once again overlapped as she had with the salt.

'Blessed be.'

Tommy's eyes widened in sheer disbelief as the creatures stepped out of the cover of trees. They were huge, pretty much the size of small horses, their flesh hung bloodied and torn from their bleached white bones, with stray patches of matted fur. Their snarling mouths contained row upon row of tiny needle-pointed teeth.

''What the fucking hell?' Tommy gasped.

'Still think it was a pack of wild dogs?' Louisa bent to quickly start lighting the blue candles, praying to every God or Goddess that ever was, that this worked otherwise she knew they were both as good as dead.

She stood and raised her hands to the sky as Tommy began firing.

'Here take this,' Jake pulled the crescent moon shaped amulet from the neck of his coat and dropped it over her head.

'What is it?' Veronica frowned.

'It's a protective amulet, it was given to Olivia by the Goddess Diana herself. Olivia, Theo and I all have one.'

'You should keep it,' she began to remove it.

'Don't,' he grasped her hand, 'don't take it off for any reason.'

She glanced into his eyes, seeing the worry for her.

'Promise me?'

'I promise,' she finally agreed.

'Nodding he turned back to the circle, trying to light the green coloured candles but frustratingly the light kept sputtering out.

'God damn it not now,' he hissed. 'Where's Olivia when you need her.'

'Here.'

'He turned and caught the lighter Veronica tossed at him.

'What?' she shrugged as she caught him staring at her. 'I smoke the odd cigarette when I'm stressed.'

'You shouldn't,' he shook his head as he started to light the candles, 'it's not good for you.'

'God, now you sound like my brothers.'

'Yeah?' he asked in interest, 'how many?'

'Two, both older,' she frowned, 'in fact they're the reason I learned to shoot.'

'They took you shooting?'

'No,' she laughed, 'my therapist thought it would be a good way for me to work out my repressed anger issues. Of course he was a member of the NRA so I think he may have been a bit biased. Still, turns out I was quite good at it and I enjoyed it.'

'You know you're nothing like I expected Roni,'

he looked up at her.

'Is that a compliment?' she smiled.

'I guess so.'

She looked up and her breath suddenly caught in her throat.

'Jake,' she whispered urgently.

He looked out past the circle to the open space beyond. Creatures were moving slowly towards them, grey and slimy looking, and although they walked upright they moved with an uneven jerky gait, like something out of a really bad zombie movie. Their heads were bald apart from a few spare tufts of grey hair. Their arms, much longer than those of a human, hung down past their knees.

'What the hell are they?' Jake breathed.

'I have no idea,' Veronica raised her gun.

'Remember aim for the faces.'

'Er Jake, I don't think they have faces.'

He looked back to find she was right. They had no eyes or nose, just a gaping maw with sparse rotting brown human looking teeth.

'Aim for the legs then,' he turned back to the circle and moved the jar of earth into the pentagram.

Veronica started shooting and for a moment he was transfixed by the sight of her. Gone was the cute klutzy girl he had become accustomed to and in her place stood a calm confident woman. Her stance widened for perfect balance, her gaze sharp and focused as she took out the legs of several of them, dropping them to the ground one by one. Christ, he swallowed, there wasn't anything hotter than a woman with a gun.

Shaking his head to try and focus his mind he finished lighting the green candles and stood, throwing his arms up to the sky.

'I do summon, stir and call thee element of earth. Uriel, guardian of the watchtower of the North I invoke thee, I entreat thee appear before us and lend of us your strength and power.'

Veronica had discarded the shotgun and now held

two handguns which she fired simultaneously hitting the grey men dead centre of what should have been their foreheads. The force of the shot knocked them backwards to the ground, but they rolled over and climbed slowly back to their feet. She switched tactics and started taking them out at the kneecaps, but even as they hit the ground they continued to claw their way along the snow towards them.

'Uriel, I invoke thee, grant us the power to banish these creatures of the nether, let us walk in your light.'

'Jake,' Veronica called out urgently, 'I can't stop them, nothing's working.'

'Uriel, I invoke thee, I entreat thee grant us the power to hold back the darkness.'

The creatures had reached the edge of the circle and were reaching towards Veronica. She stumbled and fell backwards, still shooting as she went down. Jake turned to grab her and they both hit the ground.

'Uriel,' Jake shouted to the sky, *'I invoke thee.'*

The outer edge of the circle suddenly erupted into bright green flames and burst outwards. The creatures, caught by the fire, recoiled screaming, their slimy grey flesh blackening and collapsing in on itself until they were no more than hollowed out charred husks, filling the air with an unpleasant smell of burnt flesh.

'I hope that's a yes,' Jake crawled across the circle and dropped the burlap bag into the hole he'd dug and pressed the earth over the top to seal it in.

'Bag of dirt and bones, a net I seek, bound with magic, sealed with blood,' he pulled out his knife and cut his palm allowing his blood to mingle with the soil, *'to hold until the morning sun,'* he kept pressing the dirt, *'bag of dirt and bones, a net I seek, bound with magic, sealed with blood, to hold until the morning sun, bag of dirt and bones, a net I seek...'*

He continued to murmur the words over until the ground began to glow with an eerie phosphorescent glow. The bright green light began to rise from the ground filling the circle with light. He fell backwards, tangling up with Veronica who had been watching him intently.

The light kept rising higher and higher, beginning to unfold. As it reached a full twenty feet they realised it had taken the shape of a being. Still it kept going, up and up, until it towered thirty feet above them. Then it unfurled its wingspan another forty feet in width, lighting up the sky with a vivid green glow, a gigantic angel composed entirely of light.

With a mighty cry that made the ground beneath them tremble it bent down and thrust its hand into the ground at its feet. The ground split, the cracks lighting up with green light. It continued to travel along the ground splitting again and again until it resembled a network of blood vessels. It reached the lake and began to spread across its surface, melting the snow as it went and covering the ice in a throbbing green net.

Danae stood panting hard, her silver whip dangling from her hand, her clothes splattered with blood and other gruesomeness. The area around the circle was littered with corpses and various monster body parts as she gazed up at the giant angel of yellow light towering above her and her brother. She watched calmly as it bent and speared its hand into the ground sending out vines of yellow light across the lake, which laced together with the green ones spreading over from the other side. As soon as the new net settled over the ice the angel crouched down using his huge wingspan to encircle them and create a dome of soft warm yellow light.

'That's two down,' Danae breathed hard, as her heart rate began to settle, 'it's coming from the North. That's Veronica and Jake. See I told you the girl would come through.'

'So you say,' he replied pulling out his two way. 'For all you know she could be dead.'

'Charming,' she muttered dryly.

'Just being realistic,' he shrugged hitting the button. 'Jake…Jake come in…are you both okay?'

He listened to the static for a few moments before the line crackled.

'We're both good,' came the reply, 'bit freaked out about the giant green angel though.'

Davis chuckled lightly.

'Just whatever you do stay inside the circle until we say otherwise, you'll be safe in there.'

'Yeah, if we don't freeze first.'

'You won't freeze; do you feel cold at all?'

'No, now that you mention it.'

'That's because you've just released enough power to heat three Olympic sized swimming pools. Trust me, you'll be fine in there.'

'Okay, have you heard from the others?'

'Not yet, sit tight for now. We'll let you know when there's been a change.'

'Okay.'

Danae looked up as she saw another ray of light illuminate the night sky, this time pure blue. A head and shoulders, followed by a massive wingspan, appeared above the tree line and then suddenly disappeared. Moments later thin ribbons of blue light crawled across the ice like tentacles, weaving themselves seamlessly between the yellow and green ones.

'Got another,' Danae murmured.

'That's Louisa and Tommy,' Davis replied looking up. 'Just Charles and Mac to go; what the hell are they up to?'

Mac let loose another shot as the bodies began to pile up. He had no idea what the creatures were but they didn't seem to be able to withstand the silver bullets. Another shrieked and flapped across the sky as Mac aimed and fired. It crashed violently to the ground in a mad tumble of wings and claws, sliding towards the edge of the circle spraying them with snow. Behind him he could hear Charles but he didn't have time to pay attention to the words, as something crashed through the tree line on four legs and headed straight for them.

'Charles!' he shouted in alarm as the bullets punched through its body, not even slowing it down. 'CHARLES!'

Mac fell back as it bunched its powerful muscles and leapt for the circle.

Suddenly the perimeter of the circle burst into deep red flames and the creature exploded. He could hear Charles kneeling close to the ground burying the strange cloth covered ball and muttering the same words over and over, but he barely paid attention. His mouth fell open and he tilted his head upwards to watch as a huge angel appeared and unfolded it's wings high above them. It suddenly crouched down and punched its hand through the dirt, which cracked and lit up like red veins spreading across to the lake and stretching out across the ice. He was so engrossed watching the red threads weave their way through the multi-coloured net coating the surface he didn't even register Charles standing behind him. There was a sudden sharp pain across the back of his head and then he was falling into blackness.

Charles tucked the gun into the back of his jeans and rolled Mac over, checking his pulse. Satisfied that it was strong and steady he took the two way and laid it on Mac's chest, wrapping his fingers around it. He looked up and saw the angel's wings descending towards him. He jumped to his feet and leapt head first out of the circle seconds before its wings enveloped the circle and bathed it in a protective red glow.

Charles hit the ground, growling in pain. His muscles locked up and his body felt as if it were on fire. It couldn't have been helped, he didn't have time to open a proper exit from the circle and it was always painful trying to cross a magic barrier that was designed not only to keep things out but to keep you in. Climbing slowly to his feet as the pain began to subside he took a deep shaky breath before looking at Mac's unconscious form on the other side of the, now impenetrable, shield.

'I'm sorry Mac,' he whispered, 'but Isabel is my responsibility.'

Satisfied that Mac would be safe he turned and disappeared into the night.

Olivia tracked through a deep snow drift, weaving through the trees with her flash light highlighting the path in front of her. Theo kept pace silently next to her. They'd parked the truck as close as they could but Louisa was right, the road was thick with almost two decades of fallen branches and trees and there was no way to get through. With no other alternative they made their way through the woods to the lake, where they could cross to the private beach at the foot of the cliff.

They broke through the trees and the lake came into view. Olivia's eyes widened as she saw the brightly coloured tapestry woven across the surface of the lake. In the distance she could just about make out the muted colours glowing through the trees and she could only pray that her friends were safe.

'I guess the spell worked,' Theo spoke quietly in the stillness.

She glanced at him, not saying a word as she made her way down to the lake edge. Theo stepped down from the rocky outcropping onto the ice and slid slightly but remained upright. Turning towards Olivia he held out his hand to help her.

She stepped down, ignoring his offered hand as she continued to walk carefully across the ice. It wasn't far to the private beach, she could see it from where they were.

'Olivia?' he called to her but she kept on walking.

'Olivia?' he caught up with her and stopped her.

'Is this the way it's going to be between us from now on, with you ignoring me? You've barely said anything to me since last night.'

'Really?' she retorted, 'you want to do this right now?'

'Olivia,' he sighed, 'look I'm sorry I didn't tell you about Mary.'

'You think that's what this is about?' she glared angrily at him. 'You think that's why I'm mad at you?'

'Then what?' he asked as she started walking again.

'Olivia,' he caught her arm once again and stepped in front of her so she had no choice but to face him. 'You're not running away, not this time, talk to me.'

'You want the truth?' she snapped.

'Yes.'

'I don't care that you were married before you met me, I don't even care that you didn't tell me about her. I even understand why you didn't.' She took a deep breath, 'what I'm upset about is that you knew,' her eyes narrowed, 'you knew, she was in my house and you didn't tell me.'

'Olivia,' he began as he shook his head.

'Theo, she could have slit my throat in the middle of the night, or yours. She could have burned the house down around us, did that not occur to you?'

She could tell by the sudden stunned realisation on his face that the thought hadn't occurred to him.

'She was in my house Theo, the one place,' her voice broke angrily, 'the one place I'm supposed to feel safe and you took that from me. Now you tell me, how am I supposed to trust you now?'

'God,' he breathed as a heavy weight settled on his chest, 'I'm so sorry Livy.'

The ice beneath their feet suddenly trembled alarmingly and the night air reverberated with an ominous cracking sound. They both turned to look out towards the centre of the lake.

'What is that?' Olivia frowned.

A shard of ice suddenly punched through the surface lifting the brightly coloured net, another breached the surface at an odd angle, followed by another. Even from this distance she could hear the whoosh of the water as it was forced up through the hole. The ice continued to snap and break, spearing up in great jagged spires.

'We're running out of time,' Olivia gasped as Theo grabbed her hand and hauled her towards the beach.

They tried to run as fast as they could but slipped and slid across the ice, hanging onto each other trying to keep their balance. They could feel the ice heaving and vibrating beneath their feet but they didn't dare turn back. They finally made it to the beach, trudging through the snow as quickly as they could, looking for the steps leading up.

'Here,' Theo yanked a thick branch out of the way and snapped it off.

Olivia stopped at the base of the steps and looked at Theo nervously. The stairs themselves looked stable enough as they were carved into the rock face winding upwards, but they were very narrow and steep and the guardrail was rusty and was swaying alarmingly halfway up, where the wind was stronger.

Olivia glanced back towards the lake and then looked up at the sheer height of the cliff. Biting back a wave of nausea and taking a deep resolute breath she began to climb, with Theo right behind her. The iron railing creaked and groaned, causing her heart to skip a beat every time it pulled under her hand. They'd made it almost three quarters of the way up the cliff face when the wind picked up, tearing at them viciously as if it were trying to pluck them from the rock itself. The railing whined and groaned and broke away from the rock. At the sudden loss of support Olivia fell forward, but her foot slipped and as she went down she cracked her shin against the step and toppled to the side.

Her breath caught in her throat and then came a curious feeling of weightlessness. Theo dived forward and grasped her wrist, desperately hanging on as she dangled over the sheer drop down to the ice below.

'Olivia, look at me,' he panted. 'Give me your other hand.'

He could see the terror in her eyes as she reached for him. The wind buffeted her body and she missed. He felt her slipping further.

'Olivia,' he called desperately, 'take my hand.'

'Theo,' she cried out in panic.

'You can do it,' he answered over the shriek of the wind. 'I won't let you go I swear, now reach for my hand.'

She tried again and this time he caught her fingers and pulled. As she scrambled against the wall one of her boots caught the sheared off bolt protruding from the wall and she was able to push her body further up. Letting go of one hand Theo wrapped his arms around her body and hauled her over the side. They collapsed on to the hard unforgiving steps, with his arms wrapped around her like vices as he buried his face in her neck. She trembled in his arms, her heart thumping so loudly she could hear it in her ears.

'Is now a good time to mention I don't like heights,' she panted.

'We need to get off this ledge,' Theo answered. 'It's not safe.'

'You think?'

He climbed carefully to his feet bringing her with him and they edged their way slowly and painfully up the remaining stairs with their backs pressed against the rock face. Olivia breathed a sigh of relief when they climbed the top step and at last stood out on the top of the cliff, looking down at the lake. From this angle they could see the jagged ice spiking upwards as if to form a gateway and hundreds of dark shadowy figures pressing up through the hole, snared in the brightly coloured net. They writhed and surged against it, trying to find a way to break through with arms and claws, reaching up through the gaps in the net.

'Dear God, look at them all,' Olivia breathed her stomach dropping like lead. She turned to Theo her voice barely more than a whisper above the howl of the wind. 'The net is not going to hold them.'

24.

Isabel glanced out over the lake, watching the commotion below with disdain. The dark sky was lit with muted throbbing colours, like an Aurora Borealis and the lake itself looked like a crazy disco dance floor with threads of red, blue, green and yellow woven together in a huge net. Even from this distance she could see the centre of the lake heaving and pulsing like a heartbeat.

Fools, she thought, that wasn't going to hold. Even now she could see the edges of the magic pulling taut. Soon it would give and the creatures would swarm across the lake and scatter through the surrounding woods. All that wasted effort for nothing.

She felt Nathaniel behind her watching silently, his black eyes unreadable.

'They're trying to block the doorway,' Isabel murmured. 'If they don't know we're here already it won't be long before they figure it out.' She turned back to Nathaniel, 'we need to move.'

'What about Charon?'

'Have you managed to get anything from him?' she frowned.

'No,' Nathaniel replied calmly, 'he's still not talking.'

'Losing your touch are you Nathaniel?'

'Not at all,' he shrugged. 'I have taken him apart piece by piece and he still won't give in, from which I can only conclude that he is incapable of retrieving Hester's soul, otherwise he would have broken by now.'

'Or perhaps you're just not as good as you think,' she replied coolly.

'Careful Isabel,' his eyes glittered dangerously, 'or you may get the chance to find out for yourself.'

She sneered and turned back to the window.

'You don't scare me Nathaniel' she scowled, as her mind returned to the problem of Charon. 'If he is unable to retrieve Hester's soul, he is of absolutely no use to me.'

'For all his power, he remains nothing more than a servant,' Nathaniel told her. 'I warned you when we first went after him that he was Hades' creature but you wouldn't listen. You need someone higher up the food chain.'

'What do you suggest?' she replied sarcastically, 'that we go after Hades?'

'No,' he replied, 'even I am not stupid enough to go up against a God.'

'Then what use are you to me?' her eyes flashed. 'Perhaps I should shove you back in the devil's trap I found you in and let you rot for another three hundred years.'

'Three hundred years to me is no more than a nap,' he replied coldly. 'Trust me I have infinitely more patience than you and far more time.'

She sniffed in disgust, turning away from him.

His fingers twitched infinitesimally and he swallowed slowly. He wanted to wrap his fingers around her throat and slowly squeeze and squeeze until she lost consciousness. Then he would strap her to a table and peel the flesh from her body in tiny little one inch strips, taking his time. After all he liked to be meticulous when he worked and took pride in the exquisite amount of agony he liked to inflict on his victims.

His mouth curved as he thought of all the things he wanted to do to the witch but he could wait. She couldn't, she was impatient, prideful and selfish, like a child denied a treat. She wanted desperately, that which she could not have. He had no intention of allowing her to get her hands on the Hell Book; Infernum was his. He had not spent three millennia tracking it down to be thwarted at the final hurdle by a spoiled brat, who at best was a second rate witch. His lip curled in disdain; he despised humans with their stinking pig flesh and over inflated self-importance. They truly believed the whole of existence revolved around them. They were incredibly arrogant for a swarm of insects.

'You do know,' his voice was smooth and cajoling, 'there is another way.'

'What?' Isabel asked suspiciously.

'There is another way to get to Hester.'

'You lie,' her eyes narrowed. 'If there had been another way you would have already tried it.'

'I can't because I'm not human,' his mouth curved into a slow smile, 'but you are.'

'Keep talking.'

'We need to find a crossroad, not just any crossroad but a very special one.'

'How is a crossroad supposed to help?' she scoffed.

'It's not the crossroad itself we want but the keeper of the crossroad. They are incredibly powerful beings.' Knowing that he had snared her attention he pressed on. 'They are able to grant one's deepest desires...for a price.'

'What's the price?'

'Does it matter?' he replied softly, 'the question is how badly do you want Infernum and what are you willing to pay?'

'I've paid enough already, I didn't give up my family and become a murderer to turn back now,' her eyes flashed hungrily. 'I want the book; I don't care what it costs.'

'Then I shall make sure that you have it,' he smiled coldly, knowing he had her now. 'All I ask is that you hold to your end of our bargain, and when you have Infernum in your possession you use its power to raise my brother from Hell.'

'Of course,' she promised insincerely.

And he had no intention of the book ever falling into her grubby undeserving hands, he thought beneath his cool smile. Once he'd used her to locate the book he would take it and use its power to free his brother himself. Then they would rule, side by side, Gods over the mortal infestation that had spawned on this world.

'Where are these crossroads?' she asked.

'Scattered throughout the underworld,' he replied carefully.

'The underworld?'

Nathaniel nodded. 'But luckily for you I know the location of one of them.'

'We need to dispose of Charon,' she told him coldly.

'Consider it done.'

'Then you'd better be quick before my husband or my daughter decide to interfere.'

Smiling, he turned to leave the room.

Olivia and Theo kept to the shadows, knowing that if Nathaniel or Isabel happened to look out of any of the windows at the back of the building they would more than likely be able to see them. Crawling through the underbrush and overhanging branches they made it to the side of the building, where several of the windows were broken exposing the rooms beyond to the elements.

They climbed as quietly as they could through the

nearest window, and as Olivia dropped to the floor and flicked her flashlight on, she kept the beam low so as not to attract attention. A small snowdrift sloped down to a black and white checked floor and piles of dried curled up leaves littered the corners of the bay shaped room. Above them she could see a domed glass roof which seemed for the most part to be intact, with only a few missing panes of glass. The ornate curved frame of what was once a table stood in the centre of the room, it's wooden surface long since rotted away. Several metal chair frames were also scattered around the room, some laid forlornly on their sides in drifts of snow, their upholstered cushions long since lost to the elements.

Crossing the once elegant little sun room Theo pushed open the interior door which led into a small parlor. Sheltered from the weather, this had at least fared a little better than the sunroom. Some of the tables remained upright, their matching chairs still retaining tattered cushions, while the lamps in the corners, with their faded tasselled lampshades, spoke of a lost elegance.

They moved on as quickly and quietly as they could, finding themselves in a hallway with peeling walls and wall sconces mounted on elegant black geometric shapes. To either side were doors to more rooms but a quick look was enough to confirm these hadn't been used recently. They passed through another set of glass paneled doors, inset with intricate coloured stained glass, and came upon a small tiled room with low benches. Beyond, an archway opened up into a cavernous room with high arched ceilings and walls decorated with slim rectangular tiles in a dreamy sea foam green. Stepping further in they saw that the whole middle section dropped down to another two staggered levels, which were also tiled in the same color. Spaced at intervals were small ladders bolted to the walls and leading down into the empty space.

'What is this place?' Theo whispered in her ear.

'The swimming pool,' she explained, 'come on,

this way.'

Skirting around the empty pool she headed for the exit at the other end of the room. Moving quietly through the next two archways they came upon another tiled room which, from its design, Olivia assumed must be the Turkish baths, although she'd never actually been to one.

She heard a small rustle, a clink of metal and turned in the direction of the sound, straining to make it out. Following the sound through another huge archway and into a smaller circular room she found herself looking down where the floor dropped into a deep tiled hole. Once a plunge pool, it was now empty of water. She heard the chink of metal again and glanced down into the hole, shining her torch into the void.

A bloodied face peered back at her, one eye swollen almost completely shut and the other bruised and puffy.

'Oh my God,' Olivia breathed. Swinging her legs over the edge of the plunge pool she dropped down to the floor next to him.

'I've already told you Isabel,' he rasped, as if it were painful to speak, 'I can't give you what you want no matter what you do to me.'

This was no good, he couldn't see past the glare of the flashlight and in the poor light he would not be able to see or believe she wasn't her mom. Switching it off she shoved the flashlight into her backpack. As she snapped her fingers gently, four of her dragonflies burst into flame, hovering above them burning a soft warm red and yellow and bathing them in a muted golden light which would be easier on his eyes.

He stared at Olivia his one eye blinking in confusion, 'you're not Isabel.'

'No,' Olivia reassured him. 'It's a long story but we're here to help you Charon.'

He looked up as Theo also dropped down into the hole and stepped into the circle of light. He studied Theo intently and then glanced up at the fiery dragonflies dancing around his shoulders.

'You're her daughter aren't you?'

'Yes I am.'

'How did you find me?' he frowned, looking from one to the other.

'Charlotte told me how to find you' Olivia answered.

'Charlotte?' his gaze snapped back to her and he grasped her jacket with his bound hands. 'You've seen her?'

Olivia nodded gently.

'She was locked in a death cycle,' his voice betrayed pain of a different kind. 'I tried to reach her but I couldn't.'

'She's trying desperately to break free,' Olivia told him, 'for you.'

He tipped his head back against the tiles and gulped down a deep emotional breath.

'We need to get you out of here, can you walk?' She glanced down at his bloodied and battered body, covered only by a scrap of material tied around his hips.

'I can't leave' he sighed, rattling the metal manacles around his torn raw wrists.

'I can deal with those' Olivia murmured, having a good look at the metal. 'It won't be pretty but it'll get you loose.'

'Even if you could it's not those that are the problem.' He lifted his chin and Olivia saw the black metallic collar around his chafed and swollen neck.

'What is that?'

'It's a Demon collar,' Charon whispered, 'forged in Hell fire. Once it's on there's no way to unlock it, unless you cut my head off and as you can imagine I'd rather you didn't.'

'Forged in Hell fire?' Olivia repeated thoughtfully.

Charon inclined his head, 'they are designed to

enslave souls. Once it's on, any supernatural abilities are neutralized. While I'm wearing this none of my powers will work.'

'We need to get it off,' Olivia looked up at Theo, 'otherwise all this is for nothing. He won't be able to close the doorway.'

'What's happening?' Charon asked suspiciously.

'Spirits have been escaping through the doorway ever since you went missing. The town is overrun with them and now creatures from the underworld have realized it's open.'

'They're trying to break through?' he replied.

Olivia nodded. 'We've cast a net but it's not strong enough. There are too many of them trying to come through at once, not to mention the ones already here. We haven't much time before it fails and they are all turned loose.'

'I was afraid of this,' he whispered brokenly. 'I cannot stop them as there is no way to remove the collar.'

'Olivia? Can you?' Theo asked.

'Maybe,' she looked up at him. 'If it's forged in Hell fire I might be able to do something with it.'

'What?' Charon looked at her with a skeptical expression. 'You are a mortal, what would a mortal know of Hell fire.'

'Quiet,' Olivia murmured to him, her attention already fixed on the collar.

She gently laid her fingertips on the metal. It felt cool to the touch but vibrated like a plucked string. As she traced her fingers along the surface writing appeared, glowing with sapphire blue fire. As the room faded from her awareness and her eyes drifted closed, she could hear a low murmur, a whisper in the furthest corner of her mind. It was a language so ancient it had not been spoken in millions of years, a language from the very beginning of time. It spoke to her soul and she realized with a start that she recognized it.

When she opened her eyes they were no longer their warm whiskey colour, but deep, deep blue and held within their depths endless eons and a vastness of power beyond measure. The words rose unbidden to her lips as she murmured the language that came to her so easily. The collar grew warm under her touch and as she wrapped her fingers around the sides and tugged, it came apart in her hands with an audible click.

'It's not possible,' Charon gasped.

Ignoring him Olivia reached up and wrapped her hands around the chains attached to the manacles at his wrists. The metal burned bright blue and melted, breaking the links. His hands dropped and she shook her head lightly as if to lift the fog from her mind. When she blinked her eyes were once again their usual colour.

'Charon, do you know where my mother and Nathaniel are?'

He was staring at her silently, his one good eye wide with shock.

'Charon please,' she shook him lightly, 'we don't have much time. Do you know where they are?'

He shook his head mutely.

'We need to get him out of here,' she looked up at Theo.

He reached down and wrapped Charon's arm around his neck helping him to his feet. As they made their way to the pool side Olivia scooped up the two halves of the demon collar and dropped them in her bag, before slinging it over her back. She moved to join the other two, taking Charon's weight against her as Theo hauled himself up and onto the ledge. He reached down and grabbed the Ferryman, pulling him up behind him, while Olivia hooked her hands under his dirty feet and gave him a boost. When he lay breathing heavily at the side of the plunge pool Theo stretched down and grasping Olivia's arms pulled her up easily.

Taking one of his arms each and wrapping them

around their necks for support they managed to half walk, half drag Charon out into the Turkish baths, back past the main swimming pool and out into the hallway, the way ahead illuminated by Olivia's dragonflies which danced and flitted ahead of them.

'Wait,' Charon gasped.

'We can't,' Olivia replied. 'I know you're tired but we need to get to the lake.'

'It's not that,' he breathed heavily, 'you need to get the book.'

'What book?'

'Hester's Grimoire' he replied, 'you have to have the book. You cannot leave it in Isabel's hands. Without the book all this is for nothing.'

'I don't know where it is,' Olivia frowned.

'He indicated the doors they had just passed, 'in there is the ballroom. That was where Nathaniel kept me while he questioned me. The book is being kept in there.'

She looked to Theo and then back to the double doors. Swiftly making a decision she lifted Charon's arm from around her neck and his weight slumped against Theo.

'Go,' she told him, 'get him to the lake.'

'Olivia no,' Theo argued.

'There's no time,' she began walking backwards towards the doors, 'go… I'll be right behind you.'

Taking a deep doubtful breath, torn at the idea of leaving her, he hesitated.

'GO!' she told him and as she turned and ran back down the hallway, two of her dragonflies broke away and followed her. The other two hovered over Theo and Charon.

Gritting his teeth and with a quiet growl of frustration Theo turned and headed towards the exit dragging Charon with him.

Olivia stopped and listened at the door, her heart

pounding in her chest. She couldn't hear anything, nor could she see any light or movement through the glass panels. Cracking the door open slowly she winced when it creaked loudly, as her dragonflies swept into the room lighting her way. Like a burglar she crept forward, her wary gaze scanning the room. She caught sight of a sad old grand piano across the room, one leg collapsed beneath it leaving it propped at an awkward angle. Recognizing the dark leather bound object balanced on top of the piano she moved purposefully towards it, stripping off her backpack as she went. Letting out a breath of relief as she laid her hand on it, she balanced her bag on the piano and unzipped it. Picking up Hester's Grimoire she tucked it safely into her bag.

'Well what do we have here?' a coldly familiar voice spoke from behind her, 'a thief in the night. What have you got there little thief?'

Olivia froze, her hand still tucked in her bag and then she slowly turned to look into Nathaniel's face, her heart knocking painfully in her chest. She hadn't seen the Demon since that night at Boothe's Hollow and although she had been foggy with pain at the time she could see he had somehow deteriorated. His face was still a patched, unevenly stitched mismatch of features but the flesh was now a drawn, sickly looking grey and looked as if it were flaking. One of his eyes was drained of colour, almost white and there was the unmistakable stench of decomposing flesh about him.

'You don't look too good there Nathaniel,' she replied, her voice deceptively steady. 'You should get more sun.'

His mouth curved as his gaze dropped, trailing slowly down her body and then back up to her face, leaving her feeling unclean.

'You are a lot more interesting than your mother,' he replied softly.

The tone of his voice made her cringe and her

flesh felt as if it were crawling with ants.

'Olivia,' another familiar voice intruded, breaking the uncomfortable silence.

Her gaze slowly slid across to her mother who appeared next to Nathaniel.

'Hello Mom,' Olivia replied coolly.

'I believe you have something that belongs to me,' she answered dangerously. 'Give me Hester's book.'

A quick glance around the room told Olivia that there was no escape except back past her mother and the Demon. Her fingers which were still buried in her backpack flexed involuntarily and they snagged on a cord. A sudden idea occurred to her, a way out, but she just needed to buy herself some time.

'It was left to me, not you.'

'Only because they believed I was dead, you simply got it by default.'

'Now we both know that's not true, don't we?' Olivia's eyebrow rose insultingly. 'Aunt Evie knew the truth about you, she knew you were still alive and what you had done.'

'Regardless, the book is mine. Give it to me.'

Her fingertips stealthily pulled and tugged at the chord of the binding spell, which she knew was tied around the small mirror in her backpack.

'Why? What possible good could it do you? It's simply a collection of day to day spells and housewives' charms. It's nothing earth shattering.'

Something in Isabel's expression spoke volumes, causing Olivia to come to a surprising conclusion.

'You can't read it can you?'

Isabel's eyes narrowed but she remained silent.

Olivia laughed in a show of amusement she did not feel, as her fingers tugged at the last knot and her hand closed around the cold glass which now vibrated beneath her skin. 'Shall we re-evaluate just who it belongs to then, seeing as I'm the only person who can read it?'

Isabel growled. 'GIVE ME THE BOOK OLIVIA!'

'Or what?' her voice was low and full of contempt, 'I'm grounded?'

'I won't ask again,' Isabel replied dangerously.

'You want it?' Olivia smiled coldly, 'fine you can have it.'

She yanked the mirror from her bag and hurled it towards the floor. The glass smashed and the room exploded with a bright silver coloured light. Olivia dived behind the wreck of the piano as the furious spirit was released. Nathaniel, caught unawares, was picked up and swept across the room to crash into the opposite wall. The spirit caught sight of Isabel and mistaking her for Olivia let out a bone chilling screech of madness. He dived for her, churning up the dirt and debris from the floor in a cyclone of rage. She was scooped from the floor like a rag doll and pinned to the wall three feet from the ground.

Olivia quickly zipped up her backpack and slung it over her back, then peeking out from piano she made a dash for the exit.

'OLIVIA!' Nathaniel roared as he climbed back to his feet and stalked towards her. Knowing she wouldn't get far with him behind her, she knew she only had one slim chance. Skidding to a halt she spun to face him, her Hell fire bursting into flame and flooding her body as she pulled her hands apart and her bow of living flame burst into life.

Nathaniel bared his teeth and hissed, breaking into a run as he rushed towards her. With calm detachment Olivia aimed and released a bolt, hitting him dead centre of his chest. It penetrated his body with a sickening thud, the sheer force of it taking his feet out from under him and throwing him backward to where Isabel was struggling against the enraged spirit.

Fired with adrenalin Olivia stood watching as his body lay prone on the dirty ground. For a few seconds she wondered if she had actually killed him but he twitched and then he began to move. Olivia took a hesitant step backward towards the exit as he climbed slowly to his feet.

'Itches a little,' he sneered and looked down at the smoking, bloodied cavity gaping at his chest. 'Now that wasn't very nice was it Olivia?' he spoke slowly as he took a step towards her.

'Nathaniel' Isabel croaked, clawing at the invisible hands around her throat as her lips began to turn blue.

He turned and studied her dispassionately for a moment as if he would love nothing better than to watch her die slowly as the life was choked from her. But thinking better of it, he let out a longsuffering sigh and reached out, his fist gripping around something only he could see. Suddenly a writhing mass of silver smoke appeared in front of him, twisting and shrieking as it tried to escape from his clutches. His fingers tightened and the sound of screaming intensified before the smoke suddenly began to pour to the ground as it transformed to ash.

Isabel slid down the wall and leaned over coughing as she tried to suck much needed oxygen into her starved lungs.

'Ashes to ashes,' Nathaniel murmured as he watched the last of the smoke pool on the floor as a small pile of harmless dirt.

Olivia took another step backwards her eyes wide and wary.

'Now,' his smile was chilling, 'where were we Olivia?'

Suddenly she saw a blurred shape speed past her with a shout of defiance and barrel straight into Nathaniel, knocking him to the floor. As Nathaniel was knocked out of her way Olivia looked up to see her mother staring at her, her eyes filled with anger. Fumbling at her belt, Olivia's hand wrapped around the hilt of the tranq gun Davis had given her and before Isabel could so much as raise her hand Olivia had flicked off the safety and let loose two shots.

Isabel swayed slightly, taking an unsteady step forward and her mouth fell open as she looked down at the two darts protruding from her chest. Even as she pulled them out they fell from her lax fingers, as her eyes rolled back in her head and she collapsed to the ground.

Theo and Nathaniel skidded across the floor. Before Nathaniel could do anything Theo had his knife in his hand and jammed it up under the Demon's chin. Twisting his hand and locking his shoulder he shoved the blade deep, up through the soft pallet of his mouth and into the brain cavity. Nathaniel made a revolting burbling noise, his gaze twisting to meet Theo's.

With surprising strength, he gripped Theo's hand and slowly withdrew the knife. He knocked Theo back across the floor, watching as he rolled agilely to his feet and placed Olivia protectively behind him.

Nathaniel once again climbed to his feet, congealed blood oozed and crawled unpleasantly down what was left of his chest and when his lips split in a grotesque grin his teeth were covered in black decaying blood.

'You think that tiny little pig sticker is going to kill me boy?' His voice was a mixture between a rasp and a gurgle, a trail of bloody spittle hanging down from his lip.

Theo didn't answer but edged back towards the door, his body pushing Olivia as he went. His gaze focused on his enemy and in his hand, wet and slimy with blood, he held his knife out in front of him.

'Surely you don't think you're getting out of here alive do you Theodore,' he rasped. 'I'm going to take my time with you boy. I owe you for the inconvenience you caused me when you let the little West bitch and her sister escape.' He took another menacing step towards them. 'I'm going to peel the flesh from your bones and then carve open your chest, letting you watch in agony as I pull your organs out one by one. Then once you're dead…would you like to know what I'm going to do to your little whore there, the one you're protecting so sweetly.'

Theo growled, his eyes flat and hard.

'If you lay one finger on her I am going to make you suffer like you never would have believed possible,' he grated from between clenched teeth.

'Shall we put it to the test then?' Nathaniel grinned and rushed towards them. He barely made it two feet across the floor when he smashed into a pale blue barrier. He fought and clawed against it, snarling and drooling like a rabid dog, enraged that he could see his prey but couldn't reach them.

Olivia turned and saw her father standing in the doorway, hands outstretched, breathing hard with exertion.

'Dad!' Olivia gasped.

'Go now,' he panted, 'I'll hold him.'

'No!' she shook her head desperately, 'not without you.'

'Olivia go now! You have to get Charon to the lake, the net is breaching,' he shouted. 'Theo, get her out of here!'

Theo grabbed her and dragged her towards the door, while she struggled against him.

'No!' she tried to pull away from him as he dragged her down the hallway. 'I can't leave him; he doesn't stand a chance against Nathaniel.'

'Olivia,' he grabbed her arms forcing her to look into his eyes. 'I don't want to leave him either but we have to get Charon to the lake. Your father will be alright, he hasn't survived this long without learning a few tricks but if we don't stop those creatures from escaping, a lot of people will die.'

The ground suddenly groaned and trembled beneath their feet, and they both stumbled and crashed against the wall.

With one last haunted look in the direction of her

father Olivia turned to Theo and nodded. They ran down the hallway and out into the parlor where Charon was sitting on the floor, resting weakly against the wall, his half naked damaged body wrapped in an old drape Theo had ripped down from the window. They grabbed an arm each, wrapping them around their shoulders for support and half carried, half dragged him into the sun room. No point now in climbing back out of the window and Theo kicked the door open, no longer concerned about making a noise. They stumbled out into the freezing air towards the edge of the cliff and the treacherous steps down to the lake.

The wind howled up from below as they moved down the steps one by one, with Charon supported between them. The climb down was easier than it had been coming up and they kept their backs pressed against the cliff wall, away from the dizzying drop and the fragments of guardrail which still creaked and groaned alarmingly in the wind. They'd almost made it half way down when the rock began to shake and groan once more. A huge cracking sound filled the air as part of the rock face sheared away. Olivia pushed Charon towards Theo and as the stairs behind her crashed down into the dark abyss below, she leapt.

25.

Charon instinctively caught her and stumbled back into Theo, who barely stopped all three of them from toppling over the side into the icy blackness below. Her eyes wide with shock and her breath trapped in her throat, Olivia desperately gripped the rock face as the cliff shook again.

'The net is breaking,' Theo called above the screaming wind. They looked down and saw a huge rent appear at the centre of the lake amidst the monolithic looking shards of ice.

'Hurry,' Charon urged Theo and the three of them started moving again. At last they made it to the base of the stairs, Theo and Olivia once again supporting his weight as they all stepped onto the ice.

'Get me as close to the center as you can,' he cried above the cracking noise.

They kept on inexorably, stumbling as the ice shifted and heaved beneath their feet while an alarming splintering noise filled the air, accompanied by the splash of water. Deep cracks ran along the ice snapping at their heels. The multi coloured net shredded and tore away, shrieks and howls filling the air as they got closer to the center.

'Do you have my staff?' Charon shouted above the chaos.

She reached behind her for the end of the staff which was still protruding out of the top of her backpack and yanking it loose she handed it to Charon.

They came to a halt letting him move forward to stand unaided. As his fingers gripped around the staff the lettering burst into flame and the pole extended to a full six feet. The sky swirled and boiled above him as he held it up to the sky and cried out in a deep ringing voice. Olivia couldn't understand the words he used but she knew they were Greek. The sky lit up with jagged spears of lightening and boomed impossibly loud with the terrifying roar of thunder. Grasping the staff with both hands he drove it down into the ice, which split and fanned out like a web. The frozen surface heaved again violently and Olivia stumbled and fell heavily on the ice, knocking the wind from her lungs. As she looked up she saw Theo was also lying on the ice a few feet from her, on the other side of Charon. Her gaze was drawn to the center of the lake where the water churned and frothed up, breaking over the splintered ice like waves upon the sand. She realized with a jolt something was rising from the shadowy depths of the lake, something colossal.

Her mouth fell open and her eyes widened in shock as a great archway appeared, water pouring from its huge pillars and draining away as it rose higher and higher into the sky. It was covered in engravings and ancient lettering which bore a distinct similarity to Greek. Suddenly she felt herself sliding towards the gigantic gateway, caught in a riptide of air.

'Hold on to something,' Charon yelled in warning.

She tried to but she was surrounded by a frozen wasteland. She fought valiantly as she clawed to find some purchase but she was dragged along the ice. She raised her head and saw shadowy shapes being pulled through the air towards the gate. The gateway she realized, was like a giant vortex, pulling all the spirits back through to the other side. The creatures which had been trying to claw their way through to her world were also sucked back in, squealing and scratching, trying to stop themselves being dragged back through.

She dug the tips of her boots in but it was no good, she was still sliding dangerously close to the gateway. Plunging her hands into the ice, in desperation she reached for the heat of her magic, forcing it roughly into her frozen fingertips. She dug her hands into the ice like claws, letting the heat in her fingers melt grips for her. It wasn't perfect but at least she'd stopped moving. She glanced around and saw Theo not far from her, the blue black of his Hell fire blade dug into the ice and as he held on for dear life his eyes looked up and met hers.

Theo watched uneasily as her eyes suddenly widened at something behind him. He turned his head in the direction of her shocked gaze and his heart jolted in his chest at the sight of Mary's face hissing next to his. Unable to do anything he hung on to the knife and prayed. He felt something cold grip his leg and when he looked down he could see Mary hanging onto him, trying to keep herself from flying backwards through the gateway or trying to take him with her, he wasn't sure which. He kicked his legs in an effort to shake her loose but his hands kept slipping. He gripped the knife tighter but the blade began to slide loose.

'Theo!' Olivia reached a hand out for him desperately.

The blade slipped again, gouging a deep trench along the ice. He scrambled against the slippery surface but Mary held tight, her lips peeled back in a snarl as she yanked hard.

Theo's eyes met Olivia's and something passed silently between them as the knife ripped free from the ice and he was sucked backwards to the gateway, with his dead wife still clinging to him.

'THEO!' she screamed in anguish, but with a huge grind the ice tore itself apart and split beneath her. Her head cracked sharply against a deep ledge of ice which speared up in front of her and she toppled into the freezing water with an icy splash. Urgently kicking her legs, she breached the surface, sucking in a sharp gasp of air. The water was so cold it was like her skin was being pieced by thousands of tiny needles. She scrambled to grasp onto the ice and pull herself out of the water but it was no good, it simply bobbed and slid away from her numb fingers. Blood dripped into her eyes from the cut at her temple and her vision wavered and blurred.

She went under again but she didn't have the strength to kick for the surface again. She could see the glow of light above the face of the water as she stopped struggling and sank down. She blinked as her body swirled in the water and all she could see was the dark deep depths of the lake engulfing her. A strange kind of acceptance passed over her, there was no use fighting. Theo was gone, she had nothing left that mattered.

Her vision began to waver and she could no longer hold her breath, briefly she saw a white shape in the water beneath her, cutting and weaving through the shadows and as her mouth opened and she felt the water rush in she thought she saw Charlotte's pale face and white eyes. Then darkness consumed her and she let go. She didn't feel Charlotte take her hand, nor was she aware of being pulled towards the surface.

Olivia rolled over, coughing violently as the lake water was heaved unmercifully from her lungs. Dragging in a deep shuddering breath she blinked, trying to clear her vision. For a moment she couldn't move but sprawled face down on a hard wet surface as her body shook violently from the cold. She flexed her numb fingers and felt snow mixed with rough grains of sand. With a tremendous effort she raised her throbbing head and realized she was lying on the small sandy patch of beach near the dock by her house. Pushing herself up on shaky arms she looked out over the lake.

It was so calm now, the creatures and spirits were all gone and there was no sign of the net. The ice had broken up and bobbed harmlessly on the surface of the lake, like the ice floes of the North Atlantic. The huge and imposing gateway remained in the middle of the lake and although it still shimmered in the moonlight, it was silent and still.

Aware someone was close by Olivia turned her head slowly, her breath catching as her gaze fell on a hunched wet dirty figure kneeling in the snow, slowly rocking back and forth. Charlotte's long dark matted hair hung forward, trailing in the snow, hiding her white face.

'Charlotte?' a soft voice called from behind them.

Olivia turned to look and saw Charon's wooden skiff anchored at the edge of the lake, bobbing serenely in the water, its lantern lit. Charon stepped down onto the beach, clean and healed, dressed in a white tunic of linen with matching pants. On his feet were leather sandals, a leather thong hung at his neck and from it hung a pendant, which looked like an ancient coin. He stepped towards them and leaving his pole planted firmly in the soft ground he approached Charlotte slowly. His face no longer bore the swelling and bruising of his captivity and his matted bloodied hair was once again clean and sat in soft, dark brown curls.

'Charlotte he called again softly as he knelt down beside her, his hand outstretched. 'Come back to me…' he whispered, 'agapiméni, i kardiá mou ítan ádeio chorís eséna.'

She stopped rocking for a moment as if responding to his voice. Slowly she raised her head, her white eyes locking with his.

He smiled and reached out to her. 'Gýrna píso se

ména,' he whispered.

She reached out her hand and for a second Olivia held her breath.

Their hands met and when she looked up at him, her eyes were no longer white but the same deep whiskey colour of Olivia's. Charon stood, slowly pulling Charlotte to her feet and when she stood to face him her dress was no longer soaked and dirty but the same pristine snowy white soft linen that he now wore. Her hair fell down her back in soft clean, dark brown waves and her face was a warm flesh colour. With rose coloured lips she smiled at him as if he were the most precious thing in the world.

'My love,' she whispered, cupping his face gently and pressing her forehead against his.

'I waited for you,' he whispered taking her lips gently.

He pulled away from her and turned to Olivia.

Thank you Olivia,' he replied softly, 'I am in your debt.'

'Charon,' her voice betrayed her emotions as her body was racked with deep shudders, 'where is Theo?'

Charon's face fell and he shook his head sadly.

'He was pulled through the doorway Olivia; he is trapped on the other side now.'

'Give him back to me,' she whispered brokenly, as her eyes filled with tears. 'Please…'

'Olivia,' he replied remorsefully, 'I can't, it is beyond my authority. I cannot return a soul once it has crossed over.'

'Then who's authority does it need?' she asked harshly.

'Mine,' a voice spoke firmly from behind her.

All three of them turned to look. She could feel Charlotte drop into a curtsy behind her and somehow knew Charon bowed low but she paid them no mind. All her attention was fixed on the tall stranger in front of her. He was extremely handsome, tall and well-built, immaculately dressed in a tailor made suit which could only have come from Savile Row in London. His hair was so black it looked almost blue and he carried in his hand a polished black walking cane, with a huge blue jewel instead of a handle.

The stranger's eyes flicked to Charlotte and Charon, scrutinizing them carefully.

'You may go Charon,' his voice was low and smooth but carried within it great authority.

'My lord?' Charon asked hesitantly, 'what of Charlotte?'

The stranger continued to study her for a moment longer before inclining his head the barest fraction of an inch.

Letting out a relieved breath Charon retrieved his staff and stepped into the boat. Helping Charlotte in beside him he pushed away from the shore and began to pole the boat towards the huge archway. Olivia watched them numbly as they reached the centre of the lake until they and the gateway both disappeared.

Olivia turned back to the stranger; her teeth were chattering loudly and her body was shaking so violently now her head almost bobbed on her neck.

'W...who...a...re you?' she managed to stutter out her, body wracked so badly from the cold all she wanted to do was lie down, go to sleep and never wake up again.

'Do you not know?' he replied, 'let me give you a hint.'

Suddenly his hair burst into blue black flames.

'Hades?' she gasped.

He crouched down low to where she was huddled on the freezing ground and took her hand, helping her to rise to a standing position.

'Mortals,' he murmured studying her. 'Such fragile creatures.'

He pressed his hand to her chest and she felt a

sudden warmth flood her body. She gasped loudly at the sensation and as he stepped back she realized not only had her body stopped shaking but her clothes and hair were now dry.

'That's better' Hades replied, taking a seat on thick chunk of driftwood, placing his cane between his legs and folding his hands neatly on the jewelled hilt. 'Now we can have a proper conversation.'

'You're Hades,' Olivia whispered in stunned disbelief, 'what...THE Hades?'

'Olivia West,' he continued as if she hadn't spoken, 'you have caused quite a stir.'

'I have?' she asked in confusion.

'The human girl who can wield Hell fire.' He studied her carefully like she was a fascinating specimen, his sharp dark eyes unreadable. 'The human girl who understands our language and speaks the ancient tongue as if born to it; you are quite the enigma, aren't you?'

'I'm just a regular girl, there's nothing special about me,' she replied.

'I don't think you understand, no human...NO human has ever been able to summon and control Hell fire, yet you do so with ease. It comes as naturally to you as breathing.'

She kept her mouth shut as she had no idea what to say. She'd only come face to face with the Goddess Diana before and she had felt nothing but love, warmth and comfort from the Deity she had chosen to serve, but now standing on the shore of a freezing cold lake in front of an ancient and powerful God, she fought the urge to tremble with nerves. Locking her spine, she stared him straight in the eyes, hoping she looked more confident than she felt.

'You interest me Olivia, nothing has interested me enough to visit the surface for more than two thousand years and yet here I am...so what am I going to do with you?' he mused.

'Nothing,' she replied carefully, 'I serve Diana. You have no authority over me.'

'Is that so,' he smiled slowly in amusement, 'it seems the little mouse has a backbone after all.'

Olivia's mouth tightened, she could feel a wave of belligerence building inside her.

'I'm not a mouse,' she answered indignantly, 'and I would have thought you'd be a little more grateful since I managed to save your friend Charon and help stop all your little prisoners from escaping from the underworld, despite what it cost me.'

'And what did it cost you?'

'It cost me Theo,' she whispered as her heart lurched painfully in her chest, bringing with it a fresh wave of grief.

'Ah yes Theodore,' Hades replied thoughtfully. 'Would you like to have him back Olivia?'

'My pain is not a game for your amusement,' she bit back.

'No games Olivia, tell me and I will know if you are lying to me…tell me truthfully, why you want him back. Because you feel guilty?'

'No.'

'Then why?' he pressed.

'Because I love him,' she breathed painfully, 'because it feels like there is a part of me missing without him.'

'Is it really so hard to admit child?' he replied softly. 'Mortals… I will never understand all of your complexities.'

'That's because, with all due respect Hades, you're a God,' she looked at him. 'You see what you want and you take it, you don't have to worry if that person will love you back or betray you.'

'You think a God cannot feel such doubt?' he asked curiously.

'You tell me,' she asked. 'Is it true what they say

about Persephone? Did you take her against her will and bind her to you?'

Hades scoffed lightly. 'Humans,' he shook his head, 'they get more wrong than they get right.'

He fell silent for a moment, watching her, as if coming to a decision.

'My wife remains with me because it is what she wishes,' he finally replied. 'The love of a God is vast, all-encompassing and eternal. Now do you want Theodore back or not?'

'You can give him back to me?'

'No.'

'But you just said…'

'I asked if you wanted him back. Now what are you willing to risk, for that to happen?'

'Everything,' she whispered.

'I can't just give him back to you Olivia,' he tapped his fingers against the hilt of his cane, the moonlight catching on the fiery blue stone embedded deeply in the signet ring he wore. 'It sets a bad precedent and if I were to just go around returning souls I'd be hounded constantly. But like I said, you interest me…' he pursed his lips thoughtfully, 'I can send you to the other side. Once there it's up to you to find him and convince him to come back.'

'Convince him?'

'Mr Beckett carries his own demons with him,' Hades shrugged. 'Guilt like that can do strange things to one's mind on the other side.'

'If I go and I find him, how do we get back?' she asked.

'That is up to you' he replied, his eyes glittering with entertainment. 'There is a way, we'll just have to see if you're clever enough to figure it out.'

'So this is a game to you?'

'Not at all,' he smiled, 'but it doesn't mean I can't enjoy the show. I've spent the last several thousand years surrounded by demons and damned souls, this will be a delightful change of pace for me.'

'Fine,' she agreed.

'There is of course something I want in return.'

'What?' Olivia asked suspiciously.

'Regarding the matter of your mother and Nathaniel.'

'What about them?'

'Let's just say I am well aware of their search for Infernum,' his eyes narrowed dangerously. 'I am not too concerned with your mother; she and I will come to terms eventually and when that day comes I can't say that I'll be feeling too...charitable.'

Olivia resisted the shiver of fear that tickled the length of her spine. For all of his smooth charm, Hades was not a God she wanted to cross and for a moment she almost felt sorry for what her mother obviously had in store.

'I am more concerned with that filthy creature Nathaniel.' Hades hair flared suddenly, as if he'd momentarily lost his composure. 'I have his brother Seth as my permanent...guest shall we say, still I would have liked to have had the set.'

'What exactly is it that you want me to do?'

'Stop him from gaining possession of the book.'

'Why me? Like you said I'm only a human, couldn't you...'

Hades shook his head. 'I cannot interfere with the book, that is not my destiny.'

'You want me to stop a Demon?' Olivia breathed, 'how am I supposed to do that?'

'Again I'm sure you will figure it out,' his mouth curved again, 'but I will give you a little help to set you on your path.'

'And that is?'

'Information,' he replied. 'Aren't you mortals fond of the aphorism, knowledge is power?'

'Alright then.'

'Your mother and Nathaniel escaped from the hotel; even now Nathaniel has taken Isabel into the Underworld where they search for one of the five lost crossroads.'

'I've never heard of any lost crossroads?' she frowned.

'Of course you haven't, they existed a long time before your race was even created.'

'Why are these crossroads so important?'

'Crossroad, singular, he only needs to find one,' he told her. 'Each crossroad has a Keeper, a cursed soul who committed such terrible deeds during their lifetime they are sentenced to the crossroad for a minimum of one thousand years, depending on the severity of their earthy transgressions. Each Keeper must guard the crossroad and any human traveller who makes it to the crossroad may ask a boon of the Keeper.'

'What sort of boon?' Olivia asked in fascination.

'Anything their heart desires, fame, wealth, beauty, love, immortality or...the location of something they desperately want.'

'So it's like a genie?'

He sighed and rolled his eyes as if he were trying to explain something to a four-year-old.

'No, nothing is free especially not in the Underworld, the traveller may ask for anything but the Keeper has to demand payment.'

'And what is the payment?'

'Anything the Keeper wants,' he shrugged, 'they are fickle capricious creatures. It can be anything from a treasured memory, a year of your life, your youth and beauty, your first born child...your soul.'

'Why hasn't Nathaniel used the crossroad before now?'

'Because he isn't human, but now he has your mother to make a deal for him.'

'God,' Olivia breathed.

'You people throw that word around an awful lot.'

'How am I supposed to stop them from making a deal?'

'By finding the crossroad before they do.'

'And how am I supposed to do that?'

'There you go again, always expecting to have the answers handed to you,' Hades replied irritably, 'dealing with mortals makes my teeth itch.'

He reached into his pocket and retrieved a golden object, which looked a bit like a fob watch suspended on a long gold chain.

'Here take this,' he tossed it to her.

She caught it easily and turned it over in her hands. It was beautifully engraved with constellations and star charts. She pushed the tiny gold button and the lid flipped open with a barely audible click. Inside was an incredibly complex compass.'

'It's a compass,' she replied, but as she turned, the needle remained still. 'It doesn't work.'

'It most certainly does work,' Hades answered, 'you just need to figure out how to use it.'

Olivia clicked it shut again and pulled the chain over her neck tucking the compass into her clothes.

'You have everything you need now Olivia,' he told her his dark eyes intense, 'I'll be watching you.'

'But…'

He flicked his wrist and she disappeared, leaving him staring up at the sky which was brightly lit with stars.

'You could have been a little more patient with the child,' a smooth warm, amused female voice spoke up behind him.

'Dealing with humans is like trying to have a conversation with a rock sometimes,' he sighed and turned around, his eyes sliding appreciatively down her body. 'My love,' he smiled slowly, 'the Valentino looks exquisite on you.'

Wendy Saunders

Persephone smoothed her hands down the midnight blue, shimmering beaded gown with girlish delight.

'It appears the human tailor has some talent,' she agreed before glancing up at the sky and taking a deep breath. 'I haven't been topside in over a millennium,' she laughed in delight.

Hades rose elegantly and held out his arm to her.

'What would you like to do first my love?' he asked her as she slipped her slender arm through his.

'I would like to visit a place called Broadway.'

Hades sighed. 'Bards and playwrights give me a headache.'

'I'm sure it's not that bad my husband,' her beautiful face lit in a captivating smile. 'They have had over two thousand years, perhaps they have improved.'

'Can we not see a sporting tournament instead?' he asked hopefully.

And as her delighted laughter carried on the wind, they disappeared into the darkness.

406

Coming soon
The Guardians Series 1
Book 3

Crossroads

The doorway to the Otherworld has been closed but at a terrible cost. Theo has been trapped on the other side while the Demon Nathaniel searches for one of the lost crossroads of the Underworld. With the help of the God Hades, who she doesn't trust, Olivia crosses over and with nothing but a flashlight, a broken Demon collar, a Grimoire and a compass that doesn't work she must risk everything to find him. As she searches she keeps catching glimpses of the real world. It's only then Olivia realizes when they closed the doorway something dark and ancient was left behind, trapped in Mercy. She watches helplessly from other side as the residents of Mercy begin falling into mysterious comas and it becomes clear that whatever is stalking the streets of her town is stealing human souls.

Olivia is torn, faced with an impossible situation and the clock is ticking. Even if she manages to find Theo she knows she must make a choice, stop the soul collector or go after Nathaniel, knowing that if he reaches the crossroad before her, she will have to make a deal with the Keeper of the crossroad and the price may be her own soul.

Turn the page for an exclusive preview of chapter 1.

1.

Louisa was bandaging three deep nasty claw marks in Tommy's shoulder, but paused and looked up as Jake stalked back into the library in Olivia's house.

'Any sign of the others?' she asked hopefully.

Jake shook his head, looking over at Veronica who was holding an icepack to the bleeding lump at the back of Mac's head. Beau jumped up at his legs and bending down absently he scooped the pup into his arms and stroked him soothingly. 'Don't worry buddy we'll find them for you,' he murmured to the dog who, seeming to understand the promise, leaned forward and licked Jake's face.

'Danae and Davis are still out looking and we haven't accounted for Charles yet,' Jake told them.

Louisa's mouth settled into a thin line of worry as she turned back to her husband and taped up the end of the bandage before helping him back into his shirt.

'I need a drink,' Tommy headed for the kitchen, reappearing moments later with a bottle of Glenfidditch and a stack of plastic cups.

'Anyone?'

'I certainly wouldn't say no,' Mac winced as Veronica pressed a little too hard.

'Sorry Mac,' she sighed and handed him the bag of

ice. I don't make a very good Florence Nightingale, do I?'

'No' he smiled, 'but you make a hell of a G.I Jane.'

She looked up at him and laughed in amusement. 'My parents would never believe you.'

'I expect most people wouldn't believe the half of what we saw last night,' he replied seriously as Tommy handed him a full cup.

'Ain't that the truth,' Tommy downed his own drink in one.

They all looked up hopefully as the front door slammed again, but a collective sigh of disappointment rippled around the room as Danae entered alone.

'Any news?' Jake asked.

She shook her head frowning. 'No, Davis is still looking. There's no sign of Theo and Olivia and Charles is still MIA.'

Mac's face darkened at the mention of Charles' name.

'He'd better be dead,' he muttered, 'or by the time I'm finished with him he's going to wish he was.'

'What did you say?' Danae's eyes narrowed.

'You heard,' he growled.

'Look, I don't know what happened between you two out there but I'm sure it was necessary.'

'Necessary?' Mac laughed mirthlessly. 'I don't consider someone sneaking up on me and cracking me across the skull a necessity.'

'Charles must have had his reasons.'

'Oh he had his reasons alright, it's because he's a selfish self-important, stubborn son of a bitch.'

'How dare you,' Danae hissed. 'You know nothing about my brother.'

'I know plenty and he should be thanking me for not hauling his ass back to Morley Ridge instead of trying to give me a brain hemorrhage.'

'That's enough you two,' Veronica came abruptly to her feet, glaring at them sharply. 'We're all worried and this isn't helping.'

She turned to the window and stared out into the cold pale morning light.

'They'll be okay,' Jake put his hand on her shoulder reassuringly, forcing her to look up into his eyes.

'But what I saw,' she whispered as her eyes brimmed with tears.

'You could've been wrong,' he told her. 'It was dark and we were both pumped full of adrenalin…they'll be okay; I know they will.'

The front door slammed again and they all turned to the library doorway. Another disappointed sigh as Davis stormed through, looking frustrated.

'Any luck?' Danae asked although she knew the answer from the look on her twin's face.

He shook his head.

There's no sigh of Theo and Olivia anywhere. The truck is still parked at the foot of the private road leading up to The Boatman, the keys in the ignition. I couldn't get up to the hotel to look around, the road is blocked and the ice on the lake has completely broken up now. Which means we'll need a boat to get to the private beach at the foot of the cliff but even then I don't know if there's a way to reach it. I hiked through the woods the way they would've gone, but when I reached the edge of the lake I could see that part of the cliff face had sheared away. It's crushed the Jetty and taken out part of the steps leading up.'

'God,' Jake growled in frustration.

'I could scale the cliff face but I don't have any climbing gear,' Davis frowned.

'How long would it take to get some?' Jake asked.

'I could probably have some here by mid-afternoon.' He pulled his phone from his pocket and began to scroll through his list of contacts.

'Could you make that two sets of ropes and harnesses?' Jake asked.

'You have experience?'

Jake nodded. 'It's been a while but I know what I'm doing.'

'Alright then,' Davis agreed but before he could make the call the front door slammed again.

This time they were not disappointed. As they turned to look Charles limped through the doorway, his clothes torn and dirty. One side of his face was heavily bruised and scratched and from the angle at which he was cradling his arm, it was fair to assume it was broken.

'Charles,' Davis breathed a sigh of relief.

'What happened?' Danae frowned.

But Charles ignored them, scanning the faces in the room, disregarding the angry glare Mac was throwing in his direction.

'Where's my daughter?'

'Mr Connell,' Louisa interrupted, glancing at the state of his various injuries. 'Maybe you should come and take a seat and let me have a look at you.'

'Where's Olivia?' he asked again angrily.

'We haven't been able to find them yet Charles,' Davis told him quietly, 'both Olivia and Theo are missing.'

'Charles, we're going to find them,' Danae told him 'Why don't you sit and let Louisa have a look at you and tell us what happened. We've been looking for you for hours. You were supposed to be with Mac, what the hell were you thinking?'

'He was thinking about revenge,' Mac shot back, 'that's what he was thinking about.'

'It wasn't about revenge,' Charles glared back at him, 'it was about protecting my daughter.'

'You can pretty it up all you like Charles but going up to the hotel last night wasn't about protecting Olivia, it was about getting to Isabel.'

'You're wrong.'

'Am I?' he replied, 'then why stop me from going with you?' 'It's because you knew I would have arrested her,' he continued mercilessly, 'and the simple fact is you want her dead…you want her dead for betraying you.'

'NO!' Charles shouted furiously, 'I want her dead because it's the only way to make sure she can't harm Olivia. You think a prison can hold Isabel? It couldn't hold me; I could have walked out at any time but I didn't because it didn't suit my purpose. Isabel feels no such restraint and as long as she's loose she is a threat to my daughter. So yes, you're damn right I want that bitch dead, it's the only way to make sure Olivia is safe.'

'All right calm down,' Jake stepped in between them. 'We're all on the same side here and we all want to make sure Theo and Olivia are okay, so why don't you tell us what happened as you seem to be the last person to see them both.'

Charles sighed and shook his head, clearing his thoughts.

'When I got to the hotel Olivia and Theo had Charon. Nathaniel and Isabel were also there. Olivia shot Isabel with the tranq darts and I was holding back Nathaniel to give them time to escape. I told them to get him to the lake. I don't know what happened after that, a few moments after they were gone the whole cliff shook.'

'Part of the face sheered away,' Davis explained.

'Anyway the force of it brought down part of the ceiling in the ballroom, which is where I was. I was knocked unconscious and by the time I came round Nathaniel and Isabel were gone. I managed to free myself from under the debris but when I got outside I saw that the lake was still and quiet. I headed for the stairs but part of them are gone and there was no way down. I had no choice but to try and climb through the fallen trees and branches blocking the road. It took me the rest of the night and part of this morning but I made a path through. It's narrow but there is a way through. I headed back here expecting them to have been back by now. Has no one seen them?'

They all shook their heads, except for Veronica.

'Veronica?' Charles asked quietly, 'what is it?'

'I saw,' she shook her head, 'I mean I thought I saw, it was dark and everything happened so fast I can't be sure.'

'Why don't you just tell me what it is you think you saw.'

'They were heading into the centre of the lake, at least I think it was them. I was quite far away...but.'

'But what?'

'They were still in the middle of the lake when the ice started to break up, there's no way they could have made it back to shore, not with the temperature of the water.'

'You think they went in?' Charles let out his breath slowly, closing his eyes in pain.

'I think I saw one of them go in, I couldn't tell which,' she replied miserably as her eyes filled with tears.

'No' Charles whispered, shaking his head.

'They're not dead you know,' a new calm voice spoke from the doorway.

They all turned to look in confusion.

'Mayor Burnett?' Jake frowned, 'what are you doing here?'

'I came to put your minds at rest,' she replied softly. 'Theo was pulled through the gateway to the Otherworld and Olivia went in after him. They're stranded in the Otherworld but they are alive.'

'And how exactly would you know that?' Charles asked suspiciously.

'I know a great many things Mr Connell,' her mouth curved.

'What the hell is going on Tammy,' Mac moved closer, 'how do you know about Olivia and Theo?'

'Because' she answered slowly, 'my name isn't Tammy Burnett. It's Beckett...Temperance Beckett.'

She glanced around the room at the bewildered

faces.
'Theo is my brother.'

Author Bio.

Wendy Saunders lives in Hampshire, England with her husband and three children. After initially training as a hairdresser, she has spent twelve years caring for her grandmother but when her grandmother passed away she decided the time was right to pursue her own dream of writing. The Ferryman is the second book of the five book Guardian series.

Book 1 Mercy (Available from Amazon)
Book 2 The Ferryman (Available from Amazon)
Book 3 Crossroads (Coming Summer 2016)
Book 4 Witchfinder (Coming Soon)
Book 5 Infernum (Coming Soon)

Come find me
On my official website
www.wendysaundersauthor.com
Don't forget to subscribe to my mailing list via my website or Facebook page to be e-mailed new book releases dates!

On Facebook
www.facebook.com/wendysaundersauthor

On Twitter
www.twitter.com/wsaundersauthor

On Instagram
www.instagram.com/wendysaundersauthor

If you would like to rate this book and leave a review at Amazon I would be very grateful. Thank You.

Made in the USA
Lexington, KY
31 January 2018